NickCunard.co.uk

About the Author

VICTORIA HISLOP writes travel features for *The Sunday Telegraph* and *The Mail on Sunday*, along with celebrity profiles for *Woman & Home*. She lives in Kent, England, with her husband and their two children.

the Island

Victoria Hislop

HARPER

NEW YORK . LONDON . TORONTO . SYDNEY

HARPER

This book is a work of fiction. The characters, incidents, and dialogue are drawn from the author's imagination and are not to be construed as real. Any resemblance to actual events or persons, living or dead, is entirely coincidental.

First published in Great Britain in 2005 by Headline Book Publishing, a division of Hodder Headline.

HarperCollins books may be purchased for educational, business, or sales promotional use. For information please write: Special Markets Department, HarperCollins Publishers, 10 East 53rd Street, New York, NY 10022.

First Harper paperback published 2007.

Library of Congress Cataloging-in-Publication Data is available upon request.

ISBN: 978-0-06-134032-1
ISBN-10: 0-06-134032-4

07 08 09 10 11 RRD 10 9 8 7 6 5

For my mother, Mary

With special thanks to:

The Spinalonga Island Museum
Professor Richard Groves, Academic Dermatology, Imperial College
Dr Diana Lockwood, London School of Hygiene and Tropical Medicine
Stelios Kteniadakis
LEPRA

The island of Spinalonga, off the north coast of Crete, was Greece's main leper colony from 1903 until 1957.

Plaka, 1953

A cold wind whipped through the narrow streets of Plaka and the chill of the autumnal air encircled the woman, paralysing her body and mind with a numbness that almost blocked her senses but could do nothing to alleviate her grief. As she stumbled the last few metres to the jetty she leaned heavily on her father, her gait that of an old crone for whom every step brought a stab of pain. But her pain was not physical. Her body was as strong as any young woman who had spent her life breathing the pure Cretan air, and her skin was as youthful and her eyes as intensely brown and bright as those of any girl on this island.

The little boat, unstable with its cargo of oddly shaped bundles lashed together with string, bobbed and lurched on the sea. The elderly man lowered himself in slowly, and with one hand trying to hold the craft steady reached out with the other to help his daughter. Once she was safely on board he wrapped her protectively in a blanket to shield her from the elements. The only visible indication then that she was not simply another piece of cargo were the long strands of dark hair that flew and danced freely in the wind. He carefully released his vessel from its mooring – there was nothing more to be said or done – and their journey began. This was not the start of a short trip to deliver supplies. It was the beginning of a one-way journey to start a new life. Life on a leper colony. Life on Spinalonga.

Part 1

Chapter One

Plaka, 2001

UNFURLED FROM ITS mooring, the rope flew through the air and sprayed the woman's bare arms with droplets of seawater. They soon dried, and as the sun beat down on her from a cloudless sky she noticed that her skin sparkled with intricate patterns of salty crystals, like a tattoo in diamonds. Alexis was the only passenger in the small, battered boat, and as it chugged away from the quay in the direction of the lonely, unpeopled island ahead of them she shuddered, as she thought of all the men and women who had travelled there before her.

Spinalonga. She played with the word, rolling it around her tongue like an olive stone. The island lay directly ahead, and as the boat approached the great Venetian fortification which fronted the sea, she felt both the pull of its past and an overpowering sense of what it still meant in the present. This, she speculated, might be a place where history was still warm, not stone cold, where the inhabitants were real not mythical. How different that would make it from the ancient palaces and sites she had spent the past few weeks, months – even years – visiting.

Alexis could have spent another day clambering over the ruins of Knossos, conjuring up in her mind from those chunky fragments how life had been lived there over four thousand years before. Of late, however, she had begun to feel that this was a past so remote as to be almost beyond the reach of her imagination, and certainly beyond her caring. Though she had a degree in archaeology and a job in a museum, she felt her interest in the subject waning by the day. Her father was an academic with a passion for his subject, and in a childlike way she had simply grown up to believe she would follow in his dusty footsteps. To someone like Marcus Fielding there was no ancient civilisation too far in the past to arouse his interest, but for Alexis, now twenty-five, the bullock she had passed on the road earlier that day had considerably more reality and relevance to her life than the Minotaur at the centre of the legendary Cretan labyrinth ever could.

The direction her career was taking was not, currently, the burning issue in her life. More pressing was her dilemma over Ed. All the while they soaked up the steady warmth of the late summer rays on their Greek island holiday, a line was slowly being drawn under the era of a once promising love affair. Theirs was a relationship that had blossomed in the rarefied microcosm of a university, but in the outside world it had withered and, three years on, was like a sickly cutting that had failed to survive being transplanted from greenhouse to border.

Ed was handsome. This was a matter of fact rather than opinion. But it was his good looks that sometimes annoyed her as much as anything and she was certain that they added to his air of arrogance and his sometimes enviable self-belief.

They had gone together, in an 'opposites attract' sort of way, Alexis with her pale skin and dark hair and eyes and Ed with his blond, blue-eyed, almost Aryan looks. Sometimes, however, she felt her own wilder nature being bleached out by Ed's need for discipline and order and she knew this was not what she wanted; even the small measure of spontaneity she craved seemed anathema to him.

Many of his other good qualities, most of them regarded as assets by the world at large, had begun to madden her. An unshakeable confidence for a start. It was the inevitable result of his rock-solid certainty about what lay ahead and had always lain ahead from the moment of his birth. Ed was promised a lifetime job in a law firm and the years would unfold for him in a preordained pattern of career progression and homes in predictable locations. Alexis's only certainty was their growing incompatibility. As the holiday progressed, she had spent more and more time mulling over the future and did not picture Ed in it at all. Even domestically they did not match. The toothpaste was being squeezed from the wrong end. But it was she who was the culprit, not Ed. His reaction to her sloppiness was symptomatic of his approach to life in general, and she found his demands for things to be shipshape unpleasantly controlling. She tried to appreciate his need for tidiness but resented the unspoken criticism of the slightly chaotic way in which she lived her life, often recalling that it was in her father's dark, messy study that she felt at home, and that her parents' bedroom, her mother's choice of pale walls and tidy surfaces, made her shiver.

Everything had always gone Ed's way. He was one of life's golden boys: effortlessly top of the class and unchallenged victor ludorum year after year. The perfect head boy. It would hurt to see his bubble burst. He had been brought up to believe that the world was his oyster, but Alexis had begun to see that she could not be enclosed within it. Could she really give up her independence to go and live with him, however obvious it might seem that she should? A slightly tatty rented flat in Crouch End versus a smart apartment in Kensington – was she insane to reject the latter? In spite of Ed's expectations that she would be moving in with him in the autumn, these were questions she had to ask herself: What was the point of living with him if their intention wasn't to marry? And was he the man she would want as father of her children, in any case? Such uncertainties had circled in her mind for weeks, even months now, and sooner or later she would have to be bold enough to do something about them. Ed did so much of the talking, the organising and the managing on this holiday he seemed scarcely to notice that her silences were getting longer by the day.

How different this trip was from the island-hopping holidays she had taken round the Greek islands in her student days when she and her friends were all free spirits and nothing but whim dictated the routine of their long, sun-drenched days; decisions on which bar to visit, what beach to bake on and how long to stay on any island had been made with the toss of a twenty-drachma coin. It was hard to believe that life had ever been so carefree. This trip was so full of conflict, argument and self-questioning; it was a struggle that had begun long before she had found herself on Cretan soil.

How can I be twenty-five and so *hopelessly* uncertain of the future? she had asked herself as she packed her bag for the trip. Here I am, in a flat I don't own, about to take a holiday from a job I don't like with a man I hardly care about. What's wrong with me?

By the time her mother, Sofia, was Alexis's age, she had already been married for several years and had two children. What were the circumstances that had made her so mature at so young an age? How could she have been so settled when Alexis still felt such a child? If she knew more about how her mother had approached life, perhaps it would help her to make her own decisions.

Sofia had always been extremely guarded about her background, though, and over the years her secrecy had become a barrier between herself and her daughter. It seemed ironic to Alexis that the study and understanding of the past was so encouraged in her family and yet she was prevented from holding up a magnifying glass to her own history; this sense that Sofia was hiding something from her children cast a shadow of mistrust. Sofia Fielding appeared not just to have buried her roots but to have trodden down hard on the earth above them.

Alexis had only one clue to her mother's past: a faded wedding picture which had stood on Sofia's bedside table for as long as Alexis could remember, the ornate silver frame worn thin with polishing. In early childhood when Alexis used her parents' big lumpy bed as a trampoline, the image of the smiling but rather stiffly posed couple in the picture had floated up and down in front of her. Sometimes she asked her mother questions about the beautiful lady in lace and the chiselled platinum-haired man. What were their names? Why did he have grey hair? Where were they now? Sofia had given the briefest of answers: that they were her Aunt Maria and Uncle Nikolaos, that they had lived in Crete and that they were now both dead. This information had satisfied Alexis then – but now she needed to know more. It was the status of this picture – the only framed photograph in the entire house apart from those of herself and her younger brother, Nick – that intrigued her as much as anything. This couple had clearly been significant in her mother's childhood and yet Sofia always seemed so reluctant to talk about them. It was more than reluctance, in fact; it was stubborn refusal. As Alexis grew into adolescence she had learned to respect her mother's desire for privacy – it was as keen as her own teenage instinct to lock herself away and avoid communication. But she had grown beyond all that now.

On the night before she was to leave for her holiday, she had gone to her parents' home, a Victorian terraced house in a quiet Battersea street. It had always been a family tradition to eat out at the local Greek taverna before either Alexis or Nick left for a new university term or a trip abroad, but this time Alexis had another motive for the visit. She wanted her mother's advice on what to do about Ed and, just as importantly, she planned to ask her a few questions about her past. Arriving a good hour early, Alexis had resolved to try and get her mother to lift the shutters. Even a little light would do.

She let herself into the house, dropped her heavy rucksack on to the tiled floor and tossed her key into the tarnished brass tray on the hall shelf. It landed with a loud clatter. Alexis knew there was nothing her mother hated more than being taken by surprise.

'Hi, Mum!' she called into the silent space of the hallway.

Guessing that her mother would be upstairs, she took the steps two at a time, and as she entered her parents' room she marvelled as usual at its extreme orderliness. A modest collection of beads was strung across the corner of the mirror and three bottles of perfume stood neatly lined up on Sofia's dressing table. Otherwise the room was entirely devoid of clutter. There were no clues to her mother's personality or past, not a picture on the wall, not a book by the bedside. Just the one framed photograph next to the bed. Even though she shared it with Marcus, this room was Sofia's space, and her need for tidiness dominated here. Every member of the family had his or her own place and each was entirely idiosyncratic.

If the sparse minimalism of the master bedroom made it Sofia's, Marcus's space was his study, where books were piled in columns on the floor. Sometimes these heavyweight towers would topple and the tomes would scatter across the room; the only way across to his desk then was to use the leather-bound volumes as stepping stones. Marcus enjoyed working in this ruined temple of books; it reminded him of being in the midst of an archaeological dig, where every stone had been carefully labelled even if they all looked to the untrained eye like so many bits of abandoned rubble. It was always warm in this room, and even when she was a child Alexis had often sneaked in to read a book, curling up on the soft leather chair that continually oozed stuffing but was somehow still the cosiest and most embracing seat in the house.

In spite of the fact that they had left home long ago, the children's rooms remained untouched. Alexis's was still painted in the rather oppressive purple that she had chosen when she was a sulky fifteen year old. The bedspread, rug and wardrobe were in a matching shade of mauve, the colour of migraines and tantrums – even Alexis thought so now, though at the time she had insisted on having it. One day her parents might get round to repainting it, but in a house where interior design and soft furnishings took low priority it might be another decade before this happened. The colour of the walls in Nick's room had long since ceased to be relevant – not a square inch could be seen between the posters of Arsenal players, heavy metal bands and improbably busty blondes. The drawing room was a space shared by Alexis and Nick, who during two decades must have spent a million and one hours silently watching television in the semi-darkness. But the kitchen was for everyone. The round 1970s pine table – the first piece of furniture that Sofia and Marcus had ever bought together – was the focal point, the place where everyone came together, talked, played games, ate and, in spite of the heated debates and disagreements that often raged around it, became a family.

'Hello,' said Sofia, greeting her daughter's reflection in the mirror. She was simultaneously combing her short blonde-streaked hair and rummaging in a small jewellery box. 'I'm nearly ready,' she added, fastening some coral earrings that matched her blouse.

Though Alexis would never have known it, a knot tightened in Sofia's stomach as she prepared for this family ritual. The moment reminded her of all those nights before her daughter's university terms began when she feigned jollity but felt anguished that Alexis would soon be gone. Sofia's ability to hide her emotions seemed to strengthen in proportion to the feelings she was suppressing. She looked at her daughter's mirrored image and at her own face next to it, and a shock wave passed through her. It was not the teenager's face that she always held in her mind's eye but the face of an adult, whose questioning eyes now engaged with her own.

'Hello, Mum,' Alexis said quietly. 'When's Dad back?'

'Quite soon, I hope. He knows you've got to be up early tomorrow so he promised not to be late.'

Alexis picked up the familiar photograph and took a deep breath. Even in her mid-twenties she still found herself having to summon up courage to force her way into the no-go region of her mother's past, as though she was ducking under the striped tape that cordoned off the scene of a crime. She needed to know what her mother thought. Sofia had married before she was twenty, so was she, Alexis, foolish to throw away the opportunity of spending the rest of her life with someone like Ed? Or might her mother think, as she did herself, that if these thoughts were even present in her head then he was, indeed, not the right person? Inwardly, she rehearsed her questions. How had her mother known with such certainty and at such an early age that the man she was to marry was 'the one'? How could she have known that she would be happy for the next fifty, sixty, perhaps even seventy years? Or had she not thought of it that way? Just at the moment when all these questions were to spill out, she demurred, suddenly fearful of rejection. There was, however, one question she *had* to ask.

'Could I . . .' asked Alexis, 'could I go and see where you grew up?' Apart from a Christian name that acknowledged her Greek blood, the only outward sign Alexis had of her maternal origins were her dark brown eyes, and that night she used them to full effect, locking her mother in her gaze. 'We're going to Crete at the end of our trip and it would be such a waste to travel all that way and miss the chance.'

Sofia was a woman who found it hard to smile, to show her feelings, to embrace. Reticence was her natural state and her immediate response was to search for an excuse. Something stopped her, however. It was Marcus's often-repeated words to her that Alexis would always be their child, but not forever *a* child that came back to her. Even if she struggled against the notion, she knew it was true, and seeing in front of her this independent young woman finally confirmed it. Instead of clamming up as she usually did when the subject of the past even hovered over a conversation, Sofia responded with unexpected warmth, recognising for the first time that her daughter's curiosity to know more about her roots was not only natural; it was possibly even a right.

'Yes . . .' she said hesitantly. 'I suppose you could.'

Alexis tried to hide her amazement, hardly daring to breathe in case her mother changed her mind.

Then, more certainly, Sofia said: 'Yes, it would be a good opportunity. I'll write a note for you to take to Fotini Davaras. She knew my family. She must be quite elderly now but she's lived in the village where I was born for her whole life and married the owner of the local taverna – so you might even get a good meal.'

Alexis shone with excitement. 'Thanks, Mum . . . Where exactly is the village?' she added. 'In relation to Hania?'

'It's about two hours' east of Iraklion,' Sofia said. 'So from Hania it might take you four or five hours – it's quite a distance for a day. Dad will be home any minute, but when we get back from dinner I'll write that letter for Fotini and show you exactly where Plaka is on a map.'

The careless bang of the front door announced Marcus's return from the university library. His worn leather briefcase stood, bulging, in the middle of the hallway, stray scraps of paper protruding through gaps in every seam. A bespectacled bear of a man with thick silvery hair who probably weighed as much as his wife and daughter combined, he greeted Alexis with a huge smile as she ran down from her mother's room and took off from the final stair, flying into his arms in just the way she had done since she was three years old.

'Dad!' said Alexis simply, and even that was superfluous.

'My beautiful girl,' he said, enveloping her in the sort of warm and comfortable embrace that only fathers of such generous proportions can offer.

They left for the restaurant soon after, a five-minute walk from the house. Nestling in the row of glossy wine bars, over-priced patisseries and trendy fusion restaurants, Taverna Loukakis was the constant. It had opened not long after the Fieldings had bought their house and in the meantime had seen a hundred other shops and eating places come and go. The owner, Gregorio, greeted the trio as the old friends they were, and so ritualistic were their visits that he knew even before they sat down what they would order. As ever, they listened politely to the day's specials, and then Gregorio pointed to each of them in turn and recited: '*Meze* of the day, moussaka, stifado, kalamari, a bottle of retsina and a large sparkling water.' They nodded and all of them laughed as he turned away in mock disgust at their rejection of his chef's more innovative dishes.

Alexis (moussaka) did most of the talking. She described her projected trip with Ed, and her father (kalamari) occasionally interjected with suggestions on archaeological sites they might visit.

'But Dad,' Alexis groaned despairingly, 'you *know* Ed's not really interested in looking at ruins!'

'I know, I know,' he replied patiently. 'But only a philistine would go to Crete without visiting Knossos. It would be like going to Paris and not bothering with the Louvre. Even Ed should realise that.'

They all knew perfectly well that Ed was more than capable of bypassing anything if there was a whiff of high culture about it, and as usual there was a subtle hint of disdain in Marcus's voice when Ed came into the conversation. It was not that he disliked him, or even really disapproved of him. Ed was exactly the sort that a father was meant to hope for as a son-in-law, but Marcus could not help his feelings of disappointment whenever he pictured this well-connected boy becoming his daughter's future. Sofia, on the other hand, adored Ed. He was the embodiment of all that she aspired to for her daughter: respectability, certainty and a family tree that lent him the confidence of someone linked (albeit extremely tenuously) with English aristocracy.

It was a light-hearted evening. The three of them had not been together for several months and Alexis had much to catch up on, not least all the tales of Nick's love life. In Manchester doing postgraduate work, Alexis's brother was in no hurry to grow up and his family were constantly amazed at the complexity of his relationships.

Alexis and her father then began to exchange anecdotes

about their work and Sofia found her mind wandering back to when they had first come to this restaurant and Gregorio had stacked up a pile of cushions so that Alexis could reach the table. By the time Nick was born, the taverna had invested in a highchair and soon the children had learned to love the strong tastes of taramasalata and tzatziki that the waiters brought out for them on tiny plates. For more than twenty years almost every landmark of their lives had been celebrated there, with the same tape of popular Greek tunes playing on a loop in the background. The realisation that Alexis was no longer a child struck Sofia more strongly than ever and she began to think of Plaka and the letter she was soon to write. For many years she had corresponded quite regularly with Fotini and over a quarter of a century earlier had described the arrival of her first child; within a few weeks, a small, perfectly embroidered dress had arrived in which Sofia had dressed the baby for her christening, in the absence of a traditional robe. The two women had stopped writing a while back, but Sofia was certain that Fotini's husband would have let her know if anything had happened to his wife. Sofia wondered what Plaka would be like now, and tried to block out an image of the little village overrun with noisy pubs selling English beer; she very much hoped Alexis would find it just as it was when she had left.

As the evening progressed Alexis felt a growing excitement that at last she was to delve further into her family history. In spite of the tensions she knew would have to be faced on her holiday, at least the visit to her mother's birthplace was something she could look forward to. Alexis and Sofia exchanged smiles and Marcus found himself wondering whether his days of playing mediator and truce-maker between his wife and daughter were drawing to a close. He was warmed by the thought and basked in the company of the two women he loved most in the world.

They finished their meal, politely drank the complimentary raki to the halfway mark and left for home. Alexis would sleep in her old room tonight, and she looked forward to those few hours in her childhood bed before she had to get up and take the underground to Heathrow in the morning. She felt strangely contented in spite of the fact that she had singularly failed to ask her mother's advice. It seemed much more important at this very moment that she was going, with her mother's full co-operation, to visit Sofia's birthplace. All her pressing anxieties over the more distant future were, for a moment, put aside.

When they returned from the restaurant, Alexis made her mother some coffee and Sofia sat at the kitchen table composing the letter to Fotini, rejecting three drafts before finally sealing an envelope and passing it across the table to her daughter. The whole process was conducted in silence, absorbing Sofia completely. Alexis had sensed that if she spoke the spell might be broken and her mother might have a change of heart after all.

For two and a half weeks now, Sofia's letter had sat in the safe inner pocket of Alexis's bag, as precious as her passport. Indeed, it was a passport in its own right, since it would be her way of gaining access to her mother's past. It had travelled with her from Athens and onwards on the fume-filled, sometimes storm-tossed ferries to Paros, Santorini and now

Crete. They had arrived on the island a few days earlier and found a room to rent on the seafront in Hania – an easy task at this stage of the season when most holidaymakers had already departed.

These were the last days of their vacation, and having reluctantly visited Knossos and the archaeological museum at Iraklion, Ed was keen to spend the few days before their long boat journey back to Piraeus on the beach. Alexis, however, had other plans.

'I'm going to visit an old friend of my mother's tomorrow,' she announced as they sat in a harbourside taverna waiting to give their order. 'She lives the other side of Iraklion, so I'll be gone most of the day.'

It was the first time she had mentioned her pilgrimage to Ed and she braced herself for his reaction.

'That's terrific!' he snapped, adding resentfully: 'Presumably you're taking the car?'

'Yes, I will if that's okay. It's a good hundred and fifty miles and it'll take me days if I have to go on local buses.'

'Well I suppose I don't really have a choice, do I? And I certainly don't want to come with you.'

Ed's angry eyes flashed at her like sapphires as his suntanned face disappeared behind his menu. He would sulk for the rest of the evening but Alexis could take that given that she had rather sprung this on him. What was harder to cope with, even though it was equally typical of him, was his total lack of interest in her plan. He did not even ask the name of the person she was going to visit.

Not long after the sun had risen over the hills the following morning, she crept out of bed and left their hotel.

Something very unexpected had struck her when she looked Plaka up in her guidebook. Something her mother had not mentioned. There was an island opposite the village just off the coast, and although the entry for it was minimal, miss-able even, it had captured her imagination:

> *SPINALONGA: Dominated by a massive Venetian fortress, this island was seized by the Turks in the eighteenth century. The majority of Turks left Crete when it was declared autonomous in 1898 but the inhabitants refused to give up their homes and their lucrative smuggling trade on Spinalonga. They only left in 1903 when the island was turned into a leper colony. In 1941, Crete was invaded by the Germans and occupied until 1945, but the presence of lepers meant Spinalonga was left alone. Abandoned in 1957.*

It appeared that the *raison d'être* of Plaka itself had been to act as a supply centre for the leper colony, and it intrigued Alexis that her mother had made no mention of this at all. As she sat at the wheel of the hired Cinquecento, she hoped she might have time to visit Spinalonga. She spread the map of Crete out on the empty passenger seat and noticed, for the first time, that the island was shaped like a languid animal asleep on its back.

The journey took her eastwards past Iraklion, and along the smooth, straight coastal road that passed through the insanely overdeveloped modern strips of Hersonisos and Malia. Occasionally she would spot a brown signpost indicating some ancient ruin nestling incongruously among the sprawling hotels. Alexis ignored all these signs. Today her destination was a settlement that had thrived not in the twentieth century BC but in the twentieth century AD and beyond.

Passing mile upon mile of olive groves and, in places where the ground became flatter on the coastal plains, huge plantations of reddening tomatoes and ripening grapes, she eventually turned off the main road and began the final stage of her journey towards Plaka. From here, the road narrowed and she was forced to drive in a more leisurely way, avoiding small piles of rocks which had spilled down from the mountains into the middle of the road and, from time to time, a goat ambling across in front of her, its devilishly close-set eyes glaring at her as she passed. After a while the road began to climb, and after one particularly sharp hairpin bend she drew in to the side, her tyres crackling on the gravelly surface. Way below her, in the blindingly blue waters of the Gulf of Mirabello, she could see the great arc of an almost circular natural harbour, and just where the arms of it seemed to join in embrace there was a piece of land that looked like a small, rounded hillock. From a distance it appeared to be connected to the mainland, but from her map Alexis knew this was the island of Spinalonga and that to reach it there was a strip of water to be crossed. Dwarfed by the landscape around it, the island stood proud of the water, the remains of the Venetian fortress clearly visible at one end, and behind it, fainter but still distinct, a series of lines mapped out; these were its streets. So there it was: the empty island. It had been continuously inhabited for thousands of years and then, less than fifty years ago, for some reason abandoned.

She took the last few miles of her journey down to Plaka slowly, the windows of her cheap rented car wound down to let in the warm breeze and the fragrant smell of thyme. It was two o'clock in the afternoon when she finally rattled to a halt in the silent village square. Her hands were glistening with sweat from gripping the hard plastic steering wheel and she noticed that her left arm had been scorched by the early afternoon sun. It was a ghostly time to arrive in a Greek village. Dogs played dead in the shade and a few cats prowled for scraps. There were no other signs of life, simply some vague indications that people had been there not long before – an abandoned moped leaning against a tree, half a packet of cigarettes on a bench and a backgammon set lying open next to it. Cicadas kept up their relentless chorus that would only be silenced at dusk when the fierce heat finally cooled. The village probably looked exactly as it had done in the 1970s when her mother had left. There had been few reasons for it to change.

Alexis had already decided that she would try to visit Spinalonga before she tracked down Fotini Davaras. She was enjoying this sense of complete freedom and independence, and once she had found the old woman it might then seem rude to go off on a boat trip. It was clear to Alexis that she would be pushed to get back to Hania that night, but just for now she would enjoy her afternoon and would deal with the logistics of ringing Ed and finding somewhere to stay later on.

Deciding to take the guidebook at its word ('Try the bar in the small fishing village of Plaka where, for a few thousand drachma, there is usually a fisherman willing to take you across'), she made her way purposefully across the square and pushed aside the sticky rainbow of plastic strips that hung in the doorway of the village bar. These grubby ribbons were an attempt to keep the flies out and the coolness in, but all they actually did was gather dust and keep the place in a permanent state of semi-darkness. Staring into the gloom, Alexis could just about make out the shape of a woman seated at a table, and as she groped her way towards her, the shadowy figure got up and moved behind the bar. By now Alexis's throat was desiccated with dust.

'*Nero, parakalo*,' she said, hesitantly.

The woman shuffled past a series of giant glass vats of olives and several half-empty bottles of clear, thick ouzo and reached into the fridge for some chilled mineral water. She poured carefully into a tall, straight-edged glass, adding a thick wedge of rough-skinned lemon before passing it to Alexis. She then dried her hands, wet with condensation from the icy bottle, on a huge floral apron that just about reached around her generous waist, and spoke. 'English?' she asked.

Alexis nodded. It was a half-truth after all. It took her just one word to communicate her next wish. 'Spinalonga?' she said.

The woman turned on her heel and vanished through a little doorway behind the bar. Alexis could hear the muffled yells of 'Gerasimo! Gerasimo!' and, soon after, the sound of footsteps on a wooden staircase. An elderly man, bleary-eyed from his disturbed siesta, appeared. The woman gabbled away at him, and the only word that meant anything to Alexis was 'drachma', which was repeated several times. It was quite clear that, in no uncertain terms, he was being told that there was good money to be earned here. The man stood there blinking, taking in this torrent of instructions but saying nothing.

The woman turned to Alexis and, grabbing her order pad from the bar, scribbled down some figures and a diagram. Even if Alexis had spoken fluent Greek it could not have been clearer. With the help of plenty of pointing and circular movements in the air and marks on the paper, she deduced that her return trip to Spinalonga, with a two-hour stop on the island, would cost 20,000 drachma, around £35. It wasn't going to be a cheap day out, but she was in no position to negotiate – and besides, she was more committed than ever to visiting the island. She nodded and smiled at the boatman, who nodded gravely back at her. It was at that moment that it dawned on Alexis that there was more to the ferryman's silence than she had at first realised. He could not have spoken even if he had wished. Gerasimo was dumb.

It was a short walk to the quayside where Gerasimo's battered old boat was moored. They walked in silence past the sleeping dogs and the shuttered buildings. Nothing stirred. The only sounds were the soft padding of their own rubber-soled feet and the cicadas. Even the sea was flat and soundless.

So here she was being ferried on this 500-metre journey by a man who occasionally smiled, but no more. He was as leather-faced as any Cretan fisherman who had spent decades on storm-tossed seas, battling the elements by night and mending his nets in the baking sunshine by day. He was probably somewhere beyond sixty years old, but if wrinkles were like the rings of an oak tree and could be used to measure age, a rough calculation would leave him little short of eighty. His features betrayed nothing. No pain, no misery, but no particular joy either. They were simply the quiet features of resigned old age and a reflection of all that he had lived through in the previous century. Though tourists had been Crete's most recent invaders, following the Venetians, the Turks and, in the old man's lifetime, the Germans, few of them had bothered to learn any Greek. Alexis now castigated herself for not getting her mother to teach her some useful vocabulary – presumably Sofia could still speak fluently even if her daughter had never heard her utter a word. All Alexis could now offer the boatman was a polite '*efharisto*' – 'thank you' – as he helped her on board, at which he touched the brim of his battered straw hat in reply.

Now approaching Spinalonga, Alexis gathered up her camera and the plastic two-litre bottle of water that the woman in the café had pressed upon her, indicating that she must drink plenty. As the boat bumped against the jetty, old Gerasimo offered her a hand and she stepped across the wooden seat on to the uneven surface of the deserted quay. She noticed then that the engine was still running. The old man was not, it appeared, intending to stay. They managed to communicate to each other that he would return in two hours, and she watched as he slowly turned the boat and set off back in the direction of Plaka.

Alexis was now stranded on Spinalonga and felt a wave of fear sweep over her. Supposing Gerasimo forgot her? How long would it take before Ed came in search? Could she swim the distance back to the mainland? She had never been so entirely alone, had rarely been more than a few metres from the next human being and, except in her sleep, never out of touch with other people for more than an hour or so. Her dependency suddenly felt like a millstone and she resolved to pull herself together. She would embrace this period of solitude – her few hours of isolation were a mere pinprick of time compared with the life sentence of loneliness that past inhabitants of Spinalonga must have faced.

The massive stone walls of the Venetian fortification loomed above her. How was she to get past this apparently impregnable obstacle? It was then that she noticed, in the rounded section of the wall, a small entrance that was just about head height. It was a tiny, dark opening in the pale expanse of stonework, and as she approached she saw that it was the way into a long tunnel which curved away to block the view of what lay at its far end. With the sea behind her and the walls in front, there was only one way to go – forward into the dark, claustrophobic passageway. It went on for some metres, and when she emerged from the semi-darkness once again into the dazzling early afternoon light she saw that the scale of the place had changed completely. She stopped, transfixed.

She was at the lower end of a long street lined on both sides with small two-storey houses. At one time this might have looked like any village in Crete, but these buildings had been reduced to a state of semi-dereliction. Window frames hung at strange angles on broken hinges, and shutters twitched and creaked in the slight sea breeze. She walked hesitantly down the dusty street, taking in everything she saw: a church on her right with a solid carved door, a building which, judging by its large ground-floor window frames, had evidently been a shop, and a slightly grander detached building with a wooden balcony, arched doorway and the remains of a walled garden. A profound, eerie silence hung over it all.

In the downstairs rooms of the houses clumps of bright

wild flowers grew in abundance, and on the upper storeys wallflowers peeped out from between cracks in the plaster. Many of the house numbers were still visible, the fading figures – 11, 18, 29 – focusing Alexis's imagination on the fact that behind each of these front doors real lives had been lived. She continued to stroll, spellbound. It was like sleep-walking. This was not a dream and yet there was something entirely unreal about it all.

She passed what must have been a café, a larger hall and a building with rows of concrete basins, which she deduced must have been a laundry. Next to them were the remains of an ugly three-storey block with functional cast-iron balcony railings. The scale of the building was in strange contrast with the houses, and it was odd to think that someone must have put this building up only seventy years ago and thought it the height of modernity. Now its huge windows gaped open to the sea breeze and electric wires hung down from the ceilings like clumps of coagulated spaghetti. It was almost the saddest building of all.

Beyond the town she came to an overgrown path that led away to a spot beyond all signs of civilisation. It was a natural promontory with a sheer drop into the sea hundreds of feet below. Here she allowed herself to imagine the misery of the lepers and to wonder whether in desperation they might ever have come to this place to contemplate ending it all. She stared out towards the curved horizon. Until now she had been so absorbed by her surroundings, so entirely immersed in the dense atmosphere of the place, that all thoughts of her own situation had been suspended. She was the only person on this entire island and it made her face a fact: solitude did not have to mean loneliness. You could be lonely in a crowd. The thought gave her strength for what she might have to do when she returned: begin the next stage of her life alone.

Retracing her steps into the silent town, Alexis rested for a while on a stone doorstep, gulping back some of the water she had carried with her. Nothing stirred except for the occasional lizard scuttling through the dry leaves that now carpeted the floors of these decaying homes. Through a gap in the derelict house in front of her she caught a glimpse of the sea, and beyond it the mainland. Each day the lepers must have looked across at Plaka and been able to see every building, every boat – perhaps even people going about their daily business. She could only begin to imagine how much its proximity must have tantalised them.

What stories could the walls of this town tell? They must have seen great suffering. It went without saying that being a leper, stuck out here on this rock, must have been as bad a card as life could deal. Alexis was, however, well practised in making deductions from archaeological fragments, and she could tell from what remained of this place that life here had held a more complex range of emotions for the inhabitants than simply misery and despair. If their existence had been entirely abject, why would there have been cafés? Why was there a building that could only have been a town hall? She sensed melancholy, but she also saw signs of normality. It was these that had taken her by surprise. This tiny island had been a community, not just a place to come and die – that much was clear from the remains of the infrastructure.

Time had passed quickly. When Alexis glanced at her watch

she saw that it was already five o'clock. The sun had seemed so high still and its heat so intense that she had lost all track of time. She leapt up, her heart pounding. Though she had enjoyed the silence and the peace here, she did not relish the idea of Gerasimo leaving without her. She hurried back through the long dark tunnel and out on to the quay the other side. The old fisherman was sitting in his boat waiting for her, and immediately she appeared, he twisted the key to start the motor. Clearly he had no intention of staying around longer than necessary.

The journey back to Plaka was over within minutes. With a sense of relief she spotted the bar where her journey had begun and saw the comfortingly familiar hire car parked just opposite. By now the village had come to life. Outside doorways women sat talking, and under the trees in the open space by the bar a group of men were huddled over a game of cards, a pall of smoke from their strong cigarettes hanging in the air. She and Gerasimo walked back to the bar in their now accustomed silence and were greeted by the woman, who Alexis deduced was Gerasimo's wife. Alexis counted out a handful of scruffy notes and handed them to her. 'Do you want drink?' asked the woman in her rough English. Alexis realised that it was not only a drink she needed, but also food. She had eaten nothing all day and the combination of heat and the sea journey had left her feeling shaky.

Recalling that her mother's friend ran a local taverna, she hastily rummaged inside her backpack for the crumpled envelope containing Sofia's letter. She showed the address to the woman, who registered immediate recognition. Taking Alexis by the arm, she led her out into the street and along the seafront. About fifty metres down the road, and extending on a small pier out into the sea, was a taverna. Like an oasis, its painted blue chairs and checked indigo and white tablecloths seemed to summon Alexis, and the moment she was greeted by its owner, the restaurant's eponymous Stephanos, she knew she would be happy to sit there and watch the sun go down.

Stephanos had one thing in common with every other taverna owner Alexis had met: a thick, well-clipped moustache. Unlike the majority of them, however, he did not look as though he ate as much as he served. It was much too early for local people to eat, so Alexis sat alone, at a table right on the edge by the sea.

'Is Fotini Davaras here today?' Alexis asked tentatively. 'My mother knew her when she was growing up here and I have a letter for her.'

Stephanos, who spoke a great deal more English than the couple at the bar, warmly replied that his wife was indeed there and would come out to see her as soon as she had finished preparing today's dishes. He suggested meanwhile that he bring her a selection of local specialities so that she didn't have to bother with a menu. With a glass of chilled retsina in her hand and some coarse bread on the table in front of her to sate her immediate hunger, Alexis felt a wave of contentment pass over her. She had derived great pleasure from her day of solitude and relished this moment of freedom and independence. She looked across at Spinalonga. Freedom was not something any of the lepers would ever have enjoyed, she thought, but had they gained something else instead?

Stephanos returned with a series of small white plates stacked up his arm, each one charged with a tiny portion of something tasty and freshly prepared from his kitchen – prawns, stuffed zucchini flowers, tzatziki and miniature cheese pies. Alexis wondered if she had ever felt such hunger or been presented with such delicious-looking food.

As he approached her table Stephanos had noticed her gazing out towards the island. He was intrigued by this lone Englishwoman who had, as Andriana, Gerasimo's wife, explained, spent the afternoon alone on Spinalonga. In high summer several boatloads of tourists a day were ferried across – but most of them only stayed for half an hour at most and then were driven back by coach to one of the big resorts further down the coast. The majority only came out of ghoulish curiosity, and judging by the snatches of conversation he sometimes overheard if they ever bothered to stop in Plaka for a meal, they were usually disappointed. It seemed that they expected to see more than a few derelict houses and a boarded-up church. What did they want? he was always tempted to ask. Bodies? Abandoned crutches? Their insensitivity never failed to arouse his irritation. But this woman was not like them.

'What did you think of the island?' he asked.

'It surprised me,' she replied. 'I expected it to be terribly melancholy – and it was – but there was much more to it than that. It was obvious that the people who lived there did more than just sit around feeling sorry for themselves. At least that's how it seemed to me.'

This was not at all the usual reaction from visitors to Spinalonga, but the young woman had obviously spent more time there than most. Alexis was happy to make conversation, and since Stephanos was always keen to practise his English he was not going to discourage her.

'I don't really know why I think that – but am I right?' she asked.

'May I sit down?' asked Stephanos, not waiting for an answer before scraping a chair across the floor and perching on it. He felt instinctively that this woman was open to the magic of Spinalonga. 'My wife had a friend who used to live there,' he said. 'She is one of the few people round here who still has any connections at all with the island. Everyone else went as far away as possible once the cure had been found. Apart from old Gerasimo, of course.'

'Gerasimo . . . was a leper?' asked Alexis, slightly aghast. It would certainly explain his haste to get away from the island once he had dropped her off there. Her curiosity was fully aroused now. 'And your wife, did she ever visit the island?'

'Many, many times,' replied Stephanos. 'She knows more about it than anyone else around here.'

By now, other customers were arriving, and Stephanos got up from the wicker-seated chair to show them to their tables and present them with menus. The sun had now fallen below the horizon and the sky had turned a deep pink. Swallows dived and swooped, catching insects on the rapidly cooling air. What seemed like an age went by. Alexis had eaten everything that Stephanos had put in front of her but she was still hungry.

Just as she was wondering whether to go into the kitchen to choose what to have next, as was perfectly acceptable for customers in Crete, her main course arrived.

'This is today's catch,' said the waitress, setting down an oval platter. 'It is *barbouni*. I think that is red mullet in English. I hope I have cooked it as you like it – just grilled with fresh herbs and a little olive oil.'

Alexis was astonished. Not just by the perfectly presented dish. Not even by the woman's soft, almost accentless English. What took her by surprise was her beauty. She had always wondered what kind of face could possibly have launched a thousand ships. It must have been one like this.

'Thank you,' she said finally. 'That looks wonderful.'

The vision seemed about to turn away, but then she paused. 'My husband said you were asking for me.'

Alexis looked up in surprise. Her mother had told her that Fotini was in her early seventies, but this woman was slim, scarcely lined, and her hair, piled high on her head, was still the colour of ripe chestnuts. She was not the old woman Alexis had been expecting to meet.

'You're not . . . Fotini Davaras?' she said uncertainly, getting to her feet.

'I am she,' the woman asserted gently.

'I have a letter for you,' Alexis said, recovering. 'From my mother, Sofia Fielding.'

Fotini Davaras's face lit up. 'You're Sofia's daughter! My goodness, how wonderful!' she said. 'How is she? How is she?'

Fotini accepted with huge enthusiasm the letter which Alexis held out to her, hugging it to her chest as though Sofia herself were there in person. 'I am so happy. I haven't heard from her since her aunt died a few years ago. Until then she used to write to me every month, then she just stopped. I was very worried when some of my last letters went unanswered.'

All of this was news to Alexis. She had been unaware that her mother used to send letters to Crete so regularly – and certainly had no idea that she had ever received any. How odd during all those years that Alexis herself had never once seen a letter bearing a Greek postmark – she felt sure she would have remembered it, since she had always been an early riser, and invariably the one to sweep up any letters from the doormat. It seemed that her mother had gone to great lengths to conceal this correspondence.

By now Fotini was holding Alexis by the shoulders and scrutinising her face with her almond-shaped eyes.

'Let me see – yes, yes, you do look a bit like her. You look even more like poor Anna.'

Anna? On all those occasions when she had tried to extract information from her mother about the sepia-toned aunt and uncle who had brought her up, Alexis had never heard this name.

'Your mother's mother,' Fotini added quickly, immediately spotting the quizzical look on the girl's face. Something like a shudder went down Alexis's spine. Standing in the dusky half-light, with the now ink-black sea behind her, she was all but knocked backwards by the scale of her mother's secretiveness, and the realisation that she was talking to someone who might hold some of the answers.

'Come on, sit down, sit down. You must eat the *barbouni*,' said Fotini. By now Alexis had almost lost her appetite, but she felt it polite to co-operate and the two women sat down.

In spite of the fact that she wanted to ask all the questions – she was bursting with them – Alexis allowed herself to be interviewed by Fotini, whose enquiries were all more searching than they appeared. How was her mother? Was she happy? What was her father like? What had brought her to Crete?

Fotini was as warm as the night, and Alexis found herself

answering her questions very openly. This woman was old enough to be her grandmother, and yet was so unlike how she would expect a grandmother to be. Fotini Davaras was the antithesis of the bent old lady in black that she had imagined when her mother had handed her the letter. Her interest in Alexis seemed totally genuine. It was a long time – if it had ever happened at all – since Alexis had talked to someone like this. Her university tutor had occasionally listened to her as though what she said really mattered, but in her heart she knew that was only because she was paid to do so. It wasn't long before Alexis was confiding in Fotini.

'My mother has always been terribly secretive about her early life,' she said. 'All I really know is that she was born near here and brought up by her uncle and aunt – and that she left altogether when she was eighteen and never came back.'

'Is that *really* all you know?' Fotini asked. 'Hasn't she told you any more than that?'

'No, nothing at all. That's partly why I'm here. I want to know more. I want to know what made her turn her back on the past like that.'

'But why now?' enquired Fotini.

'Oh, lots of reasons,' said Alexis, looking down at her plate. 'But mostly it's to do with my boyfriend. I've realised lately how lucky my mother was to find my father – I'd always assumed that their relationship was typical.'

'I'm glad they're happy. It was a bit of a whirlwind at the time, but we were all very hopeful because they seemed so blissfully content.'

'It's odd, though. I know so little about my mother. She never talks about her childhood, never talks about living here—'

'Doesn't she?' interjected Fotini.

'What I feel,' said Alexis, 'is that to find out more about my mother might help me. She was fortunate to meet someone she could care so much about, but how did she *know* he would be the right person for ever? I've been with Ed for more than five years, and I'm not sure whether we should be together or not.'

This statement was very uncharacteristic of the normally pragmatic Alexis, and she was aware that it might sound rather nebulous, almost fanciful, to someone she had known for less than two hours. Besides, she had strayed off the agenda; how could she expect this Greek woman, kindly as she was, to be interested in her?

Stephanos approached at this moment to clear the dishes, and within minutes he was back with cups of coffee and two generous balloons of molasses-coloured brandy. Other customers had come and gone during the evening and, once again, the table Alexis occupied was the only one in use.

Warmed by the hot coffee and even more so by the fiery Metaxa, Alexis asked Fotini how long she had known her mother.

'Practically from the day she was born,' the older woman replied. But she stopped there, feeling a great weight of responsibility. Who was she, Fotini Davaras, to tell this girl things about her family's past that her own mother had clearly wanted to conceal from her? It was only at that moment that Fotini remembered the letter she had tucked into her apron.

She pulled it out and, picking up a knife from the next table, quickly slit it open.

Dear Fotini,

Please forgive me for being out of touch for so long. I know I don't need to explain the reasons to you, but believe me when I tell you that I think of you often. This is my daughter, Alexis. Will you treat her as kindly as you always treated me – I hardly need to ask it, do I?

Alexis is very curious about her history – it's understandable, but I have found it almost impossible to tell her anything. Isn't it odd how the passage of time can make it harder than ever to bring things out into the open?

I know she will ask you plenty of questions – she is a natural historian. Will you answer them? Your eyes and ears witnessed the whole story – I think you will be able to give her a truer account than I ever could.

Paint a picture of it all for her, Fotini. She will be eternally grateful. Who knows – she may even return to England and be able to tell me things I never knew. Will you show her where I was born – I know she will be interested in that – and take her to Agios Nikolaos?

This comes with much love to you and Stephanos – and please send warm best wishes to your sons too.

Thank you, Fotini.

Yours ever,
Sofia

When she had finished reading the letter, Fotini folded it carefully and returned it to its envelope. She looked across at Alexis, who had been studying her every expression with curiosity as she scanned the crumpled sheet of paper.

'Your mother has asked me to tell you all about your family,' said Fotini, 'but it's not really a bed-time story. We close the taverna on Sunday and Monday and I have all the time in the world at this end of the season. Why don't you stay with us for a couple of days? I would be delighted if you would.' Fotini's eyes glittered in the darkness. They looked watery – with tears or excitement, Alexis couldn't tell.

She knew instinctively that this might be the best investment of time she could ever make, and there was no doubt that her mother's story could help her more in the long term than yet another museum visit. Why examine the cool relics of past civilisations when she could be breathing life into her own history? There was nothing to stop her staying. Just a brief text message telling Ed that she was going to be here for a day or so would be all it would take. Even though she knew it was an act of almost callous disregard for him, she felt this opportunity justified a little selfishness. She was essentially free to do what she pleased. It was a moment of stillness. The dark, flat sea almost seemed to hold its breath, and in the clear sky above, the brightest constellation of all, Orion, who had been killed and placed in the sky by the gods, seemed to wait for her decision.

This might be the one chance Alexis was offered in her lifetime to grab at the fragments of her own history before they were dissipated in the breeze. She knew there was only one response to the invitation. 'Thank you,' she said quietly, suddenly overwhelmed with tiredness. 'I'd love to stay.'

Chapter Two

ALEXIS SLEPT DEEPLY that night. When she and Fotini finally went to bed, it was after one o'clock in the morning, and the cumulative effect of the long drive to Plaka, the afternoon on Spinalonga and the heady mix of meze and Metaxa drew her into a deep and dreamless sleep.

It was nearly ten when luminous sunshine came streaming through the gap between the thick hessian curtains and threw a beam across Alexis's pillow. As it woke her, she instinctively slid further under the sheets to hide her face. In the past fortnight she had slept in several unfamiliar rooms, and each time she surfaced there was a moment of confusion as she adjusted to her surroundings and dragged herself into the here and now. Most of the mattresses in the cheap pensions where she and Ed had stayed had either sagged in the middle or had metal springs protruding through the ticking. It had never been hard to get up from those beds in the morning. But this bed was altogether different. In fact the whole room was different. The round table with a lace cloth, the stool with its faded woven seat, the group of framed watercolours on the wall, the candlestick thickly coated with organ pipes of wax, the fragrant lavender which hung in a bunch on the back of the door, and the walls painted in a soft blue to match the bed linen: all of these things made it homelier than home.

When she drew back the curtains she was greeted by the dazzling vista of a sparkling sea and the island of Spinalonga, which, in the shimmering haze of heat, seemed further away, more remote than it had yesterday.

When she had set off from Hania early the previous day, she had had no intention of staying in Plaka. She had imagined a brief meeting with the elderly woman from her mother's childhood and a short tour of the village before rejoining Ed. For that reason she had brought nothing more than a map and her camera – and had certainly not anticipated needing spare clothes or a toothbrush. Fotini, however, had been quick to come to her rescue, lending her everything she needed – one of Stephanos's shirts to sleep in, and a clean if rather threadbare towel. This morning, at the end of her bed, she found a floral shirt – not at all her style, but after the heat and dust of the previous day she was glad for the change of clothing. It was a gesture of such maternal kindness that she could hardly ignore it – even if the pale pinks and blues of the blouse looked rather incongruous with her khaki shorts, what did it really matter? Alexis splashed her face with cold water at the tiny sink in the corner and then scrutinised her tanned face in the mirror. She was as excited as a child who was about to be read the crucial chapter of a story. Today Fotini was going to be her Scheherazade.

Dressed in the unfamiliar feel of crisp, ironed cotton, she wandered down the dark back stairway and found herself in the restaurant kitchen, drawn there by the powerful aroma of strong, freshly brewed coffee. Fotini sat at a huge, gnarled table in the middle of the room. Though thoroughly scrubbed, it still seemed to bear the stains from every piece of meat that had been pulverised there and every herb that had been crushed on its surface. It must have also witnessed a thousand moments of frayed temper which had simmered and boiled over in the intense heat of the kitchen. Fotini rose to greet her.

'*Kalimera*, Alexis!' she said warmly.

She was wearing a blouse similar to the one she had lent Alexis, though Fotini's was in shades of ochre that matched the full skirt that billowed out from her slender waist and nearly reached her ankles. The first impression of her beauty that had struck Alexis so forcibly the night before in the kindly dusk light had not been wrong. The Cretan woman's statuesque physique and large eyes reminded her of the images on the great Minoan fresco at Knossos, those vivid portraits which had survived several thousand years of time's ravages and yet had a remarkable simplicity that made them seem so contemporary.

'Did you sleep well?' asked Fotini.

Alexis stifled a yawn, nodded and then smiled at Fotini, who was now busily loading a tray with a coffee pot, some generously proportioned cups and saucers and a loaf that she had just removed from the oven.

'I'm sorry – it's reheated. That's the only bad thing about Sundays here – the baker doesn't get out of bed. So it's dry crusts or fresh air,' Fotini said laughingly.

'I'd be more than happy with fresh air, as long as it was washed down with fresh coffee,' responded Alexis, following Fotini out through a set of the ubiquitous plastic strips and on to the terrace, where all last night's tables had been stripped of their paper cloths and now looked strangely bare with their red Formica tops.

The two women sat overlooking the sea which lapped the rocks below. Fotini poured and the dense black liquid gushed in a dark stream into the white china. After the endless disappointing cups of Nescafé, served as though the tasteless dissolving granules of instant coffee were a delicacy, Alexis felt no cup of coffee had ever tasted as powerful and delicious as this. It seemed that nobody had the heart to tell the Greeks that Nescafé was no longer a novelty – it was this old-fashioned thick and treacly fluid that everyone, including her, craved. The September sunshine had a clear brilliance and a kindly warmth that, after the intensity of the August heat, made it one of the most welcome months in Crete. The furnace-strong temperatures of midsummer had dropped and the hot, angry winds had gone too. The two women sat opposite each other beneath the shade of the awning and Fotini put her dark, lined hand on Alexis's.

'I'm so pleased you have come,' she said. 'You can't imagine how pleased. I was very hurt when your mother stopped writing – I understood perfectly, but it broke such an important link with the past.'

'I had no idea she used to write to you,' said Alexis, feeling as though she should apologise on her mother's behalf.

'The very beginning of her life was difficult,' continued Fotini, 'but we all tried, we really did, to make her happy and to do our best for her.'

Looking at Alexis's slightly puzzled expression, Fotini realised that she had to slow her pace. She poured them both another cup of coffee, giving herself a moment to think about where to start. It seemed she would have to go back even further than she had originally imagined would be necessary.

'I could say, "I'll begin at the beginning", but there is no real beginning here,' she said. 'Your mother's story is your grandmother's story, and it is also your great-grandmother's story. It's your great-aunt's story too. Their lives were intertwined, and that's what we really mean when we talk about fate in Greece. Our so-called fate is largely ordained by our ancestors, not by the stars. When we talk about ancient history here we always refer to destiny – but we don't really mean the uncontrollable. Of course events seem to take place out of the blue that change the course of our lives, but what really determines what happens to us are the actions of those around us now and those who came before us.'

Alexis began to feel slightly edgy. The impregnable safe of her mother's past, which had been so resolutely locked for her entire life, was now to be opened. All the secrets would come spilling out, and she found herself questioning whether she really wanted that. She stared out across the sea at the pale outline of Spinalonga and remembered her solitary afternoon there, already with nostalgia. Pandora regretted opening her box. Would it be the same for her?

Fotini spotted the direction of her gaze.

'Your great-grandmother lived on that island,' she said. 'She was a leper.' She didn't expect her words to sound quite so blunt, quite so heartless, and she saw straightaway that they had made Alexis wince.

'A *leper*?' Alexis asked in a voice that was almost choked with shock. She was repelled by this thought even though she knew her reaction was probably irrational, and found it difficult to hide her feelings. She had learned that the old boatman had been a leper and had seen for herself that he was not visibly disfigured. Nevertheless, she was horrified to hear that her own flesh and blood had been leprous. That was entirely different, and she felt strangely disgusted.

For Fotini, who had grown up in the shadow of the colony, leprosy had always been a fact of life. She had seen more lepers arrive in Plaka to cross over the water to Spinalonga than she could count. She had also seen the varied states of the victims of the disease: some cripplingly disfigured, others apparently untouched. Untouchable had, in fact, been the last thing they seemed. But she understood Alexis's reaction. It was the natural response for someone whose knowledge of leprosy came from Old Testament stories and the image of a bell-swinging sufferer crying, 'Unclean! Unclean!'

'Let me explain more,' she offered. 'I know what you imagine leprosy to be like, but it's important that you know the truth of it, otherwise you will never understand the real Spinalonga, the Spinalonga that was home to so many good people.'

Alexis continued to gaze at the little island across the shimmering water. Her visit there yesterday had seemed so full of conflicting images: the remains of elegant Italianate villas, gardens and even shops, and overshadowing them all the spectre of a disease which she had seen portrayed in epic films as a living death. She took another gulp of the thick coffee.

'I know it's not fatal in every case,' she said, almost defensively, 'but it is always horribly disfiguring, isn't it?'

'Not to the extent that you might think,' replied Fotini. 'It's not a rampantly fast-spreading disease like the plague. It sometimes takes ages to develop – those images you have seen of people who are so terribly maimed are of those who have suffered for years, maybe decades. There are two strains of leprosy, one much slower to develop than the other. Both are curable now. Your great-grandmother was unfortunate, though. She had the faster-developing of the two types and neither time nor history was on her side.'

Alexis was feeling ashamed of her initial reaction, humbled by her ignorance, but the revelation that a member of her family had been a leper had been a bolt out of the bluest of skies.

'Your great-grandmother may have been the one with the disease, but your great-grandfather, Giorgis, bore deep scars too. Even before his wife was exiled to Spinalonga, he used to make deliveries to the island with his fishing boat, and he continued to do so when she went there. It meant that he watched on an almost daily basis as she was gradually destroyed by the disease. When Eleni first went to Spinalonga hygiene was poor, and though it improved a great deal during the time she was there, some irreparable damage was done in her early years. I shall spare you the details. Giorgis spared Maria and Anna from them. But you do know how it happens, don't you? Leprosy can affect nerve endings, and the result of this is that you can't feel it if you burn or cut yourself. That's why people with leprosy are so vulnerable to inflicting permanent damage on themselves, and the consequences of that can be disastrous.'

Fotini paused. She was concerned not to offend this young

woman's sensibilities, but was also very aware that there were elements of the story that were nothing less than shocking. It was simply a case of treading carefully.

'I don't want your image of your mother's family to be dominated by disease. It wasn't like that,' she added hastily. 'Look. I've got some photographs of them here.'

On the big wooden tray propped against the coffee pot there was a tatty manila envelope. Fotini opened it and the contents spilled out on to the table. Some of the photographs were no bigger than train tickets, others were postcard size. Some were shiny, with white borders, others were matt, but all were monochrome, many faded almost to invisibility. Most had been taken in a studio in the days before the spontaneous snapshot was possible, and the stiffness of the subjects made them seem as distant and remote as King Minos.

The first photo Alexis focused on was one she recognised. It was the picture that her mother had next to her bed of the lady in lace and the platinum-haired man. She picked it up.

'That's your great-aunt Maria and great-uncle Nikolaos,' said Fotini, with a detectable hint of pride. 'And this one,' she said, pulling out a battered picture from the bottom of the pile, 'was the last picture taken of your great-grandparents and their two girls all together.'

She passed it to Alexis. The man was about the same height as the woman, but broad-shouldered. He had dark, wavy hair, a clipped moustache, a strong nose, and eyes that smiled even though the expression he maintained for this photograph was serious and posed. His hands seemed big in comparison with his body. The woman next to him was slim, long-necked and strikingly beautiful; her hair was wound into plaits which were coiled up on top of her head, and her smile was broad and spontaneous. Seated in front of them were two girls in cotton dresses. One had strong, thick hair worn loose about her shoulders and her eyes were slanted almost like a cat's. She had mischief in her eyes and plump lips that did not smile. The other had neatly plaited hair, more delicate features and a nose that wrinkled as she smiled at the camera. She could almost be described as skinny and, of the two girls, was much more like the mother, with her hands held softly in her lap in a demure pose while her sister had her arms folded and glared, as if in defiance, at the person taking the photograph.

'That's Maria,' said Fotini, pointing at the child who smiled. 'And that's Anna, your grandmother,' she said, indicating the other. 'And those are their parents, Eleni and Giorgis.'

She spread the pictures out on the table, and occasionally the breeze lifted them gently from its surface and seemed to bring them to life. Alexis saw pictures of the two sisters when they were babes in arms, then as schoolgirls, and then as young women, by that stage just with their father. There was also a picture of Anna arm in arm with a man in full traditional Cretan dress. It was a wedding picture.

'So that must be my grandfather,' said Alexis. 'Anna looks really beautiful there,' she added admiringly. 'Really happy.'

'Mmm . . . the radiance of young love,' said Fotini. There was a hint of sarcasm in her voice that took Alexis by surprise, and she was about to quiz her further when another picture surfaced which seized her interest.

'That looks like my mother!' she exclaimed. The little girl

in the photograph had a distinctive aquiline nose and a sweet but rather shy smile.

'It *is* your mother. She must have been about five then.'

Like any collection of family photographs, it was a random selection that told only fragments of a story. The real tale would be revealed by the pictures that were missing or never even taken at all, not the ones that had been so carefully framed or packed away neatly in an envelope. Alexis was aware of that, but at least she had now been given a glimpse of these family members that her mother had kept so secret for so long.

'It all began here in Plaka,' said Fotini. 'Just behind us, over there. That's where the Petrakis family lived.'

She pointed to a small house on the corner, a pebble's throw from where they sat sipping their coffee. It was a tatty, whitewashed building, as shabby as every other home in the ramshackle village, but charming nevertheless. Its plastered walls were flaking and the shutters, repainted time and time again since Alexis's great-grandparents had lived there, were a shade of bright aqua that had peeled and cracked in the heat. A balcony, perched above the doorway, sagged under the weight of several huge urns from which flame-red geraniums cascaded downwards, as though making their escape through the carved wooden railings. It was typical of almost every home on every Greek island and could have been built at any time in the past few hundred years. Plaka, like any village lucky enough to have been spared the ravages of mass tourism, was timeless.

'That's where your grandmother and her sister grew up. Maria was my best friend; she was just over a year younger than Anna. Their father, Giorgis, was a fisherman, like most of the local men, and Eleni, his wife, was a teacher. In fact she was really much more than a teacher – she more or less ran the local elementary school. It was just down the road in Elounda, the town you must have come through to reach us here. She loved children – not just her own daughters, but *all* the children who were in her classes. I think Anna found that difficult. She was a possessive child and hated sharing anything, especially her mother's affection. But Eleni was generous in every way and had enough time for all her children, whether they were her own flesh and blood or simply her pupils.

'I used to pretend that I was another of Giorgis and Eleni's daughters. I was always at their house; I had two brothers so you can imagine how my own home differed from theirs. My mother, Savina, didn't seem to mind. She and Eleni had been friends since childhood and had shared everything from an early age, so I don't think she worried about losing me. In fact, I believe she always harboured a fantasy that either Maria or Anna would end up marrying one of my brothers.

'When I was little I probably spent more time at the Petrakis place than I did at my own, but the tables turned later on and Anna and Maria more or less lived with us.

'Our playground at that time, and for our whole childhood, was the beach. It was ever-changing and we never tired of it. We would swim each day from late May to early October and would have restless nights from the unbearable grittiness of the sand that had hidden in between our toes and then worked its way out on to our sheets. In the evenings we fished for our own picarel, tiny fish, and in the morning we'd go and see what the fishermen had brought in. The winters bring higher tides and there was usually something washed up for us to inspect: jellyfish, eels, octopus, and a few times the sight of a turtle lying motionless on the shore. Whatever the season, we would go back to Anna and Maria's as it was getting dark and the fragrant smell of warm pastry often greeted us when we arrived – Eleni would make us fresh cheese pies and I'd usually be nibbling on one as I trudged up the hill to my own house when it was time for bed—'

'It does sound an idyllic way to grow up,' interrupted Alexis, beguiled by Fotini's descriptions of this perfect and almost fairy-tale childhood. What she really wanted to find out, though, was how it all came to an end. 'How did Eleni catch leprosy?' she asked abruptly. 'Were lepers allowed off the island?'

'No, of course they weren't. That was why the island was feared so much. Back at the beginning of the century, the government had declared that all lepers in Crete should be confined on Spinalonga. The moment that doctors were certain of the diagnosis, people had to leave their families for good and go there. It was known as "The Place of the Living Dead" and there was no better description.

'In those days people did everything they could to conceal symptoms, mostly because the consequences of being diagnosed were so horrific. It was hardly surprising that Eleni was vulnerable to leprosy. She never gave a second thought to the risk of catching infections from her pupils – she couldn't teach them without having them sitting close, and if a child fell in the dusty schoolyard she would be the first to scoop them up. And it turned out that one of her pupils did have leprosy.' Fotini paused.

'So you think the parents knew their child was infected?' asked Alexis incredulously.

'Almost certainly,' replied Fotini. 'They knew they would never see the child again if anyone found out. There was only one responsible action Eleni could take once she knew she was infected – and she took it. She gave instructions that every child in the school should be checked so that the sufferer could be identified, and, sure enough, there was a nine-year-old boy, called Dimitri, whose wretched parents had to endure the horror of having their son taken away from them. But the alternative was a great deal worse. Think of the contact that children have with each other when they play! They're not like adults, who keep their distance. They scuffle and wrestle and fall in heaps on top of each other. We know now that the disease is generally only spread through persistent close contact, but what people were afraid of in those days was that the school in Elounda would become a leper colony in its own right if they didn't pull out the infected child as soon as they possibly could.'

'That must have been a very difficult thing for Eleni to do – particularly if she had that kind of relationship with her pupils,' said Alexis thoughtfully.

'Yes, it was awful. Awful for everyone concerned,' replied Fotini.

Alexis's lips had dried and she hardly trusted herself to speak in case no sound came. To help the moment pass, she moved her empty cup towards Fotini, who filled it once more and pushed it back across the table. As she carefully stirred sugar into the dark swirling liquid, Alexis felt herself being pulled into Eleni's vortex of grief and suffering.

What had it felt like? To sail away from your home and be effectively imprisoned within sight of your family, everything that was precious to you stripped away? She thought not only of the woman who had been her great-grandmother, but also of the boy, both of them innocent of any crime and yet condemned.

Fotini reached out and put her hand on Alexis's. Perhaps she had been in too much of a hurry to tell the story, without really knowing this young woman well enough. It was no fairytale, however, and she could not simply choose which chapters to tell and which ones to omit. If she trod too carefully now, the real story might never be told. She watched the clouds pass across Alexis's face. Unlike the pale wisps that hung in the blue sky that morning, these were sombre and brooding. Until now, Fotini suspected, the only darkness in Alexis's life had been the vague shadow of her mother's hidden past. It had been nothing more than a question mark, nothing that had kept her awake at night. She had not seen disease, let alone death. Now she had to learn about them both.

'Let's go for a walk, Alexis.' Fotini stood up. 'We'll get Gerasimo to take us out to the island later – everything will make more sense when we're over there.'

A walk was exactly what Alexis needed. These fragments of her mother's history and a surfeit of caffeine had made her head spin, and as they descended the wooden steps on to the shingly beach below, Alexis gulped in the salty air.

'Why has my mother never told me any of this?' she asked.

'She had her reasons, I'm sure,' said Fotini, knowing that there was so much more left to tell. 'And perhaps when you get back to England she'll explain why she was so secretive.'

They strolled the length of the beach and began to ascend the stony path lined with teasels and lavender that led away from the village. The breeze was stronger here and Fotini's walk slowed. Though she was fit for a woman in her seventies, she didn't always have her old stamina, and her pace became more careful and more faltering as the path began to steepen.

Occasionally she stopped, once or twice pointing out places on Spinalonga that came into view. Eventually they came to a huge rock worn smooth by wind, rain and its long use as a bench. They sat down and looked out to sea, the wind rustling the scrubby bushes of wild thyme that grew in profusion around them. It was here that Fotini began to relate Sofia's story.

Over the next few days Fotini told Alexis everything she knew of her family's history, leaving no pebble unturned – from the small shingle of childhood minutiae to the larger boulders of Crete's own history. In the time they had together, the two women strolled along the coastal paths, sat for hours over the dinner table and made journeys to local towns and villages in Alexis's hired car, with Fotini laying the pieces of the Petrakis jigsaw before them. These were days during which Alexis felt herself grow older and wiser, and Fotini, in retelling so much of her past, felt herself young again. The half-century that separated the two women disappeared to vanishing point, and as they strolled arm in arm, they might even have been mistaken for sisters.

Part 2

Chapter Three

1939

EARLY MAY BRINGS Crete its most perfect and heaven-sent days. On one such day, when the trees were heavy with blossom and the very last of the mountain snows had melted into crystal streams, Eleni left the mainland for Spinalonga. In cruel contrast to this blackest of events, the sky was brilliant, a cloudless blue. A crowd had gathered to watch, to weep, to wave a final goodbye. Even if the school had not officially closed for the day out of respect for the departing teacher, the classrooms would have echoed with emptiness. Pupils and teachers alike had deserted. No one would have missed the chance to wave goodbye to their beloved 'Kyria Petrakis'.

Eleni Petrakis was loved in Plaka and the surrounding villages. She had a magnetism that attracted children and adults alike to her and was admired and respected by them all. The reason was simple. For Eleni, teaching was a vocation, and her enthusiasm touched the children like a torch. 'If they love it they will learn it' was her mantra. These were not her own words, but the saying of the teacher with fire in his belly who had been her own doorway into learning twenty years before.

The night before she left her home for ever, Eleni had filled a vase with spring flowers. She put this in the centre of the table and the small spray of pale blooms magically transformed the room. She understood the potency of the simple act, the power of detail. She knew, for example, that recollection of a child's birthday or favourite colour could be the key to winning the heart and then the mind. Children absorbed information in her classroom largely because they wanted to please her, not because they were forced to learn, and the process was helped by the way she displayed facts and figures, each one written on a card and suspended from the ceiling so it seemed as though a flock of exotic birds hovered permanently overhead.

But it was not just a favourite teacher who would be making her way over the water to Spinalonga that day. They were saying goodbye to a friend as well: nine-year-old Dimitri, whose parents had gone to such lengths for a year or more to conceal the signs of his leprosy. Each month there had been some new attempt to hide his blemishes – his knee-length shorts were replaced by long trousers, open sandals by heavy boots, and in the summer he was banned from swimming in the sea with his friends lest the patches on his back should be noticed. 'Say you're afraid of the waves!' pleaded his mother, which was of course ridiculous. These children had all grown up to enjoy the exhilarating power of the sea and actually looked forward to those days when the Meltemi wind turned the glassy Mediterranean into a wild ocean. Only a sissy was afraid of the breakers. The child had lived with the fear of discovery for many months, always knowing in his heart that this was a temporary state and that sooner or later he would be found out.

Anyone unacquainted with the extraordinary circumstances of this summer morning might well have assumed that the crowd had gathered for a funeral. They were nearly one hundred in number, mostly women and children, and there was a sad stillness about them. They stood in the village square, one great body, silent, waiting, breathing in unison. Close by, in an adjacent side street, Eleni Petrakis opened her front door. She was confronted by the unusual sight of this great mass of people in the normally empty space and her instinct was to retreat inside. This was not an option. Giorgis was waiting for her by the jetty, his boat already loaded up with some of her possessions. She needed few, since Giorgis could bring more to her during the following weeks, and she had no desire to remove anything but bare essentials from the family home. Anna and Maria remained behind the closed door. The last few minutes with them had been the most agonising of Eleni's life. She felt the strongest desire to hold them, to crush them in her embrace, to feel their hot tears on her skin, to still their shaking bodies. But she could do none of these things. Not without risk. Their faces were contorted with grief and their eyes swollen with crying. There was nothing left to say. Almost nothing left to feel. Their mother was leaving. She would not be coming back early that evening weighed down with books, sallow with exhaustion, but beaming with pleasure to be at home with them. There would be no return.

The girls had behaved precisely as Eleni would have anticipated. Anna, the elder, had always been volatile, and there was never any doubt about what she was feeling. Maria, on the other hand, was a quieter, more patient child who was slower to lose her temper. True to form, Anna had been more openly distressed than her sister in the days leading up to her mother's departure, and her inability to control her emotions had never been more on display than on this day. She had begged her mother not to go, beseeched her to stay, ranted, raved and torn her hair. By contrast, Maria had wept, silently at first and then with huge racking sobs that could be heard out in the street. The final stage for both of them, however, was the same: they both became subdued, exhausted, spent.

Eleni was determined to contain the volcanic eruption of grief that threatened to overwhelm her. She could vent it in full once she was away from Plaka, but the only hope any of them had at this moment was that her self-possession would remain intact. If she caved in, they were all done for. The girls were to stay in the house. They would be spared the vision of their mother's receding figure, a sight that might burn itself for ever on to their memory.

This was the hardest moment of Eleni's life and now the least private. She was watched by rows of sad eyes. She knew they were there to wish her farewell but never before had she yearned so much to be alone. Every face in the crowd was familiar to her, each was one she loved. 'Goodbye,' she said softly. 'Goodbye.' She kept her distance from them. Her old instincts to embrace had died a sudden death ten days ago, that fateful morning when she had noticed the strange patches on the back of her leg. They were unmistakable, especially when she compared them with a picture on the leaflet that had been circulated to warn people of the symptoms. She hardly needed to see a specialist to understand the awful truth. She knew, even before she visited the doctor, that she had somehow contracted that most dreaded of diseases. The words from Leviticus, read out with more frequency than strictly necessary by the local priest, had resounded inside her head:

> *As the leprosy appeareth in the skin of the flesh, he is a leprous man, he is unclean and the priest shall pronounce him utterly unclean. And the leper in whom the plague is, his clothes shall be rent and his head bared and he shall put a covering upon his upper lip and shall cry 'Unclean, Unclean.'*

Many people still believed that the Old Testament's brutal instructions for the treatment of lepers should be followed. This passage had been heard in church for hundreds of years, and the image of the leper as a man, woman or even child to be cast out of society was deeply ingrained.

As she approached through the crowd Giorgis could just make out the top of Eleni's head, and he knew the moment he had been dreading was upon him. He had been to Spinalonga a thousand times, for years supplementing his meagre fisherman's income by making regular deliveries to the leper colony, but he had never imagined making a journey such as this. The boat was ready and he stood watching her as she approached, his arms wrapped tightly across his chest, his head bowed. He thought that if he stood like this, his body tense, rigid, he could subdue his raging emotions and prevent them from spilling out as huge involuntary cries of anguish. His built-in ability to hide his feelings was bolstered by his wife's exemplary self-control. Inside, though, he was stricken with grief. I must do this, he told himself, as though it is just another ordinary boat journey. To the thousand crossings he had already made would be added this one and a thousand more.

As Eleni approached the jetty, the crowd remained silent. One child cried, but was hushed by its mother. One false emotional move and these grieving people would lose their composure. The control, the formality would be gone and the dignity of this farewell would be no more. Though the few hundred metres had seemed an impossible distance, Eleni's walk to the jetty was nearly over, and she turned round to look at the throng for the last time. Her house was out of sight now, but she knew the shutters would remain closed and that her daughters would be weeping in the darkness.

Suddenly there were cries to be heard. They were the loud, heartbreaking sobs of a grown woman, and her display of grief was as unchecked as Eleni's was controlled. For a moment Eleni halted. These sounds seemed to echo her own emotional state. They were the precise outward expression of everything she felt inside, but she knew she was not their author. The crowd stirred, taking their eyes off Eleni and looking back towards the far corner of the square where a mule had been tethered to a tree and, close by, a man and a woman stood. Though he had all but disappeared within the woman's embrace, there was also a boy. The top of his head barely reached her chest and she was bent over him, her arms wrapped around his body as though she would never let go. 'My boy!' she cried despairingly. 'My boy, my darling boy!' Her husband was at their side. 'Katerina,' he coaxed. 'Dimitri must go. We have no choice. The boat is waiting.' Gently he prised the mother's arms away from the child. She spoke her son's name one final time, softly, indistinctly: 'Dimitri . . .' but the boy did not look up. His gaze was fixed on the dusty ground. 'Come, Dimitri,' his father said firmly. And the boy followed.

He kept his eyes focused on his father's worn leather boots. All he had to do was plant his own feet in the prints they made in the dust. It was mechanical – a game they had played so many times, when his father would take giant strides and Dimitri would jump and leap until his legs could stretch no more and he would fall over, helpless with laughter. This time, however, his father's pace was slow and faltering. Dimitri had no trouble keeping up. His father had relieved the sad-faced mule of its burden and now balanced the small crate of the boy's possessions on his shoulder, the very same shoulder on which his son had been carried so many times. It seemed a long way, past the crowd, to the water's edge.

The final goodbye between father and son was a brief, almost manly one. Eleni, aware of this awkwardness, greeted Dimitri, her focus now solely on the boy whose life, from this moment on, would be her greatest responsibility. 'Come,' she said, encouragingly. 'Let's go and see our new home.' And she took the child's hand and helped him on to the boat as though they were going on an adventure and the boxes packed around them contained supplies for a picnic.

The crowd watched the departure, maintaining its silence. There was no protocol for this moment. Should they wave? Should they shout goodbye? Skin paled, stomachs contracted, hearts felt heavy. Some had ambivalent feelings about the boy, blaming him for Eleni's situation and for the unease they now had about their own children's health. At the very moment of their departure, though, the mothers and fathers felt only pity for the two unfortunates who were leaving their families behind for ever. Giorgis pushed the boat away from the jetty and soon his oars were engaged in the usual battle with the current. It was as though the sea did not want them to go. For a short while the crowd watched, but as the figures became less distinct they began to disperse.

The last to turn away and leave the square were a woman of about Eleni's own age and a girl. The woman was Savina Angelopoulos, who had grown up with Eleni, and the girl was her daughter Fotini, who, in the way of small village life, was the best friend of Eleni's youngest daughter, Maria. Savina wore a head scarf, which hid her thick hair but accentuated her huge kind eyes; childbearing had not been kind to her body and she was now stocky, with heavy legs. By contrast, Fotini was as slim as an olive sapling but she had inherited her mother's beautiful eyes. When the little boat had all but disappeared, the two of them turned and walked swiftly across the square. Their destination was the house with the faded green door, the house from which Eleni had emerged some time earlier. The shutters were closed, but the front door was unlocked and mother and daughter stepped inside. Soon Savina would hold the girls and provide the embrace that their own mother, in her wisdom, had been unable to give.

As the boat neared the island, Eleni held Dimitri's hand ever more tightly. She was glad that this poor boy would have someone to care for him and at this moment did not give a second thought to the irony of this position. She would teach him and nurture him as though he was her own son, and do her best to ensure that his schooling was not cut short by this terrible turn of events. She was now close enough to see that there were a few people standing just outside the fortress wall and realised they must be waiting for her. Why else would they be there? It was unlikely that they were on the point of leaving the island themselves.

Giorgis guided the boat expertly towards the jetty and soon he was helping his wife and Dimitri on to dry land. Almost subconsciously, he found himself avoiding contact with the boy's bare skin, taking his elbow not his hand as he helped him out of the boat. He then concentrated fiercely on tying the boat fast so that he could unload the boxes safely, distracting himself from the thought of leaving the island without his wife. The small wooden crate that was the boy's and the larger one that belonged to Eleni soon sat on the quayside.

Now that they were on Spinalonga, it seemed to both Eleni and Dimitri that they had crossed a wide ocean and that their old lives were already a million miles away.

Before Eleni had thought to look around once more, Giorgis had gone. They had agreed the night before that there would be no goodbyes between them, and they had both been true to their resolve. Giorgis had already set off on the return journey and was a hundred metres away, his hat pulled down low so that the boat's dark strips of wood were all that lay in his field of vision.

Chapter Four

THE CLUSTER OF people Eleni had noticed earlier now moved towards them. Dimitri remained silent, staring down at his feet, while Eleni held out her hand to the man who came forward to greet them. It was a gesture that demonstrated an acceptance that this was her new home. She found herself reaching out to take a hand that was as bent as a shepherd's crook, a hand so badly deformed now by leprosy that the elderly man could not grasp Eleni's outstretched hand. But his smile said enough, and Eleni responded with a polite '*Kalimera*.' Dimitri stood back, silent. He would remain in this state of shock for several more days.

It was a custom on Spinalonga for new members of the colony to be received with some degree of formality, and Eleni and Dimitri were welcomed just as if they had finally reached a far-off, long-dreamed-of destination. The reality was that for some lepers this was truly the case. The island could provide a welcome refuge from a life of vagrancy; many of the lepers had spent months or even years living outside society, sleeping in shacks and surviving off pilfered scraps. For these victims of the disease, Spinalonga was a relief, respite from the abject misery they had endured as outcasts.

The man who greeted them was Petros Kontomaris, the island leader. He had been voted in, along with a group of elders, by the three hundred or so inhabitants in the annual election; Spinalonga was a model of democracy and the regularity of the elections was intended to ensure that dissatisfaction never festered. It was Kontomaris's duty to welcome all newcomers, and only he and a handful of other appointed individuals were permitted to come and go through the great gateway.

Eleni and Dimitri followed Petros Kontomaris through the tunnel, their hands locked together. Eleni probably knew more about Spinalonga than most people on the mainland because of Giorgis's first-hand knowledge. Even so, the scene that greeted her was a surprise. In the narrow street ahead of them was a throng of people. It looked just like market day in Plaka. People went to and fro with baskets full of produce, a priest emerged from a church doorway and two elderly women made their way slowly up the street, riding side-saddle on their weary-looking donkeys. Some turned to stare at the new arrivals and several nodded their heads in a gesture of greeting. Eleni looked around her, anxious not to be rude but unable to contain her curiosity. What had always been rumoured was true. Most of the lepers looked as she did: ostensibly unblemished.

One woman, however, whose head was obscured by a shawl, stopped to let them pass. Eleni glimpsed a face deformed by lumps the size of walnuts and shuddered. Never had she seen anything more hideous, and she prayed that Dimitri had not noticed the woman.

The group of three continued to walk up the street,

followed by another elderly man who led two donkeys bearing the weight of their possessions. Petros Kontomaris chatted to Eleni. 'We have a house for you,' he explained. 'It became vacant last week.'

In Spinalonga, vacancies were only created by death. People continued to arrive regardless of whether there was space, and this meant that the island was overcrowded. Since it was the government's policy to encourage lepers to live on Spinalonga, it was entirely in its own interests to minimise unrest on the island, so from time to time it would provide funds for new housing or small grants to restore the old. The previous year, just when existing buildings were reaching the limit of their capacity, an ugly but functional block had been completed and a housing crisis averted. Once again, every islander had some privacy. The man who made the final decision on where newcomers should live was Kontomaris. He regarded Eleni and Dimitri as a special case; they were to be treated as mother and son, and for that reason he had decided that they should not be housed in the new block, but should take over the newly vacant house in the high street. Dimitri at least might be there for many years to come.

'Kyria Petrakis,' he said. 'This is to be your home.'

At the end of the central street where the shops ended, standing back from the road, stood a single house. It struck Eleni that it bore more than a little resemblance to her own home. Then she told herself she must stop thinking in this way – this old stone house in front of her *was* now her home. Kontomaris unlocked the door and held it open for her. The interior was dark, even on this luminously bright day, and her heart sank. For the hundredth time that day, the limits of her bravery were tested. This was undoubtedly the best there was and it was imperative that she pretend to be pleased. Her best acting skills, the ability to perform that contributed so much to her remarkable teaching style, were in heavy demand.

'I'll leave you to settle in,' Kontomaris said. 'My wife will be over to see you later and she will show you round the colony.'

'Your wife?' exclaimed Eleni with more surprise in her voice than she had quite intended. But he was used to such a reaction.

'Yes, my wife. We met and married here. It's not unusual, you know.'

'No, no, I'm sure it isn't,' said Eleni, abashed, realising that she had much to learn. Kontomaris gave the slightest of bows and left. Eleni and Dimitri were now alone, and they both stood looking about them in the daytime darkness. Apart from a threadbare rug, all that furnished the room was a wooden chest, a small table and two spindly wooden chairs. Tears pricked Eleni's eyes. Her life was reduced to this. Two souls in a sombre room and a pair of fragile chairs that looked as though they might crumble with a hand's touch, let alone the full weight of a human body. What difference between she and Dimitri and those frail pieces of furniture? Once again, there was an imperative for false cheer.

'Come on, Dimitri, shall we go and look upstairs?'

They crossed the unlit room and climbed the stairs. At the top were two doors. Eleni opened the left-hand one and went in, throwing open the shutters. The light poured in. The windows looked over the street and from here the sparkle of the sea could be seen in the distance. A metal bed and yet another decrepit chair was all that this bare cell contained. Eleni left Dimitri standing there and went into the other bedroom, which was smaller and somehow greyer. She returned to the first, where Dimitri still stood.

'This one will be your room,' she announced.

'My room?' he asked incredulously. 'Just for me?' He had always shared a room with his two brothers and two sisters. For the first time his small face showed some expression. Quite unexpectedly he found that one thing at least had improved in his life.

As they descended the stairs a cockroach scuttled across the room and disappeared behind the wooden chest which stood in the corner. Eleni would hunt it out later, but for now she would light the three oil lamps which would help to brighten this gloomy dwelling. Opening her box of possessions – which contained mostly books and other materials that she would need for teaching Dimitri – she found paper and pencil and began to make a list: three lengths of cotton for curtains, two pictures, some cushions, five blankets, a large saucepan and a few pieces of her best china. She knew her family would enjoy the idea that they were all eating from the same flower-sprigged plates. Another important item she requested was seeds. Although the house was dismal, Eleni was greatly cheered by the little courtyard in front of it and had already begun to plan what she would grow. Giorgis would be back in a few days, so within a week or two she would have this place looking as she wanted it. This would be the first of many lists for Giorgis, and Eleni knew that he would fulfil her requirements to the very last letter.

Dimitri sat and watched Eleni as she drew up her inventory of essentials. He was slightly in awe of this woman who only yesterday had been his teacher and now was to care for him not just between the hours of eight in the morning and two in the afternoon but for all the others as well. She was to be his mother, his *meetera*. But he would never call her by any name other than 'Kyria Petrakis'. He wondered what his real mother was doing now. She would probably be stirring the big cooking pot, preparing the evening meal. In Dimitri's eyes that was how she seemed to spend most of her time, while he and his brothers and sisters played outside in the street. He wondered if he would ever see them again and wished with all his heart that he was there now, messing about in the dust. If he missed them this much after only a few hours, how much more would he miss them each day, each week, each month? he wondered. His throat tightened until it hurt so much the tears flowed down his face. Then Kyria Petrakis was by his side, holding him close and whispering: 'There, there, Dimitri. Everything will be all right . . . Everything will be all right.' If only he believed her.

That afternoon they unpacked their boxes. Surrounding themselves with a few familiar objects should have lifted their mood, but each time a new possession emerged it came with all the associations of their past lives and did not help them forget. Every new trinket, book or toy reminded them more intensely than the last of what they had left behind.

One of Eleni's treasures was a small clock, a gift from her parents on her wedding day. She placed it in the centre of the mantelpiece and a gentle tick-tock now filled the long silences. It struck on the hour, and at precisely three o'clock, before the chimes had quite died away, there was a gentle knock on the door.

Eleni opened the door wide to admit her visitor, a small, round-faced woman with flecks of silver in her hair.

'*Kalispera*,' said Eleni. 'Kyrios Kontomaris told me to expect your visit. Please come in.'

'This must be Dimitri,' said the woman immediately, walking over to the boy, who remained seated, his head resting in his hands. 'Come,' she said, holding out her hand to him. 'I am going to show you round. My name is Elpida Kontomaris, but please call me Elpida.'

There was a note of forced jollity in her voice and the kind of enthusiasm you would summon up if you were taking a terrified child to have a tooth pulled. They emerged from the gloom of the house into the late afternoon light and turned right.

'The most important thing is the water supply,' she began, her matter-of-fact tone betraying that she had taken new arrivals on a tour of the island many times before. Whenever a woman arrived, her husband would dispatch Elpida to welcome her. This was the first time that she had given her talk with a child present, so she knew she would have to modify some of the information she usually imparted. She would certainly have to control the vitriol that rose up inside her when she was describing the island's facilities.

'This,' she said brightly, pointing to a huge cistern at the foot of the hill, 'is where we collect our water. It's a sociable place and we all spend plenty of time here chatting and catching up with each other's news.'

In truth, the fact that they had to trudge several hundred metres downhill to fetch water and then all the way back with it angered her beyond words. She could cope, but there were others more crippled than her who could barely lift an empty vessel let alone one that brimmed with water. Before she lived on Spinalonga she had rarely lifted more than a glassful of water, but now carrying bucketfuls was part of life's daily grind. It had taken her several years to get used to this. Things had perhaps changed more drastically for Elpida than for many. Coming from a wealthy family in Hania, she had been a stranger to manual work until she arrived in Spinalonga ten years earlier; the hardest assignment she had ever undertaken prior to that was to embroider a bedspread.

As usual, Elpida put on a brave front for her introduction to the island and presented only the positive aspects of it all. She showed Eleni Petrakis the few shops as though they were the finest in Iraklion, pointed out where the bi-weekly market was held and where they did their laundry. She also took her to the pharmacy, which for many was the most important building of all. She told her the times when the baker's oven was lit and where the *kafenion* was situated, tucked away down a little side street. The priest would call on her later, but meanwhile she indicated where he lived and took them to the church. She enthused to the boy about the puppet shows which were put on for the children once a week in the town hall and finally she pointed out the schoolhouse, which stood empty today, but on three mornings each week contained the island's small population of children.

She told Dimitri about other children of his own age and attempted to prise a smile out of him by describing the fun and games they had together, but no matter how hard she tried, his face remained impassive.

What she refrained from speaking of today, especially in

front of the boy, was the restlessness that was brewing on Spinalonga. Though many of the lepers were initially grateful for the sanctuary that the island provided, they became disenchanted after a while and believed themselves abandoned, feeling their needs were met only minimally. Elpida could see that Eleni would soon become aware of the bitterness that consumed many of the lepers. It hung in the very air.

As the wife of the island leader she was in a difficult position. Petros Kontomaris had been elected by the people of Spinalonga, but his most important task was to act as mediator and go-between with the government. He was a reasonable man and knew where the boundaries lay with the authorities on Crete, but Elpida saw him battling continually against a vociferous and sometimes radical minority in the leper colony who felt that they were being badly treated and who agitated constantly for improvements to the island's facilities. Some felt that they were mere squatters in the Turkish rubble even though Kontomaris had done everything he could in the years he had been in charge. He had negotiated a monthly allowance of twenty-five drachma for every inhabitant, a grant to build the new block of flats, a decent pharmacy and clinic and regular visits from a doctor from the mainland. He had also constructed a plan which allocated land to each person on Spinalonga who wished to cultivate their own fruit and vegetables either to eat themselves or to sell at the weekly market. In short, he had done everything he humanly could, but the population of Spinalonga always wanted more and Elpida was not sure that her husband had the energy to fulfil their expectations. She worried about him constantly. He was in his late fifties, like her, but his health was failing. Leprosy was beginning to win the battle for his body.

Elpida had seen huge changes since she had arrived, and most of these had been achieved through her husband's endeavours. Still the rumbles of dissatisfaction grew by the day. The water situation was the main focus of unrest, particularly in the summer. The Venetian water system, constructed hundreds of years earlier, collected rainwater in tunnelled watersheds and stored it in underground tanks to prevent evaporation. It was ingeniously simple, but the tunnels were now beginning to crumble. Additionally, fresh water was brought over from the mainland every week, but there was never enough to keep more than two hundred people well washed and watered. It was a daily struggle, even with the help of mules, especially for the elderly and crippled. In the winter it was electricity they needed. A generator had been installed a couple of years earlier and everyone had anticipated the pleasure of warmth and light in the dark, chilly days from November to February. This was not to be. The generator packed up after only three weeks and had never worked again; requests for new parts were ignored and the machinery stood abandoned, almost entirely covered now with a tangle of weeds.

Water and electricity were not luxuries but necessities, and they were all aware that the inadequacy of the water supply in particular could shorten their lives. Elpida knew that, although the government had to keep their lives tolerable, its commitment to making them better was perfunctory. The inhabitants of Spinalonga seethed with anger and she shared their fury. Why, in a country where huge mountains reared up into the sky, their snowy peaks clearly visible on a wintry day, were they rationed? They wanted a reliable fresh water supply. They wanted it soon. There had been, as far as there could be amongst men and women, some of whom were crippled, violent arguments about what to do. Elpida remembered the time when one group had threatened to storm the mainland and another suggested the taking of hostages. In the end they had realised what a pathetic straggling crew they would make, with no boats, no weapons and, above all, very little strength.

All they could do was try and make their voices heard. And that was where Petros's powers of argument and diplomacy became the most valuable weapon they had. Elpida had to maintain some distance between herself and the rest of the community but her ear was continually bent, mostly by the women, who regarded her as a conduit to her husband. She was tired of it all and secretly pressurised Petros not to stand in the next elections. Had he not given enough?

As she led Eleni and Dimitri around the little streets of the island, Elpida kept all these thoughts to herself. She saw Dimitri clutch the edge of Eleni's billowing skirt as they walked, as if for comfort, and sighed to herself. What sort of future did the boy have in this place? She almost hoped it would not be a long one.

Eleni found the gentle tug at her skirt reassuring. It reminded her that she was not alone and had someone to care for. Only yesterday she had had a husband and daughters, and the day before a hundred eager faces at school had looked up into hers. All of them had needed her and she had thrived on that. This new reality was hard to grasp. For a moment she wondered if she had already died and this woman was a chimera showing her round Hades, telling where the dead souls could wash their shrouds and buy their insubstantial rations. Her mind, however, told her it was all real. It had not been Charon but her own husband who had brought her to hell and left her here to die. She came to a halt and Dimitri stopped too. Her head dropped to her chest and she could feel huge tears well up in her eyes. For the first time she lost control. Her throat contracted as if to deny her another breath and she took one desperate gasp to drag air into her lungs. Elpida, until now so matter-of-fact, so businesslike, turned to face her and grasped her by the arms. Dimitri looked up at both women. He had seen his own mother cry for the first time that day. Now it was the turn of his teacher. The tears coursed freely down her cheeks.

'Don't be afraid to cry,' said Elpida gently. 'The boy will see plenty of tears here. Believe me, they're shed freely on Spinalonga.'

Eleni buried her head in Elpida's shoulder. Two passers-by stopped and stared. Not at the sight of a woman weeping, but simply because they were curious about the newcomers. Dimitri looked away, doubly embarrassed by Eleni's weeping and the strangers' stares. He wished the ground beneath him would part just like in the earthquakes he had learned about in school, and then swallow him up. He knew that Crete was regularly shaken, but why not today?

Elpida could see what Dimitri was feeling. Eleni's sobbing had begun to affect her too: she sympathised terribly but she wanted her to stop. By good fortune they had come to a halt outside her own house, and she led Eleni firmly inside. For a moment she felt self-conscious about the size of her home, which she knew contrasted starkly with the place Eleni and Dimitri had just moved into. The Kontomaris house, the official residence of the island leader, was one of the buildings from the island's period of occupation by the Venetians, with a balcony that could almost be described as grand and a porticoed front door.

They had lived here for the past six years, and so sure was Elpida of her husband's majority in the yearly elections that she had never even imagined what it would be like to live anywhere else. Now, of course, it was she who was discouraging him from staying on in his position, and this was what they would give up if Petros chose not to stand. 'But who is there to take over?' he would ask. It was true. The only others who were rumoured to be putting themselves up had few supporters. One of them was the chief among the agitators, Theodoros Makridakis, and though many of his causes were sound, it would be disastrous for the island if he was given any power. His lack of diplomacy would mean that any progress that had already been made with the government would be undone and it was quite likely that privileges could be subtly withdrawn rather than added to. The only other candidate for the role was Spyros Kazakis, a kind but weak individual whose only real interest in the position was to secure himself the house everyone on Spinalonga secretly coveted.

The interior provided an extraordinary contrast with almost every other home on the island. Floor-to-ceiling windows allowed light to flood in on three sides, and an ornate crystal lamp hung down into the middle of the room on a long dusty chain, the small, irregular shapes of coloured crystal projecting a kaleidoscopic pattern on to the pastel walls.

The furniture was worn but comfortable, and Elpida gestured to Eleni to take a seat. Dimitri wandered about the room, examining the framed photos and staring into a glass-fronted cabinet that housed precious pieces of Kontomaris memorabilia: an etched silver jug, a row of lace bobbins, some pieces of precious china, more framed pictures and, most intriguingly of all, row upon row of tiny soldiers. He stood gazing into the cabinet for some minutes, not looking beyond the glass at these objects but mesmerised by his own reflection. His face seemed as strange to him as the room where he stood and he met his own gaze with some disquiet, as though he did not recognise the dark eyes that stared back at him. This was a boy whose entire universe had encompassed the towns of Agios Nikolaos, Elounda and a few hamlets in between where cousins, aunts and uncles lived and he felt he had been transported into another galaxy. His face was mirrored in the highly polished pane and behind him he could see Kyria Kontomaris, her arms wrapped around Kyria Petrakis, comforting her as she wept. He watched for some moments and then refocused his eyes so that they could once more study the soldiers so neatly arranged in their regiments.

When he turned around to face the women, Kyria Petrakis had regained her composure and reached out both hands towards him. 'Dimitri,' she said, 'I am sorry.' Her crying had shocked as well as embarrassed him and the thought suddenly occurred to him that she might be missing her children as much as he was missing his mother. He tried to imagine what his mother would be feeling if she had been sent to Spinalonga instead of him. He took Kyria Petrakis's hands and squeezed them hard. 'Don't be sorry,' he said.

Elpida disappeared into her kitchen to make coffee for Eleni and, using sugared water with a twist of lemon, some lemonade for Dimitri. When she returned she found her visitors sitting, talking quietly. The boy's eyes lit up when he saw his drink and he had soon drained it to the bottom. As for Eleni, whether it was the sweetness of the coffee or the kindness, she could not tell, but she felt herself enveloped in Elpida's warm concern. It had always been her role to dispense such sympathy and she found it harder to receive than to give. She would be challenged by this reversal.

The afternoon light was beginning to fade. For a few minutes they sat absorbed in their own thoughts, the silence broken only by the careful clink of their cups. Dimitri nursed a second glass of lemonade. Never had he been in a house like this one, where the light shone in rainbow patterns and the chairs were softer than anything he had ever slept on. It was so unlike his own home, where every bench became a sleeping place at night and every rug doubled up as a blanket. He had thought that was how everyone lived. But not here.

When they had all finished their drinks, Elpida spoke.

'Shall we continue our walk?' she asked, rising out of her seat. 'There's someone waiting to meet you.'

Eleni and Dimitri followed her from the house. Dimitri was reluctant to leave. He had liked it there and hoped he might go back one day and sip lemonade, and perhaps pluck up courage to ask Kyria Kontomaris to open the cabinet so that he could take a closer look at the soldiers, maybe even pick them up.

Further up the street was a building several hundred years

newer than the leader's residence. With its crisp, straight lines, it lacked the classical aesthetics of the home they had just left. This functional structure was the hospital and was their next stop.

Eleni and Dimitri's arrival had coincided with one of the days on which the doctor came from the mainland. This innovation and the building of the hospital had been the result of Petros Kontomaris's campaign to improve medical treatment for the lepers. The first hurdle had been to persuade the government to fund such a project and the second to convince them that a careful doctor could treat and help them without danger of infection to himself. Finally they relented on all counts, and every Monday, Wednesday and Friday a doctor would arrive from Agios Nikolaos. The doctor who had put himself forward for what many of his colleagues thought was a dangerous and foolhardy assignment was Christos Lapakis. He was a jovial, red-faced fellow in his early thirties, well liked by the staff in the dermatovenereology department at the hospital and loved by his patients on Spinalonga. His great girth was evidence of his hedonism, in itself a reflection of his belief that the here and now was all you had so you might as well enjoy it. It disappointed his respectable family in Agios Nikolaos that he was still a bachelor, and he knew himself that he was not helping his marriage prospects by working in a leper colony. This did not bother him unduly, however. He was fulfilled in this work and enjoyed the difference, albeit limited, that he could make to these poor people's lives. In his own opinion, there was no afterlife, no second chance.

Dr Lapakis spent his time on Spinalonga treating wounds

and advising his patients on all the extra precautions they could take and how exercise could help them. With new arrivals he would always do a thorough examination. The introduction of the Doctor's Days, as they became known throughout the community, had done a huge amount to lift morale on the island and had already improved the health of many of the sufferers. His emphasis on cleanliness, sanitation and physiotherapy gave them a reason to get up in the morning and a feeling that they were not simply rising from their beds in order to continue their gradual degeneration. Dr Lapakis had been shocked when he arrived on Spinalonga at the conditions many of the lepers lived in. He knew it was essential for good health that they keep their wounds clean, but when he had first arrived, he had discovered something akin to apathy among many of them. Their sense of abandonment was catastrophic and the psychological damage inflicted by being on the island was actually greater than the physical harm caused by the disease. Many could simply no longer be bothered with life. Why should they? Life had ceased to bother with them.

Christos Lapakis treated both their minds and their bodies. He told them that there always had to be hope and that they should never give up. He was authoritative but often blunt: 'You will die if you don't wash your wounds,' he would say. He was pragmatic and told them the truth dispassionately, but also with enough feeling to show that he cared, and he was practical too, telling them precisely how they needed to care for themselves. 'This is how you wash your wounds,' he would say, 'and this is how you exercise your hands and legs if you don't want to lose your fingers and toes.' As he told them these things, he demonstrated the movements. He made them all realise more than ever the vital importance of clean water. Water was life. And for them the difference between life and death. Lapakis was a great supporter of Kontomaris and gave him all the backing he could in lobbying for the fresh water supply that could transform the island and the prognosis of many who lived there.

'Here's the hospital,' said Elpida. 'Dr Lapakis is expecting you. He has just finished seeing his regular patients.'

They found themselves in a space as cool and white as a sepulchre and sat on the bench that ran down one side of the room. They were not seated for long. The doctor soon came out to greet them, and in turn, the woman and the boy were examined. They showed him their patches and he studied them carefully, examining their naked skin for himself and looking for signs of development in their condition that they might not even have noticed themselves. The pale-faced Dimitri had a few large, dry patches on his back and legs, indicating that at this stage he had the less damaging, tuberculoid strain of the disease. The smaller, shinier lesions on Eleni Petrakis's legs and feet worried Dr Lapakis much more. Without any doubt she had the more virulent, lepromatous form and there was a distinct possibility that she might have had it for some time before these signs had appeared.

The boy's prognosis is not too bad, Lapakis mused. But that poor woman, she's not long for this island. His face, however, did not betray the merest hint of what he had discovered.

Chapter Five

When Eleni left for Spinalonga, Anna was twelve and Maria ten. Giorgis was faced with managing the job of home-making single-handedly and, more importantly, the task of bringing up the girls without their mother. Of the two, Anna had always been the more difficult. She had been obstreperous to the point of uncontrollability even before she could walk, and from the day her younger sister was born it seemed she was furious with life. It was no surprise to Giorgis that once Eleni was no longer there Anna rebelled furiously against domesticity, refusing to take on the maternal mantle just because she was the elder of the two girls. She made this painfully clear to her father and to her sister.

Maria had an altogether gentler nature. Two people with her sister's temper could not have lived under the same roof, and Maria fell into the role of peacekeeper even if she often had to fight an instinct to react against Anna's aggression. Unlike Anna, Maria did not find domestic work belittling. She was naturally practical and sometimes enjoyed helping her father clean and cook, a tendency for which Giorgis silently thanked God. Like most men of his generation he could no more darn a sock than fly to the moon.

To the world at large, Giorgis seemed a man of few words. Even those endless lonely hours at sea had not made him yearn for conversation when he was on dry land. He loved the sound of silence, and when he passed the evening at the *kafenion* table – a requirement of manhood rather an optional social activity – he remained quiet, listening to the people around him just as though he was out at sea listening to the lap of the waves against the hull of his boat.

Though his family knew his warm heart and his affectionate embrace, casual acquaintances found his uncommunicative behaviour almost antisocial at times. Those who knew him better saw it as a reflection of a quiet stoicism, a quality that stood him in good stead now that his circumstances had changed so drastically.

Life for Giorgis had rarely been anything but tough. He was a fisherman like his father and grandfather before him, and like them he had become hardened to long stretches spent at sea. These would usually be whiled away in tedious hours of chilly inactivity, but sometimes the long, dark nights would be spent battling against the wild waves, and at times like those there was a distinct danger that the sea might have its way and consume him once and for all. It was a life spent crouched low in the hull of a wooden caique, but a Cretan fisherman never questioned his lot. For him it was fate, not choice.

For several years before Eleni had been exiled there, Giorgis had supplemented his income by making deliveries to Spinalonga. Nowadays he had a boat with a motor and would go there once a week with crates of essential items, dropping them off on the jetty for collection by the lepers.

For the first few days after Eleni left, Giorgis dared not leave his daughters for a moment. Their distress seemed to intensify the longer their mother was away, but he knew that sooner or later they would have to find a new way of living. Although kind neighbours came with food, Giorgis still had the responsibility of getting the girls to eat. One evening, when he faced the task of cooking a meal himself, his woeful inadequacy at the stove almost brought a smile to Maria's lips. Anna, though, could only mock her father's efforts.

'I'm not eating this!' she cried, throwing her fork down into her plate of mutton stew. 'A starving *animal* wouldn't eat it!' With that she burst into tears for the tenth time that day and flounced from the room. It was the third night that she had eaten nothing but bread.

'Starvation will soon crack her stubbornness,' her father said lightly to Maria, who patiently chewed a piece of the over-cooked meat. The two of them sat at opposite ends of the table. Conversation did not flow and the silence was punctuated by the occasional chink of their forks on china and the sound of Anna's anguished sobs.

The day eventually came when they had to return to school. This worked like a spell. As soon as their minds had something other than their mother to focus on, their grief began to abate. This was also the day when Giorgis could point the prow of his boat once more in the direction of Spinalonga. With a curious mix of dread and excitement he made his way across the narrow strip of water. Eleni would not know he was coming, and a message would have to be sent to alert her to his arrival. But news travelled fast on Spinalonga, and before he had even tied his boat to the mooring post, Eleni had appeared round the corner of the huge wall and stood in its shadow.

What could they say? How could they react? They did not touch though they desperately wanted to. Instead they just spoke each other's names. They were words they had uttered a thousand times before, but today their syllables sounded like noises with no meaning. At that moment Giorgis wished he had not come. He had mourned his wife this last week, and yet here she was, just as she always had been, as vivid and lovely as ever, which only added to the unbearable ache of their impending separation. Soon he would have to leave the island again and take his boat back to Plaka. Each time he visited there would be this painful parting. His was a gloomy soul and for a fleeting moment he wished them both dead.

Eleni's first week on the island had been full of activity and had passed more quickly than it had done for Giorgis, but when she heard that his boat had been spotted on its way from Plaka, her emotions were thrown into a state of turmoil. Since her arrival she had had plenty of distractions, almost enough to keep her mind away from the sea change which had taken place, but now that Giorgis was standing there before her, his deep green eyes gazing into hers, there was only one focus for her thoughts: how much she loved this strong, broad-shouldered man and how much it hurt her to the very core of her being to be separated from him.

They asked almost formally about each other's health, and Eleni enquired after the girls. How could he respond, except with an answer that only just brushed the surface of the truth? Sooner or later they would get used to it all, he knew that, and then he would be able to tell her honestly how they were. The only truth today was in Eleni's answer to Giorgis's question.

'What's it like in there?' He nodded in the direction of the great stone wall.

'It is not as dreadful as you imagine, and things are going to get better,' she replied, with such conviction and determination that Giorgis found his fears for her instantly suppressed.

'Dimitri and I have a house all to ourselves,' she told him, 'and it's not unlike our home in Plaka. It's more primitive but we're making the best of it. We have our own courtyard and by next spring we should have a herb garden, if you can bring me some seeds. There are roses already in bloom on our doorstep and soon there'll be hollyhocks out too. It's not bad really.'

Giorgis was relieved to hear such words. Eleni now produced a folded sheet of paper from her pocket and gave it to him.

'Is it for the girls?' enquired Giorgis.

'No, it's not,' she said apologetically. 'I thought it might be too early for that, but I'll have a letter for them next time you come. This is a list of things we need for the house.'

Giorgis noted the use of 'we' and a pang of envy hit him. Once, 'we' had included Anna, Maria and himself, he reflected. Then a bitter thought of which he was almost instantly ashamed came into his head: now 'we' meant the hated child who had taken Eleni away from them. The 'we' of his family no longer existed. It had been split asunder and redefined, its rock solidity replaced by such fragility he hardly dared contemplate it. Giorgis was finding it hard to believe that God had not deserted them all. One moment he had been the head of a household; the next he was just a man with two daughters. The two states were as far apart as different planets.

It was time for Giorgis to go. The girls would be back from school soon and he wanted to be there for their return.

'I shall be across again soon,' he promised. 'And I'll bring everything you've asked for.'

'Let's agree on something,' said Eleni. 'Shall we *not* say goodbye? There's no real sense in the word.'

'You're right,' responded Giorgis. 'We'll have no goodbyes.'

They smiled and simultaneously turned away from each other, Eleni towards the shadowy entrance in the high Venetian wall and Giorgis to his boat. Neither looked back.

On his next visit, Eleni had written a letter for Giorgis to take back for the girls, but the moment her father held out the envelope, Anna's impatience got the better of her and, as she tried to snatch it out of his hands, it was ripped in two.

'But that letter's for both of us!' protested Maria. 'I want to read it too!'

By now Anna was at the front door.

'I don't care. I'm the oldest and I get to look at it first!' and with that she turned on her heels and ran off down the street, leaving Maria weeping tears of frustration and anger.

A few hundred yards from their home was a little alleyway that ran between two houses, and this was where Anna, crouched in the shadows and, holding the two halves together, read her mother's first letter:

Dear Anna and Maria,

I wonder how you both are? I hope you are being good and kind and working hard at school. Your father tells me that his first attempts at cooking were not very successful but I am sure he will get better at it and that soon he will know the difference between a cucumber and a courgette! I hope it won't be long before you are helping him in the kitchen too, but meanwhile be patient with him while he is learning.

Let me tell you about Spinalonga. I am living in a small, tumbledown house in the main street with one room downstairs and two bedrooms upstairs, rather like at home. It is quite dark but I am planning to whitewash the walls, and once I have put my pictures up and displayed my pieces of china I think it will look quite pretty. Dimitri likes having his own room – he has always had to share so it is quite a novelty for him.

I have a new friend. Her name is Elpida and she is the wife of the man who is in charge of the government of Spinalonga. They are both very kind people and we have had a few meals at their home, which is the biggest and the grandest on the whole island. It has chandeliers and every table and every chair has some kind of lace draped across it. Anna especially would love it.

I have already planted some geranium cuttings in the courtyard and roses are beginning to bloom on our doorstep, just like at home. I will write and tell you lots more in my next letter. Meanwhile, be good, I think of you every day.

With love and kisses,
Your loving Mother xxxxx

P.S. I hope the bees are working hard – don't forget to collect the honey.

Anna read the letter over and over again before walking slowly home. She knew she would be in trouble. From that day on, Eleni wrote separate letters to the two girls.

Giorgis visited the island much more regularly now than before and his meetings with Eleni were his oxygen. He lived for those moments when she would appear through the archway in the wall. Sometimes they would sit on the stone mooring posts; at other times they would remain standing in the shade of the pines that grew, as if for the purpose, out of the dry earth. Giorgis would tell her how the girls were, what they had been doing, and would confide in her about Anna's behaviour.

'Sometimes it's as though she has the devil in her,' said Giorgis one day as they sat talking. 'She doesn't seem to get any easier with time.'

'Well, it's just as well that Maria isn't the same,' replied Eleni.

'That's probably why Anna is so disobedient half the time, because Maria doesn't seem to have a wicked bone in her body,' reflected Giorgis. 'And I thought tantrums were meant to be something children grew out of.'

'I'm sorry to leave you with such a burden, Giorgis, I really am,' sighed Eleni, knowing that she would give anything to be facing the daily battle of wills involved in bringing Anna up instead of being stuck here on this island.

★ ★ ★

Giorgis was not even forty when Eleni left, but he was already stooped with anxiety, and over the next few months he was to age beyond recognition. His hair turned from olive black to the silvery grey of the eucalyptus, and people seemed always to refer to him as 'Poor Giorgis'. It became his name.

Savina Angelopoulos did as much as she was able, whilst managing her own home too. On still, moonless nights, knowing that there could be a rich catch, Giorgis would want to fish, and it became a regular event for Maria and Fotini to sleep, top to tail, in the latter's narrow bed, with Anna on the floor next to them, two thick blankets for her mattress. Maria and Anna also found they were eating more meals at the Angelopoulos home than their own, and it was as if Fotini's own family had suddenly grown and she had the sisters she had always wanted. On those nights there would be eight at the table: Fotini and her two brothers, Antonis and Angelos, her parents, and Giorgis, Anna and Maria. Some days, if she had the time, Savina would try to teach Anna and Maria how to keep their house tidy, how to beat a carpet and how to make up a bed, but quite often she would end up doing it all for them. They were just children, and Anna for one had no interest in anything domestic. Why should she learn to patch a sheet, gut a fish or bake a loaf? She was determined that she would never need such skills and from an early age had a powerful urge to escape and get away from what she regarded as pointless domestic drudgery.

The girls' lives could not have been more altered if a tornado had snatched them and dropped them on Santorini. They acted out their days with a fixed routine, for only with a rigid, unthinking pattern of activity could they rise in the morning.

Anna battled against it all, constantly complaining and questioning why things were as they were; Maria simply accepted. She knew that complaining achieved nothing at all and probably just made things worse. Her sister had no such wisdom. Anna always wanted to fight the status quo.

'Why do *I* have to go and get the bread every morning?' she complained one day.

'You don't,' her father replied patiently. 'Maria gets it every other day.'

'Well why can't she get it *every* day? I'm the oldest and I don't see why I have to get bread for her.'

'If everyone questioned why they should do things for each other, the world would stop turning, Anna. Now go and get the bread. Right this minute!'

Giorgis's fist came down with a bang on the table. He was weary of Anna turning every small domestic task she was asked to perform into an argument and now even she knew that she had pushed her father to the edge.

On Spinalonga, meanwhile, Eleni tried to grow accustomed to what would be regarded as unacceptable on the mainland but on the colony passed for normality; she failed, however, and found herself wanting to change whatever she could. Just as Giorgis did not protect Eleni from his worries, she in turn shared her concerns about her life and her future on Spinalonga.

The first really disagreeable encounter she experienced on the island was with Kristina Kroustalakis, the woman who ran the school.

'I don't expect her to like me,' she commented to Giorgis, 'but she's acting like an animal that's been driven into a tight corner.'

'Why does she do that?' asked Giorgis, already knowing the answer.

'She's a useless teacher, who doesn't care a drachma for the children – and she knows that's what I think of her,' answered Eleni.

Giorgis sighed. Eleni had never been reticent about her views.

Almost as soon as they had arrived, Eleni had seen that the school had little to offer Dimitri. After his first day, he returned silent and sullen, and when she enquired what he had done in class his reply was 'Nothing.'

'What do you mean, nothing? You must have done something.'

'The teacher was writing all the letters and numbers on the board and I was sent to the back of the class for saying that I already knew them. After that the oldest children were allowed to do some really easy sums and when I shouted out one of the answers I was sent out of the room for the rest of the day.'

After this, Eleni started to teach Dimitri herself, and his friends then began to come to her for lessons. Soon children who had barely been able to distinguish their letters and numbers could read fluently and do their sums and within a few months her small house was filled with children on five long mornings a week. They ranged in age from six to sixteen and, with one exception, a boy who had been born on the island, they had all been sent to the island from Crete when they had shown the symptoms of leprosy. The majority of them had received some basic education before they arrived, but most of them, even the older ones, had made little progress in all the time they had spent in a classroom with Kristina Kroustalakis. She treated them like fools, so fools they remained.

The tension between Kristina Kroustalakis and Eleni began to build up. It was evident to almost everyone that Eleni should take over the school and that the valuable teacher's stipend should be hers. Kristina Kroustalakis fought her own corner, refusing to concede or even consider the possibility of sharing her role, but Eleni was tenacious. She drove the situation to a conclusion, not for her own gain but for the good of the island's seventeen children, who deserved so much more than they would ever get from the lackadaisical Kroustalakis. Pedagogy was an investment in the future, and Kristina Kroustalakis saw little point in expending much energy on those who might not be around for long.

Finally, one day, Eleni was invited to put her case before the elders. She brought with her examples of the work the children had been doing both before and after she arrived on the island. 'But this simply shows natural progress,' protested one elder, known to be a close friend of Kyria Kroustalakis. To most of them there, however, the evidence was plain. Eleni's zeal and commitment to her task showed results. Her driving force was the belief that education was not a means to some nebulous end but had intrinsic value, and made the children better people. The strong possibility that several of them might not live to see their twenty-first birthdays was of no relevance to Eleni.

There were a few dissenting voices, but the majority of elders were in favour of the controversial decision to remove the established teacher from her position and install Eleni instead. For ever after there would be people on the island who regarded Eleni as a usurper, but she was profoundly unbothered by such an attitude. The children were what mattered.

The school provided Dimitri with almost everything he needed: a structure to his day, stimulation for his mind, and companionship, in the form of a new friend, Nikos, who was the only child to have been born on the island but not taken to the mainland for adoption. The reason for this was that he had developed signs of the disease as a baby. If he had been healthy he would have been taken away from his parents, who, although they were overwhelmed with guilt that the child shared their affliction, were also overjoyed to be able to keep him.

Every moment of Dimitri's life was filled, successfully keeping him from dwelling on how things used to be. In some ways this life was an improvement. The small, dark-eyed boy now endured less hardship, less anxiety and fewer worries than had burdened him as the oldest of five children in a peasant family. Each afternoon, however, when he left the school building to return to the semi-darkness of his new home, he would become aware of the undercurrents of adult disquiet. He would hear snatches of conversation as he passed the *kafenion* or whispered discussions between people as they talked in the street.

Sometimes there were new rumours mixed in with the old. There was the endlessly recycled discussion over whether they would be getting a new generator and the perennial debate over the water supply. In the past few months there had been whispers about a grant for new accommodation and an increased 'pension' for every member of the colony. Dimitri listened to a great deal of adult talk and observed that grown-ups endlessly chewed over the same matter, like dogs with old bones long since stripped of their flesh. The smallest events, as well as the larger ones such as illness and death, were anticipated and mulled over. One day, though, something took place for which there had been no build-up and little forewarning but which was to have a huge impact on the life of the island.

One night a few months after Dimitri and Eleni had arrived they were eating supper when they were disturbed by an insistent banging on the door. It was Elpida, and the elderly woman was out of breath and flushed with excitement.

'Eleni, please come,' she panted. 'There are boatloads of them – *boatloads* – and they need our help. Come!'

Eleni knew Elpida well enough by now to realise that if she said help was called for, no questions needed to be asked. Dimitri's curiosity was aroused. He dropped his cutlery and followed the women as they hastened down the twilit street, listening as Kyria Kontomaris blurted out the story, her words tumbling out one after the other.

'They're from Athens,' she gasped. 'Giorgis has already brought over two boatloads and he's about to arrive with the third. They're mostly men but I noticed a few women as well. They look like prisoners, sick prisoners.'

By now they had reached the entrance to the long tunnel which led to the quay, and Eleni turned to Dimitri.

'You'll have to stay here,' she said firmly. 'Please go back to the house and finish your supper.'

Even from the end of the tunnel Dimitri could hear the

muffled echo of male voices, and he was more curious than ever about what was causing such commotion. The two women hurried on and were soon out of sight. Dimitri aimlessly kicked a stone about at the tunnel entrance and then, looking furtively behind him, darted into the dark passageway, making sure he kept close to the sides. As he turned the corner he could see quite clearly what the fuss was all about.

New inhabitants usually arrived one by one and after a quiet welcome from Petros Kontomaris slipped as discreetly into the community as they could. Initially, the best anyone hoped for on Spinalonga was anonymity, and most people remained silent as they were welcomed. On the quayside tonight, however, there was no such calm. As they tumbled off Giorgis's small boat, many of the new arrivals lost their balance before landing heavily on the stony ground. They shouted, writhed and howled, some of them clearly in pain, and from his shadowy position, Dimitri could see why they had fallen. The newcomers seemed not to have arms, at least not arms that hung freely by their sides, and when he looked closer, he realised that they were all wearing strange jackets that trapped their arms behind their backs.

Dimitri watched as Eleni and Elpida bent down, one by one undid the straps that kept these people tied up like packages, and released them from their hessian prisons. Lying in heaps on the dusty ground these creatures seemed less than human. One of them then staggered to the water's edge, leant towards the sea and vomited copiously. Another did the same – and then a third.

Dimitri watched both fascinated and fearful, as still as the rocky wall which screened him. As the newcomers unfurled themselves and slowly stood upright they regained a little dignity. Even from a hundred metres, he could feel the anger and aggression that emanated from them. Gathering round one particular man who appeared to be attempting to calm them, several talked at once, their voices raised.

Dimitri counted. There were eighteen of them here, and Giorgis was turning his boat around again to return to Plaka. One more boatload was still to arrive.

Close to the quayside in Plaka, a crowd had gathered in the square to study this curious group. A few days before, Giorgis had taken a letter from Athens across to Petros Kontomaris warning him of the lepers' imminent arrival. Between them they had agreed to keep their own counsel. The prospect of nearly two dozen new patients arriving simultaneously on Spinalonga would send the islanders into a state of panic. All Kontomaris had been told was that these lepers had created trouble at the hospital in Athens – and as a consequence had been dispatched to Spinalonga. They had been shipped like cattle from Piraeus to Iraklion on two days of rough seas. Stricken with sunstroke and sea sickness, they were then transferred to a smaller vessel bound for Plaka. From there Giorgis was to bring them, six at a time, on the final stretch of their journey. It was plain for anyone to see that this bedraggled mob of abused and uncared-for humanity would not survive such treatment for long.

The village children in Plaka, unafraid to stare, had gathered to watch. Fotini, Anna and Maria were among them, and Anna questioned her father as he took a short break before taking the final load across the water.

'Why are they here? What have they done? Why couldn't they stay in Athens?' she demanded. Giorgis had no real answers to her persistent questions. But he did tell her one thing. While he was transporting his first batch of passengers to the island, he had listened intently to their conversation and, in spite of their anger and disenchantment, the voices he heard were those of educated and articulate men.

'I have no answers for you, Anna,' he told her. 'But Spinalonga will make room for them, that's what matters.'

'What about our mother?' she persisted. 'Her life will be worse than ever.'

'I think you might be wrong,' said Giorgis, drawing on the deep well of patience that he held in reserve for his elder daughter. 'These newcomers could be the best thing that ever happened to that island.'

'How can that *possibly* be?' Anna cried, dancing up and down in disbelief. 'What do you mean? They look like *animals*!' She was right about that. They did indeed resemble animals and, bundled into crates like cattle, had been treated like little more than that.

Giorgis turned his back on his daughter and returned to his boat. There were just five passengers this time. When they reached Spinalonga, the other new arrivals were wandering about. It was the first time in thirty-six hours that they had stood upright. The four women among them remained in a quiet huddle. Petros Kontomaris was walking from one person to another asking for names, ages, occupations, and number of years since diagnosis.

All the while he did this task, his mind was spinning. Every additional minute that he could detain them here with this bureaucracy gave him more time for some kind of inspiration about where, in heaven's name, these people were going to be housed. Each second of procrastination delayed the moment when they would be led through the tunnel to find that they did not have homes and that, potentially, they were even worse off than they had been in the Athenian hospital. Each short interview took a few minutes, and by the time he had finished, one thing was very clear to him. In the past, when he had taken details of new arrivals, the majority had been fishermen, smallholders or shopkeepers. This time, he had a list of trained professionals: lawyer, teacher, doctor, master stonemason, editor, engineer . . . the catalogue went on. This was an entirely different category of folk from those who made up the bulk of the population on Spinalonga, and for a moment, Kontomaris felt slightly fearful of this band of Athenian citizens who had arrived in the guise of beggars.

It was time now to take them into their new world. Kontomaris led the group through the tunnel. Word had got around that newcomers had arrived and people came out of their houses to stare. In the square, the Athenians drew to a halt behind the leader, who now turned to face them, waiting until he had their attention before he spoke.

'As a temporary measure, apart from the women, who will be housed in a vacant room at the top of the hill, you will be accommodated in the town hall.'

A crowd had now gathered around them and there was a murmur of unrest as they too listened to the announcement. Kontomaris, however, was prepared for hostility to the plan and continued.

'Let me assure you that this is only a temporary measure.

Your arrival swells our population by nearly ten per cent and we now expect the government to provide money for new housing, as they have long promised.'

The reason for the antagonism to the town hall being used as a dormitory was that it was where the social life of Spinalonga, such as it was, took place. It represented, as much as anything could, the social and political normality of life on Spinalonga, and to commandeer it was to strip the islanders of a key resource. But where else was there? There was one empty room in 'the block', the soulless new apartment building, and this was where the Athenian women would be housed. Kontomaris would ask Elpida to take them there while he got the men settled into their makeshift quarters. His heart sank when he thought about his wife's task; the only difference between the new block and a prison was that the doors there were bolted from the inside rather than from the outside. But for the men it had to be the town hall.

That night, Spinalonga became home to the twenty-three Athenian newcomers. Soon, many of those who had come to gawp realised that more constructive action was needed and made offers of food, drink and bedding. Any donation from their meagre stores meant significant sacrifice, but all, bar very few, managed some gesture.

The first few days were tense. Everyone waited to see what impact these new arrivals would have, but for forty-eight hours most of them were hardly seen, many lying impassively on their improvised bedding. Dr Lapakis visited them and noted that they were all suffering not just from leprosy but also from the rigours of a journey without adequate food or water and without shade from the relentless sun. It would take each one of them several weeks to recover from the months, perhaps years, of mistreatment they had endured even before they had embarked on their journey from Athens. Lapakis had heard that there was no discernible difference between conditions in the leprosy hospital and those in the gaol just a few hundred metres away on the edge of the city. The story went that the lepers were fed on scraps from the prison and that their clothes were cast-offs stripped from corpses in the city's main hospital. He soon learned that this was not just a myth.

All the patients had been treated barbarically, and this group who had arrived in Crete had been the driving force behind a rebellion. Mostly professional, educated people, they had led a hunger strike, drafted letters which were smuggled out to friends and politicians and stirred up dissent throughout the hospital. Rather than agreeing to any change, however, the governor of the hospital decided to evict them; or, as he preferred to term it, 'transfer them to more suitable accommodation'. Their expulsion to Spinalonga marked an end for them, and a new beginning for the island.

The women were visited each day by Elpida and were soon recovered enough to have their tour of the island and to take coffee at the Kontomaris house, and even to begin planning how they would make use of the small plot of ground which had been cleared for them to grow vegetables. They recognised very quickly that this life was an improvement on the old. At least it *was* a life. Conditions at the Athenian hospital had been horrific. The fires of hell could not have been more stifling than the suffocating summer heat in their mean, claustrophobic rooms. Add to that the rats that scratched about on the floors during the night, and they had felt no worthier than vermin.

Spinalonga, by contrast, was paradise. It offered unimagined freedom, with fresh air, birdsong and a street to amble down; here they could rediscover their humanity. During the long days of their journey from Athens, some had considered taking their own lives, assuming that they were being sent to an even worse place than the vile Hades where they had been struggling to survive. On Spinalonga, from their window on the second floor, the women could see the sun rise, and during their first days on the island they were entranced by the sight of the slow-breaking dawn.

Just as Eleni had done, they turned the space they were given into a home. Embroidered cotton cloths hung across the windows at night and woven rugs spread across their beds transformed the room and made it look like any simple Cretan dwelling.

For the men, it was a different story. They languished on their beds for several days, many of them still weakened by the hunger strike they had staged in Athens. Kontomaris organised for food to be brought to the hall and left in the vestibule, but when the dishes were collected on the first day the islanders saw that their offerings had scarcely been touched. The great metal cooking pot was still full to the brim with lamb stew; the only indication that there was any life in the building was that of the five loaves brought to the town hall, only three remained.

On the second day all the bread was eaten, and on the third, a pan of rabbit casserole was scraped clean. Each day such signs of increased appetite signified the revival of these pitiful creatures. On the fourth day, Nikos Papadimitriou emerged, blinking, into the dazzling sunlight. Forty-five years old and a lawyer, Papadimitriou had once been at the centre of Athenian life. Now he was the leader and spokesman for a group of lepers, playing this role with just as much energy as he had put into his legal career. Nikos was a natural trouble-maker, and if he had not gone into law, he might have chosen crime instead. His attempts to oppose the Athenian authorities by organising the revolt in the hospital had not been entirely successful, but he was more determined than ever to win better conditions for his fellow lepers now that they were on Spinalonga.

Though sharp-tongued, Papadimitriou had great charm and could always gather supporters. His great ally and friend was Mihalis Kouris, an engineer who had, like Papadimitriou, been in the Athenian hospital for nearly five years. That day, Kontomaris took them around Spinalonga. Unlike the majority of newcomers shown the island for the first time, a constant stream of questions flowed from these two men: 'So where is the water source?' 'How long have you been waiting for the generator?' 'How often does the doctor visit?' 'What is the mortality rate?' 'What are the current building plans?'

Kontomaris answered their questions as well as he could, but could tell by their every grunt and sigh that they were rarely satisfied with the answers. The island leader knew perfectly well that Spinalonga was underresourced. He had worked tirelessly for six years to improve things and in many areas he had succeeded, though never to the degree that everyone wanted. It was a thankless task, and as he strolled out beyond the town towards the cemetery, he wondered why he had bothered at all. This was where they would all end up, however hard he strived to make things better. All three of them would eventually lie beneath a stone slab in one of these subterranean concrete bunkers until their bones were moved to one side to make way for the next corpse. The futility of it all and the distant sound of Papadimitriou's insistent questioning made him want to sit down and weep. He decided at that very moment that he would tell the Athenians the bald facts. If they were more interested in reality than in simply being made to feel welcome, then so be it.

'I'll tell you,' he said, stopping in his tracks and turning round to face them both, 'everything you want to know. But if I do that, the burden becomes yours too. Do you understand?'

They nodded in assent, and Kontomaris began to give them the details of the island's shortcomings. He described every hoop he had jumped through in order to make any changes and told them about all the issues currently under negotiation. Then the three of them went back to the leader's house and, with Papadimitriou and Kouris's fresh perspective on the island's facilities, drew up a new plan. This included works in progress, projects to be started and finished within the coming year and an outline of what would be undertaken in the forthcoming five-year period. Such prospects in themselves would create the sense of moving forward that these people needed so much.

From that day, Papadimitriou and Kouris became Kontomaris's great supporters. No longer did they feel like condemned men, but as though they had been given a new start. Life had not held so much potential for a very long time. Within weeks, the proposals, which included specifications for building and reconstruction, were ready to be submitted to the government. Papadimitriou knew how to lean on the politicians, and his law firm in Athens, a family practice of some influence, became involved. 'Everyone on this island is a citizen of Greece,' he insisted. 'They have rights and I'm damned if I won't fight for them.' To the amazement of everyone – apart from Papadimitrou himself – within a month the government had agreed to provide the sum of money they had asked for.

The other Athenians, once they had risen from their torpor, threw themselves into new building projects. No longer were they abandoned invalids but members of a community where everyone had to pull their weight. It was now late September, and though temperatures were more moderate, the issue of water was still pressing – the addition of twenty-three new inhabitants had placed more demand than ever on the supply from the mainland and the crumbling water tunnels. Something had to be done, and Mihalis Kouris was the man to do it.

Once repairs were complete, everyone looked to the heavens for rain, and one night in early November their prayers were answered. In a spectacular display of sound and light, the skies opened, noisily emptying their contents on to the island, the mainland and the sea all around. Pebble-sized hailstones bounced down, breaking windows and sending goats scampering for safety on the hillsides, as flashes of lightning bathed the landscape in an apocalyptic luminescence. Next morning the islanders woke to find their watersheds brimful of cool, clear water. Having resolved the most pressing issue of all, the Athenians then turned their attention to creating homes for themselves. There was a derelict area between the main street and the sea; it was where the Turks had built their first houses. The dwellings, mere shells, were constructed right up against the fortress walls and would have been among the most sheltered of all enclaves. With the sort of industry and efficiency rarely seen on Crete, the old houses were restored and raised up out of the rubble, with good-as-new masonry and skilfully planed carpentry. Well before the first snowfall crowned Mount Dhikti they were ready to be occupied and the town hall was once again available for everyone. Not that the initial resentment against the Athenian lepers had lasted for long. It had only been a matter of weeks before the population of Spinalonga had recognised the potential of the new islanders and realised that what they might give would far exceed what they could ever take.

Then, as winter approached, the campaign for the generator began again in earnest. Heat and light would become the most valuable commodities as the winds began to find their way through chinks in every door and window, whipping through the draughty homes in the fading mid-afternoon light. Now that the government had discovered that Spinalonga had a more strident voice, one that could not be disregarded, it was not long before a letter came promising everything that was required. Many of the islanders were cynical. 'I wouldn't put money on them keeping their word,' some would say. 'Until I can turn on a lamp in my own house, I won't trust them to deliver,' agreed others. The general view among people who had been on Spinalonga for more than a few years was that the government's promise was worth no more than the flimsy paper it was written on.

Just ten days before all the parts arrived, labelled and complete, the anticipation of the generator was the main topic of Eleni's identical letters to Anna and Maria:

> *The generator is going to make so much difference to our lives. There was one here once before so some of the electric fittings are already in place and two of the men from Athens are expert in how to make it all work (thank goodness). Every house is promised at least one light and a small heater and those are due to arrive at the same time as the rest of the equipment.*

Anna read her letter in the dying light of a winter's afternoon. A low fire burned in the grate but she could see her breath on the cold air. A candle cast a flickering light across the page and she idly poked a corner of the sheet into its flame. Slowly the fire crept across, melting the paper until she held nothing but a fingertip-sized piece which she then dropped into the wax. Why did her mother have to write so often? Did she really think that they all wanted to hear of her warm, contented and now well-lit life with that boy? Her father made them reply to every letter, and Anna struggled over every word. She was not happy and she was not going to pretend.

Maria read her letter and showed it to her father.

'It's good news, isn't it?' Giorgis commented. 'And it's all thanks to those Athenians. Who would have thought that a ragbag like that could make such a difference?'

By the beginning of winter, before the sharpness of the December winds arrived, the island had warmth and, after darkness fell, those who wished could now read by the dimmest of dim electric lights.

When Advent began, Giorgis and Eleni needed to decide how to deal with Christmas. It was to be their first one apart for fifteen years. The festival did not have the importance of Easter, but it was a time for ritual and feasting within the family and Eleni's absence would be a gaping void.

For a few days before and after Christmas Giorgis did not cross the choppy waters to visit Eleni. Not just because the vicious wind would bite into his hands and face until they were raw, but because his daughters needed him to stay. Similarly, Eleni's attentions had to be on Dimitri and they played out in parallel the age-old traditions. As they always had, the girls sang tuneful *kalanda* from house to house and were rewarded with sweets and dried fruit, and after early morning mass on Christmas Day they feasted with the Angelopoulos family on pork and delicious *kourambiethes*, sweet nutty biscuits baked by Savina. Things were not so very different on Spinalonga. The children sang in the square, helped bake the ornate seasonal loaves known as *christopsomo*, Christ's bread, and ate as never before. For Dimitri it was the first time he had enjoyed such plentiful quantities of rich food and witnessed such hedonism.

Throughout the twelve days of Christmas, Giorgis and Eleni sprinkled a little holy water in each room of their respective houses to deter the *kallikantzari*, seasonal goblins that were said to play havoc in the home, and on 1 January, St Basil's Day, Giorgis visited Eleni once again, bringing her presents from the children and from Savina. The ending of the old year and the beginning of the new was a watershed, a milestone that had been safely passed, taking the Petrakis family into a different era. Although Anna and Maria still missed their mother, they now knew that they could survive without her.

Chapter Six

1940

AFTER ITS BEST winter in years came Spinalonga's most glorious spring. It was not just the carpets of wild flowers that spread across the slopes of the island's north side and peeped out of every crack in the rocks that made it so, but also the sense of new life that had been breathed into the community.

Spinalonga's main street, only a few months earlier a series of dilapidated buildings, was now a smart row of shops with shutters and doors freshly painted in deep blues and greens. They were now places where shopkeepers displayed their wares with pride and islanders shopped not just out of necessity but for pleasure too. For the first time, the island had its own economy. People were productive: they bartered, bought and sold, sometimes at a profit, sometimes at a loss.

The *kafenion* was flourishing too and a new taverna opened which specialised in *kakavia*, fish soup, freshly made each day. One of the busiest places in the main street was the barber. Stelios Vandis had been the top hair stylist in Rethimnon, Crete's second city, but had abandoned his trade when he had been exiled to Spinalonga. When Papadimitriou learned that they had such a man in their midst, he insisted Vandis resume his work. The Athenian men were all peacocks. They had the swaggering vanity of the city type and in their former days had all enjoyed the ritual of the fortnightly trim to both hair and moustache, the condition and shape of which almost defined their manliness. Life took a turn for the better now that they had found someone who could make them handsome again. It was not individual style that they aspired to but identically luxurious and well-coiffed hair.

'Stelios,' Papadimitriou would say, 'give me your best Venizelos.' Venizelos, the Cretan lawyer who had become prime minister of Greece, was thought to have had the most handsome moustache in the Christian world, and it was appropriate, the menfolk joked, that Papadimitriou should emulate him, since he clearly aspired to a position of leadership on the island.

As Kontomaris's strength began to fail, the leader relied more and more on Papadimitriou, and the popularity of the Athenian grew among the islanders. The men respected him for what he had achieved in such a short time; the women were grateful too; and soon he enjoyed a sort of hero-worship, no doubt enhanced by his silver-screen looks. Like most of the Athenians he had always lived in the city, and one result of this was that he did not have the bent and grizzled appearance of the average Cretan male who had spent the best part of his life in the open air, scraping a living off the land or out of the sea. Until the past few months of manual labour, his skin had seen little sunlight and even less wind.

Although the Athenian had ambitions, he was not a ruthless man, and he would not stand for election unless Kontomaris was ready to retire.

'Papadimitriou, I'm more than ready to give up this position,' the older man said one night in early March over a game of backgammon. 'I've told you that a thousand times. The job needs fresh blood – and look at what you have done for the island already! My supporters will back you, there's no question of it. Believe me, I'm just too weary now.'

Papadimitriou was unsurprised at this last comment. During the six months since his arrival he had seen Kontomaris's condition deteriorate. The two men had been close for some time and he had known that the elderly leader was grooming him as his successor.

'I'll take it on if you really are ready to let go,' he said quietly, 'but I think you should give it a few more days' thought.'

'I've given it *months* of thought already,' replied Petros grumpily. 'I know I can't go on.'

The two men played on in a silence only broken by the clack of the counters.

'There's one other thing I want you to know,' said Papadimitriou when the game finished and it was time for him to go. 'If I do win the election, I shall not want to live in your house.'

'But it isn't my house,' retorted Kontomaris. 'It's the leader's house. It goes with the position and always has done.'

Papadimitriou drew on his cigarette and paused a moment as he exhaled. He decided to let the matter rest. The issue might be hypothetical in any case since the election was not entirely a fait accompli. It would be contested by two others, one of whom had been on the island for some six or seven years and had a large following; the election of Theodoros Makridakis seemed, to Papadimitriou at least, a distinct possibility. A large contingent of the population responded to Makridakis's negativity, and although they loved to lap up the benefits of all Papadimitriou's hard work and the dramatic changes of the past six months, they also felt that their interests could be better served by someone who was driven by anger. It was easy to believe that the fire that propelled Makridakis might help him achieve things that reason and diplomacy could not.

The annual elections in late March were the mostly hotly contested in the history of the island, and this time the results actually mattered. Spinalonga was somewhere worth governing and leadership was no longer a poisoned chalice. Three men stood: Papadimitriou, Spyros Kazakis and Theodoros Makridakis. On the day of the election every man and woman placed a vote, and even the lepers who were confined in the hospital with little chance of ever emerging again from their sickbeds were taken a ballot paper which was duly returned to the town hall in a sealed envelope.

Spyros Kazakis won a mere handful of votes and Makridakis, to Papadimitriou's relief and surprise, gained fewer than one hundred. This left the lion's share and the clear majority to the Athenian. The population had voted with their hearts, but also with wisdom. Makridakis's posturing was all very well, but achievement counted for more, and for this Papadimitriou knew at last that he was recognised. It was a pivotal moment in the civilising of the island.

'Fellow inhabitants of Spinalonga,' he said. 'My wishes for this island are your wishes too.' He was speaking to the crowd gathered in the small square outside the town hall on the night following the election. The count had just been double-checked and the results announced.

'We have already made Spinalonga a more civilised place, and in some ways it is now an even better place to live than the towns and villages that serve us.' He waved his hand in the direction of Plaka. 'We have electricity when Plaka does not. We have diligent medical staff and the most dedicated of teachers. On the mainland, many people are living at subsistence level, starving when we are not. Last week, some of them rowed out to us from Elounda. Rumours of our new prosperity had reached them and they came to ask *us* for food. Is that not a turnaround?' A murmur of assent rippled through the throng. 'No longer are we the outcasts with begging bowls crying, "Unclean! Unclean!"' he continued. 'Now others come to us to seek alms.'

He paused for a moment, enough time for someone to shout out from the crowd: 'Three cheers for Papadimitriou!' When the cheers died down, he added one final note to his message.

'There is one thing that binds us together. The disease of leprosy. When we have our disagreements, let us not forget there is no escape from one another. While we have life, let us make it as good as we can – this must be our common purpose.' He raised his hand in the air, pointing his finger upwards into the sky, a sign of celebration and victory. 'To Spinalonga!' he shouted.

The crowd of two hundred mirrored the gesture, and with

a cry that was heard across the water in Plaka they cried out in unison: 'To Spinalonga!'

Theodoros Makridakis, unnoticed by anyone, sloped away into the shadows. He had long yearned to be the leader and his disappointment was as bitter as an unripe olive.

The next afternoon, Elpida Kontomaris began to pack her possessions. Within a day or two she and Petros would need to move out of this house and into Papadimitriou's current accommodation. She had expected this moment for a long time but it did not lessen the feeling of dread that weighed her down so that she could scarcely summon the energy to move one foot in front of the other. She went about packing in a desultory fashion, her heavy body unwilling to do the task and her misshapen feet more painful than ever before. As she stood contemplating the prospect of tidying away the precious contents of the glass-fronted cabinet – the rows of soldiers, the tiny pieces of porcelain and the engraved silver that had been in her family for many generations – she asked herself where these valuables would go when she and Petros were no more. The two of them were the end of the line.

A gentle tap on the door interrupted her thoughts. That must be Eleni, she thought. Though busy with school and the task of motherhood, Eleni had promised to come by that afternoon to help her, and she was always true to her word. When Elpida opened the door, however, expecting to see her slim, fine-featured friend, a large, darkly dressed male figure filled the frame instead. It was Papadimitriou.

'*Kalispera*, Kyria Kontomaris. May I come in?' he asked gently, conscious of her surprise.

'Yes . . . please do,' she answered, moving away from the door to let him in.

'I have only one thing to say,' he told her as they stood facing each other, surrounded by the half-filled crates of books, china and photographs. 'There is no need for you to move out of here. I have no intention of taking this house away from you. There is no need. Petros has given so much of his life to being leader of this island that I have decided to endow him with it – call it his pension, if you like.'

'But it's where the leader has always lived. It's yours now, and besides, Petros wouldn't hear of it.'

'I have no interest in what has happened in the past,' replied Papadimitriou. 'I want you to stay here, and in any case I want to live in the house I'm restoring. Please,' he insisted. 'It will suit all of us better this way.'

Elpida's eyes glistened with tears. 'It's so kind of you,' she said, extending both her hands towards him. 'So very kind. I can see that you mean it, but I don't know how we are going to persuade Petros.'

'He has no choice,' said Papadimitriou with determination. 'I'm in charge now. What I want you to do is unpack all your things from these boxes and put them back exactly where they were. I'll come back later to make sure you've done that.'

Elpida could see that this was no idle gesture. The man meant what he said and was used to getting what he wanted. This was why he had been elected leader, and as she repositioned the lead soldiers in their ranks she tried to analyse what it was that made Papadimitriou so hard to disagree with. It was not merely his physical stature. That on its own might simply have made him a bully. He had other, more subtle techniques. Sometimes he moved people round to his point of view simply through the modulations of his voice. On other occasions he would achieve the same end by overpowering them with the force of his logic. His lawyer's skills were as sharp as ever, even on Spinalonga.

Before Papadimitriou went on his way, Elpida asked him to eat with them when he returned that evening. Her great talent was in the kitchen. She cooked as no one else on Spinalonga, and only a fool would ever turn down such an invitation. As soon as he had gone she went about preparing the meal, fashioning her favourite *kefethes*, meat balls in egg-lemon sauce, and measuring out the ingredients for *revani*, a sweet cake made with semolina and syrup.

When Kontomaris came home that evening, his duties as leader finally completed, there was a lightness in his step. As he entered his home, the fragrant smells of baking wafted over him and an apron-clad Elpida came towards him, her arms outstretched in welcome. They embraced, his head resting on her shoulder.

'It's all over,' he murmured. 'At long last it's over.'

As he glanced up, he noticed that the room looked just as it always had. There was no sign of the half-filled crates that had been standing about the room when he had left that morning.

'Why haven't you packed?' There was more than a note of irritation in his voice. He was weary and he so much wanted the next few days to be over. Wishing they were already transported to their new house, the fact that nothing seemed even vaguely ready to go upset him greatly and made him feel more exhausted than ever.

'I packed and then I unpacked,' Elpida replied mysteriously. 'We're staying here.'

Precisely on cue, there was a firm knock at the door. Papadimitriou had arrived.

'Kyria Kontomaris invited me to eat with you,' he said simply.

Once they were all seated and a generous glass of ouzo had been poured for each of them, Kontomaris regained his composure.

'I think there's been some kind of conspiracy,' he said. 'I should be angry, but I know you both well enough to realise I've no choice in this matter.'

His smile belied his stern tone and the formality of his words. He was secretly delighted at Papadimitriou's generosity, not least because he knew how much it meant to his wife. The three of them toasted each other in ratification of the deal that had been struck, and the issue of the leader's house was never mentioned between them again. There were a few rumbles of dissent among the council members and fervent discussions about what would happen if a future leader wished to reclaim the splendid house, but a compromise was eventually reached: tenancy of the house would be reassessed every five years.

After the election, work continued apace with the renovation of the island. Papadimitriou's efforts had not merely been an electioneering ploy. Repairing and rebuilding went on until everyone had a decent place to live, their own oven, usually in the courtyard in front of their home, and, even more importantly for their sense of pride, a private outdoor latrine.

Now that water was being collected efficiently there was

plenty for everyone, and an extensive communal laundry was built with a long row of smooth concrete sinks. It was little less than a luxury for the women, who would linger over their washing, making the area a vibrant social focus.

The social aspect of their lives was also enhanced, however, in less workaday situations. For Panos Sklavounis, an Athenian who had once been an actor, the working day began when everyone else's had ended. Not long after the election, he took Papadimitriou to one side. Sklavounis's approach was aggressive, which was typical of the man's manner. He liked confrontation and as an actor back in Athens had been used to hustling.

'Boredom is growing like a fungus here,' he said. 'What people need is entertainment. Lots of them can't look forward to next year, but they might as well have something to look forward to next week.'

'I see your point and I agree entirely,' responded Papadimitriou. 'But what do you propose?'

'Entertainment. Large-scale entertainment,' replied Sklavounis rather grandly.

'Which means what?' asked Papadimitriou.

'Movies,' said Sklavounis.

Six months earlier, such a proposal would have seemed ambitious beyond words and as laughable as telling the lepers they could swim across to Elounda to visit the cinema. Now, however, it was not beyond the realms of possibility.

'Well, we have a generator,' said Papadimitriou, 'which is a good start, but it's not all that's required, is it?'

Keeping the islanders happy and occupied in the evening might indeed help rule out much of the discontent that still lingered. While people sat in rows in the dark, thought Papadimitriou, they could not be drinking to excess or hatching plots in the *kafenion*.

'What else do you need?' he asked.

Sklavounis was quick to reply. He had already worked out how many people could fit into the town hall and where he could get a projector, a screen and the film reels. He had also, very importantly, done the figures. The missing element, until he had committee approval, was money, but given that so many of the lepers were now earning some kind of income, an entry fee could be charged to the new cinema and the cost of the entire enterprise might eventually cover itself.

Within a few weeks of his initial request, posters appeared around the town:

Saturday 13 April
7.00 p.m.
Town Hall
The Apaches of Athens
Tickets 2 drachma

By six o'clock that evening, over one hundred people were queuing outside the town hall. At least another eighty had arrived by the time the doors opened at six-thirty, and the same enthusiasm greeted the film the following Saturday.

Eleni bubbled with excitement when she wrote to her daughters about the new entertainment:

We are all so enjoying the films – they're the highlight of the week. Things don't always go to plan, though. Last Saturday the reels did not arrive from Agios Nikolaos. There was such disappointment when people realised that the film was cancelled that there was nearly a riot, and for several days people went about long-faced, as though the harvest had failed! Anyway, everyone cheered up as the week progressed, and we were all so relieved when your father was spotted carrying the reels ashore.

Within weeks, however, Giorgis began to bring more than the latest feature film from Athens. He also had a newsreel, which brought the audience sharply up to date with the sinister events that were taking place in the outside world. Though copies of Crete's weekly newspaper made their way to the island and radios occasionally crackled with the latest news bulletin, no one had had any idea of the scale of the growing havoc being wreaked across Europe by Nazi Germany. At this stage these outrages seemed remote and the inhabitants of Spinalonga had other more immediate things to concern them. With the elections behind them, Easter was approaching.

In previous years, the observance of this, the greatest of Christian festivals, had been subdued. The festivities taking place in Plaka made plenty of noise, and although a reduced version of the same dramatic rituals was always held in Spinalonga's little church of St Pantaleimon, there was a sense that it was not the same as the full-scale celebrations taking place across the water.

This year it was to be different. Papadimitriou would make sure of that. The commemoration of Christ's resurrection in Spinalonga was to be no less extravagant in expression than anything held on Crete or in mainland Greece itself.

Lent had been strictly observed. Most people had gone without meat and fish for forty days, and in the final week, wine and olive oil had been consigned to the darkest recesses. By Thursday of Passion Week the wooden cross in the church that was big enough to accommodate perhaps one hundred souls (so long as they were as tight-packed as grains in an ear of wheat) was laden with lemon blossom and a long line formed down the street to mourn Christ and kiss his feet. The throng of worshippers both inside and outside the church stood hushed. This was a melancholy moment, and all the more so when they looked on the icon of St Pantaleimon, who was, as the more cynical of the lepers described him, the supposed patron saint of healing. Many had lost faith in him some time earlier, but his life story had made him the perfect choice for such a church. A young doctor in Roman times, Pantaleimon followed his mother's lead and became a Christian, an act which would almost certainly result in persecution. His success in healing the sick aroused suspicions and he was arrested, stretched out on a wheel and finally boiled alive.

However cynical the islanders might be about the healing powers of the saint, they all joined in Christ's great funeral procession the next day. A coffin was decorated in the morning, and in the late afternoon the floral *epitaphoi* was carried through the streets. It was a solemn procession.

'We have plenty of practice at this, don't we?' Elpida commented sardonically to Eleni as they walked slowly along the street, the two-hundred-strong snake of people winding its way through the little town and up on to the path that led round to the north side of the island.

'We do,' she agreed, 'but this is different. This man comes alive again—'

'Which is more than we'll ever do,' interjected Theodoros Makridakis, who happened to be walking behind them and who was always ready with a negative comment. Resurrection of the body seemed an unlikely concept, but the strong believers among them knew that this was what was promised: a new, unblemished, resurrected body. It was the whole point of the story and the meaning of the ritual. The believers clung to that.

Saturday was a quiet day. Men, women and children were meant to be in mourning. Everyone was busy, however. Eleni organised the children into a working party to paint eggs and then decorate them with tiny leaf stencils. Meanwhile other women baked the traditional cakes. By contrast with such gentle activities, the men all helped in the slaughter and preparation of the lambs which had been shipped over a few weeks before. Once all such chores were done, people again visited the church to decorate it with sprigs of rosemary, laurel leaves and myrtle branches, and by early evening a bittersweet smell emanated from the building and the air was heavy with anticipation and incense.

Eleni stood in the doorway of the crowded church. The people were silent, subdued and expectant, straining to hear the initial whispers of the Kyrie Eleison. It began so softly it might have been the breeze stirring the leaves but then grew into something almost tangible, filling the building and exploding into the world outside. The candles which had burned inside the church were now extinguished and under a starless, moonless sky, the world was plunged into darkness.

For a few moments Eleni could sense nothing but the heavy scent of molten tallow that pervaded the air.

At midnight, when the bell from the church in Plaka could be heard tolling resonantly across the still water, the priest lit a single candle.

'Come and receive the light,' he commanded. Papa Kazakos spoke the sacred words with reverence, but also with directness, and the islanders were in no doubt that this was a command to approach him. One by one those closest reached out with tapers, and from these the light was shared around until both inside and outside the church there was a flickering forest of flames. In less than a minute darkness had turned to light.

Papa Kazakos, a warm-natured, heavily bearded man with a love for good living – making some justifiably sceptical about whether he had observed any kind of abstinence during Lent – now began to read the Gospel. It was a familiar passage and many of the older islanders moved their lips in perfect synchronicity.

'*Christos anesti!*' he proclaimed at the end of the passage. Christ is risen.

'*Christos anesti! Christos anesti!*' the crowd shouted back in unison.

The great triumphant cry carried on in the street for some time as people wished each other many happy years – '*Chronia polla!*' – responding with enthusiasm: '*E pisis*' – 'Same to you'.

Then it was time to carry the lighted candles carefully home.

'Come, Dimitri,' Eleni encouraged the boy. 'Let's see if we can get this home without it going out.'

If they could reach their house with the candle still lit, it would bring good luck for a whole year, and on this still April night it was perfectly feasible to do so. Within a few minutes every home on the island had a candle glowing in its window.

The final stage of the ritual was the lighting of the bonfire, the symbolic burning of the traitor Judas Iscariot. All day people had brought their spare kindling, and bushes had been stripped of dry branches. Now the priest lit the pyre and there was more rejoicing as it crackled and then finally went up with a roar while rockets soared into the sky all around. The real celebrations had begun. In every far-flung village, town and city, from Plaka to Athens, there would be great merrymaking, and this year it would be as noisy on Spinalonga as anywhere across the land. Sure enough, over in Plaka, they could hear the lively blasts of the bouzouki as the dancing on the island began.

Many of the lepers had not danced for years, but unless they were so crippled that they could not walk, they were encouraged to get up and join the circle as it slowly rotated. Out of their dust-filled trunks had come pieces of traditional costume, so that among them there were several men in fringed turbans, long boots and knickerbockers, and many of the women had donned their embroidered waistcoats and bright headscarves for the night.

Some of the dances were stately, but when they were not, the fit and active would take their turn, spinning and whirling as though it was the last time they would ever dance. After the dances came the songs, the *mantinades*. Some were sweet, some melancholy; some were ballads telling long stories that lulled the old folk and children almost to a slumber.

By the time day broke, most people had found their way to bed, but some had passed out across rows of chairs in the taverna, full not just of raki but of the sweetest lamb they had ever feasted on. Not since the Turks had occupied the island had Spinalonga seen such high spirits and hedonism. It was in God's name that they were celebrating. Christ was risen and in certain ways there had been some kind of rising from the dead for them too, a resurrection of their spirits.

What was left of April became a period of intense activity. Several more lepers had arrived from Athens in March, adding to the half-dozen who had come from various parts of Crete during the winter months. This meant more restoration work was needed, and everyone was aware that once the temperatures had soared there would be many tasks that would be abandoned until the autumn. The Turkish quarter was finally finished and the repairs to the Venetian water tanks were completed. Front doors and shutters had another coat of paint and the tiles on the church roof were all fastened into place.

As Spinalonga rose from its own ashes, Eleni began to decline. She watched the continuing restoration process and could not help comparing it to her own gradual deterioration. For months she had pretended to herself that the disease had met resistance in her body and that there was no development, but then she began to notice changes, almost by the day. The smooth lumps on her feet had multiplied, and for many weeks now she had walked without feeling in them.

'Isn't there anything the doctor can do to help?' Giorgis asked quietly.

'No,' she said. 'I think we have to face that.'

'How is Dimitri?' he asked, trying to change the subject.

'He's fine. He's being very helpful now that I'm finding it harder to walk, and in the last few months he's grown a lot and can carry all the groceries for me. I can't help thinking that he is happier here than he was before, though I don't doubt that he misses his parents.'

'Does he ever mention them?'

'He hasn't said a word about them for weeks and weeks. Do you know something? He hasn't received one letter from them all the time that he's been here. Poor child.'

By the end of May, life had settled into its usual summer pattern of long siestas and sultry nights. Flies buzzed around and a haze of heat settled over the island from midday till dusk. Scarcely anything moved during these hours of simmering heat. There was a sense of permanence here now and, though it was unspoken, the majority of people felt that life was worth living. As Eleni hobbled slowly to school on a typical morning, she relished the strong smell of coffee mingling with the sweet scent of mimosa in the street; the sight of a man walking down the hill, his donkey laden with oranges; the sound of ivory backgammon counters click-clacking as they were pushed about the baize and the rattle of the dice punctuating a buzz of conversation in the *kafenion*. Just as they did in any Cretan village, elderly women sat in doorways facing the street and nodded a greeting as she passed. These women never looked directly at each other when they spoke in case they should miss any comings and goings.

There was plenty happening on Spinalonga. Occasionally

there was even a marriage. Such major events, the burgeoning social life on the island and other significant information which the population needed to know soon created the need for a newspaper. Yiannis Solomonidis, formerly a journalist in Athens, took charge and, once he had got hold of a press, printed fifty copies of a weekly newssheet, *The Spinalonga Star.* These were passed around and devoured with interest by everyone on the island. To start with the newspaper contained the parochial affairs of the island, the title of that week's film, the opening times of the pharmacy, items lost, found and for sale, and, of course, marriages and deaths. As time went on it began to include a digest of events on the mainland, opinion pieces and even cartoons.

One day in November there was a significant event that went unreported by the newspaper. Not a sentence, not a word recorded the visit of a mysterious dark-haired man whose smart appearance would have made him blend into a crowd in Iraklion. In Plaka however, he was noticed by several people because it was rare for someone to be seen in the village wearing a suit, unless of course there was a wedding or a funeral, and there was neither that day.

Chapter Seven

Dr Lapakis had informed Giorgis that he was expecting a visitor who would need to be brought across to Spinalonga and returned to Plaka a few hours later. His name was Nikolaos Kyritsis. In his early thirties, with thick, black hair, he was slight by comparison with most Cretans and a well-cut suit accentuated his slender build. His skin was taut across his prominent cheek bones. Some considered him distinguished-looking, while others thought he appeared undernourished, and neither view was wrong.

Kyritsis looked incongruous on the Plaka quayside. He had no baggage, no boxes and no tearful family as did most of the people Giorgis took across, just the slimmest of leather portfolios which he held to his chest. The only other people who went to Spinalonga were Lapakis and the very occasional government representative making a quick visit to assess financial requests. This man was the first real visitor Giorgis had ever taken there, and he overcame his usual reticence with strangers and spoke to him.

'What's your business on the island?'

'I'm a doctor,' the man replied.

'But there's already a doctor there,' said Giorgis. 'I took him this morning.'

'Yes, I know. It's Dr Lapakis I'm going to visit. He is a friend and colleague of mine from many years back.'

'You aren't a leper, are you?' asked Giorgis.

'No,' answered the stranger, his face almost creasing into a smile. 'And one day none of the people on the island will be either.'

This was a bold statement and Giorgis's heart quickened at the thought. Snippets of news – or was it just rumour? – occasionally filtered through that so-and-so's uncle or friend had heard something about a development in the cure for leprosy. There had been talk of injections of gold, arsenic and snake venom, for example, but there was a hint of madness about such treatments, and even if they were affordable, would they really work? Only the Athenians, people gossiped, could possibly entertain thoughts of paying for such quack remedies. For a moment, Giorgis day-dreamed as he loosened the boat from its moorings and prepared to take this new doctor across. Eleni's condition had been getting visibly worse in the past few months and he had begun to lose hope that a cure would ever be found to bring her home, but for the first time since he had taken her to Spinalonga, eighteen months earlier, his heart lifted. Just a little.

Papadimitriou was waiting on the quayside to greet the doctor, and Giorgis watched as they both disappeared out of sight through the tunnel, the dapper figure with his slim leather case and the powerful figure of the island's leader towering over him.

An icy blast of wind blew across the water, fighting against

Giorgis's boat, but in spite of this, he found himself humming. He would not be perturbed by the elements today.

As the two men walked up the main street together, Papadimitriou grilled Kyritsis. He had enough information at his fingertips to know what questions to ask.

'Where are they with the latest research? When are they going to start testing it out? How long will it take to reach us here? How closely involved are you?' It was a cross-examination that Kyritsis had not expected, but then he had not anticipated meeting someone like Papadimitriou.

'It's early days,' he said cautiously. 'I'm part of a widespread research programme being funded by the Pasteur Foundation, but it's not just the cure we're hunting for. There are new guidelines on treatment and prevention that were set down at the Cairo Conference a couple of years ago, and that's my main interest in coming here. I want to make sure that we are doing all we can – I don't want the cure, if and when it's found, to be too late for everyone here.'

Papadimitriou, a consummate actor, concealed his mild disappointment that the longed-for cure was still out of reach by laughing it off: 'That's too bad. I'd promised my family I'd be back in Athens by Christmas, so I was relying on you for a magic potion.'

Kyritsis was a realist. He knew it could be some years until these people received successful treatment and he would not raise their hopes. Leprosy was a disease almost as old as the hills themselves and was not going to vanish overnight.

As the men walked together to the hospital, Kyritsis took in the sights and sounds around him with some incredulity.

It looked like any normal village, albeit less run-down than many in that part of Crete. Except for the occasional inhabitant he spotted with an enlarged earlobe or perhaps a crippled foot – signs which might not have been noticed by most – the people living there could have been ordinary folk going about their business. At this time of year there were few faces in full view. Men wore their caps pulled down and their collars turned up and women had their woollen shawls furled tightly around their heads and shoulders, protecting themselves from the elements, the wind which grew wilder by the day and the rain which fell in torrents and turned streets into streams.

The two men passed the glass-fronted shops with their brightly painted shutters, and the baker, removing a batch of sandy-coloured loaves from his oven, caught Kyritsis's eye and nodded. Kyritsis touched the brim of his hat in reply. Just before the church, they turned off the central street. High above them was the hospital. Particularly from below, it was an imposing sight, a building far grander than any other on the island.

Lapakis was at the front entrance to greet Kyritsis, and the two men embraced in a spontaneous display of genuine affection. For a few moments greetings and questions overlapped each other in a helter-skelter of enthusiasm. 'How are you? How long have you been here? What's happening in Athens? Tell me your news!' Eventually, their mutual delight at seeing each other gave way to practicalities. Time was running away. Lapakis took Kyritsis on a swift guided tour of the hospital, showing him the outpatients' clinic and treatment rooms and finally the ward.

'We have so few resources at present. More people should

be coming in for a few days, but we simply have to treat the majority and send them back home,' said Lapakis wearily.

In the ward, ten beds were packed in with no more than half a metre between each. All of them were occupied, some by men and some by women, though it was hard to tell which was which, since the shutters were closed and only a few faint streaks of light filtered through. Most of these patients were at the end of the line. Kyritsis, who had spent some time in the leprosy hospital in Athens, was unshocked. The conditions, the overcrowding and the smell there had been a hundred times worse. Here, at least, there was some attention to hygiene, which could mean the difference between life and death for someone with infected ulcers.

'All of these patients are in a reactive state,' said Lapakis quietly, leaning against the doorframe. This was the phase of leprosy where the symptoms of the disease intensified, sometimes for days or even weeks. During their time in this state patients were in terrible pain, with a raging fever and sores that were more agonising than ever. Lepra reaction could leave them sicker than before, but sometimes it indicated that the body was struggling to eliminate the disease and when their suffering subsided they might find themselves healed.

As the two men stood looking into the room, most of the patients were quiet. One moaned intermittently and another, whom Kyritsis thought was a woman but could not be sure, groaned. Lapakis and Kyritsis withdrew from the doorway. It seemed intrusive to stand there.

'Come to my office,' said Lapakis. 'We'll talk there.'

He led Kyritsis down a dark corridor to the very last door on the left. Unlike the ward, this was a room with a view.

Huge windows which reached from waist height almost to the lofty ceiling looked out towards Plaka and the mountains that rose up behind it. Pinned up on the wall was a large architectural drawing of the hospital as it was now and, in red, the outline of an additional building.

Lapakis saw that the drawing had caught Kyritsis's eye.

'These are my plans,' he said. 'We need another ward and several more treatment rooms. The men and women ought to be separated – if they can't have their lives, the very least we can give them is their dignity.'

Kyritsis strolled over to look at the scheme. He knew how low a priority the government gave to health, particularly of those they regarded as terminally ill, and he could not help but let his cynicism show.

'That's going to cost some money,' he said.

'I know, I know,' replied Lapakis wearily, 'but now that our patients are coming from mainland Greece as well as Crete, the government is obliged to come up with some funding. And when you meet a few more of the lepers we have here, you'll see they're not the sort to take no for an answer. But what brought you back to Crete? I was so glad to get your letter, but you didn't really say why you were coming here.'

The two men began to speak with the easy intimacy of those who had spent their student years together. They had both been at medical school in Athens, and although six years had passed since they had last met, they were able to pick up their friendship as if they had never been apart.

'It's quite simple, really,' said Kyritsis. 'I'd grown tired of Athens, and when I saw a post advertised at the hospital in Iraklion in the Department of Dermatovenereology I applied.

I knew I'd be able to continue my research, especially with the large number of lepers you now have here. Spinalonga is altogether a perfect place for a case study. Would you be happy for me to make occasional visits – and, more importantly, do you think the patients would tolerate it?'

'I certainly have no objection, and I am sure they wouldn't either.'

'At some point, there might even be some new treatments to try out – though I'm not promising anything dramatic. To be honest, the results of the latest remedies have been singularly unimpressive. But we can't stand still, can we?'

Lapakis sat at his desk. He had listened intently and his heart had lifted with every word that Kyritsis had spoken. For five long years he had been the only doctor prepared to visit Spinalonga, and during that time he had treated a relentless stream of the sick and the dying. Every night when he undressed for bed he checked his ample body for signs of the disease. He knew this was ridiculous and that the bacteria could be living in his system for months or even years before he was aware of their presence, but his deep anxieties were one of the reasons he only came across to Spinalonga on three days a week. He had to give himself a fighting chance. His role here was a calling that he had felt obliged to follow, but he feared the possibility of his remaining free of leprosy was no greater than the prospect of a long life for a man who regularly played Russian roulette.

Lapakis did have some help now. It was at precisely the moment when he could no longer cope with the slow wave of the sick who hobbled up the hill each day, some to stay for weeks and others just to have their bandages and dressings replaced, that Athina Manakis arrived. She had been a doctor in Athens before discovering that she had leprosy and admitting herself to the leprosarium there before being sent to Spinalonga with the rest of the Athenian rebels. Here she had a new role. Lapakis could not believe his luck: here was someone not only willing to live in at the hospital but who also had an encyclopaedic knowledge of general practice; just because they were leprous it did not stop the inhabitants of Spinalonga from suffering from a whole gamut of other complaints, such as mumps, measles and simple earache, and these ailments were often left unattended. Athina Manakis's twenty-five years' experience and her willingness to work every hour except those when she slept made her invaluable, and Lapakis did not at all mind the fact that she treated him as though he was a younger brother who needed knocking into shape. If he had believed in God, he would have thanked Him heartily.

Now, out of the blue – or, more accurately, out of the grey of this November day when sea and sky competed with each other for drabness – Nikolaos Kyritsis had arrived, asking if he could make regular visits. Lapakis could have wept with relief. His had been a lonely and thankless job and now his isolation had come to an end. When he left the hospital at the end of each day, washing himself down with a sulphurous solution in the great Venetian arsenal that now served as the disinfection room, there would no longer be a nagging sense of inadequacy. There was Athina, and now there would sometimes be Kyritsis.

'Please,' he said. 'Come as often as you wish. I can't tell you how delighted I would be. Tell me what you'd be doing exactly.'

'Well,' said Kyritsis, taking off his jacket and hanging it carefully over the back of the chair, 'there are people in the field of leprosy research who are sure that we are getting closer to a cure. I'm still attached to the Pasteur Institute in Athens and our director-general is very keen on pushing things forward as fast as we can. Imagine what it would mean, not just to the hundreds of people here but to thousands around the world – millions even in India and South America. The impact of a cure would be enormous. In my cautious opinion we're still a long way off, but every piece of evidence, every case study, helps build a picture of how we can prevent the disease spreading.'

'I'd like to think you're wrong about it being a long way off,' responded Lapakis. 'I'm under such pressure these days to use quack remedies. These people are so vulnerable and they'll grasp at any straw, particularly if they have the resources to pay. So what's your plan here exactly?'

'What I need are a few dozen cases that I can monitor very minutely over the next few months, even years, if it works out that way. I've been rather stuck in Iraklion on the diagnosis side and after that I lose my patients because they all come here! Nothing could be a better outcome for them from what I've seen, but I need to do some follow-ups.'

Lapakis was smiling. This was an arrangement that would suit them both equally. Along one wall of his office, reaching from floor to ceiling, were rows of filing cabinets. Some contained the medical records of every living inhabitant of Spinalonga. Others were where the records were transferred when they died. Until Lapakis had volunteered to work on the island, no papers had been kept. There had scarcely been any treatment worth noting and the only progress had been towards gradual degeneration. All that remained to remember the lepers by during the first few decades of the colony's existence was a large black ledger listing name, date of arrival and date of death. Their lives were reduced to a single entry in a macabre visitors' book and their bones now lay jumbled and indistinguishable under the stone slabs of the communal graves on the far side of the island.

'I've got records of everyone who has been here since I came in 1934,' said Lapakis. 'I make detailed notes on their state when they arrive, and record every change as it happens. They're in age order – it seemed as logical a way as any. Why don't you go through them and pull out the ones you'd like to see, and when you next visit I can make appointments for them to come and meet you.'

Lapakis tugged open the heavy top drawer of the cabinet nearest to him. It overflowed with papers, and with a sweep of his arm he gave Kyritsis an open invitation to browse.

'I'll leave you to it,' he said. 'I'd better get back to the ward. Some of the patients will be in need of attention.'

An hour and a half later, when Lapakis returned to his office, there was a stack of files on the floor; the name on the front of the top one was 'Eleni Petrakis'.

'You met her husband this morning,' commented Lapakis. 'He's the boatman.'

They made a note of all the chosen patients, had a brief discussion about each and then Kyritsis glanced at the clock on the wall. It was time to go. Before he entered the disinfectant room to spray himself – though he knew this measure to try and limit the spreading of bacteria was futile – the two men shook hands firmly. Lapakis then led him back down the hill to the tunnel entrance, and Kyritsis continued alone to the quayside, where Giorgis was waiting, ready to take him on the first stage of his long journey back to Iraklion.

Few words were exchanged on the return journey to the mainland. It seemed that they had run out of things to say on the way over. When they reached Plaka, however, Kyritsis asked Giorgis whether he could be there on the same day the following week to take him across to Spinalonga. For some reason he could not quite fathom, Giorgis felt pleased. Not just because of the fare. He was simply glad to know that the new doctor, as he thought of him, would be back.

Through the bitter cold of December, the arctic temperatures of January and February and the howling gales of March, Nikolaos Kyritsis continued to visit every Wednesday. Neither he nor Giorgis was a man for small talk, but they did strike up short conversations as they crossed the water to the leper colony.

'Kyrie Petrakis, how are you today?' Kyritsis would ask.

'I'm well, God willing,' Giorgis would reply with caution.

'And how is your wife?' the doctor would ask, a question that made Giorgis feel like a man with an ordinary married life. Neither of them dwelt on the irony that the person asking the question knew the answer better than anyone.

Giorgis looked forward to Kyritsis's visits, and so did twelve-year-old Maria, as they brought a hint of optimism and the possibility that she might see her father smile. Nothing was said, it was just something she could sense. In the late afternoon she would go to the quayside and wait for them to return. Wrapping her woollen coat tightly around her, she would sit and watch the little boat making its way back across the water in the greyness of dusk, catching the rope from her father and tying it expertly to the post to secure it for the night.

By April, the winds had lost their bite and there was a subtle change in the air. The earth was warming up. Purple spring anemones and pale pink orchids had broken through, and migrating birds flew over Crete making their way back from Africa after winter. Everyone welcomed the change of season and the keenly anticipated warmth that would now arrive, but there were also less positive changes in the air.

War had raged in Europe for some time, but that very month Greece itself was overrun. The people of Crete were now living under the sword of Damocles; the colony's newspaper, *The Spinalonga Star*, carried regular bulletins on the situation, and the newsreels that came with the weekly film stirred the population into a state of anxiety. What they feared most then happened: the Germans turned their sights on Crete.

Chapter Eight

'MARIA, MARIA!' SCREAMED Anna from the street below her sister's window. 'They're here! The Germans are here!' There was panic in her voice, and as Maria galloped two steps at a time down the stairs, she fully expected to hear the sound of steel-tipped boots marching down the central street of Plaka.

'Where?' Maria demanded breathlessly, colliding with her sister in the street. 'Where are they? I can't see them.'

'They're not right here, you idiot,' retorted Anna. 'Not yet anyway, but they are here on Crete and they could be coming this way.'

Anyone who knew Anna well would have spotted a hint of excitement in her voice. Her view was that anything that broke the monotony of an existence governed by the predictable pattern of the seasons and the prospect of living the rest of her life in this same village was to be welcomed.

Anna had run all the way from Fotini's house, where a group of them had been gathered around a crackling radio. They had just about made out the news that German paratroopers had landed in the west of Crete. Now the girls both raced to the village square where, at times like this, everyone would gather.

It was late afternoon but the bar was overflowing with men and, unusually, women, all clamouring to listen to the radio, though of course drowning much of it out with their din.

The broadcast information was stark and limited. 'At around six o'clock this morning a number of paratroopers landed on Cretan soil near the airfield of Maleme. They are all believed to be dead.'

It seemed after all that Anna was wrong. The Germans had not really arrived at all. As usual, thought Maria, her sister had overreacted.

There was tension in the air, however. Athens had fallen four weeks earlier and the German flag had fluttered over the Acropolis since then. This had been disturbing enough, but to Maria, who had never been there, Athens seemed a long way off. Why should events there bother the people of Plaka? Besides, thousands of Allied troops had just arrived on Crete from the mainland, so surely that would make them safe? When Maria listened to the adults around her arguing and debating and throwing in their opinions on the war, her sense of security was reinforced by what they said.

'They haven't got a chance!' scoffed Vangelis Lidaki, the bar owner. 'The mainland's one thing, but not Crete. Not in a million years! Look at our landscape! They couldn't *begin* to get across our mountains with their tanks!'

'We didn't exactly manage to keep the Turks out,' retorted Pavlos Angelopoulos pessimistically.

'Or the Venetians,' piped up a voice in the crowd.

'Well, if this lot come anywhere near here, they'll get more than they bargained for,' growled another, punching a fist into his open palm.

This was not an empty threat, and all those in the room knew it. Even if Crete had been invaded in the past, the inhabitants had always put up the fiercest resistance. The history of their island was a long catalogue of fighting, reprisals and nationalism, and there wasn't a single house to be found that was not equipped with a bandolier, rifle or pistol. The rhythm of life might have appeared gentle, but behind the façade there often simmered feuds between families or villages, and among males over the age of fourteen there were few untrained in the use of a lethal weapon.

Savina Angelopoulos, who stood in the doorway with Fotini and the two Petrakis girls, well knew why the threat was real this time. The speed of flight was the simple reason. The German planes that had dropped the paratroopers could cover the distance from their base in Athens to this island in not much more time than it took the children to walk to school in Elounda. But she kept quiet. Even the presence of the tens of thousands of Allied troops evacuated from the mainland to Crete made her feel more vulnerable than safe. She did not have the confidence of the menfolk. They wanted to believe that the killing of a few hundred Germans who had landed by parachute was the end of the story. Savina felt instinctively that it was not.

Within a week, the true picture was clearer. Each day everyone congregated at the bar, spilling out into the square on those late May evenings which were the first of the year when the warmth of the day did not disappear with the sun. A hundred or so miles as they were from the centre of the action, the people of Plaka were relying on rumours and fragments of information, and every day more pieces of the story would drift over from the west like thistle seeds carried on the air. It seemed that although many of the men who had dropped from the sky had died, some of them had miraculously survived and fled into hiding, from where they were now managing to take up strategic positions. The early stories had told only of spilt German blood and of men speared by bamboo canes, strangled by their own parachutes in the olive trees or dashed on to rocks, but now the truth emerged that a worrying number of them had survived, the airfield had been used to land thousands more and the tide was turning in the Germans' favour. Within a week of the first landing, Germany claimed Crete as its own.

That night, everyone gathered in the bar once again. Maria and Fotini were outside, playing tick-tack-toe by scratching the dusty ground with sharp sticks, but their ears pricked up when they heard the sound of raised voices.

'Why weren't we ready?' demanded Antonis Angelopoulos, banging his glass down on the metal table. 'It was obvious they'd come by air.' Antonis had enough passion for both himself and his brother, and at the best of times it took little to arouse it. Beneath dark lashes, his hooded green eyes flashed with anger. The boys were unalike in every way. Angelos was soft-edged in both body and mind, while Antonis was sharp, thin-faced and eager to attack.

'No it wasn't,' said Angelos, with a dismissive wave of his pudgy hand. 'That's the last thing anyone expected.'

Not for the first time Pavlos wondered why his sons could never agree on anything. He drew on his cigarette and delivered his own verdict.

'I'm with Angelos,' he said. 'No one imagined an air attack.

It's a suicidal way to invade this place – dropping out of the sky to be shot as you land!'

Pavlos was right. For many of them it had been little more than suicide, but the Germans thought nothing of sacrificing a few thousand men in order to achieve their aim, and before the Allies had organised themselves to react, the key airport of Maleme, near Hania, was in their hands.

For the first few days, Plaka went about its business as usual. No one knew what it would actually mean for them having Germans now resident on Cretan soil. For several days they were in a state of shock that it had been allowed to happen at all. News filtered through that the picture was bleaker than they had ever imagined. Within a week the 40,000 combined Greek and Allied troops on Crete had been routed and thousands of Allies had to be evacuated with huge numbers of casualties and loss of life. Debate at the bar intensified and there were further mutterings about how the village should prepare to defend itself for when the Germans came east. The desire to take up arms began to spread like a religious fervour. The villagers were not afraid of bloodshed. Many of them looked forward to picking up a weapon.

It became reality for the people of Plaka when the first German troops marched into Agios Nikolaos and a small unit was dispatched from there to Elounda. The Petrakis girls were walking home from school when Anna stopped and tugged her sister's sleeve.

'Look, Maria!' she urged. 'Look! Coming down the street!'

Maria's heart missed a beat. This time Anna was right. The Germans really were here. Two soldiers were walking purposefully towards them. What did occupying troops do once they invaded? She assumed they went about killing everyone. Why else come? Her legs turned to jelly.

'What shall we do?' she whispered.

'Keep walking,' hissed Anna.

'Shouldn't we run back the other way?' Maria asked pleadingly.

'Don't be stupid. Just keep going. I want to see what they look like close up.' She grabbed her sister's arm and propelled her along.

The soldiers were inscrutable, their blue gazes fixed straight ahead of them. They were dressed in heavy grey woollen jackets, and their steel-capped boots clicked rhythmically on the cobbled street. As they passed they appeared not to see the girls. It was as if they did not exist.

'They didn't even look at us!' cried Anna, as soon as they were out of earshot. Now nearly fifteen years old, she was affronted if anyone of the opposite sex failed to notice her.

Only days later Plaka was given its own small battalion of German soldiers. At the far end of the village one family had a rude early morning awakening.

'Open up!' shouted the soldiers, banging on the door with their rifle butts.

Despite not having a word of common language, the family understood the command, and those that followed. They were to vacate their home by midday or face the consequences. From that day, the presence Anna had excitedly predicted was in their midst, and the atmosphere in the village darkened.

Day to day, there was little substantial news of what was going on elsewhere on Crete, but there was plenty of rumour, including talk that some small groups of Allies were moving eastwards towards Sitia. One night, as dusk fell, four heavily disguised British soldiers came down from the hills where they had been sleeping in an abandoned shepherd's hut and strolled insouciantly into the village. They would not have received a warmer welcome had they appeared in their own villages in the Home Counties. It was not just the hunger for first-hand news that drew people to them; it was also the innate desire of the villagers to be hospitable and to treat every stranger as though he might have been sent from God. The men made excellent guests. They ate and drank everything that was offered, but only after one member of the group, who had a good grasp of Greek, had given a first-hand account of the previous week's events on the north-west coast.

'The last thing we expected was for them to come by air – and certainly not in those numbers,' he said. 'Everyone thought they would come by sea. Lots died immediately but plenty of them landed safely and then regrouped.' The young Englishman hesitated. Almost against his better judgement, he added: 'There were a few, however, who were helped to die.'

He made it sound almost humane, but when he went on to explain, many of the villagers paled.

'Some of the wounded Germans were hacked to pieces,' he said, staring into his beer. 'By local villagers.'

One of the other soldiers then took a folded sheet of paper from his breast pocket and, carefully flattening it out, spread it on the table in front of him. Below the original printed German someone had scribbled translations in both Greek and English.

'I think you all ought to see this. The head of the German

air corps, General Student, issued these orders a couple of days ago.'

The villagers crowded round the table to read what was written on the paper.

There is evidence that Cretan civilians have been responsible for the mutilation and murder of our wounded soldiers. Reprisals and punishment must be carried out without delay or restraint.

I hereby authorise any units which have been victims of these atrocities to carry out the following:

1. *Shooting*
2. *Total destruction of villages*
3. *Extermination of the entire male population in any village harbouring perpetrators of the above crimes*

Military tribunals will not be required to pass judgement on those who have assassinated our troops.

'Extermination of the entire male population'. The words leapt off the paper. The villagers were as still as dead men, the only sound was their breathing; but how much longer would they be free to breathe at all?

The Englishman broke the silence. 'The Germans have never before encountered the kind of resistance they are meeting in Crete. It has taken them completely by surprise. And it's not just from men but from women and children too – and even priests. They expected a full and uncompromising surrender, from you as well as the Allies. But it's only fair to warn you that they have already dealt brutally with several villages over in the west. They've razed them to the ground – even the churches and the schools—'

He was unable to continue. Uproar broke out in the room.

'Shall we resist them?' roared Pavlos Angelopoulos over the hubbub.

'Yes,' shouted the forty or so men in reply.

'To the death!' roared Angelopoulos.

'To the death!' echoed the crowd.

Even though the Germans rarely ventured out after dark, men took turns to keep watch at the door of the bar. They talked long into the small hours of the morning, until the air was thick with smoke and silvery forests of empty raki bottles sat on the tables. Knowing it would be a fatal error to be spotted in daylight, the soldiers rose to go just before dawn. From now on they were in hiding. Tens of thousands of Allied troops had been evacuated to Alexandria a few days earlier and those left had to avoid capture by the Germans if they were to perform their vital intelligence operations. This group was on its way to Sitia, where the Italians had already landed and taken control.

In the Englishmen's view, the farewells and embraces were long and affectionate for such a short acquaintance, but the Cretans thought nothing of putting on such an effusive emotional display. While the men had been drinking, some of the wives had come to the bar with parcels of provisions almost too heavy for the soldiers to lift. They would have enough to last them a fortnight and were fulsome in their gratitude. '*Efharisto, efharisto*,' repeated one of them over and over again, using the only word of the Greek language he knew.

'It's nothing,' the villagers said. 'You are helping us. It is we who should be saying thank you.'

While they were all still in the bar, Antonis Angelopolous, the older of Fotini's brothers, had slipped away, crept into the house and gathered a few possessions: a sharp knife, a woollen blanket, a spare shirt and his gun, a small pistol which his father had given him at the age of eighteen. At the last minute he grabbed the wooden pipe which lived on a shelf along with his father's more precious and ornate lyre. This was his *thiaboli*, a wooden flute, which he had played since he was a child, and since he did not know when he would be home again, he could not leave it behind.

Just as he was fastening the buckle of his leather bag, Savina appeared in the doorway. For everyone in Plaka sleep had been elusive in the past few days. They were all on alert, restless with worry, occasionally roused from their beds by bright flashes in the sky that told of enemy bombs blasting their towns and cities. How could they sleep when they half expected their own homes to be rocked by the impact of shell fire or even to hear the strident voices of the German soldiers who now lived at the end of the street? Savina had been sleeping only lightly and was easily woken by the sound of footsteps on the hard earth floor and the scrape of the pistol on the rough wall as it was lifted from its hook. Above all, Antonis had not wanted to be seen by his mother. Savina might try to stop him.

'What are you doing?' she asked.

'I'm going to help them. I'm going to guide those soldiers – they won't last a day in the mountains without someone who knows the terrain.' Antonis launched into a passionate defence of his actions, like a man who expected fierce opposition. To his surprise, however, he realised his mother was nodding in agreement. Her instinct to protect him was as strong as ever, but she knew that this was how it had to be.

'You're right,' she said, adding in a rather matter-of-fact fashion: 'It's our duty to support them however we can.'

Savina held her son for a fleeting moment and then he was gone, anxious not to miss the four strangers who might already be making their way out of the village.

'Keep safe,' his mother murmured to his shadow, though he was already out of earshot. 'Promise me you'll keep safe.'

Antonis ran back to the bar. By now the soldiers were in the square and the last farewells had been said. He raced up to them.

'I'm going to be your guide,' he informed them. 'You'll need to know where the caves, crevasses and gorges are because on your own you could die out there. And I can teach you how to survive – where to find bird's eggs, edible berries and water where you wouldn't expect it.'

There was a murmur of appreciation from the soldiers and the Greek-speaker stepped forward. 'It's treacherous out there. We have already discovered that to our cost, on many occasions. We are very grateful to you.'

Pavlos stood back. Like his wife, he felt sick with fear at what his firstborn was committing himself to, but he also felt admiration. He had brought his two boys up to understand how the land worked and he knew Antonis had the knowledge to help these men sustain themselves, like goats on apparently barren land. He knew what would poison them and what would nourish them; he even knew which type of scrub made the best tobacco. Proud of Antonis's courage and touched by his almost naïve enthusiasm, Pavlos embraced his son, then, before the five men were out of sight, he turned away and began walking home, knowing that Savina would be waiting for him.

Giorgis related all of this to Eleni when he visited the following day.

'Poor Savina!' she exclaimed hoarsely. 'She'll be worried sick.'

'Someone has to do it – and that young man was ready for an adventure,' replied Giorgis flippantly, trying to make light of Antonis's departure.

'But how long will he be away?'

'Nobody knows. That's like asking how long this war is going to last.'

They looked out across the strait to Plaka. A few figures moved about on the waterfront, going about their daily business. From this distance everything looked normal. No one would have known that Crete was an island occupied by an enemy force.

'Have the Germans been causing any trouble?' asked Eleni.

'You would hardly know they were there,' answered Giorgis. 'They patrol up and down in the day but at night they're nowhere to be seen. Yet it's as though we're being watched all the time.'

The last thing Giorgis wanted to do was make Eleni aware of the sense of menace that now pervaded the atmosphere. He changed the subject.

'But how are you feeling, Eleni?'

His wife's health was beginning to fail. The lesions on her face had spread and her voice had become gravelly.

'My throat is a bit sore,' she admitted, 'but I'm sure it's just a cold. Tell me about the girls.'

Giorgis could tell that she wanted to change the subject. He knew not to dwell on the subject of her health.

'Anna seems a bit happier at the moment. She's working hard at school but she's not much better round the house. In fact she's probably lazier than ever. She can just about clear away her own plate but she wouldn't dream of picking up Maria's. I've almost given up nagging her—'

'You shouldn't let her get away with it, you know,' interjected Eleni. 'She's just going to get into worse and worse habits. And it puts so much more pressure on Maria.'

'I know it does. And Maria seems so quiet at the moment. I think she's even more anxious about the occupation than Anna.'

'She's had enough upheaval in her life already, poor child,' said Eleni. At moments like these she felt overwhelmed with guilt that her daughters were growing up without her.

'It's so strange,' she said. 'We're almost completely unaffected by the war here. I feel more isolated than ever. I can't even share the danger you're in.' Her quiet voice shook and she fought against the possibility of breaking down in front of her husband. It would not help. Not in any way at all.

'We're not in danger, Eleni.'

His words were a lie, of course. Antonis was not the only one of the local boys to have joined the resistance, and tales of the Germans' infamously vicious behaviour at the slightest whiff of espionage made the people of Plaka shiver with fear. But somehow life appeared to go on as normal. There were daily tasks and those that the seasons dictated. When the late summer came, the grapes had to be trodden; when the autumn arrived it was time for the olives to be harvested; and all year round there were goats to be milked, cheese to be churned and weaving to be done. The sun rose, the moon saturated the night sky with its silver light and the stars blazed, indifferent to the events happening below them.

Always, however, there was tension in the air and the expectation of violence. The Cretan resistance became more organised, and several more men from the village disappeared to play their role in the unfolding events of the war. This added to the sense of anticipation that sooner or later life might change dramatically. Villages just like theirs, where men had become *andarte*, members of the resistance, were being marked out by the Germans and targeted for the most brutal reprisals.

One day early in 1942 a group of children, including Anna and Maria, were taking the long walk home from school along the water's edge.

'Look!' shouted Maria. 'Look – it's snowing!'

Snow had ceased to fall some weeks ago and it would only be a matter of time before there was a thaw on the mountaintops. So what was this flurry of white around them?

Maria was the first to realise the truth. It was not snow that was falling from the sky. It was paper. Moments earlier a small aircraft had buzzed overhead, but they had barely looked up, so common was it for German planes to fly low along this part of the coast. It had dropped a blizzard of leaflets, and Anna grabbed one as it floated down towards her.

'Look at this,' she said. 'It's from the Germans.' They clustered round to read the leaflet.

A WARNING
TO
THE PEOPLE OF CRETE

IF YOUR COMMUNITY GIVES SHELTER OR SUPPLIES TO ALLIED SOLDIERS OR MEMBERS OF THE RESISTANCE MOVEMENT, YOU WILL BE PUNISHED SEVERELY. IF YOU ARE FOUND GUILTY, RETRIBUTION WILL BE HARSH AND SWIFT FOR YOUR ENTIRE VILLAGE.

The paper continued to drift down, creating a carpet of white that swirled around their feet before being lifted into the sea and merging into the foamy surf. The children stood quietly.

'We must take some of these back to our parents,' suggested one, gathering a handful before they blew away. 'We need to warn them.' They trudged on, their pockets full of propaganda and their hearts pounding with fear.

Other villages had been similarly targeted with this warning, but the effect was not the one the Germans had hoped for.

'You're crazy,' said Anna, as her father read the leaflet and shrugged his shoulders. 'How can you dismiss it like that? These *andarte* are putting all our lives at risk. Just for the sake of their own little adventures!'

Maria cowered in the corner of the room. She could sense

an impending explosion. Giorgis took a deep breath. He was struggling to control his temper, resisting the urge to tear his daughter to shreds in his anger.

'Do you really think they are doing it for themselves? Freezing to death in caves and living off grass like *animals*! How dare you?'

Anna shrank. She loved to provoke these scenes but had rarely seen her father vent such fury.

'You haven't heard their stories,' he continued. 'You haven't seen them when they stagger into the bar at dead of night, almost dying of hunger, the soles of their shoes worn down as thin as onion skin and their bones almost piercing their cheeks! They're doing it for you, Anna, and me and Maria.'

'And for our mother,' said Maria quietly from the corner.

Everything Giorgis said was true. In the winter, when the mountains were capped with snow and the wind moaned round the twisted ilexes, the men of the resistance nearly froze to death; cowering in the network of caves high above the villages in the mountains, where the only drink was the moisture from the dripping stalactites, some reached the limits of their endurance. In the summer, when the weather was the very opposite, they experienced the full blaze of the island's heat and a thirst which was unquenchable when the streams lay dry.

Such leaflets only reinforced the Cretan determination to resist. There was no question of surrender and they would carry the risks that went with it. With increasing regularity, the Germans appeared in Plaka, searching houses for signs of the resistance, such as radio equipment, and interrogating Vangelis Lidaki since, as the owner of the bar, he was generally the only male in the village during daylight hours. Other working men were in the hills or on the sea. The Germans did not come at night and this was a certainty that the Cretans came to value; the foreigners were too fearful to go anywhere after dusk, suspicious of the island's rocky and difficult terrain and aware of their vulnerability to attack in the dark.

One night in September, Giorgis and Pavlos were at their usual corner table in the bar when three strangers walked in. The two elderly men looked up briefly but soon resumed their conversation and the rhythmic clicking of their worry beads. Before the occupation and the development of the resistance it had been rare to see any outsiders in the village, but now it was commonplace. One of the strangers walked over to them.

'Father,' he said quietly.

Pavlos looked up, open-mouthed with amazement. It was Antonis, almost unrecognisable from the boyish youth who had joined up so idealistically the previous year. His clothes hung off him and his belt was wrapped twice around his waist to keep his trousers in place.

Pavlos's face was still damp with tears when Savina, Fotini and Angelos arrived. Lidaki's son had been hastily dispatched to bring them to the bar, and it was just as a reunion should be between people who loved each other and who had not, until then, been separated for even a day in their lives. There was not just pleasure, there was pain too when they saw Antonis, who looked starved, drawn and not just one year but a whole decade older than when they had last seen him.

Antonis was accompanied by two Englishmen. There was nothing, however, in their appearance to betray their true nationality. Swarthy-skinned and with extravagant moustaches that they had trained to curl in the local style, they now had enough grasp of Greek to be able to converse with their hosts, and they told tales of encountering enemy soldiers and, in the guise of shepherds, fooling them into believing that they were Cretan. They had travelled across the island several times in the past year, and one of their tasks was to observe Italian troop movements. The Italian headquarters was in Neapoli, the largest town in their own region of Lasithi, and the troops there seemed to do little but eat, drink and be merry, particularly with the local prostitutes. Other troops, however, were stationed around the west of the island, and their manoeuvres were more arduous to monitor.

With their shrunken stomachs now bloated with lamb stew and their heads whirling with *tsikoudia*, the three men told stories long into the night.

'Your son is an excellent cook now,' one of the Englishmen told Savina. 'Nobody can make acorn bread like his.'

'Or snail and thyme stew!' joked the other.

'No wonder you're all so thin,' answered Savina. 'Antonis hadn't cooked much more than a potato before all this began.'

'Antonis, tell them about the time we fooled the krauts into thinking we were brothers,' said one, and so the evening continued, with their moments of fear and anxiety turned into humorous anecdotes for everyone's entertainment. Then the lyres were brought out from behind the bar and the singing began. *Mantinades* were sung and the Englishmen struggled to learn the lines which told of love and death, struggle and freedom, their hearts and voices now blending almost completely with those of their Cretan hosts who owed them so much.

Antonis spent one night with his family, and the two

Englishmen were garrisoned with other families willing to take the risk. It was the first time any of them had slept on anything but hard ground in nearly a year. Since they had to leave before dawn, the luxury of their straw-filled mattresses was a short-lived one, and as soon as they had pulled on their long boots and put their fringed black turbans back on their heads, they walked out of the village. Not even a local would have questioned whether these were true natives of Crete. There was nothing to give them away. Nothing, that is, except someone who might succumb to a bribe.

Levels of starvation in Crete were, by now, reaching such high levels that it was not unheard of for local people to accept what was known as the 'Deutsche drachma' for a tip-off about the whereabouts of resistance fighters. Famine and hunger could corrupt even honest people, and such betrayals led to some of the worst atrocities of the war, with mass executions and the destruction of whole villages. The old and sick were incinerated in their beds and men forced to hand over their weapons before being shot in cold blood. The dangers of betrayal were real and meant that Antonis and all like him made only rare and brief visits to their families, knowing that their presence might endanger those they loved the most.

Throughout the war, the only place that really remained immune from the Germans was Spinalonga, where the lepers were protected from the worst disease of all: the occupation. Leprosy might have disrupted families and friends but the Germans made an even more effective job of destroying everything they touched.

As a result of the occupation, Nikolaos Kyritsis's visits to Plaka immediately ceased, since unnecessary travel to and from

Iraklion was regarded with suspicion by the occupying troops. Loath as he was to do it, Kyritsis abandoned his research for the time being; the needs of the wounded and dying all around him in Iraklion could not be ignored. The repercussions of this insane invasion meant that anyone with any medical expertise found himself working round the clock to help the ill and the mutilated, applying dressings, fixing splints and treating the symptoms of dysentery, tuberculosis and malaria, which were rife in the field hospitals. When he returned from the hospital at night, Kyritsis was so exhausted he rarely thought of the lepers who, for such a tantalisingly brief time, had been the focus of his efforts.

The absence of Dr Kyritsis was perhaps the worst side-effect of the war on the inhabitants of Spinalonga. In the months during which he had been making his weekly visits they had nurtured hopes for the future. Now, once again, the present was their only certainty.

Giorgis's routine of coming and going from the island was more fixed than ever. He was soon aware that the Athenians had no difficulty in affording the same luxuries as they had done before the war, in spite of the soaring prices they had to pay.

'Look,' he said to his friends on the quayside one evening as they sat repairing their nets, 'I'd be a fool to ask too many questions. They have the money to pay me, so what right do I have to question their being able to afford to buy on the black market?'

'But there are people round here who are down to their last handful of flour,' protested one of the other fishermen.

Jealousy of the Athenians' wealth dominated conversation in the bar.

'Why should they eat better than we do?' demanded Pavlos. 'And how come they can afford chocolate and good tobacco?'

'They have money, that's why,' said Giorgis. 'Even if they don't have their freedom.'

'Freedom!', scoffed Lidaki. 'You call this freedom? Our country taken over by the bloody Germans, our young men brutalised and the old people burnt to death in their beds? *They're* the ones who are free!' he said, stabbing his finger in the direction of Spinalonga.

Giorgis knew it was pointless arguing with them and said nothing more. Even the friends who had known her well now occasionally forgot that Eleni was on the island. Sometimes he would get a muttered apology for their lack of tact. Only he and Dr Lapakis knew the reality, and even then Giorgis was conscious that he only knew the half of it. He saw little more than the gateway and the lofty walls but he heard plenty of stories from Eleni.

On his last visit, there had been a further change in her condition. First it had been the unsightly lumps that had spread to her chest and back and, most horrifyingly, to her face. Now her voice was becoming less and less audible, and though Giorgis thought this could sometimes be attributed to emotion, he knew it was not the entire cause. She said her throat felt constricted and promised she would go and see Dr Lapakis to get something for it. Meanwhile she tried to remain cheerful with Giorgis so that he did not take his downcast face back home to the girls.

He knew the disease was taking her over and that she, like the majority of the lepers on the island, whether they were impoverished or sitting on a fortune, was losing hope.

These men with whom Giorgis mended nets and sat in the bar whiling away the time playing backgammon and cards were the same people he had grown up with. Their bigoted, narrow views would have been his too if he had not been set apart by his connection with Spinalonga. This one element in his life had given him an understanding they would never have. He would keep his temper and excuse their ignorance, for that was all it was.

Giorgis continued to take his packages and parcels to the island. What did he care if the contents were procured under the counter? Would everyone not have bought the best if only they had the resources of the Athenians? He himself yearned to be able to buy the luxuries for his daughters that only some of the inhabitants of Spinalonga could now afford. For his own part, he very consciously took the best of his catch – once Anna and Maria had eaten their fill – to the leper colony. Why should they not have his biggest bream or bass? These people were sick and cast out of society, but they were not criminals. That was something the people of Plaka conveniently forgot.

The Germans feared Spinalonga with its hundreds of lepers living just across the water and allowed deliveries to continue, since the last thing they wanted was for any of them to leave the island to search out their own supplies on the mainland. One of them did, however, take his chance to escape. It was in the late summer of 1943, and the Italian armistice had led to a heavier German presence in the province of Lasithi.

Late one afternoon, Fotini, Anna, Maria and a group of five or six others were playing as usual on the beach. They were accustomed now to the presence of German soldiers among them, and the fact that there was one patrolling close by on the beach did not attract their interest.

'Let's skim stones,' shouted one of the boys.

'Yes, first to twenty!' replied another.

There was no shortage of smooth, flat pebbles on the beach, and soon their stones were flying across the water, bouncing lightly across the still surface, as they all tried to reach the ambitious target.

Suddenly one of the boys was shouting at them all: 'Stop! Stop! There's someone out there!'

He was right. There was a figure swimming out from the island. The German soldier could see it too and was watching, his arms folded in contempt. The children jumped up and down, screaming at the swimmer to turn back, anticipating the awful outcome.

'What's he doing?' cried Maria. 'Doesn't he know he's going to get killed?'

The leper's progress was slow but relentless. He was either unaware of the soldier's presence or just prepared to take the risk – however suicidal it was – because he could no longer bear life on the colony. The children continued to shout at the tops of their voices, but at the moment when the German raised his gun to fire they were all silenced by fear. He waited until the man had swum to within fifty metres of the beach and then shot him. It was a cold-blooded execution. Simply target practice. At that stage of the war the air was thick with stories of bloodshed and execution but the children had witnessed none of it themselves. In that moment they saw the difference between stories and reality. A single shot ricocheted across the water, the noise amplified by the echo from the mountains behind, and a crimson blanket spread itself slowly across the still sea.

Anna, the oldest among them, screamed abuse at the soldier. 'You bastard! You German bastard!'

A few of the younger children wept with fear and shock. These were the tears of lost innocence. By now dozens of people had rushed from their homes and saw them huddled together, sobbing and crying. Rumours had reached Plaka only that week that the enemy had adopted a new tactic: whenever they suspected the possibility of a guerrilla attack, the Germans would take all the young girls from a village and use them as hostages. Knowing that the safety of their children was far from guaranteed, the villagers' first thought was that some atrocity had been committed against one of them by the lone soldier who stood facing them a few metres down the beach. They were ready, although unarmed, to tear him to shreds. But with the utmost sang-froid he turned to face the sea and gestured defiantly towards the island. The body had long since disappeared but the patch of crimson still floated, clinging to the surface like an oil slick.

Anna, always the ringleader, broke from the wailing group and shouted to the group of anxious adults: 'A leper!'

They understood immediately and turned away from the German soldier. Their attitude had changed now. Some of them were less than bothered by the death of a leper. There were still plenty left. In the short time it took for the parents to reassure themselves that their children were unharmed, the soldier had vanished. So too had the victim and all traces of him. Everyone could forget all about him.

Giorgis, however, would not find it so easy. His feelings about the inhabitants of Spinalonga were anything but neutral. That night, when he took his battered old caique across the water, Eleni told him that the leper whose cold-blooded execution they had all witnessed was a young man called Nikos. It transpired that he had been making regular forays from the island when it was pitch dark to visit his wife and child. Rumour had it that it had been his son's third birthday on the day he died and he wished for once to see him before nightfall.

The children on the shore at Plaka had not been Nikos's only audience. A crowd had also gathered to watch him on Spinalonga. There were no rules or regulations to protect people from such folly and few felt the restraining hand of husband, wife or lover when they were spurred to some spontaneous act of insanity as this. Nikos had been like a starving man and his hunger dominated his every thought and waking moment. He craved the company of his wife, but even more the sight of his son, his own flesh and blood, the image of his unscarred, unblemished boyhood, a mirror of himself as a child. He had paid for his desire with his life.

Nikos was mourned on the little island that night. Prayers were said in the church and a wake was held for him even though there was no body to bury. Death was never ignored on Spinalonga. It was handled with as much dignity there as it would be anywhere else on Crete.

After this incident, Fotini, Anna and Maria and all the other children playing with them that day lived under a cloud of anxiety. In a single moment on this stretch of warm pebbles where they had enjoyed so much carefree childhood happiness, everything had changed.

Chapter Nine

ALTHOUGH THE LEPER executed just metres off their shore had meant little to most of them personally, the hatred the people of Plaka felt for the Germans intensified after this incident. It had brought the reality of war to the very threshold of their homes and made them realise that their village was now as vulnerable as anywhere in this worldwide conflict. Reactions varied. For many people, God was the only source of true peace, and the churches were sometimes full to overflowing with people bent in prayer. A few of the old people, Fotini's grandmother, for instance, spent so much time in the company of the priest that they permanently carried the sweet perfume of incense with them. 'Grandma smells like candle wax!' Fotini would cry, dancing around the old lady, who smiled indulgently at her only granddaughter. Even if He did not appear to be doing much to help them win it, her faith told her that God was on their side in this war, and when stories of the destruction and desecration of churches reached her, it only intensified her belief.

The *panegyria*, saints' days, were still celebrated. Icons would be taken from their safe places and carried in procession by the priests, the town band following them with an almost unholy cacophony of brass and drums. Lavish feasting and the sound of fireworks may have been missing, but when the relics had been safely returned to the church, people still danced wildly and sang their haunting songs with even more passion than in times of peace. Fury and frustration at the continuing occupation would be washed away with the best wines, but as dawn broke and sobriety returned, everything was as it had been before. It was then that those whose faith was less than rock solid began to question why God had not answered their prayers.

The Germans were no doubt bemused by these displays of the sacred and the curiously profane but knew better than to ban them. They did, however, do what they could to interfere, demanding to question the priest just as he was about to begin a service or to search houses as the dancing got into full swing.

On Spinalonga, candles were lit daily for those suffering on the mainland. The islanders were well aware that the Cretans were living in fear of German cruelty, and prayed for a swift end to the occupation.

Dr Lapakis, who believed in the power of medicine rather than divine intervention, began to grow disillusioned. He knew that research and testing had been more or less abandoned. He had sent letters to Kyritsis in Iraklion, but since they had gone unanswered for many months, he came to the conclusion that his colleague must be dealing with more pressing issues and resigned himself to a long wait before he saw him again. Lapakis increased the number of visits he made to Spinalonga from three to six days a week. Some of the lepers needed constant attention, and Athina Manakis could not cope alone. One such patient was Eleni.

Giorgis would never forget the day he came to the island and saw, instead of the slender silhouette of his wife, the squatter figure of Elpida, her friend. His heartbeat had quickened. What had happened to Eleni? It was the first time she had not been there to greet him. Elpida spoke first.

'Don't worry, Giorgis,' she said, trying to inject reassurance into her voice. 'Eleni is fine.'

'Where is she then?' There was an unmistakable note of panic in his tone.

'She has to spend a few days in the hospital. Dr Lapakis is keeping her under observation for a while until her throat improves.'

'And *will* it improve?' he asked.

'I hope so,' said Elpida. 'I'm sure the doctors are doing everything they can.'

Her statement was noncommittal. Elpida knew no more about the chances of Eleni's survival than Giorgis himself.

Giorgis left the packages he was delivering and quickly returned to Plaka. It was a Saturday, and Maria noticed that her father was back much earlier than usual.

'That was a short visit,' she said. 'How is Mother? Did you bring a letter?'

'I'm afraid there's no letter,' he replied. 'She hasn't had time to write this week.'

This much was entirely true, but he left the house quickly before Maria could ask any more questions.

'I'll be back by four,' he said. 'I need to go and mend my nets.'

Maria could tell something was wrong, and the feeling lingered with her all day.

For the next four months Eleni lay in the hospital, too ill to struggle through the tunnel to meet Giorgis. Each day when he brought Lapakis to Spinalonga he looked in vain, expecting her to be waiting under the pine trees for him. Every evening Lapakis would report to him, at first with a diluted version of the truth.

'Her body is still fighting the disease,' he would say, or 'I think her temperature has gone down slightly today.'

But the doctor soon realised that he was building false hopes, and that the more these were reinforced the harder it would be when the final days came, as he knew, in the pit of his stomach, they would. It was not as though he was lying when he said that Eleni's body was fighting. It was engaged in a raging battle, with every tissue fighting the bacteria that struggled to dominate. Lepra fever had two possible outcomes: deterioration or improvement. The lesions on Eleni's legs, back, neck and face had now multiplied, and she lay racked with pain, finding no comfort whichever way she turned. Her body was a mass of ulcers which Lapakis did everything he could to treat, holding on to the basic principle that if they were kept clean and disinfected he might be able to minimise the virulently multiplying bacteria.

It was during this phase that Elpida took Dimitri to see Eleni. He was now living at the Kontomaris house, an arrangement they had all hoped would be temporary but that was now looking as though it might be permanent.

'Hello, Dimitri,' Eleni said weakly. Then, turning her head towards Elpida, she managed just two more words: 'Thank you.'

Her voice was very quiet but Elpida knew what her words had acknowledged: that the thirteen-year-old boy was now in her capable hands. This at least might give her some peace of mind.

Eleni had been moved into a small room where she could be alone, away from the stares of the other patients and neither disturbed by them nor a disturbance to them in the dead of night, when the agony worsened and her sheets became saturated with fever and her groans continuous. Athina Manakis tended to her in those dark hours, spooning watery soup between her lips and sponging down her fiery brow. The quantities of soup were ever-diminishing, however, and one night she ceased to be able to swallow at all. Not even water could slip down her throat.

It was when Lapakis found his patient gasping for breath the next morning and incapable of replying to any of his usual questions that he realised Eleni had entered a new and perhaps final stage.

'Kyria Petrakis, I need to look at your throat,' he said gently. With the new sores around her lips, he knew that even getting her to open her mouth wide enough to look inside would be uncomfortable. The examination only confirmed his fears. He glanced up at Dr Manakis, who was standing on the other side of the bed.

'We'll be back in one moment,' he said, taking Eleni's hand as he spoke.

The two doctors left the room, closing the door quietly behind them. Dr Lapakis spoke quietly and hurriedly.

'There are at least half a dozen lesions in her throat and the epiglottis is inflamed. I can't even see the back of the pharynx for swelling. We need to keep her comfortable – I don't think she has long.'

He returned to the room, sat down beside Eleni and took her hand. Her breathlessness seemed to have worsened in the moments they had been away. It was the point he had reached before with so many patients, when he knew that there was nothing more he could do for them, except keep them company for the last hours. The hospital's elevated position gave it the best views of anywhere in Spinalonga, and as he sat by Eleni's bedside, listening to her increasingly laboured breathing, he gazed through the huge window which looked out across the water to Plaka. He thought of Giorgis, who would be setting off towards Spinalonga later that day to race with the white horses across the sea.

Eleni's breathing now came in short gasps, and her eyes were wide open, brimming with tears and full of fear. He could see there would be no peace at the end of this life and gripped her hands in both of his as if to try and reassure her. It may have been for two, maybe even three hours that he sat like this before the end finally came. Eleni's last breath was a futile struggle for another which failed to arrive.

The best any doctor could tell a bereaved family was that their loved one had died peacefully. It was an untruth Lapakis had told before and would willingly tell again. He hurried out of the hospital. He wanted to be waiting at the quayside when Giorgis arrived.

Some way off shore, the boat lurched up and down in the high, early spring waves. Giorgis was puzzled that Dr Lapakis was already waiting. It was unusual for his passenger to be there first, but there was also something in his manner that made Giorgis nervous.

'Can we stay here a moment?' Lapakis asked him, conscious that he must break the news here and now and give Giorgis time to compose himself before they were back in Plaka and he had to confront his daughters. He held out his hand to Giorgis to help him off the boat, then folded his arms and stared at the ground, nervously moving a stone about with the tip of his right shoe.

Giorgis knew even before the doctor spoke that his hopes were about to be destroyed.

They sat down on the low stone wall that had been built around the pine trees and both men looked out across the sea.

'She's dead,' Giorgis said quietly. It was not just the lines of distress left on Lapakis's face by a gruelling day that had given the news away. A man can simply feel it in the air when his wife is no longer there.

'I am so, so sorry,' said the doctor. 'There was nothing we could do in the end. She died peacefully.'

He had his arm around Giorgis's shoulder, and the older man, head in hands, now shed such heavy and copious tears that they splashed his dirty shoes and darkened the dust around his feet. They sat like this for more than an hour, and it was nearly seven o'clock, the sky almost dark and the air now crisp and cold, when the tears no longer coursed down his face. He was as dry as a wrung cloth and had reached the moment of grieving when exhaustion and a strange sense of relief descend as those first intense tidal waves of grief pass.

'The girls will be wondering where I am,' he said. 'We must get back.'

As they bumped up and down across the water in near darkness towards the lights of Plaka, Giorgis confessed to Lapakis that he had kept the seriousness of Eleni's condition from his daughters.

'You were right to do that,' Lapakis said comfortingly. 'Only a month ago I still believed she could win the fight. It's never wrong to have hope.'

It was much later than usual when Giorgis arrived home, and the girls had been growing anxious about him. The moment he walked in the door they knew something was terribly wrong.

'It's our mother, isn't it?' demanded Anna. 'Something has happened to her!'

Giorgis's face crumpled. He gripped the back of a chair, his features contorted. Maria stepped forward and put her arms round him.

'Sit down, Father,' she said. 'Tell us what's happened . . . please.'

Giorgis sat at the table trying to compose himself. A few minutes elapsed before he could speak.

'Your mother . . . is dead.' He almost choked on the words.

'Dead!' shrieked Anna. 'But we didn't know she was going to *die*!'

Anna had never accepted that her mother's illness could have only one real, inevitable conclusion. Giorgis's decision to keep the news of her deterioration from them meant that this came as a huge shock to them both. It was as though their mother had died twice and the distress they had felt nearly five years before had to be experienced all over again. Older, but little wiser than she had been as a twelve-year-old, Anna's first reaction was one of anger that their father had not given them any warning and that this cataclysmic event had come out of the blue.

For half a decade, the photograph of Giorgis and Eleni which hung on the wall by the fireplace had provided the image of their mother which Anna and Maria carried around in their heads. Their only memories of her were general ones, of maternal kindness and the aura of happy routine. They had long since forgotten the reality of Eleni and had only this idealised picture of her in traditional dress, a long, richly draped skirt, a narrow apron and a splendid *saltamarka*, an embroidered blouse with sleeves slit to the elbows. With her smiling face and long dark hair, braided and wound round her head, she was the archetype of Cretan beauty, captured for ever in the moment when the camera's shutters had snapped. The finality of their mother's death was hard to grasp. They had always cherished the hope that she would return, and as talk of a cure had increased, their hopes had risen. And now this.

Anna's sobs from the upstairs room were audible down the street and as far as the village square. Maria's tears did not come so easily. She looked at her father and saw a man physically diminished by grief. Eleni's death not only represented an end to his hopes and expectations, but the end of a friendship. His life had been turned upside down when she was exiled, but now it was changed beyond repair.

'She died peacefully,' he told Maria that night, as the two of them ate supper. A place had been laid for Anna but she could not be coaxed down the stairs, let alone to eat.

Nothing had prepared any of them for the impact of Eleni's

death. Their three-cornered family unit was only meant to be temporary, wasn't it? For forty days an oil lamp burned in the front room as a mark of respect and the doors and windows of their home remained closed. Eleni had been buried on Spinalonga under one of the concrete slabs that formed the communal graveyard, but she was remembered in Plaka by the lighting of a single candle in the church of Agia Marina on the edge of the village, where the sea was so close it lapped against the church steps.

After a few months, Maria, and even Anna, moved beyond the stages of mourning. For a time, their own personal tragedy had eclipsed wider world events, but when they emerged from their cocoon of grief, all continued to go on around them just as it had before.

In April, the daring kidnap of General Kreipe, commander of the Sebastopol Division in Crete, added to the state of tension across the island. With the help of members of the resistance, Kreipe had been ambushed by Allied troops disguised as Germans and, in spite of a massive manhunt, was smuggled from his headquarters outside Iraklion over the mountains to the south coast of Crete. From here he was shipped off to Egypt, the Allies' most valuable prisoner of war. There were fears that the reprisals for this audacious abduction might be more barbaric than ever. The Germans made it clear, however, that the terror they were still perpetrating would have happened in any case. One of the worst waves of all took place in May. Vangelis Lidaki had been returning from Neapoli when he saw the awful burnt-out villages.

'They've destroyed them,' he ranted. 'They've burned them to the ground.'

The men in the bar listened in disbelief to his descriptions of the smoke still rising from the ashes of the flame-engulfed villages south of the Lasithi mountains, and their hearts went cold.

A few days after this event, a copy of a newssheet published by the Germans found its way to Plaka via Antonis, who had visited briefly to reassure his parents that he was still alive. The tone of it was as threatening as ever:

The villages of Margarikari, Lokhria, Kamares and Saktouria and the nearby parts of the Nome of Iraklion have been razed to the ground and their inhabitants have been dealt with.

These villages had offered protection to Communist bands and we find the entire population guilty of failing to report these treasonable practices.

Bandits have roamed freely in the Saktouria region with the full support of the local populace and have been given shelter by them. At Margarikari, the traitor Petrakgeorgis openly celebrated Easter with the inhabitants.

Listen carefully to us, Cretans. Recognise who your real enemies are and protect yourselves from those who cause retribution to be brought down on you. We have always warned you of the dangers of collaboration with the British. We are losing patience now. The German sword will destroy everyone who associates with the bandits and the British.

The sheet was passed around, read and reread until the paper was worn thin with handling. It did not dampen the villagers' resolve.

'It just shows they're getting desperate,' said Lidaki.

'Yes, but we're getting desperate too,' answered his wife. 'How much longer can we stand it? If we stopped helping the *andarte*, we could sleep easy in our beds.'

Conversation continued long into the night. To surrender and co-operate went against everything that was instinctive to most Cretans. They should resist, they should fight. Besides, they liked fighting. From a minor argument to a decade-old blood feud between families, the men thrived on conflict. Many of the women, by contrast, prayed hard for peace and thought their prayers had been answered as they read between the lines and detected sinking morale among their occupiers.

The printing and distribution of such threats might well be an act of desperation, but, whatever the motivation behind them, it was a fact that villages had been razed to the ground. Every home in them had been reduced to a smoking ruin and the landscape around was now scarred with the eerie silhouettes of blackened, twisted trees. Anna insisted to her father that they should tell the Germans everything they knew.

'Why should we risk Plaka being destroyed?' she demanded.

'Some of it's just propaganda,' interjected Maria.

'But not all of it!' retorted Anna.

The propaganda war was not only being waged by the Germans, however. The British were orchestrating their own campaign and finding it an effective weapon. They produced newssheets that gave the impression that the enemy's position was weakening, spread rumours of a British landing and exaggerated the success of resistance activities. '*Kapitulation*' was the theme, and the Germans would wake to the sight of huge letter Ks daubed liberally on their sentry boxes, barrack walls and vehicles. Even in villages such as Plaka, mothers waited nervously for their sons to return after trips to perpetrate acts of graffiti vandalism; the boys, of course, were thrilled to be contributing something to the effort, never imagining for a minute that they were putting themselves in any danger.

Such attempts to undermine the Germans may have been small in themselves but they helped to change the bigger picture. The tide was turning throughout Europe, and cracks had appeared in the Nazis' firm hold on the continent. In Crete, morale was now so low that German troops were starting to withdraw; some, even, to desert.

It was Maria who noticed that the small garrison in Plaka had cleared out. At six o'clock sharp there was always a show of force, a supposedly intimidating march through the main street and back again with the occasional interrogation of someone en route.

'Something's strange,' she said to Fotini. 'Something's different.'

It did not take long to work it out. It was now ten past six and the familiar sound of steel-capped boots had not been heard.

'You're right,' replied Fotini. 'It's quiet.'

The tension that hung in the air seemed to have lifted.

'Let's go for a walk,' suggested Maria.

The two girls, rather than ambling on to the beach as they usually did, kept to the main street until it ran out. Right at this point was the house where the German garrison had their headquarters. The front door and the shutters were wide open.

'Come on,' said Fotini. 'I'm going to look inside.'

She stood on tiptoes and peered through the front window. She could see a table, bare but for an ashtray piled high with cigarette butts, and four chairs, two of them tipped carelessly on to the floor.

'It looks like they've gone,' she said excitedly. 'I'm going inside.'

'Are you *sure* there's no one in there?' asked Maria.

'Pretty positive,' whispered Fotini as she stepped across the threshold.

Except for a few stray bits of rubbish and a yellowing German newspaper discarded on the floor, the house was empty. The two girls ran home and reported the news to Pavlos, who went immediately to the bar. Within an hour word had swept round the village, and that evening the square was filled with people celebrating the release of their own small corner of the island.

Only days later, on 11 October 1944, Iraklion was liberated. Remarkably, given all the bloodshed of the previous few years, the German troops were calmly escorted out of the city gate without any loss of life; the violence was saved for anyone who was perceived to have collaborated. German troops did, however, continue to occupy parts of western Crete, and it was some months before that situation changed.

One morning in early summer the following year, Lidaki had the radio blaring in the bar. He was washing glasses from the night before in his customary slapdash manner, sluicing them in a bowl of grey water before wiping them with a cloth that had already been used to mop a few puddles on the floor. He was mildly irritated when the music was suddenly interrupted for a news announcement, but his ears pricked up when he caught the solemnity of the tone.

'Today, the eighth of May 1945, the Germans have officially surrendered. Within a few days all enemy troops will have withdrawn from the Hania area and Crete will once again be free.'

The music resumed and Lidaki wondered if the announcement had just been a trick of his own mind. He stuck his head out of the door of the bar and saw Giorgis hastening towards him.

'Have you heard?' he asked.

'I have!' replied Lidaki.

It was true then. The tyranny was over. Though the people of Crete had always believed that they would drive the enemy from their island, when the moment came their joy was unrestrained. A celebration to end all celebrations would have to be held.

Part 3

Chapter Ten

1945

IT WAS AS though they had been breathing in a poisonous gas and now once again there was oxygen in the atmosphere. Members of the resistance were arriving back in their villages, often after travelling hundreds of miles to reach them, and fresh bottles of raki were uncorked to toast every return. Within a fortnight of the end of occupation it was the feast of Agios Konstandinos, and the celebration of this saint's day was the excuse everyone needed to throw all caution to the wind. A cloud had lifted and madness descended in its place. Fatted goats and well-fed sheep rotated on spits the length and breadth of Crete, and fireworks crackled in the sky across the island, reminding some people of the explosions which had ripped through their cities and illuminated the skies in the early days of the war. No one dwelt on this comparison, however; they wanted to look forward now, not back.

For the feast of Agios Konstandinos, the girls of Plaka donned their finery. They had been to church, but their minds were on things other than the sacred nature of the event. These adolescent girls had few restrictions placed on them because they were still perceived as children and innocence was presumed in all they said and did. It was only later, when their womanliness was already developed, that their parents woke up to their sexuality and began to keep a close eye on them, sometimes rather too late. By then, of course, many of these girls had stolen kisses from village boys and engaged in secret trysts in the olive groves or fields on the way home from school.

Whilst neither Maria nor Fotini had ever been kissed, Anna had become a well-practised flirt. She was never happier than when she was in the company of boys and could toss her mane of hair and flash her engaging smile knowing that her audience would not look away. She was like a cat on heat.

'Tonight's going to be special,' announced Anna. 'I can feel it in the air.'

'Why's that then?' asked Fotini.

'Most of the boys are back, that's why,' she answered.

There were several dozen young men in the village, mere boys when they had left to fight with the *andarte* at the beginning of the occupation. Some of them had now chosen to join the Communists and had gone to take part in the struggle against right-wing forces that was brewing on mainland Greece, bringing new hardship and bloodshed.

Fotini's brother Antonis was one of those who had returned to Plaka. Sympathetic as he was to the ideals of the left and the new campaign on the mainland, after four years away he had been more than ready to come home. It was Crete that he had been fighting for, and here he wanted to stay. During his time away Antonis had grown wiry and strong and was unrecognisable from the emaciated figure who had staggered back after those first few months in the resistance to see his family. Now he had not only a moustache, but a beard too, which added at least five years to his twenty-three. He had lived on a diet of mountain greens, snails and whatever wild animals he could ensnare, and endured extremes of heat and cold that had given him a sense of indestructibility.

It was the romantic figure of Antonis that Anna had set her heart on that night. She was not alone in that ambition, but she was confident of winning at least a kiss from him. He was lean and slim-hipped, and when the dancing began, Anna was determined to make him notice her. If he failed to, he would be the only man in the village who had. Everyone was aware of Anna, not only because she was half a head taller than most of the other girls, but because her hair was longer, wavier and glossier than all the rest, and even when plaited it reached down to her hips. The whites of her huge oval eyes were as bright as the dazzling cotton shirts which the girls all wore, and her pearly teeth gleamed as she laughed and chattered with her friends, supremely conscious of her beauty under the watchful gaze of the groups of young men who stood about the square, anticipating the moment when music would mark the real launch of the festivities. Anna was almost luminous in the dusk of this great feast day. The other girls were in her shadow.

Tables and chairs had been set out on three sides of the square, and on the fourth a long trestle table took the weight of a dozen dishes piled high with cheese pies and spicy sausages, sweet pastries and pyramids of waxy-skinned oranges and ripe apricots. The smell of roasting lamb wafted over the square and brought with it the mouth-watering anticipation of pleasure. There was a strict order of events. Eating and drinking would come later, but before that there would be dancing.

At first the boys and men all stood talking together and the girls stood apart, giggling excitedly. The separation was not to last. The band struck up and the swirling and stamping of feet began. Men and women rose from their seats and girls and boys broke away from their huddles. Soon the dusty space was filled. Anna knew as the inner female circle rotated that sooner or later she would find herself opposite Antonis and that for a few moments they would dance together before moving on. How can I make him see me as someone more than his little sister's friend? she asked herself.

She did not have to try. Antonis stood in front of her. The slow *pentozali* dance gave her a few moments to study the pair of fathomless eyes that looked out through the black tassled fringe of his traditional headdress. The *sariki* was the warrior's hat that many young men now wore to show that they had graduated into manhood, not just through the passage of time but because they had the blood of another man on their hands. In Antonis's case, it was not merely one but several enemy soldiers. He prayed that he would never again hear the distinctive cry of surprise as his blade penetrated the soft flesh between the shoulder blades, and the strangulated gasp that followed. It never felt like victory, but it did give him the right to associate himself with the fearless warriors of Crete's past, the *pallikaria*, in their breeches and long boots.

Anna flashed her broad smile at this boy who had become a man, but he did not return it. The ebony eyes had instead fixed on hers and held them until she was almost relieved when it was time for him to move on to his next partner. As the dance ended, her heart still pounded furiously and she returned to her group of friends, who now spectated as some of the men, Antonis among them, reeled before them like human gyroscopes. It was a dizzying display. Their boots cleared the ground by several feet as they leapt into the air, and the perfectly synchronised bowing of the three-stringed lyre and the plucking of the lute urged them on, giving the dance a breathless energy right to the very end.

The married women and the widows watched the acrobatics even though the performance was not being staged for them, but for the nubile beauties who observed from the corner of the square. As Antonis rotated and the music and the drum beat built to a climax, Anna was certain that this handsome warrior was dancing for her alone. The whole audience clapped and cheered as they finished and the band, with hardly a moment's pause, launched into the next tune. A group of slightly older men now took the dusty centre stage.

Anna was bold. She broke away from her circle of friends and approached Antonis, who was pouring himself a glass of wine from a huge clay jug. Although he had seen her many times at his home, he had barely noticed her before tonight. Before the occupation Anna had seemed just a little girl; now a shapely, voluptuous woman had taken her place.

'Hello, Antonis,' she said boldly.

'Hello, Anna.'

'You must have been practising your dancing while you were away,' she said, 'to be able to do those steps.'

'We saw nothing but goats up in the mountains,' Antonis

replied laughingly. 'But they're pretty nimble on their feet, so maybe we learnt a thing or two from them.'

'Can we dance again soon?' she asked, over the noisy strains of the lyre and the beat of the drums.

'Yes,' he said, his face now breaking into a smile.

'Good. I'll be waiting. Over there.' she said, and returned to her friends.

Antonis had the feeling that Anna had offered herself to him for more than a *pentozali*. When a suitable dance began, he went up to her, took her by the hand and led her into the circle. Holding her round the waist, he now inhaled the indescribably sensual smell of her sweat, an essence of more intoxicating sweetness than anything he had ever breathed in before. Crushed lavender and rose petals would not compare. When the dance finished, he felt her hot breath in his ear.

'Meet me behind the church,' she whispered.

Anna knew that a stroll to the church, even during such wild celebrations, was perfectly normal on a saint's day, and besides, Agios Konstandinos shared his day with his wife, Agia Eleni, making it a special moment to remember her mother. She made her way swiftly to the alleyway behind the church and within a few moments Antonis was there too, fumbling to find her in the darkness. Her parted lips immediately sought his.

Not since he had been paying good money had he been kissed like this. In the last months of the war he had been a regular in the brothels of Rethimnon. The women there loved the *andarte* and gave them a special rate, particularly when they were as handsome as Antonis. Theirs had been the only business that had thrived during the occupation as men sought comfort after long absences from their wives, and young men took the opportunity to develop sexual experience that would never be tolerated under the watchful eyes of their own community. It had, however, been loveless. Here in his arms was a woman who kissed like a prostitute but was probably a virgin and, most importantly, Antonis could feel real desire. There was no mistaking it. Every part of his being craved for this lascivious kiss to continue. His mind was working swiftly. Here he was back for good and expected to marry and settle down in the community, and here was a woman eager for love who had been waiting quite literally on his doorstep, just as she had been since childhood. She had to be his. It was meant to be.

They separated from their embrace. 'We must get back to the square,' said Anna, knowing that her father would notice her absence if she was away for much longer. 'But let's go separately.'

She slipped out of the shadows and into the church, where she spent a few minutes lighting a candle before an image of the Virgin and Child, her lips, still wet from Antonis's, moving silently in prayer.

As she returned to the square there was a slight commotion in the street. A large saloon car had drawn up, one of few on an island where most people still travelled on their own two feet or on the back of a four-legged beast. Anna paused to watch the passengers as they climbed out. The driver, a distinguished man in his sixties, was immediately recognisable as Alexandros Vandoulakis, the head of the wealthy landowning family that lived on a sprawling farm near Elounda. He was a popular man, and his wife Eleftheria was liked too. They employed a dozen or so men in the village – Antonis included – several of whom had only just returned after long absences with the resistance, and had welcomed them back with open arms. They were generous with the men's wages, though some said, sarcastically, that they could afford to be. It was not just the thousands of hectares of olive groves that were the source of their wealth. They owned a similar amount of land on the fertile Lasithi plateau, where they grew huge crops of potatoes, cereals and apples, providing them with an all-year round income, and a guaranteed one at that. The cool climate of the plateau, 800 metres up, rarely failed and the green fields were verdant with moisture provided by the melting snows of the mountains that encircled it. Alexandros and Eleftheria Vandoulakis often spent the months of high summer in Neapoli, twenty or so kilometres away, where they had a grand town house, leaving the estate in Elounda to be managed by their son Andreas. Theirs was a fortune of rare magnitude.

It was, however, no surprise that such a well-to-do family should turn out to celebrate with fishermen, shepherds and men who worked the land. It was the same all over Crete. Every village member would turn out to dance and feast and the wealthy landowning families who lived on nearby farms or estates would come to join them. They could not throw a better party, however great their fortune, and they wanted to share in its exuberance. Both rich and poor had suffered and all had equal cause to celebrate their liberation. The soulful sentiment of the *mantinades* and the excitement of the energetic *pentozali* were the same whether your family owned ninety olive trees or ninety thousand.

From the back seat of the car emerged the two Vandoulakis daughters and finally their older brother, Andreas. They were immediately welcomed by some of the villagers and given a good table with the best view of the dancing. Andreas, however, did not sit for long.

'Come on,' he said to his sisters. 'Let's join in with the dancing.'

He grabbed them both and pulled them into the circle, where they blended in with the crowd of dancers, dressed as they were in the same costumes as the village girls. Anna watched. Some of her friends were in the group and it struck her that if they were going to have the opportunity to link arms and dance with Andreas Vandoulakis, then so was she. She joined the next *pentozali* and, just as she had done with Antonis not an hour earlier, fixed Andreas in her gaze.

The dance soon came to an end. The lamb was now roasted and being cut into thick chunks, platters of which were passed round for the villagers to feast on. Andreas was back with his family but his mind was elsewhere.

At the age of twenty-five, he was being pressurised by his parents to find a wife. Alexandros and Eleftheria were frustrated by his rejection of every single one of the daughters of their friends and acquaintances. Some were dour, some were drippy and others were simply dim, and although all of them would have been more than generously dowried, Andreas refused to have anything to do with them.

'Who's that girl, the one with the amazing hair?' he asked his sisters, gesturing towards Anna.

'How should we know?' they chorused. 'She's just one of the local girls.'

'She's beautiful,' he said. 'That's what I'd like my wife to look like.'

As he got up, Eleftheria gave Alexandros a knowing look. Her view was that, given the lack of impact any dowry would have on Andreas's life, what did it really matter whom he married? Eleftheria herself had come from a considerably humbler background than Alexandros, but it had not significantly affected their lives. She wanted her son to be happy, and if that involved flying in the face of convention, then so be it.

Andreas had walked right up to the crowd of girls, who were sitting in a circle eating pieces of the tender meat with their fingers. There was nothing particularly remarkable about Andreas, who had inherited his father's strong features and his mother's sallow complexion, but his family background lent him a bearing that set him apart from all the other men at the gathering, except for Alexandros Vandoulakis. The young women were embarrassed when they realised Andreas was approaching them and hastily wiped their hands on their skirts and licked the fatty juice from their lips.

'Anyone care to dance?' he asked casually, looking directly at Anna. His was the attitude of a man confident of his superior social situation and there was only one response. To get up out of her seat and take the hand which was being offered to her.

The candles on the tables had guttered and burned out, but by now the moon had risen and cast its bright glow in the otherwise sable-black sky. Both raki and wine had flowed and the musicians, emboldened by the atmosphere, played faster and faster until the dancers once again appeared to fly through the air. Andreas held Anna close. It was the time of night when the tradition of swapping partners during the dance could be ignored, and he decided he was not going to exchange her for some matronly type with few teeth and two left feet. Anna was perfect. No one else would do.

Alexandros and Eleftheria Vandoulakis watched their son courting this woman, but they were not the only ones to do so. Antonis sat at a table with his friends, drinking himself into a stupor as he realised what was unfolding in front of him. The man he worked for was in the process of seducing the girl he desired. The more he drank the more miserable he became. He had felt less dejected when he was sleeping on an open hillside during the war, lashed by storms and stinging winds. What hope did he have of keeping Anna for himself when he was in competition with a man who was heir to a sizeable chunk of Lasithi?

In the far corner of the square Giorgis sat playing backgammon with a group of older people. His eyes darted back and forth from the board to the square, where Anna continued to dance with the most eligible man this side of Agios Nikolaos.

The Vandoulakis family eventually rose to leave. Andreas's mother knew instinctively that her son would not want to come home with them, but in the interests of respectability and the reputation of this village beauty he had taken such a liking to, it was important that he should. Her son was no fool. If he was going to break away from tradition and have the liberty to select his own wife rather than be manoeuvred into accepting some choice of his parents, he needed them to be on his side.

'Look,' he said to Anna, 'I have to go now, but I want to see you again. I'll have a note delivered to you tomorrow. It'll tell you when we could meet next.'

He spoke like a man used to issuing orders and expecting them to be carried out. Anna had no objection to that, for once realising that acquiescence was the right response. It could, after all, be her route out of Plaka.

Chapter Eleven

'HEY! ANTONIS! HERE a minute!'

The summons was perfunctory, the voice of a master to his servant. Andreas had stopped his truck some distance from where Antonis was hacking down some old and now barren olive trees and was waving him over. Antonis paused from his work and leaned on his axe. He was not yet used to being at the beck and call of his young master. The roamings of the past few years, though endlessly tough and uncomfortable, had had a joyful freedom about them, and he was finding it hard to get used to both the daily routine and the idea that he must jump to attention every time the boss issued an order. If that was not enough, there was also a specific cause for resentment between himself and this man who stood shouting at him from the driving seat of his vehicle. It made him feel like planting his axe into Andreas Vandoulakis's neck.

Antonis glistened. His brow was beaded with droplets of perspiration and his shirt clung to his back. It was only the end of May but already temperatures were soaring. He would not jump to attention, not quite yet anyway. Nonchalantly he pulled the cork from the hollow gourd at his feet and took a swig of water.

Anna . . . Before last week Antonis had scarcely noticed her, and he had certainly not given her a moment's thought, but on that saint's day night she had roused in him a passion that would not let him sleep. Over and over again he relived the moment of their embrace. Ten short minutes it had lasted, perhaps even less, but to Antonis every second had been as long and lingering as a whole day. Then it was all over. Right in front of him, the possibility of love had been snatched away. He had watched Andreas Vandoulakis from the moment he had arrived and seen him dance with Anna. He knew then, even before the battle lines were drawn up, who had won the war. The odds had been heavily weighted against him.

Antonis now sauntered over to Andreas, who was oblivious to the nuances of his manner.

'You live in Plaka, don't you?' Andreas said. 'I want you to deliver this for me. Today.'

He handed over an envelope. Antonis did not need to look at it to know whose name was written on the outside.

'I'll take it some time,' he said with feigned indifference, folding the letter in two and stuffing it into the back pocket of his trousers.

'I want it delivered *today*,' said Andreas sternly. 'Don't forget.'

The engine of his truck started up noisily and Andreas hurriedly reversed out of the field, whipping the dry earth into a filthy cloud that lingered in the air and filled Antonis's lungs with dust.

'Why should I take your bloody letter?' Antonis yelled as Andreas disappeared from sight. 'God damn you!'

He knew this letter would seal his own misery but he also knew he had no choice but to make sure it was safely handed over. Andreas Vandoulakis would soon find out if he had failed in his task and there would be hell to pay. All day long the crisp envelope sat in his pocket. It crackled whenever he sat down and he tortured himself with thoughts of ripping it up, crushing it into a tight ball and hurling it into a ravine, or of watching it burn slowly in the small fire he had made to dispose of some of the debris from his day's wood-cutting. But the one thing he had not been tempted to do was open it. He could not bear to read it. Not that he needed to. It was perfectly obvious what it would say.

Anna was surprised to find Antonis standing on her doorstep early that evening. He had knocked on the door, hoping not to find her in, but there she was, with that same broad-mouthed smile that was so indiscriminately flashed at whoever crossed her path.

'I have a letter for you,' said Antonis before she had time to speak. 'It's from Andreas Vandoulakis.' The words stuck in his throat but he found a perverse satisfaction in disciplining himself to say them without betraying the slightest emotion. Anna's eyes widened with unconcealed excitement.

'Thank you,' she said, taking the now limp and crumpled envelope from him, careful not to meet his gaze. It was as though she had forgotten the fervour of their embrace. Had it meant nothing to her? wondered Antonis. At the time it had seemed like a beginning, but now he could see that the kiss which for him had been so full of expectation and anticipation had for her been merely the grasping of a moment of pleasure.

She shifted from one foot to the other and he could see that she was impatient to open the letter and wanted him gone. Taking a step back, she said goodbye and closed the door. As it banged shut it was as though he had been slapped in the face.

Inside the house, Anna sat down at the low table and with trembling hands opened the envelope. She wanted to savour the moment. What was she going to find? An articulate outpouring of passion? Words that exploded on the page like fireworks? Sentiments as moving as the sight of a shooting star on a clear night? Like any eighteen-year-old girl anticipating such poetry, she was bound to be disappointed by the letter on the table in front of her:

Dear Anna,

I wish to meet you again. Please would you come to lunch with your father on Sunday next. My mother and father look forward to meeting you both.

Yours,
Andreas Vandoulakis

Though the content excited her, taking her one step closer to her escape from Plaka, the formality of the letter chilled her. Anna thought that because Andreas had enjoyed a superior education he might be masterful with words, but there was about as much emotion in this hastily scribbled note as in the dreary books of ancient Greek grammar that she had been happy to leave behind with her school days.

* * *

The lunch duly took place, and many thereafter. Anna was always chaperoned by her father in accordance with the strict etiquette observed by people both rich and poor for such situations. On the first half-dozen occasions, father and daughter were collected at midday by a servant in Alexandros Vandoulakis's car, taken to the grand porticoed town house in Neapoli and returned home again at three-thirty precisely. The pattern was always the same. On arrival they would be shown into an airy reception room where every piece of furniture was covered with throws of intricate, ornately embroidered white lace and a huge dresser gleamed with a display of fine, almost translucent china. Here Eleftheria Vandoulakis would offer them a small plate of sweet preserve and a tiny glass of liqueur, waiting to receive the empty plates and glasses on a tray once they had finished. Then they all processed into the gloomy dining room, where oil paintings of fierce moustachioed ancestors glared down from panelled walls. Even here the formalities continued. Alexandros would appear and, crossing himself, would say, 'Welcome,' to which the visitors replied in unison with the words: 'I am fortunate to be with you.' It was the same on each occasion, until Anna knew, almost to the minute, what would happen when.

Visit after visit they perched on elaborately carved high-backed chairs at the dark overpolished table, politely accepting every course that was brought to them. Eleftheria did all she could to make her guests feel relaxed; many years earlier she had been through the same ordeal when she was vetted by the previous generation of the Vandoulakis family for her suitability as Alexandros's wife, and she remembered the unbearable stiffness of it all as though it was yesterday. In spite of the woman's kind efforts, however, conversation was stilted and both Giorgis and Anna were painfully conscious that they were on trial. It was to be expected. If this was a courtship, and no one had yet defined it as such, there were terms of engagement that needed to be established.

By the time of the seventh meeting, the Vandoulakis family had decamped to the sprawling house on the large estate in Elounda which was where they spent the months between September and April. Anna was now growing impatient. She and Andreas had not been alone together since the dance they had had in May, and, as she moaned one evening to Fotini and her mother, 'That was hardly being on our own, with the whole village watching us! Why does it all take so long?'

'Because if it's the right thing for both of you and for both families there is no need to hurry,' answered Savina, wisely.

Anna, Maria and Fotini were at the Angelopoulos house, supposedly being instructed on their needlework. In reality they were all there to chew over the 'Vandoulakis situation', as it was referred to. By now Anna was feeling like an animal at the local market being sized up for her suitability. Perhaps she should have kept her sights lower after all. She was determined not to let her enthusiasm wane, however. She had turned eighteen, her school days were long past and she had only one ambition: to marry well.

'I'll just treat the next few months as a waiting game,' she said. 'And anyway, there's Father to look after in the meantime.'

It was Maria, naturally, who was really taking care of Giorgis and who knew that she would remain in the home for some while longer, putting aside her own remote dream of becoming a teacher. She bit her tongue, however. It wasn't a good idea to seek confrontation with Anna at the best of times.

It took until spring of the following year for Alexandros Vandoulakis to satisfy himself that, in spite of the differences in their wealth and social situation, it would not be a mistake if his son made Anna his bride. She was, after all, exceedingly handsome, bright enough and clearly devoted to Andreas. One day, after yet another lunch, the two fathers returned to the reception room alone. Alexandros Vandoulakis was blunt.

'We are all aware of the inequality of this potential union but we are satisfied that it will not cause repercussions on either side. My wife has persuaded me that Andreas will be happier with your daughter than with any other woman he has ever met, so as long as Anna performs her duties as wife and mother we can find no real objections.'

'I can't offer you much of a dowry,' said Giorgis, stating the obvious.

'We are perfectly aware of that,' replied Alexandros. 'Her dowry would be her promise to be a good wife and to do all she can in helping to manage the estate. It's a significant job and needs a good woman in the wings. I'll be retiring in a few years and Andreas will have a great deal on his shoulders.'

'I am sure she'll do her best,' Giorgis said simply. He felt out of his depth. The scale of this family's power and wealth intimidated him, reflected as it was in the size of everything with which they surrounded themselves: the big dark furniture, the lavish rugs and tapestries and the valuable icons that hung on the walls were all a manifestation of this family's significance. But it did not matter whether he felt at home here, he told himself. What mattered was whether Anna could really become accustomed to such grandeur. There was no evidence that she felt anything but perfectly at ease in the Vandoulakis home, even though it was, to him, as alien as a foreign country. Anna could sip delicately from a glass, eat daintily and say the right things as though she had been born to do it. He, of course, knew that she was simply acting a role.

'What is as important as anything is that her basic education has been a good one. Your wife taught her well, Kyrie Petrakis.'

At the mention of Eleni, Giorgis maintained his silence. The Vandoulakis family knew that Anna's mother had died a few years earlier, but more than that he did not intend them to find out.

When they returned home that afternoon, Maria was waiting for them. It was as if she knew that this meeting had been a crucial one.

'Well?' she said. 'Has he asked you?'

'Not yet,' replied Anna. 'But I know it's going to happen, I just know it.'

Maria knew that what her sister wanted more than anything in the world was to become Anna Vandoulakis, and she wanted it for her too. It would take her out of Plaka and into the other world she had always fantasised about where she would not have to cook, clean, darn or spin.

'They're not under any illusions,' said Anna. 'They know what sort of house we live in and they know that I'm not bringing a fortune with me, just a few pieces of jewellery that were Mother's, that's all—'

'So they know about Mother?' interrupted Maria with incredulity.

'Only that Father is widowed,' Anna retorted. 'And that's all they're going to know.' The conversation was closed, as if it was a box with a sprung lid.

'So what happens next?' asked Maria, steering them both away from danger.

'I wait,' said Anna. 'I wait until he asks me. But meanwhile it's torture and I'm going to *die* if he doesn't do it soon.'

'He will, I'm sure. He obviously loves you. *Everyone* says so.'

'Who's everyone?' Anna asked sharply.

'I don't know really, but according to Fotini everyone on the estate seems to think so.'

'And what does Fotini know?'

Maria knew that she had said too much. Though there had been few secrets between these girls in days gone by, over the past few months this had changed. Fotini had confided in Maria about her brother's infatuation with Anna and how it aggravated him to hear all the estate workers talk of nothing but the impending engagement between their master's son and the girl from the village. Poor Antonis.

Anna bullied Maria until she told her.

'It's Antonis. He's obsessed with you, you must know that. He tells Fotini all the estate gossip and everyone's saying that Andreas is about to ask you to marry him.'

For a moment Anna basked in the knowledge that she was the focus of discussion and speculation. She loved to know she was the centre of attention and wanted to know more.

'What else are they saying? Go on, Maria, tell me!'

'They're saying he's marrying beneath him.'

It was not what Anna expected and certainly not what she wanted to hear. She responded with vehemence.

'What do I care about what they think? Why *shouldn't* I marry Andreas Vandoulakis? I certainly wouldn't have married someone like Antonis Angelopoulos. He doesn't own more than the shirt he stands up in!'

'That's no way to talk about our best friend's brother – and anyway, the reason he has nothing is that he was away fighting for his country while other people stayed at home and lined their own pockets.'

Maria's parting shot was one barbed comment too many for Anna's liking. She hurled herself at her sister, and Maria, as ever when she became embroiled in an argument with the unrestrained Anna, chose not to retaliate. She fled from the house and, being a faster runner than Anna, was soon out of sight in the maze of little streets at the far end of the village.

Maria was a mistress of restraint. Unlike her volatile sister, whose feelings, thoughts and actions were simultaneously played out for all to see, she was thoughtful. Generally she kept her feelings and opinions to herself, observing that outbursts of emotion or careless words were often regretted. In the past few years she had learned to control her feelings better than ever. In this way she kept up the appearance of being contented, largely to protect her father. Sometimes, however, she would allow herself the luxury of a spontaneous outburst, and when it came, it could have the impact of a clap of thunder on a cloudless day.

In spite of the opinions of the estate workers and the residual misgivings of Alexandros Vandoulakis, the engagement took place in April. The pair had been left alone in the gloomy drawing room after dinner, which had been an even stiffer event than usual. The anticipation of the engagement had been such that when the moment finally came and Andreas asked for her hand, Anna felt little emotion. She had played the scene through in her mind so often that when it actually took place it was as though she were an actress on a stage. She felt numb, unreal.

'Anna,' said Andreas. 'I have something to ask you.'

There was nothing romantic, imaginative or even remotely magical about the proposal. It was as functional as the floorboards they stood on.

'Will you marry me?'

Anna had reached her goal, winning a bet with herself and cocking a snook at those who might have thought she was not up to marriage into a landed family. These were her first thoughts as she accepted Andreas's hand and kissed him fully and passionately on the lips for the first time.

As was customary during a period of engagement, gifts were then lavished on Anna by her future in-laws. Beautiful clothes, silk underwear and expensive trinkets were purchased for her so that, although her own father could provide very little, she would not be lacking for anything by the time she finally became a Vandoulakis.

'It's as though every day is my saint's day,' Anna said to Fotini, who had come to view the latest array of luxury items that had been delivered from Iraklion. The small house in Plaka overflowed with the scent of extravagance, and in this post-occupation period, when a pair of silk stockings was out of reach for all but the wealthiest women, Anna's trousseau was a spectacle that all the girls queued up to see. The oyster-coloured satin camisoles and nightgowns that sat in boxes between layers of crinkly tissue paper were the stuff of Hollywood movies. When she lifted some of the items out to show her friends, the fabric ran between her fingers like water spilling into a pool. They were beyond even her own wildest dreams.

A week before the wedding itself took place, work began in Plaka on the traditional crown of bread. Leavened seven times, a large circle of dough was decorated with intricate patterns of a hundred flowers and fronds, and in the final stage of its baking was glazed to a golden brown. The unbroken circle symbolised the bride's intention to stay with her husband from beginning to end. Meanwhile, at the Vandoulakis home, Andreas's sisters began work on decorating the nuptial quarters at the couple's future home with silk cloth and wreaths of ivy, pomegranates and laurel leaves.

A lavish party had been thrown to celebrate the engagement, and for the wedding itself in March of the following year, no expense was spared. Before the service, which was to take place in Elounda, the guests arrived at the Vandoulakis home. They were a curious mix. Wealthy people from Elounda, Agios Nikolaos and Neapoli mixed with the estate workers and dozens of folk from Plaka. When they caught sight of Anna, the people from her old village gasped. Enough gold coins to fill a bank vault jangled across her chest and heavily jewelled earrings hung from her ears. She glittered in the spring light, and in the rich red of her traditional bridal gown she could have stepped from the *Tales of the Arabian Nights*.

Giorgis looked at her with pride and some bemusement, marvelling that this was his own daughter. She was almost unrecognisable. He wished at this more than any other moment that Eleni was here to see their firstborn looking so beautiful. He wondered what she would have thought about Anna moving into such an important family. So much of his elder daughter reminded him of his wife, but there was also a part of her that was completely unfamiliar. It seemed an impossibility that he, a humble fisherman, could have anything to do with this vision.

Maria had helped Anna get ready that morning. Her sister's hands trembled so violently that she had to do up every button for her. She knew this was what Anna wanted and that she was achieving her ultimate goal. She was confident that her sister had rehearsed being the *grande dame* so often in her daydreams that she would have no trouble adapting to the reality.

'Tell me it's really happening,' Anna said. 'I can't believe I'm actually going to be Kyria Vandoulakis!'

'It's all real,' Maria reassured her, wondering as she spoke what the reality of going to live in a grand house would be like. She hoped it would mean more than fine jewellery and smart clothes. Even for Anna such things might have their limitations.

The mix of guests made this an unusual event, but even more unconventional was that the pre-nuptial feast was held in the groom's house rather than the bride's, as was the tradition. Everyone understood the reasons for this. They did not need to be articulated. What kind of feast would have been on offer at the house of Giorgis Petrakis? The smart ladies of Neapoli tittered at the very thought, just as they had done when they heard that the Vandoulakis boy was marrying a poor fisherman's daughter. 'What on *earth* is the family thinking of?' they had sneered. Whatever anyone thought of the marriage, everyone was there to enjoy the fine lunch of roast lamb, cheese and wine from Vandoulakis's own crops, and when all two hundred stomachs were full it was time for the marriage service. It was a motley procession of cars, trucks and donkeys pulling carts that finally made its way down to Elounda.

For Cretans both rich and poor the rituals of the marriage ceremony were the same. Two *stephana*, the simple marriage crowns made from dried flowers and grasses and linked by a ribbon, were placed on the heads of the couple by the priest, and then exchanged three times to cement their union. These crowns would be framed later on by Anna's mother-in-law and hung high above the couple's bed so that, as the saying went, no one could tread on the marriage. For much of the time, the words of the sacred ritual were lost in the chatter of the congregation, but when the bride and groom finally joined hands with the priest, a hush spread around the church. Now they performed a sedate dance around the altar, the Isaiah Dance, and the guests knew that soon they would be outside in the sunshine.

Following the bride and groom, who rode in a carriage, everyone trooped back to the Vandoulakis home where trestle tables were laid out for another feast. People ate, drank and danced into the night, and just before the sun rose a volley of gunshots was fired to mark the end of the celebrations.

* * *

After the wedding, Anna more or less vanished from life in Plaka. She visited once a week to see her father, but as time went on she began to send a car down to collect him instead, so her appearances in Plaka became very few and far between. As the wife of the future head of the estate, she found her social position much altered. This was, however, not a problem for her. It was exactly what she wanted – a disconnection from her past.

Anna threw herself into her new role and soon found that her duties as daughter-in-law were as weighty as those of being a wife. She spent each day in the company of Eleftheria and her friends, either calling on them or receiving them at their home, and just as she had hoped, they all enjoyed a level of leisure that bordered on idleness. Her main duty was to help manage the domestic aspects of the Vandoulakis household, which largely involved ensuring that the maid had laid on a great spread of food for the menfolk when they returned in the evening.

She longed to make changes to the two family homes, to relieve them of their dark drapes and sombre furnishings. She nagged Andreas until he took his mother aside to ask for permission, and Eleftheria in turn consulted the real head of the household. This was the way in which everything had to be done.

'I don't want the big house altered too much,' said Alexandros Vandoulakis to his wife, referring to the house in Elounda. 'But Anna can give the house in Neapoli a lick of paint if she'd like to.'

The new bride threw herself into the task and was soon carried away on a wave of enthusiasm for fabrics and wallpapers, making endless trips to an importer of fine French and Italian goods who had a smart shop in Agios Nikolaos. It kept her busy and absorbed and Andreas benefited, finding her in a lively and buoyant mood at the end of each day.

Another of her duties was to manage the *panegyria* celebrations which the Vandoulakis family threw for their workers. Anna excelled at putting on a show. At these feasts she would sometimes feel the eyes of Antonis Angelopoulos on her and she would look up to meet his steely glare. Occasionally he would even speak to her.

'Kyria Vandoulakis,' he would say with exaggerated deference, his bow rather too low. 'How are you?'

His manner made Anna flinch and her reply was appropriately curt.

'Well, thank you.'

With that she turned her back on him. Both his look and his manner challenged her right to be there as his superior. How *dare* he?

Anna's marriage brought a change not only to her own status; her departure also meant a change in Maria's. The younger sister now clearly had the role of mistress in her own household. Much of Maria's energy had gone into pleasing and pacifying her sister, and the fact that Anna was no longer there meant a lightening of her load. She put renewed energy into running the Petrakis home and now often went with her father to make deliveries to Spinalonga.

For Giorgis, who could not lay flowers on her grave, each visit to the island was an opportunity to remember Eleni. He continued to go to and fro with Dr Lapakis in both fair and stormy weather, and on these journeys the doctor talked about his work, confessing to Giorgis how many of the lepers were now dying and how much he missed the visits of Dr Kyritsis.

'He brought a hint of good things to come,' said Lapakis wearily. 'I don't believe in very much myself, but I saw how belief can be a good thing, an end in itself. For some of the lepers, having the faith that Kyritsis might be able to cure them was enough to stop them wanting to die. Many of them feel there's nothing left to live for now.'

Lapakis had received some letters from his old colleague, explaining and profusely regretting his absence. Kyritsis was still involved in putting back together the damaged hospital in Iraklion and at present could not be spared to continue his research. Privately, Lapakis began to despair and poured out his heart to Giorgis. Most people would have prayed to God on bended knee, but in the absence of faith, Lapakis leant on his loyal boatman, whose suffering would always be greater than his own.

Although people continued to die of the disease, for those with the less virulent strain life on Spinalonga was still full of the unexpected. Since the war finished, there had been two film showings every week, the market was better than ever and the newspaper thrived. Dimitri, who was now seventeen, had already begun to teach the five- and six-year-olds whilst a more experienced teacher took charge of the older children; he continued to live at the Kontomaris house, an arrangement which brought great happiness on both sides. As far as it could do, a general sense of contentment pervaded the island. Even Theodoros Makridakis no longer had the will to make trouble. He liked a good debate in the bar but had long since given up the idea of taking over the position of ultimate authority. Nikos Papadimitriou did the job far too well.

Maria and Fotini were engaged in a pattern of daily tasks that took them through the next few years like a dance, with an endlessly repeated sequence of steps. With three sons, Savina Angelopoulos needed the help of her fit and capable daughter to keep the men in the house fed and looked after, so Fotini, like Maria, had domestic duties that tied her to Plaka.

Even if Eleni might have wished for better things for her daughter than remaining in the village, she would not have wished for a more conscientious child than Maria. There was no question in the girl's mind that she should be doing anything other than looking after her father, even if she had once entertained fantasies of standing, chalk in hand, at the front of a class, as her mother had done. Like the printed pattern on their old curtains, all such aspirations had long since faded.

The two girls shared the joys and the limitations of this existence for several years, and in all the time they performed their duties it did not occur to them that they had any real cause for complaint. There was water to fetch from the village pump, wood to be collected for their ovens, sweeping, spinning, cooking and the beating of rugs. Maria would regularly collect honey from her hives on the thyme-covered hillside overlooking Plaka; it yielded such intense sweetness that for several years she had no need to buy even one gram of sugar. In the courtyards at the back of their homes old olive oil cans overflowed with basil and mint and *pithoi*, huge urns once used to store water and oil, provided a perfect home for carefully tended geraniums and lilies, when they became cracked and no longer of practical use.

The girls were heiresses to a millennium of secretly evolved folklore and were now considered old enough to be taught the crafts and skills that had been handed down through generations without written record. Fotini's grandmother was a great source of such lore and showed them how to dye wool with extracts of iris, hibiscus and chrysanthemum petals, and how to weave coloured grasses into elaborate baskets and mats. Other women passed on to them their knowledge of the magical benefits of locally grown herbs, and they would walk far into the mountains to find wild sage, cistus and camomile for their healing powers. On a good day they would return with a basket of the most precious herb of all, *origanum dictamus*, which was said to heal wounds as well as cure sore throats and stomach problems. Maria would always have the right potion to minister to her father if he was sick, and soon her reputation for mixing useful remedies spread round the village.

While they were on their long walks into the mountains they would also gather *horta*, the iron-rich mountain greens that were a staple part of every diet. The childhood games they had played on the beach when they fashioned pies out of sand were now replaced by the more adult pastime of making them out of pastry and herbs.

One of Maria's most important jobs between late autumn and early spring was to keep the home fire burning. It not only provided the warmth which kept them sane while winter winds howled outside; it also kept the spirit of the house alive. The *spiti* – the Greeks used the same word for both 'house' and 'home' – was a divine symbol of unity, and theirs, more than most, needed constant nurturing.

However onerous Maria's domestic tasks might have seemed to anyone living in a city – or indeed to Anna, who now lived in some luxury – there was always time for chatter and intrigue. Fotini's house was a focal point for this. Since idleness was considered a sin, the serious business of gossip was conducted in the innocent context of sewing and embroidery. This not only kept the girls' hands busy but also gave them the opportunity to prepare for the future. Every pillowcase, cushion, tablecloth and runner in the house of a married woman had been woven or embroidered by herself, her mother or her mother's mother. Anna had been an exception. Over the few years she had sat in a sewing circle with women older and wiser than herself, she had completed just one small corner of a pillowcase. It had been symptomatic of her continuous state of rebellion. Her stubbornness was subtle. While the other girls and women sat talking and sewing, her fingers remained idle. She would wave her needle around, gesticulating and making patterns in the air with her thread, but rarely pricked the cloth. It was just as well that she had married into a family where everything was provided.

At certain times of year, the girls turned their hands to the seasonal tasks which demanded they should be outside. They would join the fray at grape harvest and would be the first into the troughs to tread the copiously juicy fruit. Then, just before autumn turned to winter, they would be among the crowd who would beat the olive trees to make the fruit cascade down into the open baskets below. Such days were full of laughter and flirtation, and the completion of these communal tasks would be marked with dancing and merrymaking.

One by one, members of this carefree but duty-laden coterie of young women moved out of the group. They found husbands, or, as was more generally the case, husbands were found for them. On the whole they were other young men from Plaka or one of the neighbouring villages such as Vrouhas or Selles. Their parents had usually known each other for years and had sometimes planned the match between their offspring before they could even count or write their own names. When Fotini announced her own engagement Maria saw her world coming to an end. She displayed only pleasure and delight, however, quietly castigating herself for her feelings of envy as she anticipated the rest of her life spent on doorsteps with the widowed crones, crocheting lace as the sun went down.

Fotini, like Maria, was now twenty-two years old. Her father had supplied the fish taverna on the seafront for many years, and the owner, Stavros Davaras, was a good friend, as well as being a reliable customer. His son, Stephanos, was already working for his father and one day would take over the business, which had a gentle flow of customers on weekdays and a torrent of them on saints' days and Sundays. Pavlos Angelopoulous regarded Stephanos as a good match for his daughter, and the already established mutual dependence of the families was considered a desirable grounding for the marriage. The pair had known each other since childhood and were confident that they could develop feelings for each other which would add sparkle to what was, after all, just an arrangement. A modest dowry was negotiated, and once the engagement had run its usual course, the wedding took place.

The great consolation for Maria was that Fotini would be living no further away from her now than she had been before. Although Fotini now had different, more onerous duties – working in the taverna as well as running the home and negotiating the minefield of living with her in-laws – the women would still see each other every day.

Determined not to betray her dismay at finding herself the last of a diminishing group, Maria threw herself more enthusiastically than ever into her filial duties, accompanying her father with increasing frequency on his trips to Spinalonga and ensuring that their home was always immaculately tidy. For a young woman it was far from fulfilling. Her devotion to Giorgis was admired in the village, but at the same time her lack of a husband reduced her status. Spinsterhood was perceived as a curse, and to be left on the shelf was daily public humiliation in a village like Plaka. If she got any older without finding a fiancé, respect for her dutiful behaviour could quickly turn to scorn. The problem now was that there were few eligible men in Plaka, and Maria would not consider a man from another village. It was unthinkable that Giorgis should uproot himself from Plaka and therefore unimaginable that Maria would ever move either. There was, she reflected, as much chance of marriage as there was of seeing her beloved mother walk through the door.

Chapter Twelve

1951

ANNA WAS NOW four years married and thriving on her new status. She loved Andreas dutifully, and willingly responded to his passion for her. To everyone around her, Anna seemed a faultless wife. She was aware, however, that the family was awaiting the announcement of a pregnancy. The lack of a baby did not bother her at all. There would be plenty of time for children and she was enjoying this carefree time far too much to want to lose it to mother-hood. Eleftheria had broached the subject one day when they were discussing the decor for one of the spare bedrooms in Neapoli.

'This used to be the nursery,' she said, 'when our girls were little. What colour would you like to paint it?'

Eleftheria thought she was providing the perfect opportunity for her daughter-in-law to say something about her plans and aspirations for becoming a mother, and was disappointed when Anna professed a liking for pale green. 'It'll complement the fabric I've ordered to cover the furniture,' she said.

Anna and Andreas, along with his parents, lived for some

of the time during the summer months in the family's grand neoclassical villa in Neapoli, which Anna had now extensively refurbished. Eleftheria considered its fine drapes and fragile furniture very impractical, but it appeared she could not stand in this young woman's way. In September the family started to move back to the main house in Elounda, which Anna was also gradually transforming to her own taste in spite of her father-in-law's penchant for the sombre style favoured by his generation. She often had herself taken into Agios Nikolaos to shop, and one day in late autumn she arrived back from one of these trips to see her upholsterer and check up on the progress of her latest pair of curtains. She rushed into the kitchen and planted a kiss on the back of the head of the figure seated at the table.

'Hello, darling,' she said. 'How was the press today?'

It had been the first day of olive pressing, a significant date in the calendar, when the press was used for the first time in many months and it was always touch and go whether the machinery would perform. There were thousands of litres of oil to be extracted from the countless baskets of olives that sat waiting to be crushed and it was crucial that everything went smoothly. The golden liquid that poured from press to *pithoi* was the basis of the family's wealth and, as Anna saw it, each jar was another metre of fabric, another tailored dress to be hand-fitted to her curves, with tucks and darts that moulded the garment around her body. These clothes, more than anything, illustrated her separation from the village women, whose shapeless gathered skirts were no different now from those that their grandmothers had worn a hundred years before. Today, to keep the biting November winds at bay, Anna wore an emerald-green coat which hugged her breasts and hips like an embrace before falling away almost to the ground in extravagant swirls of fabric. A fur collar rose up her neck to warm her ears and stroke her cheeks.

As she walked across the room, the silk lining of her coat rustling against her legs, she chattered about the minutiae of her day. She was putting water on to prepare herself some coffee when the man at the table rose from his chair. Anna turned round and let out a scream of surprise.

'Who are *you*?' she asked in a strangulated voice. 'I . . . I thought you were my husband.'

'So I gathered.' The man smiled, clearly amused by her confusion.

As the two stood face to face, Anna saw that the man she had greeted so affectionately, though clearly *not* her husband, was in every way very like him. The breadth of his shoulders, his hair and, now that he was standing, even his height seemed to match Andreas's exactly. The strong and distinctive Vandoulakis nose was the same and the slightly slanted eyes bore an uncanny resemblance. When he spoke, Anna's mouth went dry. What trick was this?

'I'm Manoli Vandoulakis,' he said, holding out his hand. 'You must be Anna.'

Anna knew of the existence of a cousin and had heard Manoli's name mentioned a few times in conversation, but little more than that. She had never pictured him as this carbon copy of her husband.

'Manoli.' She repeated the name. It was pleasing. Now she needed to regain control of the situation, feeling foolish that she had made such a mistake and carelessly embraced a total stranger. 'Does Andreas know you're here?' she asked.

'No, I arrived an hour ago and decided to give everyone a surprise. It certainly worked with you! You look as though you've seen a ghost.'

'I feel as though I have,' answered Anna. 'The similarity between the two of you is uncanny.'

'I haven't seen Andreas for ten years, but we were very alike. People were always mistaking us for twins.'

Anna could see that, but she could also see many other things that actually made this version of her husband very different from the original. Though Manoli had the same broad shoulders as Andreas, he was actually thinner and she could see his bony shoulder blades protruding under his shirt. He had laughter in his eyes and deep lines around them. He thought it was a terrific joke that she had mistaken him for his cousin and she realised quite quickly that he had set the moment up. Life was there to be enjoyed, you could see it in his smile.

At that moment, Andreas and his father returned and there were exclamations of delight and amazement when they saw Manoli standing there. Soon the three men were sitting round a bottle of raki and Anna excused herself to make arrangements for dinner. When Eleftheria arrived an hour or so later, a second bottle of raki was already drained and both she and Manoli wept tears of joy as they embraced. Letters were immediately sent off to Andreas's sisters, and the following Sunday a great reunion party was held to mark Manoli's return after his decade of absence.

Manoli Vandoulakis was a free-spirited youth who had spent

the past ten years, largely on mainland Greece, squandering a sizeable inheritance. His mother had died in childbirth and his father had passed away five years later at the age of thirty, of a heart attack. Manoli had grown up hearing dark murmurings of how his father had died of a broken heart and whether or not this was true, it made him resolve to live as though each day might be his last. It was a philosophy that made perfect sense to him, and even his uncle Alexandros, who since the death of Yiannis Vandoulakis had been his guardian, could not stop him. As a child Manoli had noticed that everyone around him carried out a relentless round of tasks and duties, apparently only enjoying themselves when they were given permission on saints' days and Sundays. He wanted pleasure every day of his life.

Though the memory of his parents dimmed by the day, he was often told that they had lived good and dutiful lives. But what real good had their exemplary behaviour done them? It had not kept death away, had it? Fate had snatched them like an eagle plucking its defenceless prey from a bare rock face. To hell with it, he thought; if destiny could not be outwitted, he might as well see what else life had to offer him other than a few decades of living on a Cretan hillside before burial beneath it.

Ten years earlier, he had left home. Apart from the occasional letter to his aunt and uncle – some from Italy, some from Yugoslavia, but mostly from Athens – to reassure them that he was still alive, he had had little contact with his family. Alexandros was aware that if his older brother Yiannis had not died so young, it would be Manoli who would now be in line to inherit the Vandoulakis estate, rather than his own son. But such thoughts were hypothetical. Instead of the promise of land, when he had reached the age of eighteen Manoli had come into a small cash fortune. It was this money that he had largely squandered in Rome, Belgrade and Athens.

'The high life had a high price,' he confided to Andreas soon after his return. 'The best women were like good wine, expensive but worth every drachma.' Now, however, the women of Europe had cleaned him out of everything he owned and all he had left were the coins in his pocket and a promise from his uncle that he would employ him on the estate.

His return caused a great stir, not just with his uncle and aunt, but also with Andreas himself. With only six months' difference between them, the two were virtually twins. As children they had almost known each other's thoughts and felt each other's pain, but after their eighteenth birthdays their lives had taken such divergent paths that it was hard to imagine how things would be now that Manoli was back.

It was, however, timely. Alexandros Vandoulakis was due to retire the following year, and Andreas could really do with a helping hand in managing the estate. They all felt it would be better for Manoli to take on the role than for them to employ an outsider, and even if Alexandros had some doubts about whether his nephew would really buckle down to it, he would put those doubts aside. Manoli was family, after all.

For several months, Manoli lived in the house on the Elounda estate. There were plenty of rooms that were never used so his presence inconvenienced no one, but in December Alexandros provided him with a house of his own. Manoli had enjoyed this taste of family life and being part of the dynasty from which he had chosen for ten years to absent himself, but his uncle expected him to get married in the future and for this purpose insisted that he should live in his own home.

'You'll be lucky to find a girl who's prepared to live in a house where there are already two mistresses,' he said to his nephew. 'A third woman in a house is asking for trouble.'

Manoli's house had belonged to the estate manager in the days when Alexandros had paid an outsider to perform the role. It was set at the end of a short driveway a kilometre from the main house, and with its four bedrooms and large drawing room was considered a substantial home for a bachelor. Manoli, however, continued to be a regular visitor at the main house. He wanted to be fed and pampered, just like Alexandros and Andreas, and here were two women to do just that for him. Everyone loved his lively conversation and welcomed him there, but Alexandros always insisted that eventually he should go home.

Manoli had lived his life in a state of impermanence, flitting like a butterfly from one place to the next. And wherever he went he left a trail of broken promises. Even as a child, he had stretched things to the limit. Just for a dare, he once held his hand in a flame until the skin began to melt and another time he jumped off the highest rock on the Elounda coast, scraping his back so badly the sea around him turned scarlet. In the foreign capitals of Europe he would gamble until he was down to his shirt and then make a spectacular comeback. It was just the way he was. In spite of himself he found he was playing the same game in Elounda, but the difference here was that he was now obliged to stay.

He could no longer afford to fly away, even if he had wanted to.

To Alexandros's surprise, Manoli worked quite hard, though he did not have the same commitment as his cousin. Andreas would always take his lunch to the fields to save the time it took to return home, but Manoli preferred to get away from the harsh sunshine just for a few hours and had taken to coming in to eat his lunch at the spacious table in the Vandoulakis kitchen. Anna had no objection. She welcomed his presence in the house.

Their interaction was not so much conversation as flirtation. Manoli made her laugh, sometimes until tears streamed down her face, and her appreciation of his teasing humour and the way the enlarged pupils of her eyes sparkled when she held his gaze were enough to keep him from the olive groves well into the afternoon.

Sometimes Eleftheria was there rather than in Neapoli and feared that her nephew was not really pulling his weight on the estate. 'Men shouldn't hang around the house in the day,' she once remarked to Anna. 'It's a woman's territory. Theirs is outside.'

Anna chose to ignore her mother-in-law's disapproving comment and welcomed Manoli more effusively than ever. In her view, the closeness of the kinship between them sanctioned their friendship. It was the custom that a woman enjoyed much greater freedom once married than she had been allowed as a single woman, so at first no one questioned Anna's liberty to spend an hour a day, sometimes even more, with her 'cousin'. But a few people began to notice the frequency of Manoli's visits, and tongues started to wag.

One lunchtime that spring, Manoli had lingered even longer than usual. Anna sensed his recklessness and for once shuddered at the danger she was putting herself in. Nowadays when he left he would hold on to her hand and kiss it in an absurdly histrionic way. She could have passed it off as a frivolous gesture, but the way in which he pressed his middle finger into the very centre of her palm and held it there made her shiver. More significantly, he touched her hair. It was dead matter, he said laughingly, and anyway she had started it, he teased, by kissing a total stranger . . . on the hair. And so it went on. He had picked some meadow flowers that day, and presented her with a bouquet of bright, if wilting, poppies. It was a romantic gesture and she was charmed, especially when he pulled one from the bunch and carefully placed it in the front of her blouse. His touch was subtle and there was a moment when she was not entirely certain whether the contact of his rough hand with her smooth skin was accidental, or whether he had, very deliberately, brushed her breast with his fingers. A moment later, when she felt his gentle touch on her neck, the doubt was gone.

Anna was an impetuous enough woman, but something held her back. My God, she thought, this is the threshold of insanity. What am I doing? She pictured herself standing in this huge kitchen almost nose to nose with a man who, though he looked so very like him, was not her husband. She saw the situation as it would appear to someone looking in through the open window, and however hard she tried to convince herself, she knew it would not seem ambiguous. She was one second away from being kissed. She still had a choice.

Her marriage to Andreas lacked nothing. He was warm,

adoring and gave her free rein to make changes in their homes when she wished; she even got on tolerably well with her in-laws. They had, however, quickly settled into a pattern, as happened in such marriages, and life had a predictability that made it unlikely that the next half-century would hold any real surprises. After all the anticipation and excitement at starting a new life, Anna was discovering that it could be just as dull as her old one. What it lacked was the thrill of the clandestine, the frisson of the illicit. Whether such things were worth risking everything for, she did not quite know.

I ought to stop this, she thought. Otherwise I could lose everything. She addressed Manoli with her usual haughtiness. It was their game, how she always talked to him. While he was extravagantly flirtatious, she treated him as her inferior.

'Look, young man,' she said. 'As you know, I'm spoken for. You can take your flowers elsewhere.'

'Can I indeed?' Manoli answered. 'And exactly where shall I take them?'

'Well, my sister isn't yet spoken for. You could take them to her.' As if the true Anna was somewhere very distant, she heard a voice saying: 'I shall invite her to lunch next Sunday. You'll like her.'

The following Sunday was the feast of Agios Giorgis, so it was a perfect excuse for inviting Maria and her father to visit. It was a duty rather than a particular pleasure to see them both; she felt she had nothing in common with her tedious little sister and little to say to her father. For the rest of that week Anna dreamed of Manoli's lingering touch and looked forward to the next time they could be alone, but before that happened, she mused, the dull family luncheon had to take place.

There were still shortages of many kinds of food in Crete at that time, but these never seemed to affect the Vandoulakis household, especially on a saint's day, when it was conveniently considered a religious duty to feast. Giorgis was delighted to receive the invitation.

'Maria, look! Anna has invited us to lunch.'

'That's kind of her ladyship,' said Maria with uncharacteristic sarcasm. 'When?'

'On Sunday. In two days' time.'

Maria was secretly pleased that they had been invited. She yearned to strengthen the bond with her sister, knowing that this would have been what their mother wanted, but nevertheless she felt some trepidation as the day approached. Giorgis, however, who was finally emerging from his long state of grief, was happy at the prospect of seeing his elder daughter.

Anna cringed as she heard the spluttering sound of her father's newly acquired truck in the driveway and with little enthusiasm made her way slowly down the big staircase to greet them. Manoli, who had already arrived, had got to the front door well before her and thrown it open.

Maria was not at all what he had expected. She had the biggest brown eyes he had ever seen and they looked at him with wide-eyed surprise.

'I'm Manoli,' he said, striding towards her with outstretched hand, adding: 'Andreas's cousin.'

So negligent was Anna in her correspondence that Maria and Giorgis had known nothing of the arrival of the long-lost relative.

Manoli was always in his element with a pretty girl, but never more so than with one like this, who added innocence to such sweet beauty. He took in every detail: a slim waist, a neat bosom and muscular arms built up by years of hard physical work. She was at once fragile and strong.

At one o'clock they all sat down to eat. With Alexandros, Eleftheria, their two daughters and their respective families, there were at least a dozen. Chatter was noisy and animated.

Manoli had decided in advance that he would flirt with Anna's younger sister. A practised lothario such as he was did so out of habit. What he had not expected was that Maria would be so pretty and so eminently easy to tease. Throughout lunch he dominated her with his playful talk, and although she was unused to such flippancy, she parried his witty remarks. Her unaffected personality made her so different from most of the women he was used to meeting that he eventually found himself toning down his banter and asking her questions about herself. He discovered that she knew about mountain herbs and their healing powers, and they talked earnestly about their place in a world where the boundaries of science were being pushed forward by the day. Maria and Anna were as unalike as a raw pearl and a polished diamond. One had natural lustre and its own unique, irregular shape. The other had been cut and polished to achieve its glittering beauty. Manoli loved both such jewels, and this soft, gentle-eyed girl who was so clearly devoted to her father appealed strongly to him. She was without artifice and had a naïvety that he found unexpectedly alluring.

Anna watched as Manoli drew Maria into his magnetic field, telling her stories and making her laugh. She saw her sister melt in his warmth. Before the meal was over, Anna realised what she had done. She had given Manoli away, handed him like a gift-wrapped parcel to her sister, and now she wanted him back.

Chapter Thirteen

FOR THE NEXT week, Manoli was vexed. This was unusual for him. How could he pursue Maria? She was quite unlike most of the women he had met on his travels. Besides which, the accepted patterns and modes of behaviour between men and women in Plaka were very different from those governing such relationships in the cities where he had lived. Here in rural Crete, every move, every word was subject to scrutiny. He had been perfectly aware of this when he had visited Anna on all those occasions, and though he had always been careful to ensure that certain boundaries were never crossed, he had known that he was playing with fire. In Anna he had seen a bored, isolated woman who had separated herself from the village where she had grown up and achieved her ambition of being in a position where other people were paid to do those tasks which would otherwise have kept her busy and occupied. She had improved her position, but now floated in a friendless social vacuum, one in which Manoli had been happy to entertain her. A woman with eyes that so hungrily sought his and lips that spread themselves into such a generous smile: it would have been rude to ignore her.

Maria was quite different. Not only did she lack her sister's ambition to marry outside the village, she seemed without desire to marry at all. She lived in a small house with her widowed father, apparently content and yet so exceptionally marriageable. Manoli would not have admitted it to himself, but it was largely her lack of interest that attracted him. He had all the time in the world, though, and would be patient, certain that sooner or later she would be won over. Confidence was not lacking in the Vandoulakis male. It rarely occurred to them that they would not get what they wanted. Manoli had much on his side. Perhaps the most important factor was that Fotini had protected Maria from the gossip about Manoli and Anna. The source of the endlessly flowing fountain of stories was Fotini's brother Antonis. It was more than five years since that kiss which had meant nothing to Anna and far too much to Antonis, but the sense of having been cast aside still rankled. He despised Anna and had watched with malicious satisfaction the comings and goings of her husband's cousin, which had increased in regularity now that Eleftheria and Alexandros Vandoulakis were spending more time in Neapoli and less in Elounda. Antonis gave reports to Fotini whenever he called in for supper at the waterfront taverna which was now her home.

'He was there for at least two hours one lunchtime last week.' he gloated.

'I don't want to hear your stories,' Fotini said brusquely to Antonis as she poured him a raki. 'And above all, I don't want Maria to hear them either.'

'Why not? Her sister is a tart. Don't you think she knows that already?' snapped Antonis.

'Of course she doesn't know that. And nor do you. So

what if her husband's cousin comes to visit her? He's family, why shouldn't he?'

'Just the occasional visit would be one thing, but not virtually every day. Even family don't bother to visit each other that often.'

'Well, whatever you think, Maria mustn't know – and nor must Giorgis. He has suffered quite enough. Seeing Anna married to a wealthy man was the best thing that could have happened to him – so you're to keep your mouth shut. I mean it, Antonis.'

Fotini did mean it. She slammed the bottle down on the table in front of her brother and glared at him. She was as protective of Giorgis and Maria Petrakis as she would have been of her own flesh and blood, and wanted to keep these vicious and damaging rumours from them. Part of her could not believe them in any case. Why would Anna, whose whole life had turned around the night she met Andreas, risk throwing it all away? The very thought of it was baffling, ridiculous even, and besides, she held out hope that Manoli, the subject of Antonis's scurrilous rumour-mongering, might one day notice Maria. Since the lunch on the feast of Agios Giorgis, Maria had chatted incessantly about Andreas's cousin, repeating every detail of their encounter at the Vandoulakis house.

Manoli had been seen a few times in the village. With his connection to Giorgis he had found a warm welcome among the men of Plaka and soon became a regular fixture at the bar; he was found there as often as anyone, playing backgammon, passing around strong cigarettes and discussing the politics of the island beneath a thick pall of smoke. Even in this small village on a road that led only to even smaller villages, the pressing issues of world politics were high on the agenda. In spite of their remoteness from them, events on mainland Greece regularly aroused both passion and fury.

'The Communists are to blame!' exclaimed Lidaki, banging his fist on the top of the bar.

'How can you say that?' answered another voice. 'If it wasn't for the monarchy, the mainland wouldn't be in half the mess it is,' and so they went on, sometimes into the small hours. 'Two Greeks, one argument', the saying went, and here, on most nights of the week, there were twenty or more villagers and as many arguments as there were olives in a jar.

Manoli had a broader world view than others in the bar – many had been no further than Iraklion and most had never got as far as Hania – and he brought a new perspective to argument and conversation. Though he was careful not to brag of the casual conquests that had been a recurring theme of his travels, he entertained them all with stories of Italians, Yugoslavians and their brothers on mainland Greece. His was a light touch and everyone liked him, enjoying the gaiety that he brought to the bar. Whenever there was a pause in the argument Manoli would have an anecdote or two to tell and the assembled company were happy to indulge him. His tales of the old Turkish quarter in Athens, the Spanish Steps in Rome and the bars of Belgrade were mesmerising and while he spoke there was silence, except for the occasional clack of worry beads. He did not need to embroider the facts to entertain. The stories of his brief imprisonment, being adrift on a ship in the middle of the Mediterranean, and fighting a duel in the back streets of a Yugoslavian port were all true enough. They were the tales of a man who had travelled without responsibilities and initially without cares. They showed him to be a wild but not uncaring man, but as he spoke, Manoli was conscious that he did not wish to be perceived as an unsuitable match for Giorgis's daughter and accordingly toned down his stories.

Even Antonis, who had ceased to skulk in the corner whenever his boss's rakish cousin appeared, now greeted him warmly. Music was their common bond, plus the fact that they had both spent a few years away from this province; though decades younger than the grizzled men they drank with, they were in some ways more worldly-wise than their elders would ever be. As a child, Manoli had learned to play the lyre and during his travelling years it had been both a companion and his security, at one point the only thing that stood between him and starvation. Often he had found himself singing and playing for his supper, and his lyre was the only possession of any value that he had not gambled away. This precious instrument now hung on the wall behind the bar, and when the raki was low in the bottle he would remove it from its hook and play, the bow sending the sound of its vibrating strings shuddering through the night air.

Likewise, Antonis's wooden flute, his *thiaboli*, had been his constant companion during his years away from home. Its mellow sounds had filled a hundred different caves and shepherds' huts, the notes soothing the hearts and souls of his companions and, more prosaically, helping them while away all those hours they had spent watching and waiting. As different as Manoli and Antonis were, music was a neutral space where wealth and hierarchy played no part. The two of them would play in the bar for an hour or so, their haunting melodies casting a spell over their audience and over those whose open windows captured the escaping sounds as they drifted through the stillness.

Though everyone was aware of the great wealth that Manoli's parents had enjoyed and of the fortune that he himself had frittered away, most of the villagers now accepted him as someone just like themselves, who needed to work hard for a living and who, quite naturally, aspired to having a wife and a family. For Manoli, the simplicity of this more settled life had its own rewards. Even without the possibility of seeing Maria, which had been his original motivation in visiting Plaka, he found much in this village to love. The bonds between childhood friends, the loyalty to family and a way of life that had not needed to change for centuries, all had great appeal. If he could secure a woman like Maria, or perhaps even one of the other village beauties, it would complete his sense of belonging. Apart from saints' day celebrations in the village, however, there were few legitimate occasions for him to meet her.

The formalities still observed in villages like Plaka drove him mad. Though he found the enduring traditions part of the attraction, the obscurity of the courting rituals he found nothing less than ridiculous. He knew he could not mention his intentions to Anna, and anyway, he was not visiting her so much now. It was a pattern he knew he needed to break if he wanted to achieve his planned conquest of Maria. Anna had been predictably brittle with him when he last visited.

'Well, thanks for coming to see me,' she said tartly.

'Look,' said Manoli, 'I don't think I should come at

lunchtime any more. People are beginning to mutter about me not pulling my weight.'

'Suit yourself,' she snapped, her eyes full of angry tears. 'You've obviously finished your little game with me. I assume you're now playing it with someone else.'

With that she marched out of the room, and the door slammed behind her like a thunderclap.

Manoli would miss their intimacy and the sparkle in Anna's eyes, but it was a price he was prepared to pay.

Since there was no one at home preparing him meals, Manoli often ate in one of the tavernas in Elounda or in Plaka. Each Friday he went to Fotini's taverna, which she and Stephanos had now taken over from his parents. One visit in July, he sat there looking out to sea towards Spinalonga. The island, shaped like a large, half-submerged egg, had become so familiar to him that he scarcely gave it a second thought. Like everyone else, he occasionally wondered what it must be like over there, but he did not dwell on such thoughts for long. Spinalonga was simply there, a lump of rock inhabited by lepers.

A plate of tiny *picarel* fish sat on the table in front of Manoli, and as he stabbed each one with his fork, his eye was caught by something. In the dusky half-light a little boat was chugging its way from the island, creating a broad triangular wake as it cut through the dense water. Two people were in it, and as the boat came into the harbour, he saw that one of them looked very like Maria.

'Stephanos!' he called. 'Is that Maria with Giorgis? You don't usually see a woman out fishing, do you?'

'They haven't been fishing,' replied Stephanos. 'They've

been making one of their deliveries to the leper colony.'

'Oh,' said Manoli, chewing slowly and thoughtfully. 'I suppose someone has to.'

'Giorgis has been doing it for years. It's better money than fishing – and more guaranteed,' said Stephanos, putting a plate of fried potatoes down on Manoli's table. 'But he mostly does it for—'

Fotini, who had been hovering in the background, saw where this conversation might lead. Even if he did not intend to, she knew that Stephanos was likely to forget Giorgis's desire to keep the facts of Eleni's tragic death from leprosy a secret from the Vandoulakis family.

'Here you are, Manoli!' She dived forward with a plate of sliced aubergines. 'These are freshly cooked. With garlic. I hope you like them. Would you excuse us a moment?'

She grabbed her husband's arm and led him back to the kitchen.

'You must be careful!' she exclaimed. 'We *all* have to forget that Anna and Maria's mother was ever on Spinalonga. It's the only way. We know it's nothing for them to be ashamed of, but Alexandros Vandoulakis might not see it that way.'

Stephanos was shamefaced.

'I know, I know. It slips my mind sometimes, that's all. It was really stupid of me,' he muttered. 'Manoli comes in here so often, I forget that he's connected with Anna.'

'It's not just Anna's position I'm thinking of,' admitted Fotini. 'Maria has feelings for Manoli. They met only once, up at Anna's house, but she hasn't stopped talking about him, at least not to me.'

'Really? That poor girl needs a husband, but he looks a

bit of a rogue to me,' replied Stephanos. 'I suppose there's not much choice around here, is there.'

Stephanos only saw things in black and white. He understood what his wife was getting at and realised that he and Fotini had a role to play in bringing these two together.

It was precisely a week later that the opportunity to engineer a meeting between Maria and Manoli presented itself. When Manoli appeared that Friday, Fotini slipped out of a side door and ran to the Petrakis house. Giorgis had eaten and gone to the bar to play backgammon and Maria now sat in the fading light, straining to read.

'Maria, he's there,' Fotini said breathlessly. 'Manoli is at the taverna. Why don't you come down and see him.'

'I can't,' said Maria. 'What would my father think?'

'For heaven's sake,' replied Fotini. 'You're twenty-three. Be bold. Your father needn't even know.'

She grabbed her friend by the arm. Maria resisted, but only feebly; in her heart she yearned to go.

'What do I say to him?' she asked anxiously.

'Don't worry,' Fotini reassured her. 'Men like Manoli never allow that to be your concern, at least not for long. He'll have plenty to say.'

Fotini was right. When they arrived at the taverna, Manoli was immediately in charge of the situation. He did not question why Maria was there, but invited her to join him at his table, asking her what she had been doing since they had last met, and how her father was. Then, more boldly than a man normally did in these situations, he said, 'There's a new cinema opened in Agios Nikolaos. Would you come there with me?'

Maria, already flushed from the excitement of seeing Manoli

again, blushed even more deeply. She looked down into her lap and could hardly reply.

'That would be very nice,' she said eventually. 'But it's not really the done thing around here . . . going to the cinema with someone you hardly know.'

'I tell you what, I shall ask Fotini and Stephanos to come as well. They can act as chaperones. Let's go on Monday. That's the day the taverna shuts, isn't it?'

So before she knew it and had had time to be anxious and think of all the reasons against it, the date was agreed. In a mere three days from now they would all go to Agios Nikolaos.

Manoli's manners were impeccable and their outings became a weekly event. Each Monday, the four of them would set off at about seven in the evening to spend an evening watching the latest movie, followed by supper.

Giorgis was delighted to see his daughter being wooed by this handsome and charming man, someone he had liked for many months even before his daughter had got to know him. Though it was a very modern approach – all this going out before there was any kind of formal agreement – they were, after all, moving into a more modern era, and the fact that Maria had an escort helped to contain the mutterings of disapproval from the older ladies of the village.

The four of them enjoyed each other's company and the trips out of Plaka changed the texture and pattern of their otherwise routine lives. Laughter characterised their times together, and they were often bent double with amusement at Manoli's jokes and antics. Maria began to allow herself the luxury of a daydream and to imagine that she could spend the rest of her days looking at this handsome, lined face, aged by life and laughter. Sometimes when he looked straight into her eyes she felt the invisible hairs on her neck stand on end and the palms of her hands dampen. Even on a warm evening she would feel herself shudder involuntarily. It was a new experience to be so flattered and teased. What light relief Manoli was from the colourless backdrop of the rest of her life! There were moments when she wondered if he was actually capable of taking anything seriously. The bubbles of his effervescence spread to everyone around him. Maria had never enjoyed such carefree happiness and began to think this euphoria was love.

Always weighing on her conscience, however, was what would become of her father if she should marry. With most marriage arrangements, the girl left her own family and moved in with her new husband's parents. Clearly that would not happen with Manoli since he had no parents, but equally impossible was the idea that he might move into their small Plaka home. With his background, it was inconceivable. The problem went round and round in her mind, and not once did it seem absurd that Manoli had not yet even kissed her.

Manoli was on his best behaviour and had long since decided that the only way he would win Maria was by conducting himself faultlessly. How absurd it sometimes seemed to him that in another country he might have taken a girl to bed when they had scarcely exchanged names, and yet here he had spent many dozens of hours with Maria and had not yet touched her. His desire for her was intense but the waiting had a delicious novelty. He was sure his patience would be rewarded and the wait only made him want her all the more. In the early months of this courtship, when he gazed at her pale oval face framed by its halo of dark plaited hair, she would look down bashfully, afraid to meet his eye. As time went on, however, he watched her grow bolder and stare back. If he had looked closely, he would have had the satisfaction of seeing a quickening pulse on her pretty neck before her fine features broke into a smile. If he took this virgin now he knew he would be obliged to leave Plaka. Though he had deflowered dozens of girls in his past, even he could not disgrace the lovely Maria and, more importantly, a voice inside urged him to hold back. It was time to settle down.

From a distance, Anna smouldered with envy and resentment. Manoli had hardly been to visit her since Giorgis and Maria had come for lunch, and on some occasions when there were family gatherings he had stayed away. How *dare* he treat her that way? Soon she learned from her father that Manoli was wooing Maria. Was this just to provoke her? If only she could show him that she really did not care. There was no such opportunity, however, and therefore no such catharsis. She desperately tried not to think about them together, and irritably threw herself into increasingly extravagant projects about the home to distract herself. All the while she knew that in Plaka events were inexorably unfolding, but there was no one in whom she could confide, and the fury built up inside her like steam in a pressure cooker.

Andreas, dismayed by her strange mood, repeatedly asked her what was wrong and was told not to bother her. He gave up. He had sensed for a while that the halcyon days of early marriage, with its loving looks and kind words, were over, and he now busied himself more and more on the estate. Eleftheria noticed the change too. Anna had seemed so happy and vivacious just a few months before and now she seemed permanently angry. For Anna, concealing her emotions like this was the antithesis of everything that came naturally to her. She wanted to scream, shout, yank her hair in handfuls from its roots, but when her father and Maria visited her from time to time, Manoli was not even mentioned.

By some instinct, Maria felt that her friendship with Manoli might have strayed into her sister's territory and that perhaps she regarded the Vandoulakis family as her own domain. Why make things worse by talking about it? She had no idea of the scale of Anna's anguish and assumed that her air of vagueness was something to do with the fact that she had so far failed to conceive a child.

One February evening, six months after the weekly nights out had begun, Manoli went to find Giorgis in the bar. The old man was sitting alone, reading the local newspaper. He looked up as Manoli approached, a plume of smoke curling above his head.

'Giorgis, may I sit down?' Manoli asked politely.

'Yes,' Giorgis replied, returning to the paper. 'I don't own the place, do I?'

'There's something I want to ask you. I'll get to the point. I would like to marry your daughter. Will you agree to it?'

Giorgis folded the newspaper carefully and placed it on the table. To Manoli it seemed an age before he spoke.

'Agree to it? Of course I'll agree to it! You've been courting the most beautiful girl in the village for over half a year – and I thought you might never ask. It's about time!'

Giorgis's blustering response concealed his absolute joy at the request. Not just one, but now two of his daughters were to become part of the most powerful family in the province. There was no snobbery at the heart of his sentiment, just sheer relief and pleasure that both their futures were now secure. It was the best a father could possibly hope for on behalf of his children, especially a father who was a mere fisherman. Behind Manoli's head he could see the twinkling lights of Spinalonga through the half-shuttered window of the bar. If only Eleni could share this moment.

He put out his hand to seize Manoli's, momentarily lost for words. His expression said enough.

'Thank you. I will look after her, but between us we will look after you too,' said Manoli, fully aware of the lonely situation Maria's marriage could put her father in.

'Hey! We need your best *tsikoudia*!' he called out to Lidaki. 'We have something to celebrate here. It's a miracle. I'm no longer an orphan!'

'What are you talking about?' said Lidaki, sauntering over with a bottle and two glasses, well used now to Manoli's verbal stunts.

'Giorgis has agreed to be my father-in-law. I am to marry Maria!'

There were a few others in the bar that evening, and even before the girl in question knew anything about it, the menfolk of the village were toasting her future with Manoli.

Later that night when Giorgis returned home, Maria was getting ready to retire to bed. As her father came in through the door, shutting it quickly to keep the February wind outside and the warmth of the fire in, she noticed an unfamiliar expression on his face. It was suffused with excitement and delight.

'Maria,' he said, reaching out to grab her by both arms,

'Manoli has asked for your hand in marriage.'

For a moment she bowed her head, pleasure and pain somehow mixed in equal measure. Her throat contracted.

'What answer did you give him?' she asked in a whisper.

'The one you would have wanted me to. Yes, of course!'

In all her life Maria had not felt this unfamiliar mingling of emotions. Her heart felt like a cauldron of ingredients that declined to blend. Her chest tightened with anxiety. What was this? Was happiness meant to feel so like nausea? Just as she could not imagine someone else's pain, Maria did not know what love felt like for anyone else. She was fairly certain she loved Manoli. With his charm and wit, it was not hard to do so. But her whole future with him? A host of worries began to gnaw at her. What would happen to her father? She voiced her anxieties immediately.

'It's wonderful, Father. It's really wonderful, but what about you? I can't leave you here alone.'

'Don't worry about me. I can stay here – I wouldn't want to move out of Plaka. There's still too much for me to do here.'

'What do you mean?' she asked, though she knew exactly what he meant.

'Spinalonga. The island still needs me – and as long as I'm fit to take my boat there I'll keep going. Dr Lapakis relies on me, and so do all the islanders.'

There were as many comings and goings to and from the leper colony as ever. Each month there were new arrivals and supplies to be delivered, as well as building materials for the government-funded refurbishment that was being carried out. Giorgis was an essential part of the whole operation. Maria understood his attachment to the island. They rarely spoke about it now, but it was accepted between them that this was his vocation and his way of maintaining a connection with Eleni.

Both father and daughter slept fitfully that night, and morning could not come too soon. That day, Giorgis was to take Maria to Manoli's house on the Vandoulakis estate. It was a Sunday, and Manoli was there to greet them on the doorstep. Maria had never even seen his house before, and it was now to become her home. It took her no time at all to calculate that it was four times the size of their house in Plaka and the thought of living there daunted her.

'Welcome,' Manoli said, warming her with a single word. 'Come in, both of you. Come out of the cold.'

It was indeed the coldest day they had yet had this year. A storm was brewing and the winds seemed to come from several directions, stirring up eddies of dead leaves and sending them spiralling around their ankles. Maria's first impression when they went into the house was of a lack of light and a general untidiness that she was unsurprised to find in a house that might have had a maid but did not have a mistress. Manoli took them into a reception room which was slightly tidier and more cared for, with its embroidered lace cloths and a few photographs on the walls.

'My aunt and uncle are due to arrive shortly,' he explained, almost nervously, and then to Maria he said: 'Your father has consented to my asking for your hand. Will you marry me?'

She paused a moment before answering. To both of them it seemed an age. He looked at her with pleading eyes, momentarily doubtful.

'Yes,' she said, finally.

'She says yes!' roared Manoli, suddenly regaining his confidence. He hugged her and kissed her hands and spun her round until she pleaded for mercy. There would always be surprises with Manoli, and his exuberance took her breath away. The man was a human *pentozali*.

'You're going to be my wife!' he said excitedly. 'My uncle and aunt are so looking forward to meeting you again, Maria. But before they get here we must talk about the important matter of you, Giorgis. Will you come and live with us here?'

Manoli had, typically, waded in. Asking Giorgis to live with them was the closest they could approximate to re-establishing a traditional pattern where parents were ultimately taken care of by their children. Manoli had not discussed the matter with Maria and was unaware of the sensitivities, though he knew that she would want to have her father close by.

'It's very kind of you. But I couldn't leave the village. Maria understands, don't you, Maria?' he said, appealing to his daughter.

'Of course I understand, Father. I don't mind, as long as you come to see us as often as you can – and anyway we'll be down in Plaka to see you most days.'

Giorgis knew Maria would be true to her word and that he could look forward to her visits without fear of disappointment. She would not be like Anna, whose letters and visits had virtually dried up now.

Manoli could not really understand his future father-in-law's attachment to his old house in the village, but he was not going to pursue the point. At that moment the sound of tyres could be heard on the stony track outside, and then car doors slamming shut. Alexandros and Eleftheria were at the door and Manoli ushered them in. Warm handshakes were exchanged. Although the Vandoulakis and Petrakis paths had not crossed for several months, they were pleased to see each other. Alexandros, as head of the family, had a duty to speak.

'Giorgis and Maria. It will be a pleasure, once again, to welcome you into our family. My brother and his wife, Manoli's dear late parents, would have felt as we do that Maria will make our nephew very happy.'

The words came from his heart and Maria flushed with embarrassment and pleasure. Alexandros and Eleftheria were as aware as they had been with Anna that there was no dowry attached to this bride, no more than a trousseau of embroidery and lace to soften the harsh lines of their nephew's spartan home. They would not dwell on this, however, since there was more to be gained than lost from having Manoli settled down and attached to a local girl. The match would fulfil their promise to Manoli's father to ensure his son's well-being. When the boy had disappeared to Europe, Alexandros had felt a terrible sense of failure. Everything he had promised Yiannis had been unfulfilled. Most of the time during that period of his absence Alexandros had not even known if his nephew was dead or alive, and rarely which country he was in, but once Manoli was married to Maria he would be anchored to Elounda, and would always be there to support Andreas in the management of the great Vandoulakis estate.

The five of them drank to each other's health.

'*Iassas!*' they chorused as glasses clashed together.

There was soon talk of when the wedding might take place.

'Let's get married next week,' said Manoli.

'Don't be ridiculous!' retorted Eleftheria with alarm. 'You don't realise how much goes into the preparation of a good wedding! It'll take at least six months.'

Naturally Manoli was joking, but he continued to tease.

'Surely we could do it sooner than that. Let's go and see the priest. Come on, let's go now and see if he'll marry us today!'

Part of him meant it. He was now as impatient as a tiger, eager for his prey. His mind raced forwards. Maria, beautiful, pale and firm, her hair strewn across a pillow, a shaft of moonlight cutting across the bed to illuminate a perfect body. Waiting for him. Six whole months. My God, how could he possibly wait that long?

'We must do everything as your parents would have wanted,' said Alexandros. 'Properly!' he added, fully aware of Manoli's impetuous side.

Manoli shot him a glance. He knew that his uncle thought he needed a firm hand, and he, though he had great affection for Alexandros, loved to play up to his anxieties about him.

'Of course we'll do everything properly,' he said, now with genuine sincerity. 'We'll do everything by the book. I promise.'

As soon as she could, Maria rushed to tell Fotini the news.

'There's just one thing that worries me,' she said. 'My father.'

'But we'll be around to keep an eye on him, and so will my parents,' Fotini reassured her. 'Come on, Maria. It's time for you to marry. Your father understands that, I know he does.'

Maria tried not to feel uneasy, but her concern for Giorgis always seemed to stand between her and a sense of absolute joy.

Chapter Fourteen

THE ENGAGEMENT BETWEEN Manoli and Maria was cemented with a party to which the whole of Plaka was invited. It took place just a month after Manoli's proposal. Both of them felt as if they had been blessed by good fortune. So many of Maria's childhood friends had been married off by their fathers to men they did not love and with whom they were expected to develop some kind of affection as though they were cultivating geraniums in an urn. Matches were mostly made these days for the sake of convenience, so Maria was surprised and thankful to find herself marrying for love. She felt a certain gratitude to her sister for this, but the right moment and the right opportunity to express this never presented itself, since they rarely saw each other. To everyone's amazement and concern, she did not even appear at the engagement party. She sent her excuses with Andreas, who came to join in the celebrations with his parents.

Manoli loved the idea of marriage. He felt his life as a wandering libertine was well and truly over and now relished the prospect of being looked after and even, perhaps, of having children. In contrast to Maria, who thanked the God she spoke to in church each week, he attributed his luck to various gods, mostly Aphrodite, who had delivered this beautiful girl to him on a gilded platter. He would rather not have married at all than marry where there was no love and no beauty, and he was relieved to have found both in such equal measure.

The engagement party was in full swing and the village square teemed with merrymakers. Stephanos carried round huge trays of food and Maria and Manoli mingled with the crowd.

Manoli took his cousin to one side.

'Andreas,' he asked, almost shouting to be heard above the din of the band and the singing, 'would you agree to be our wedding sponsor?'

The wedding sponsor, the *koumbaros*, was a key figure in the marriage. In the ceremony itself his role was almost as significant as the priest's and, God willing, in due course he would become the godparent of the first child.

Andreas had expected the invitation. He would have been wounded if they had not asked him, so obvious a candidate was he. Manoli and he were more than brothers, closer than twins, and he was the perfect choice to be the person who would help bind these two in marriage, particularly with the added dimension of his already being Maria's brother-in-law. His expectation of being asked, however, did not diminish the pleasure.

'Nothing would delight me more, cousin! I'd be honoured,' he said.

Andreas felt strangely protective towards Manoli. He remembered well when his uncle had died and the period that followed when Manoli had been brought into their household. Andreas, always a steady and rather serious child, and Manoli, a wilder, less disciplined boy, could not have been more different. They had rarely squabbled as children, unlike most siblings, and there had never been any jealousy between them. Five years into their lives, they were each presented with a ready-made brother and playmate. Andreas benefited from the adventurous, less responsible influence of his cousin, and there was little doubt that Manoli needed the firm hand that his uncle and aunt could provide. Andreas, six months the older, naturally assumed the protective role, though Manoli had been the one to lead his older cousin astray, and to invite him to be bolder and more daring in their escapades around the estate as they grew into the years of early adolescence.

Maria received the first of many gifts for her trousseau, and the merrymaking continued into the small hours, after which the village became the quietest place on Crete. Even the dogs would be too tired to bark until the sun was well over the horizon.

When Andreas arrived home everyone was asleep. Alexandros and Eleftheria had returned before him and the house was eerily silent and dark. He crept into the bedroom and heard Anna stir.

'Hello, Anna,' he whispered quietly, in case she was still asleep.

The truth was that Anna had not had a wink of sleep that night. She had tossed and turned, crazed with anger at the thought of the merrymaking down in Plaka. She could picture her sister's beaming smile and Manoli's dark eyes fixed on her, his hands around her waist perhaps as they lapped up the compliments from all the well-wishers.

When Andreas switched on the bedside light she rolled over.

'Well,' she said. 'Was it fun?'

'It was a great celebration,' he answered, not looking at his wife as he undressed and so failing to take in the look on her tear-stained face. 'And Manoli has asked me to be *koumbaros*!'

The issuing of such an invitation had been inevitable but Anna had still not really braced herself for the blow. Andreas's role in the lives of Manoli and Maria would now be a significant one and would bind them all together, condemning her to an eternity of having her nose rubbed in her sister's happiness. In the shadows, her eyes pricked as she rolled over to bury her face in the pillow.

'Goodnight, Anna. Sleep tight.' Andreas climbed into bed. Within seconds the bed vibrated with his snores.

The crisp-aired March days passed quickly, spring arrived with an explosion of buds and blossom, and by summertime plans for the wedding were well under way. The date was set for October and the marriage would be toasted with the first wines from the season's crops. Maria and Manoli continued their weekly outings, still in the company of Fotini and Stephanos. A girl's virginity was an unspoken prerequisite of the marriage contract and the powers of temptation were well recognised; it was in everyone's interest that a girl should not be alone with her fiancé until the wedding night.

One May evening when the four of them were sitting over a drink in Agios Nikolaos, Maria noticed that Fotini looked slightly flushed. She could tell that her friend had something she wanted to say.

'What is it, Fotini? You look like the cat that's got the cream!'

'That's exactly how I feel . . . We're having a baby!' she blurted out.

'You're pregnant! That's such wonderful news,' said Maria, grasping her friend's hands. 'When's it due?'

'I think in about seven months – it's very early days.'

'That's only a few months after our wedding – I'll have to come back to Plaka to see you every other day,' Maria said, bubbling with enthusiasm.

They all toasted the good news. To both girls it seemed only moments since they had been making castles in the sand and, now, here they were discussing marriage and maternity.

Later that summer, concerned by the length of time that had elapsed since she had seen Anna, and rather bemused by her sister's complete lack of interest in her forthcoming nuptials, Maria decided that they should call on her. It had been one of August's hottest days, when even night-time brought little relief from the soaring temperatures, and rather than their customary outing to Agios Nikolaos with Fotini and Stephanos, Manoli and Maria would instead go alone to see Anna. It was a bold move. No invitation had been issued and no word received that the rather grand and elusive Anna wanted to see them. The message was clear to Maria. Why else would her sister be behaving in this way unless she was trying to express disapproval? Maria wanted to get to the bottom of it. Several letters she had written – one describing the engagement party that Anna had missed, supposedly because of illness, and another telling her about the beautiful lingerie she had been given for her trousseau – had gone unanswered. Anna had a telephone but Maria and Giorgis did not, and communication between them had ground to a halt.

As Manoli drove up the familiar road just beyond Elounda that led to the imposing Vandoulakis home, taking the bends as would any young man who had negotiated them a thousand times, Maria was nervous. Courage, she told herself. She's only your sister. She could not understand why she felt in such a needless state of anxiety about calling on someone who was such close flesh and blood.

When they drew up, Maria was the first to get out of the car. Manoli seemed slow, fiddling to get his key out of the ignition, and then combing his hair in the rear-view mirror. Maria stood waiting for him, impatient for this encounter. Her fiancé twisted the great round door handle – this was, after all, a sort of home from home for him – but it failed to budge, so he seized the knocker and banged hard three times. Eventually the door was opened. Not by Anna, but by Eleftheria.

She was surprised to see Manoli and Maria. It was rare that anyone should call unannounced, but everyone knew that Manoli was not the type to bother about etiquette, and she embraced him warmly.

'Come in, come in,' she fussed. 'It's so nice to see you. I wish I had known you were coming, then we could have had dinner together, but I'll get us something to eat and some drinks . . .'

'We've really come to see Anna,' said Manoli, interrupting.

'How is she? She's been rather out of touch – for months.'

'Has she? Oh, I see. I didn't realise. I'll go up and let her know you're here.' Eleftheria bustled out of the room.

From her bedroom window, Anna had seen the familiar car draw up. What should she do? She had managed to avoid such a confrontation for as long as she possibly could, believing that if only she could keep away from Manoli her feelings for him might gradually fade. Each day of the week, however, she saw him. She saw his reflection in her husband when he came in from the estate, and on the nights when Andreas made love to her, Manoli was easily conjured through half-closed eyes. The intensity of her passion for this vivacious version of her husband was as strong as it had been the day he had tucked a flower between her breasts, and the merest thought of him was enough to arouse her. She longed to see that sparkling smile which ignited her passion and sent shudders down her spine, but any such meeting would now be with Maria, and that would mean a reminder that Manoli could never be hers.

She had pretended to be in control. Until this evening. Now she was cornered. The two people she loved and loathed most in the world were downstairs waiting for her.

Eleftheria tapped gently on her door.

'Anna, your sister and her fiancé are here!' she called, without entering. 'Will you come and see them?'

Without ever having been taken into her confidence, Eleftheria had harboured her suspicions about Anna's feelings for Manoli. She had been the only person who had known quite how often he had called on her, and the only person who had known full well that Anna was not ill on the day of her sister's engagement party. Even now she could feel her daughter-in-law's reluctance to leave her bedroom. It could not possibly take that long to walk across the room. It was all beginning to make sense. She stood patiently for a few moments before knocking again, this time with more insistence. 'Anna? Are you coming?'

From behind the closed door, Anna delivered a sharp retort. '*Yes* I *am* coming. I'll be down when I'm ready.'

A few moments later, her vermilion lipstick freshly applied and her glossy hair shining like glass, Anna threw open her bedroom door and went downstairs. She took a deep breath and pushed open the door to the reception room. Looking every inch the *grande dame* of the house, even though Eleftheria was its real mistress, she swept across the room to greet her sister and pecked her politely on the cheek. Then she turned to Manoli, holding out a pale, limp hand to shake his.

'Hello,' she said, smiling. 'This is such a surprise. Such a nice surprise.'

Anna had always been able to act. And in so many ways it *was* nice to see this man, this obsession of hers, in the flesh; but it was also much more than that. She had thought of him each and every day for months and now here he was standing in front of her, even more rugged, more desirable than she had remembered. What seemed many minutes later to Anna but was only a second or two, she found she was still holding his hand. Hers was damp with sweat. She pulled away.

'I felt it had been such a long time since I saw you,' said Maria. 'Time is moving on so quickly and you know we are getting married in October, don't you?'

'Yes, yes, that's marvellous news. Truly marvellous.'

Eleftheria bustled in now with a tray of glasses and a row of little plates piled with olives, cubes of feta cheese, almonds and warm spinach pies. It was a miracle that she had produced such an array of *meze* in a matter of moments, but nevertheless she apologised for not being able to honour them with a more elaborate feast. She continued to bustle about as she removed an elaborate decanter of ouzo from the sideboard and poured everyone a drink.

They all took a seat. Anna perched on the edge of hers; Manoli sat back, comfortable, totally at ease. The room was filled with a warm orange light cast through the lace curtains by the setting sun and though conversation was stilted, Anna kept some sort of dialogue going. She knew it was her role in this situation.

'Tell me about Father. How is he?'

It was hard to tell whether Anna really cared, but it had certainly never occurred to Maria that she did not.

'He's fine. He's very pleased about our wedding. We asked him to come and live with us afterwards, but he is adamant about staying where he is in Plaka,' she said.

She had always made plenty of excuses for her sister's apparent lack of concern: her distance from Plaka, her new role as a wife, and other duties that Maria presumed she must have on an estate such as this. She knew now that similar changes were going to affect her. It would be a great help if Anna would begin to play more of a role with their father, and at least try to see him more often. She was about to broach the subject when there were voices in the hallway.

Alexandros and Andreas had returned from an inspection of their land up on the Lasithi plateau, and though the cousins saw each other regularly to discuss the affairs of the estate, they embraced now like long-lost friends. More drinks were poured and the two men of the house sat down.

Maria detected a tension but could not put her finger on the cause. Anna seemed perfectly happy making conversation, but she could not help noticing that most of her comments were directed at Manoli rather than her. Perhaps it was just the positions in which they were seated. Manoli was opposite Anna, while Andreas and Maria sat to one side on a long upholstered bench with Eleftheria between them.

Manoli had forgotten the strength of his attraction to Anna. There was something so gloriously coquettish about her, and he recalled those lunchtime trysts with something approaching nostalgia. Even though he was now an officially engaged man, the old rogue in Manoli still lurked close to the surface.

Eleftheria could see a difference in Anna. So often she could be sulky and monosyllabic, but tonight she was animated, her cheeks flushed, and even in this half-light she could see that there was a breadth to her smile. Her appreciation of everything that Manoli said was almost fawning.

As usual, Manoli dominated the conversation. Anna tried not to be infuriated when he kept referring to Maria as his 'beautiful fiancée', concluding that he was doing it deliberately to annoy her. He was still teasing her, she thought, still playing with her as he had done all those months ago, and making it obvious that he had not forgotten their flirtation. The way he was looking at her now, leaning forward to speak to her as though there was no one else in the room, made that quite plain. If only there *was* no one else in the room.

This hour she had spent in the company of Manoli was both heaven and hell.

It was mostly wedding talk. When the service was going to be, who was to be invited, and Andreas's role as *koumbaros*. It was almost dark by the time Maria and Manoli rose to go. Their eyes had adjusted to the gloaming, and only now did Eleftheria put on one of the dim table lamps so that they could make their way from the room without tripping on rugs or bumping into side tables.

'There is just one thing, Anna,' Maria said, determined not to leave without achieving her mission. 'Would you come and visit Father soon? I know you are busy, but I think he would really appreciate it.'

'Yes, yes, I will,' said Anna with unusual deference to her younger sister. 'I've been neglectful. Very naughty of me. I'll come down to Plaka in a few weeks' time. What about the third Wednesday in September? Would that be convenient?'

It was a casual, throwaway question, but somehow full of malice. Anna knew perfectly well that a Wednesday in September was the same for Maria as a Wednesday in April, June or August, or, for that matter, a Monday or a Tuesday. She was engaged in the same pattern of domestic activities for six days every week and, apart from Sundays, it didn't matter in the slightest when Anna came. Also, Maria had expected Anna to suggest something a little sooner. She was impeccable in her reply, however.

'That would be lovely. I shall tell Father,' she said. 'And I know he will look forward to it. He's usually back from Spinalonga by five o'clock with Dr Lapakis.'

Damn her for mentioning the island! thought Anna. She

felt they had all done well over the past five years to make sure that the full extent of their connection with the leper colony had not reached the ears of the Vandoulakis family. She knew too that it was now as much in Maria's interest to keep their past quiet as it was in hers. Why couldn't they all just forget about it? Everyone knew that Giorgis made his deliveries to Spinalonga and ferried the island's doctor. Wasn't that shameful enough, without it being constantly referred to?

There were final embraces and Manoli and Maria eventually drove away. Even if Anna had seemed edgy at times, Maria felt that perhaps the ice had begun to thaw. She always tried not to judge her sister, and to contain her criticisms, but she was not a saint.

'It's about time Anna came to Plaka,' she said to Manoli. 'If I'm leaving Father there on his own, she'll have to start visiting him a bit more often.'

'I'll be amazed if she does,' said Manoli. 'She's rather a law unto herself. And she certainly doesn't like it when things don't go her way.'

Such knowledge of Anna puzzled Maria. He spoke of her sister as someone he understood. Anna was not a complex person, but even so it surprised her that Manoli could make such an accurate observation.

Maria was now counting the days until her marriage. There were only four weeks to go. She wished they would pass more quickly, but the fact that she would be leaving her father still weighed heavily on her mind and she resolved to do everything she possibly could to ease the transition. The most practical step she could take would be to tidy up the house for when Giorgis would be there alone. She had put this task off during the summer months when the air both outside and inside shimmered in the soaring temperatures. It was much cooler now, the perfect day to do such a job.

It was also the day that Anna had promised to visit. There were still some of her possessions in the house and she might want to take them when she went home again. Some were her childhood toys. Perhaps Anna would need them soon, mused Maria. Surely there would be a baby in the Vandoulakis home before long.

A spring-clean in autumn-time. The small house was generally tidy – Maria always saw to that – but there was an old dresser stuffed with bowls and plates that were rarely used but could do with a wash, furniture that needed a polish, candlesticks that looked tarnished and many picture frames that she had not dusted for months.

As Maria worked, she listened to the radio, humming along to the music that crackled over the airwaves. It was three o'clock in the afternoon.

One of her favourite Mikis Theodorakis songs was on the radio. Its energetic bouzouki made an ideal accompaniment to cleaning, so she turned the volume up as high as it would go. The music drowned out the sound of the door being opened, and with her back turned, Maria did not see Anna slip in and take a seat.

Anna sat there for some ten minutes watching Maria work. She had no intention of helping her, got up as she was in a dress of finest white cotton embroidered with tiny blue flowers. What perverse satisfaction she derived from seeing her sister toil in this way, but how she could seem so happy and carefree, singing while she scrubbed shelves, made no real sense to Anna. When she thought of the man Maria was about to marry, however, she understood perfectly. Her sister must be the happiest woman in the world. How she hated that. She shifted in her seat, and Maria, suddenly hearing the scrape of wood on the stone floor, started.

'Anna!' she shrieked. 'How long have you been sitting there? Why didn't you tell me you were here?'

'I've been here for ages,' said Anna languidly. She knew it would annoy Maria to know that she had been watching her.

Maria climbed down from the chair and took off her apron.

'Shall I make us some lemonade?' she asked, instantly forgiving her sister's deception.

'Yes please,' Anna said. 'It's quite hot for September, isn't it?'

Maria busily halved a few lemons, squeezing them hard into a jug, and diluted the juice with water, vigorously stirring in sugar as she did so. They both drank two glasses before either of them spoke again.

'What are you doing?' asked Anna. 'Don't you ever stop working?'

'I'm getting the house ready for when Father is on his own here,' answered Maria. 'I've cleared out a few things you might need.' She indicated a small pile of toys: dolls, a flute, even a child's weaving loom.

'You might need those just as soon as me,' snapped Anna defensively. 'No doubt you and Manoli will be hoping to continue the Vandoulakis name once you're married.'

She could barely contain her jealousy of Maria and this single sentence carried all her resentment. Even she no longer relished her childlessness. The abandoned lemon skins which lay crushed and dry on the table in front of her were no less barren and bitter than she.

'Anna, what's the matter?' There was no avoiding such a question, even if it meant treading closer than Maria felt she ought. 'Something is wrong. You can tell me, you know.'

Anna had no intention of confiding in Maria. It was the last thing she planned to do. She had come to see her father, not to have a tête-à-tête with her sister.

'There's nothing the matter,' she snapped. 'Look, I might call on Savina and come back a bit later when Father returns.'

As Anna turned to leave, Maria noticed that her sister's back was damp, the fine fabric of her tightly fitting dress transparent with sweat. That there was something troubling her was as crystal clear as the water in a rock pool, but Maria realised that she was not going to find out. Perhaps Anna would confide in Savina and Maria could find out indirectly what the problem was. For so many years her older sister's emotions had been easy to read; they were like the posters that went up on every tree and building advertising the time and date of a concert. Nothing had been hidden. Now everything seemed so tightly wrapped up, so swaddled and secret.

Maria continued cleaning and polishing for an hour or so longer until Giorgis returned. Perhaps for the first time, she did not feel anguished about leaving him. He looked strong for a man of his age and she knew for sure that he would survive without her being there. Nowadays he did not seem too bowed down with the world's worries, and she knew the companionship of his friends in the village bar meant that lonely evenings were thankfully rare.

'Anna came by earlier,' she said chattily. 'She'll be returning quite soon.'

'Where has she gone then?' Giorgis asked.

'To see Savina, I think.'

At that moment Anna walked in. She embraced her father warmly and the two sat down to chat as Maria made drinks for them both. Their conversation skimmed all the surfaces. What had Anna been doing? Had she finished all the work on her two houses? How was Andreas? The questions Maria wanted to hear her father asking – Was Anna happy? Why did she so rarely come to Plaka? – went unasked. Not a word of Maria's forthcoming wedding was mentioned, not the slightest reference was made to it. The hour went quickly and then Anna rose to go. They said their farewells and Giorgis accepted an invitation to visit the Elounda house for Sunday lunch in just over a week's time.

After supper, when Giorgis had gone to the *kafenion*, Maria decided to do one last task. She kicked off her shoes to climb on to a rickety chair so that she could reach into the back of a tall cupboard and, as she stepped up, she noticed a strange mark on her foot. Her heart missed a beat. In some lights it might scarcely have been visible. It was like a shadow but in reverse, a patch of dry skin that was slightly paler than the rest. It almost looked as though she had burned her foot in the sun and the skin had peeled off to leave the lighter pigment underneath. Perhaps it was nothing at all to worry about, but she felt sick with anxiety. Maria usually bathed at night, and in the dim light such a thing could have gone unnoticed for months. She would confide in Fotini later, but she did not plan to worry her father about it yet. They all had quite enough to think about at the moment.

That night was the most troubled Maria had ever endured. She lay awake almost until dawn. She could not know for certain and yet she entertained little doubt about this patch. The hours of darkness passed with aching slowness as she tossed and turned and fretted with fear. When she finally fell into a brief and fitful sleep, she dreamt of her mother and of huge stormy seas which wrecked Spinalonga as though it was a great ship. It was a relief when day broke. She would go and see Fotini early. Her friend was always up by six o'clock, tidying away dishes from the night before and preparing food for the following one. It seemed she worked harder than anyone in the village, which was especially tough on her given that she was now in the third trimester of her pregnancy.

'Maria! What are you doing here so early?' Fotini exclaimed. She could see that there was something on her friend's mind. 'Let's have some coffee.'

She stopped working and they sat down together at the big table in the kitchen.

'What *is* the matter?' asked Fotini. 'You look as though you haven't had a wink of sleep. Are you getting nervous about the wedding or something?'

Maria looked up at Fotini, the shadows under her eyes as dark as her untouched coffee. Her eyes welled with tears.

'Maria, what is it?' Fotini reached out and covered her friend's hand with her own. 'You must tell me.'

'It's this,' said Maria. She stood up and put her foot on the chair, pointing to the faded patch of dry skin. 'Can you see it?'

Fotini leaned over. She now understood why her friend had looked so anxious this morning. From the leaflets regularly distributed in Plaka, everyone round here was familiar with the first visible symptoms of leprosy, and this looked very like one of them.

'What do I do?' Maria said quietly, tears now pouring down her cheeks. 'I don't know what to do.'

Fotini was calm.

'For a start, you mustn't let anyone round here know about this. It could be nothing and you don't want people jumping to conclusions, especially the Vandoulakis family. You need to get a proper diagnosis. Your father brings that doctor home from the island nearly every day, doesn't he? Why don't you ask him to have a look?'

'Dr Lapakis is a good friend of Father's, but he's almost too close and someone might get to hear of it. There was another doctor. He used to come over before the war. I can't even remember his name but I think he worked in Iraklion. Father would know.'

'Why don't you try and see him then? You've plenty of excuses for going to Iraklion with your wedding round the corner.'

'But it means telling my father,' Maria sobbed. She tried to wipe the tears from her face, but still they flowed. There was no avoiding this. Even if it could be kept secret from everyone else, Giorgis would *have* to know, and he was the one Maria would most have liked to protect.

Maria returned home. It was only eight o'clock but Giorgis was already out, and she knew she would have to wait until the evening to speak to him. She would distract herself by continuing with the work she had begun the day before, and she threw herself into it with renewed vigour and energy, polishing furniture until it gleamed and picking the dust with her fingernail from the darkest corners of every cupboard and drawer.

At around eleven o'clock there was a knock at the door. It was Anna. Maria had already been awake for seven hours. She was exhausted.

'Hello, Anna,' she said quietly. 'Here again so soon?'

'I left something behind,' Anna answered. 'My bag. It must have got tucked down behind the cushion.'

She crossed the room and there, sure enough, concealed beneath a cushion, was a small bag in the same fabric as the dress she had been wearing the day before.

'There, I knew it would be there.'

Maria needed a rest.

'Would you like a cold drink?' she asked from her elevated position on a stool.

Anna stood looking at her, transfixed. Maria shifted uncomfortably and climbed down from the stool. Her sister's eyes followed her but they were trained on her bare feet. She had noticed the sinister mark and it was too late for Maria to conceal it.

'What's that patch on your foot?' she demanded.

'I don't know,' said Maria defensively. 'Probably nothing.'

'Come on, let me see it!' said Anna.

Maria was not going to fight with her sister, who now bent down to have a closer look at her foot.

'I think it's nothing, but I am going to have it checked,' she said firmly, standing her ground.

'Have you told Father about it? And has Manoli seen it?' Anna asked.

'Neither of them knows about it yet,' answered Maria.

'Well, when are they going to know? Because if you're not going to tell them, then I'm going to. It looks like leprosy to me,' Anna said. She knew as well as Maria what a diagnosis of leprosy would mean.

'Look,' said Maria, 'I shall tell Father tonight. But no one else is to know. It may be nothing.'

'You're getting married in less than a month, so don't leave it too long to find out. As soon as you know the truth, you're to come and let me know.'

Anna's tone was distinctly bullying, and the thought even crossed Maria's mind that she was relishing the thought of her sister being leprous.

'If I haven't heard from you within a fortnight or so, I'll be back.'

With that, she was gone. The door banged shut behind her. Apart from Maria's pounding heart, a faint whiff of French perfume was the only evidence that Anna had ever been there.

That night, Maria showed Giorgis her foot.

'It's Dr Kyritsis we ought to go and see,' he said. 'He works at the big hospital in Iraklion. I'll write to him straight away.

He said little more than that, but his stomach churned with fear.

Chapter Fifteen

WITHIN A WEEK of writing, Giorgis had received a reply from Doctor Kyritsis.

Dear Kyrie Petrakis,

Thank you so much for writing to me. I am sorry to hear of your concern about your daughter and would be very pleased to see you both for an appointment. I shall expect you on Monday 17th September at midday.

I would also like to express my sorrow that your lovely wife Eleni passed away. I know it was some years ago, but I only recently heard the sad news from Dr Lapakis, with whom I am once again in contact.

With kind regards.
Yours sincerely,
Nikolaos Kyritsis

The appointment was only a few days away, which was a relief to both father and daughter as they were both, by now, thinking of little else other than the mark on Maria's foot.

After breakfast on that Monday morning, they set off on

the three-hour trip to Iraklion. No one thought it strange that the two of them should be going on such a long journey together and assumed it was on some kind of business connected to the forthcoming wedding. Brides-to-be had to buy gowns and all sorts of other finery, and what smarter place to go than Iraklion? chattered the women on their doorsteps that evening.

It was a long and often windswept journey along the coast, and as they approached the city, and the mighty Venetian harbour came into view, Maria wished more than anything that they had no cause to be here. In her entire life she had not seen such dust and chaos, and the noise of trucks and construction work deafened her. Giorgis had not visited the city since the war, and apart from the hefty city walls, which had stubbornly withstood German bombardment, most of it had changed beyond recognition. They drove around in a state of confusion, catching glimpses of spacious squares with fountains playing in their centre, only to pass the same point some time later and realise to their irritation that they had been going round in circles. Eventually they spotted the newly built hospital and Giorgis pulled up outside.

It was ten minutes before midday, and by the time they had negotiated the labyrinthine corridors of the hospital and found Dr Kyritsis's department, they were late for their appointment. Giorgis, particularly, was flustered.

'I wish we had allowed more time,' he fretted.

'Don't worry, I'm sure he will understand. It's not our fault that this city has been turned into a maze – or that they've built this hospital like one as well,' said Maria.

A nurse was there to greet them and took some details as

they sat in the stifling corridor. Dr Kyritsis would be with them shortly. The two of them sat in silence, breathing in the unfamiliar antiseptic smells that characterised the hospital. They had little conversation to make but there was plenty to watch as nurses bustled about in the corridor and the occasional patient was wheeled by. Eventually the nurse came to escort them into the office.

If the war had transformed the face of Iraklion, it had left an even greater mark on Dr Kyritsis. Though his slim figure was unchanged, the thick black hair had turned silver-grey and the previously unlined face now bore clear signs of age and overwork. He looked every one of his forty-two years.

'Kyrie Petrakis,' he said, stepping from behind his desk and taking Giorgis's hand.

'This is my daughter Maria,' said Giorgis.

'Despineda Petrakis. It's over ten years since I saw you but I do remember you as a child,' said Dr Kyritsis, shaking her hand. 'Please, do sit down and tell me why you have come.'

Maria began, nervously at first, to describe her symptoms.

'Two weeks ago, I noticed a pale mark on my left foot. It's slightly dry and a little numb. With my mother's history I couldn't ignore it, so that's why we are here.'

'And is it just this one area? Or are there others?'

Maria looked across at her father. Since the discovery of the first mark, she had found several others. No one ever saw her undressed, and she had had huge difficulty craning her neck to examine her own back in a small bedroom mirror, but even in the dim light she had made out several other blemishes. The patch on her foot was no longer the only one.

'No,' she replied. 'There are some others.'

'I will need to examine them, and if I think it necessary we will have to take some skin smears.'

Dr Kyritsis got up and Maria followed him into his surgery, leaving Giorgis alone in the office to contemplate the anatomical drawings that lined the walls. First of all Kyritsis examined the lesion on her foot and afterwards those on her back. He then tested them for sensitivity, first using a feather and then a pin. There was no doubt in his mind that there was some impairment to nerve endings, but whether it was leprosy he was not one hundred per cent certain. He made detailed notes and then sketched on an outline of the body where the patches had been found.

'I am sorry, Despineda Petrakis, I will have to take some smears here. It won't take long, but I am afraid it will leave your skin a little sore afterwards.'

Maria sat in silence as Kyritsis and a nurse prepared slides and gathered the required instruments. Only a month ago she had been showing off the latest items from her trousseau to her friends, some silk stockings which floated across their hands, lighter than air, as transparent as dragonfly wings. She had tried them on and they slipped over her skin, so gossamer fine it was as though her slim legs were still naked; the dark seam that traced the back of her leg was the only clue to their existence. She had then tried on the shoes she was to wear on her wedding day, and now the same foot that had slipped into that delicate shoe was to be cut open.

'Despineda Petrakis, I need you to lie on the couch, please.' Dr Kyritsis's words broke into her reverie.

The scalpel was razor sharp. It penetrated her skin by no more than two millimetres but in her mind the incision was magnified. It felt as though she was being sliced apart like meat as the doctor gathered enough tissue pulp from below the surface of the skin to put on the slide and examine under a microscope. She winced and her eyes watered with pain and fear. Kyritsis then took a smear from her back, and the nurse quickly applied some antiseptic ointment and cotton wool.

Once the bleeding had stopped, Maria was helped from the couch by the nurse and they returned to Dr Kyritsis's office.

'Well,' said the doctor. 'I will have the results of those smears within a few days. I shall be examining them for the presence of the Hansen bacillus, which is the only definitive proof of the presence of leprosy. I can write to you or, if you prefer, you can come and see me again and I can tell you in person. Personally, I think it's better for all parties if a diagnosis can be given face-to-face.'

In spite of the long journey involved, both father and daughter knew that they did not want to receive such news by post.

'We'll come to see you,' said Giorgis on behalf of them both.

Before they left the hospital, another appointment was made. Dr Kyritsis would expect them at the same time the following week. His professionalism was absolute and he had given no hint of what he expected the result to be. He certainly did not want to worry them unnecessarily, nor did he wish to give them false hope, and his manner was therefore neutral, almost indifferent.

It was the longest week of Maria's life. Only Fotini knew

that her friend was living on the edge of a precipice. She tried to occupy herself with as many practical tasks as possible, but nothing was enough to distract her from what might happen the following Monday.

The Friday before they were due to return to Iraklion, Anna called on her. She was eager to know: had Maria been to have tests? What were the results? Why did she not know? When were they going to hear? There was no implied sympathy or concern in her questions. Maria answered her sister in monosyllables and eventually Anna went on her way.

As soon as her sister was out of sight, Maria rushed off to see Fotini. She had been disturbed by the almost vindictive note of enthusiasm she had detected in Anna's reaction to the situation.

'I suppose she's eager for information because it could affect her one way or the other,' said Fotini holding her friend's hand tightly. 'But we mustn't dwell on that. We must be optimistic, Maria.'

For a few days Maria had hidden herself away. She had sent a message to Manoli that she was unwell and would not be able to see him until the following week. Fortunately, he did not question it, and when he saw Giorgis at the bar in Plaka, his future father-in-law supported her story and assured Manoli that his daughter would be better before long. Not being able to see Manoli made Maria miserable. She missed his gaiety and felt leaden with misery at the prospect that their wedding might now be in jeopardy.

Monday arrived, eventually. Maria and Giorgis repeated the journey to Iraklion, but this time found the hospital more easily and were soon sitting outside Kyritsis's office once again.

It was his turn to be late. The nurse came out to see them and apologised for the delay. Dr Kyritsis had been detained but would be with them within half an hour, she said. Maria was nearly beside herself. So far she had managed to contain her anxiety, but the thirty minutes she now had to wait took her beyond the limits of endurance, and she paced up and down the corridor to try and calm herself.

Eventually the doctor arrived, profusely apologetic that he had made them wait, and ushered them straight into his office. His entire demeanour seemed so different from the last visit. Maria's file was on his desk and he opened it and shut it again, as though there was something he needed to check. There was not, of course. He knew exactly what he had to say and there was no reason to keep these people waiting any longer. He came straight to the point.

'Despineda Petrakis, I am afraid that there are bacteria in your skin lesions to indicate that leprosy is present in your body. I am sorry it's bad news.'

He was not sure for whom the news was more devastating, the daughter or the father. The girl was the spitting image of her late mother, and he was keenly aware of this cruel repetition of history. He hated these moments. Of course there were emollient phrases that he could use to soften the blow, such as: 'It's not too advanced so we may be able to help you', or 'I think we've caught it early'. The announcement of bad news, however it was delivered, was still just that: bad news, catastrophic and cruel.

The pair sat in silence, their worst fears realised. In their minds they both pictured Spinalonga, knowing for certain now that this was to be Maria's final destination, her destiny.

Although she had initially made herself ill with worry, over the past few days Maria had tried to persuade herself that all would be well. To imagine the worst would have been unbearable.

Kyritsis knew that he must fill the gaping silence that had opened up in the room, and while the terrible news sank in, he gave them some reassurance.

'This is very hard news for you and I am terribly sorry to deliver it. You must be reassured, however, that great advances have been made in the study of leprosy. When your wife was ill, Kyrie Petrakis, the only methods of relief and treatment were still, in my view, extremely primitive. There has been good progress in the past few years and I very much hope you will benefit from it, Despineda Petrakis.'

Maria stared at the floor. She could hear the doctor speaking but he sounded as though he was a very long distance away. It was only when she heard her name that she looked up.

'In my opinion,' he was saying, 'it could be eight or ten years before your condition develops. Your leprosy type is, at present, neural, and if you remain in otherwise good health it should not progress to the lepromatous type.'

What is he saying? thought Maria. That I am effectively condemned to death but that it will take me a long time to die?

'So,' her voice was almost a whisper, 'what happens next?'

For the first time since she had entered the room, Maria looked directly at Kyritsis. She could see from his steady gaze that he was unafraid of the truth, and that whatever needed to be told, he would not fail to tell her. For her father's sake, if not her own, she must be brave. She must not cry.

'I shall write a letter to Dr Lapakis to explain the situation, and within the next week or so you will have to join the colony on Spinalonga. It probably goes without saying, but I would advise you to say as little as possible to anyone, except those who are closest to you. People still have very out-of-date ideas about leprosy and think you can catch it just by being in the same room as a victim.'

At this point Giorgis spoke up.

'We know,' he said. 'You can't live opposite Spinalonga for long without knowing what most people think of lepers.'

'Their prejudices are completely without scientific basis,' Kyritsis reassured him. 'Your daughter could have caught leprosy anywhere and at any time – but most people are too ignorant to know that, I'm afraid.'

'I think we should go now,' Giorgis said to Maria. 'The doctor has told us what we need to know.'

'Yes, thank you.' Maria was now completely composed. She knew what she had to do and where she would be spending the rest of her life. Not with Manoli near Elounda, but alone on Spinalonga. For a moment she had an urge to get on with it all. During the last week she had been in limbo, but now she knew what was to happen. It was all so certain.

Kyritsis opened the door for them.

'Just one final thing,' he said. 'I have been in regular correspondence with Dr Lapakis and I shall be resuming my visits to Spinalonga at some time in the future. I will, therefore, be involved with your treatment.'

They both listened to his words of comfort. It was kind of him to be so solicitous, but it did not help.

Maria and Giorgis emerged from the hospital into the bright mid-afternoon sun. All around them people went about their business, oblivious to the grief of the two individuals who stood there. The lives of all those going to and fro were the same now as they had been when they got up that morning. This was just another ordinary day. How Maria envied them the trivial tasks of their routine that in a few days would be lost to her. In the space of an hour, her life and her father's had changed totally. They had arrived at the hospital with a scrap of hope and had left it with none at all.

Silence seemed the easiest place to hide. For a while at least. An hour or so into the journey, however, Maria spoke.

'Who do we tell first?'

'We have to tell Manoli, and then Anna and then the Vandoulakis family. After that there will be no need to tell anyone. They will all know.'

They talked about what needed to be done before Maria left. There was little. With her wedding imminent, everything was already prepared for her departure.

When they arrived back in Plaka, Anna's car was parked outside their house. She was the last person in the world Maria wanted to see. She would much rather have sought comfort from Fotini. Anna, however, still had a key and had let herself into the house. It was almost dark by now and she had been sitting in the twilight waiting for their return. There was no mistaking that their news was bad. Their downcast faces as they walked through the door said it all, but Anna, insensitive as ever, shattered their silence.

'Well?' she said. 'What was the result?'

'The result was positive.'

Anna was momentarily confused. Positive? That sounded good, so why the glum faces? She was in a quandary, and realised that she hardly knew herself what the best result would be. If her sister did *not* have leprosy she would marry Manoli. For Anna that would be an unwelcome outcome. If Maria *did* have leprosy, it would immediately affect Anna's status in the Vandoulakis family. They would inevitably discover that Maria was not the first Petrakis to inhabit the island of Spinalonga. Neither was a desirable outcome, but she could not decide which was the lesser of the two evils.

'Which means what?' Anna found herself asking.

'I have leprosy,' her sister replied.

The words were stark. Even Anna now let the silence linger. All three of them standing in this room knew exactly what this meant, and there was no need for questions.

'I will go and see Manoli tonight,' said Giorgis decisively. 'And Alexandros and Eleftheria Vandoulakis tomorrow. They all need to know as soon as possible.'

With that he left. His daughters sat on together for a while, though they had little to say to each other. Anna would see her parents-in-law later that evening and fretted over whether she should say anything to them before Giorgis had the opportunity. Would it soften the blow if she told them the news herself?

Although it was now late, Giorgis knew Manoli would be at the bar in the village. He strode in and spoke directly, bluntly even.

'I need to talk to you, Manoli. Alone,' he said.

They withdrew to a table in the corner of the bar, out of earshot of everyone else.

'I have bad news, I'm afraid. Maria will not be able to marry you.'

'What's happened? Why not? Tell me!' There was sheer disbelief in Manoli's voice. He knew Maria had not been well for a few days, but had assumed it was something minor. 'You have to tell me what's wrong!'

'She has leprosy.'

'Leprosy!' he roared.

The word thundered round the room, silencing everyone in it. It was a word that most here were used to, though, and within a few minutes conversations around the room had resumed.

'Leprosy,' he repeated, more quietly this time.

'Yes, leprosy. The day after tomorrow I will be taking her to Spinalonga.'

'How did she get it?' Manoli asked, immediately worried for his own health.

What should Giorgis tell him? It could take many years before the symptoms of leprosy made themselves evident, and it was very possible that Maria had been infected by her mother all that time ago. He thought of Anna and the implications this might have for her. The chances of her having leprosy as well were infinitesimally small, but he knew that the Vandoulakis family might need some persuasion of that.

'I don't know. But it's unlikely that anyone will have caught it from her,' he answered.

'I don't know what to say. It's such terrible news.'

Manoli moved his chair away from Giorgis. It was an unconscious gesture, but one full of meaning. This was not a man who was about to give comfort, nor one who needed any himself. Giorgis looked at him and was surprised by what he saw. It was not the crumpled figure of a broken-hearted man just given the news that he could not marry the woman of his dreams. Manoli was shocked, but by no means destroyed.

He felt very sad for Maria, but it was not the end of his world. Though he had loved her, he had also passionately loved a dozen other women in his life, and he was realistic. His affections would sooner or later find another object; Maria had not been his one and only true love. He did not believe in such an idea. In his experience, love was a commodity, and if you were born with it in ample supply, there was always plenty left for the next woman. Poor Maria. Leprosy, as far as Manoli knew, was the most terrible fate for any human being but, in heaven's name, he might have caught the same disease if she had discovered it any later. God forbid.

The two men talked for a while before Giorgis took his leave. He had to be up very early to call on Alexandros and Eleftheria. When he arrived at the Vandoulakis house the following morning the four of them were already waiting for him. A nervous-looking maid led Giorgis in to the gloomy drawing room where Alexandros, Eleftheria, Andreas and Anna all sat like wax-works, cold, silent, staring.

Knowing that it was only a matter of time before the truth of her family history came out, Anna had confessed to Andreas that her mother had died on Spinalonga. She calculated that her honesty might appear to be a virtue in this situation. She was to be disappointed. Even though Alexandros Vandoulakis was an intelligent man, his views on leprosy were no different from those of an ignorant peasant. In spite of Anna's protestations that leprosy could only be transmitted through close human contact, and that even then the chances of catching it were small, he seemed to believe the age-old myth that the disease was hereditary and that its presence in a family was a curse. Nothing would deter him from this.

'Why did you keep Maria's leprosy secret until the eleventh hour?' he demanded, incandescent with rage. 'You have brought shame upon our family!'

Eleftheria tried to restrain her husband, but he was determined to continue.

'For the sake of our dignity and the Vandoulakis name, we will keep Anna within our family, though we shall never forgive the way you have deceived us. Not just one leper in your family, but two, we now discover. Only one thing could have made this situation more serious and that is if our nephew Manoli had already married your daughter. From now on we would be happy if you would keep your distance from our home. Anna will visit you in Plaka, but you are no longer welcome here, Giorgis.'

There was not one word of concern for Maria, not a moment's thought for her plight. The Vandoulakis family had closed ranks, and even the kindly Eleftheria sat silently now, afraid that her husband would turn his wrath on her if she spoke in defence of the Petrakis family. It was time for Giorgis to go, and he left his daughter's home for the last time, in silence. On the drive back to Plaka, his chest heaved with sobs as he lamented the final fragmentation of his family. It was now as good as destroyed.

Chapter Sixteen

WHEN GIORGIS ARRIVED home, he found that Fotini was already there helping Maria. They both looked up from their conversation as he walked in, and knew without asking that the encounter with the Vandoulakis family had been difficult. Giorgis looked even more pale and battered than they had expected.

'Have they no pity?' Maria cried out, leaping up to comfort her father.

'Try not to be angry with them, Maria. In their position they have a lot to lose.'

'Yes, but what did they say?'

'They said that they were sorry that the marriage is not to take place.'

In its way, what Giorgis said was true. It just missed a great deal out. What was the point of telling Maria that they never wanted to see him again, that they would deign to keep Anna within the family but as far as they were concerned her father was no longer part of it? Even Giorgis understood the importance of dignity and good name, and if Alexandros Vandoulakis felt that the Petrakis family was in danger of besmirching his, what option did he have?

Giorgis's neutral words almost matched Maria's state of mind. There had been a dreamlike quality to the past few days, as though these events were not really happening to her but to someone else. Her father described to her Manoli's reaction to the news and she had no trouble reading between the lines: he was sad, but not demented with grief.

Giorgis left the two women to get on with their preparations for Maria's departure, though there was little to do. It was only a few weeks ago that she had been preparing her trousseau, so boxes already stood in the corner of the room packed with her possessions. She had been careful not to take anything that Giorgis might need himself, but she had anticipated that the place where Manoli lived lacked much of what made a house a home, and there were many items of a domestic kind carefully stowed into the boxes: bowls, wooden spoons, her scales, scissors and an iron.

What she had to decide now was what to remove from the boxes. It seemed unfair to take the things that people had given her when she was going to a leper colony rather than her marital home in an olive grove, and what use on Spinalonga were those presents of nightwear and lingerie that had been given to her for her trousseau? As she lifted them out, all these frivolous luxury items seemed to belong to another life, as did the embroidered cloths and pillowcases that she had spent so long working on. As she held these in her lap, Maria's tears dripped on to the finely stitched linen. All those months of excitement had come to an end, and the cruelty of the turnaround stung her.

'Why don't you take them?' said Fotini, putting her arm

around her friend. 'There's no reason why you shouldn't have fine things on Spinalonga.'

'You're right, I suppose; they might make life more bearable.' She repacked them and shut the box. 'So what else do you think I should take?' she asked bravely, as though she was getting ready to go on a long and agreeable journey.

'Well, your father will be delivering several times a week, so we can always send you anything you need. But why not take some of your herbs? It's unlikely they all grow on the island and there's bound to be someone there who would benefit from them.'

They spent the day going over what Maria might need on the island. It was an effective distraction from the impending catastrophe of her departure. Fotini kept up a gentle flow of conversation that lasted until it was dark. Neither of them had left the house all day, but now the moment came for Fotini to depart. She would be needed at the taverna, and besides, she felt that Maria and her father should be alone that evening.

'I'm not going to say goodbye,' she said. 'Not just because it hurts, but because it isn't goodbye. I shall be seeing you again, next week and the week after.'

'How come?' asked Maria, looking at her friend with alarm. For a fleeting moment she wondered whether Fotini was also leprous. That could not be, she thought.

'I'll be coming with your father to do the occasional delivery,' Fotini said matter-of-factly.

'But what about the baby?'

'The baby isn't due until December, and anyway Stephanos can take care of it while I come across and see you.'

'It would be wonderful to think that you might come and see me,' said Maria, feeling a sudden surge of courage. There were so many people on the island who had not seen a relative for years. She at least would have a regular chance to see her father, and now her best friend too.

'So that's that. No goodbyes,' said Fotini with bravado. 'Just a "see you next week then".' She did not embrace her friend for even she worried about such proximity, especially with her unborn child. No one, not even Fotini, could quite put to one side the fear that leprosy could be spread by even the most superficial human contact.

Once Fotini had gone, Maria was alone for the first time in several days. She spent the next few hours rereading her mother's letters, from time to time glancing out of the window and catching sight of Spinalonga. The island was waiting for her. Soon all her questions about what it was like on the leper colony would be answered. Not long now, not long. Her reverie was disturbed by a sharp knock on the door. She was not expecting anyone, and certainly no one who would knock quite so forcefully.

It was Manoli.

'Maria,' he said breathlessly, as though he had been running. 'I just wanted to say goodbye. I'm terribly sorry it's all had to end like this.'

He did not hold out his hands or embrace her. Not that she would have expected either. What she would have hoped for was a greater sense of sorrow. His demeanour confirmed to Maria what she had half suspected, that Manoli's great passion would soon find another recipient. Her throat tightened. She felt as though she had swallowed broken glass and was no more able to speak than cry. His eyes would not meet hers. 'Goodbye, Maria,' he mumbled. 'Goodbye.' Within moments he had gone and once again the door was closed. Maria felt as hollow as the silence that once again filled the house.

Giorgis was yet to return. He had spent the last day of his daughter's freedom engaged in normal humdrum activities, mending his nets, cleaning his boat and ferrying Dr Lapakis. It was on his return journey with the doctor that he told him the news. He said it so casually that Lapakis did not, at first, take it in.

'I will be bringing my daughter over to Spinalonga tomorrow,' Giorgis said. 'As a patient.'

It was perfectly usual for Maria to accompany her father on the occasional delivery, so Lapakis did not react at first, and the last few words were lost in the wind.

'We went to see Dr Kyritsis,' Giorgis added. 'He will be writing to you.'

'Why?' asked Lapakis, taking more notice now.

'My daughter has leprosy.'

Lapakis, though he tried to conceal it, was aghast.

'Your daughter has leprosy? Maria? My God! I didn't realise . . . That's why you are bringing her to Spinalonga tomorrow.'

Giorgis nodded, concentrating now on guiding the boat into Plaka's small harbour. Lapakis stepped out of the boat. He had met the lovely Maria so many times and was shocked by the news. He felt he had to say something.

'She will receive the best possible care on Spinalonga,' he said. 'You are one of the few people who knows what the place is really like. It's not as bad as people think, but still, I am so terribly sorry that this has happened.'

'Thank you,' said Giorgis, and tied the boat up. 'I will see you tomorrow morning, but I might be a little late. I have promised to take Maria over very early but I'll do my best to be back for you at the usual time.'

The elderly fisherman sounded preternaturally calm, as normal as if he was making arrangements for any other day. This was how people conducted themselves in the first few days of bereavement, thought Lapakis. Perhaps it was just as well.

Maria had made supper for her father and herself, and at about seven in the evening they sat down opposite each other. It was the ritual of the meal that mattered tonight, not the eating, since neither of them had any appetite. This was to be their last supper. What did they talk about? They spoke of trivial things, such as what Maria had packed in her boxes, as well as more important ones like when she would next see her father on the island and how often Savina would expect him for supper at the Angelopoulos house each week. Anyone eavesdropping would have thought that Maria was simply moving out to live in another house. At nine in the evening, both exhausted, they retired to bed.

By six-thirty the following morning, Giorgis had carried all of Maria's boxes down to the quayside and loaded them on to his boat. He returned to the house to collect her. Still vivid in his mind, as though it had happened only yesterday, was Eleni's departure. He remembered that May day when the sun had shone on the crowd of friends and school children as his wife had waved goodbye to them. This morning there was deadly silence in the village. Maria would simply disappear.

A cold wind whipped through the narrow streets of Plaka and the chill of the autumnal air encircled Maria, paralysing her body and mind with a numbness that almost blocked her senses but could do nothing to alleviate her grief. As she stumbled the last few metres to the jetty she leaned heavily on her father, her gait that of an old crone for whom every step brought a stab of pain. But her pain was not physical. Her body was as strong as any young woman who had spent her life breathing the pure Cretan air, and her skin was as youthful and her eyes as intensely brown and bright as those of any girl on this island.

The little boat, unstable with its cargo of oddly shaped bundles lashed together with string, bobbed and lurched on the sea. Giorgis lowered himself in slowly, and with one hand trying to hold the craft steady reached out with the other to help his daughter. Once she was safely on board he wrapped her protectively in a blanket to shield her from the elements. The only visible indication then that she was not simply another piece of cargo were the long strands of dark hair that flew and danced freely in the wind. He carefully released his vessel from its mooring – there was nothing more to be said or done – and their journey began. This was not the start of a short trip to deliver supplies. It was the beginning of Maria's one-way journey to start a new life. Life on Spinalonga.

Chapter Seventeen

AT THE MOMENT when Maria wanted time to stand still it seemed to move faster than ever, and soon she would be dumped in a cold place where the waves broke on the shore. For once she had willed the boat's engine to stall, but the gulf between mainland and island was covered in moments and there was no turning back. She wanted to cling to her father, plead with him not to leave her stranded here, alone apart from two crates into which her life was now packed. But her tears had been spent. She had saturated Fotini's shoulder many times since her initial discovery of the mark on her foot, and her pillow was limp from the tears she had shed over the past two unhappy nights. Now was not the time for weeping.

For a few minutes they stood there alone. Giorgis was not going to leave her until someone came. He was now as familiar with the routine for new arrivals on the island as the islanders themselves, and knew that in due course they would be met.

'Maria, be brave,' said Giorgis quietly. 'I'll be back tomorrow. Come and see me if you can.'

He held both her hands in his. He was bold these days, and particularly so with his daughter. To hell with it if he got leprosy. Perhaps that would be the kindest solution because he could then come and live with Maria. The real problem if that happened would be the deliveries to Spinalonga. They would be hard pushed to find anyone else to make them, and that would cause untold hardship and misery on the island.

'Of course I'll come if it's allowed,' she answered.

'I'm sure it will be. Look,' said Giorgis, pointing to the figure emerging through the long tunnel which passed through the old fortress wall. 'Here is Nikos Papadimitriou, the island leader. I sent him a note yesterday to say I'd be bringing you today. He's the man to ask.'

'Welcome to Spinalonga,' Papadimitriou said, addressing Maria. How he could have such levity in his tone baffled her, but it distracted her for a moment. 'Your father sent me a note yesterday telling me to expect your arrival. Your boxes will be carried to your home shortly. Shall we go?'

He indicated that she should follow him up the few steps into the tunnel. Only a few weeks earlier, in Agios Nikolaos, she had been watching a Hollywood film where the heroine had swept up in a limousine and was led along a red carpet into a grand hotel while a porter dealt with her luggage. Maria tried to imagine herself in that very scene.

'Before we go,' she said hastily, 'can I ask permission to come and see my father when he brings Dr Lapakis and does his deliveries?'

'Why, certainly!' boomed Papadimitriou. 'I assumed that would be the arrangement. I know you won't try to escape. At one time we had to prevent people coming through to the quayside in case they tried to get away, but nowadays most people don't want to get off the island.'

Giorgis wanted to put the moment of parting behind him.

'I know they'll be kind to you,' were the words of reassurance he heard himself saying to her. 'I know they'll be kind.'

One or other of them had to turn away first, and Giorgis waited for his daughter to make that move. He had always regretted his hasty departure when Eleni arrived on the island fourteen years ago. So great had been his grief that he had set off in his boat before they had even said goodbye, but today he must have more courage, for his daughter's sake. Giorgis knew so much about the island now, whereas all those years ago his visits there had been just a job, a functional trip once or twice a week to drop boxes off on the quayside and then make a hasty retreat. In the intervening years his view of it all had been given a human dimension, and he had followed developments on the island as no other man outside it ever had.

Nikos Papadimitriou had been island leader ever since the election in 1940 when Petros Kontomaris had finally stood down, and he had now held the position for even longer than his predecessor. He had achieved great things on Spinalonga and the island had gone from strength to strength, so few were surprised when he was re-elected by an almost unanimous vote each spring. Maria recalled the day her father had transported the Athenians to Spinalonga. It had been one of the most dramatic episodes of that era, in a life rarely punctuated by much excitement. Her mother had written a great deal about the handsome, dark-haired island leader and all he did to change the island. Now his hair was grey, but he still had the same curled moustache that Eleni had described.

Maria followed Papadimitriou into the tunnel. He walked slowly, leaning heavily on his stick, and eventually they saw the light at the other end. Maria's emergence from the darkness of the tunnel into her new world was as much of a surprise for her as for any new arrival. In spite of her mother's letters, which had been full of description and colour, nothing had prepared her for what she now saw. A long road with a row of shops, all with freshly painted shutters, houses with window boxes and urns full of late-flowering geraniums, and one or two grander homes with carved wooden balconies. Though it was still too early for many people to be up, there was one early riser. The baker. The fragrance of freshly baked bread and pastries filled the street.

'Despineda Petrakis, before I show you to your new home, come and meet my wife,' said Papadimitriou. 'She has made breakfast for you.'

They turned left into a small side street, which in turn led into a courtyard with houses opening off it. Papadimitriou opened the door of one of these and ducked to get inside. They had been built by the Turks, and anyone of Papadimitriou's stature was more than a head taller than the original inhabitants.

The interior of the house was bright and ordered. There was a kitchen off the main room and stairs that led up to another floor. Maria even caught a glimpse of a separate bathroom beyond the kitchen.

'Let me introduce my wife. Katerina, this is Maria.'

The two women shook hands. In spite of everything that Eleni had told her to the contrary in her many letters, Maria had still expected the place to be inhabited by the lame and the deformed, and she was surprised at the woman's elegance and beauty. Katerina was younger than her husband and Maria surmised that she must be in her late forties. Her hair was still dark, and she had pale, almost unlined skin.

The table was set with embroidered white linen and fine patterned china. When they were all seated, Katerina lifted a splendid silver pot and a steady stream of hot black coffee filled the cups.

'There is a small house next door which has recently become vacant,' said Papadimitriou. 'We thought you might like that, or, if you prefer, there is a room free in a shared flat up the hill.'

'I think I would rather be on my own,' said Maria. 'If it's all right with you.'

There was a plate of fresh pastries on the table and Maria devoured one hungrily. She had eaten very little for several days. She was hungry for information too.

'Do you remember my mother, Eleni Petrakis?' she asked.

'Of course we do! She was a wonderful lady and a brilliant teacher too,' replied Katerina. 'Everyone thought so. Nearly everyone anyway.'

'There were some who did not?' Maria said.

Katerina paused.

'There was a woman who used to teach in the school before your mother arrived who regarded her as an enemy. She is still alive and has a house up the hill. Some people say that the bitterness she feels for what happened to her almost keeps her going,' said Katerina. 'Her name is Kristina Kroustalakis and you need to be wary of her – she'll inevitably find out who your mother was.'

'First things first, though, Katerina,' said Papadimitriou, displeased that his wife might be unsettling their guest. 'What you need before any of this is a tour of the island. My wife will take you round, and this afternoon Dr Lapakis will be expecting to see you. He does a preliminary assessment of all new arrivals.'

Papadimitriou stood up. It was now after eight o'clock in the morning and it was time for the island leader to be in his office.

'I shall no doubt see you again very soon, Despineda Petrakis. I shall leave you in Katerina's capable hands.'

'Goodbye, and thank you for making me feel so welcome,' responded Maria.

'Shall we finish our coffee and start the tour,' Katerina said brightly when Papadimitriou had left. 'I don't know how much you know about Spinalonga – probably more than most people – but it's not a bad place to live. The only problems come from being cooped up with the same people for your whole life. Coming from Athens I found that hard to get used to at first.'

'I've spent my whole life in Plaka,' said Maria, 'so I'm quite accustomed to that. How long have you been here?'

'I arrived on the same boat as Nikos, fourteen years ago. There were four women and nineteen men. Of the four women there are two of us left now. Fifteen of the men are still alive, though.'

Maria tightened her shawl about her shoulders as they left the house. When they turned into the main street, it was a very different scene from the one she had first seen. People came and went about their business, on foot, with mules or with donkey and cart. Everyone looked busy and purposeful. A few people looked up and nodded in Katerina and Maria's direction, and some of the men lifted their hats. As wife of the island leader, Katerina merited special respect.

By now the shops were open. Katerina pointed them all out and chatted busily about the people who owned them. Maria was hardly likely to remember all this information, but Katerina loved the details of their lives and relished the intrigue and gossip that circulated. There was the *pantopoleion*, the general store that sold everything for the house, from brooms to oil lamps, and had many of its wares displayed in profusion at the front of the building; a grocer whose windows were piled high with cans of olive oil; the *mahairopoieion*, the knife-maker; the raki store; and the baker, whose rows of freshly baked golden loaves and piles of coarse Cretan rusks, *paximithia*, drew in every passer-by. Each shop had its own hand-painted sign giving the owner's name and what he offered inside. Most important of all, for the men of the island at least, was the bar, which was run by the youthful and popular Gerasimo Mandakis. Already a few customers sat in groups drinking coffee, whilst their tangled mounds of cigarettes smouldered in an ashtray.

Just before they came to the church, there was a single-storey building which Katerina told Maria was the school. They peered in through the window and saw several rows of children. At the front of the class, a young man stood talking.

'So who is the teacher?' asked Maria. 'Didn't that woman you mentioned get the school back after my mother died?'

Katerina laughed. 'No, not over St Pantaleimon's dead body. The children did not want her back and neither did most of the elders. For a while one of my fellow Athenians took over, but he then died. Your mother had trained another teacher, however, and he was waiting in the wings. He was very young when he started but the children adore him and hang on his every word.'

'What's his name?'

'Dimitri Limonias.'

'Dimitri Limonias! I remember that name. He was the boy who came over here at the same time as my mother. We were told that it was he who had infected her with leprosy – and he's still here. Still alive!'

As occasionally happened with leprosy, Dimitri's symptoms had hardly developed since he had first been diagnosed, and now here he was, in charge of the school. Maria felt a momentary pang of resentment that the dice had been so heavily loaded against her mother.

They would not go in and interrupt the class. Katerina knew there would be another opportunity for Maria to meet Dimitri.

'There seems to be a large number of children,' commented Maria. 'Where do they all come from? Are their parents here too?'

'On the whole they don't have parents here. They're children who contracted leprosy on the mainland and were sent here. People try not to have children at all when they come to Spinalonga. If a baby is born healthy it's taken away from the parents and adopted on the mainland. We've had one or two such tragic cases recently.'

'That's desperately sad. But who looks after these children, the ones who are sent here?' asked Maria.

'Most of them are adopted. Nikos and I had one such child until he was old enough to move out and live on his own. The others live together in a house run by the community, but they're all well cared for.'

The two women continued on up the main street. High up above them on the hill towered the hospital, the biggest building of all.

'I'll take you up there later on,' said Katerina.

'You can see that building from the mainland,' said Maria. 'But it looks even bigger close to.'

'It was extended quite recently, so it's larger than it used to be.'

They walked round to the north side of the island, where human habitation ran out and eagles soared in the sky above. Here Spinalonga took the full blast of the wind from the north-east and the sea crashed on the rocks far below them, sending its spray high into the air. The texture of the water changed here, from the usual calmness of the channel that divided Spinalonga from Plaka to the galloping white horses of the open sea. Hundreds of miles away lay the Greek mainland and, in between, dozens of small islands, but from this vantage point there was nothing. Just air and sky and birds of prey. Maria was not the first to look over the edge and wonder, just for a moment, what it would be like to hurl herself off. Would she hit the sea first or be dashed against the serrated edges of the rocks?

It began to drizzle now and the path was becoming slippery.

'Come on,' Katerina said. 'Let's go back. Your boxes will have been brought up by now. I'll show you your new home and help you unpack if you like.'

As they descended the path, Maria noticed dozens of separate, carefully cultivated areas of land where, against the odds created by the elements, people were growing vegetable crops. Onions, garlic, potatoes and carrots were all sprouting on this windswept hillside and their neat weed-free rows were an indication of how much effort and attention went into the process of nursing them out of this rocky landscape. Each allotment was a reassuring sign of hope and showed that life was tolerable on this island.

They passed a tiny chapel that looked across the huge expanse of sea and finally reached the walled cemetery.

'Your mother was buried here,' Katerina said to Maria. 'It's where everyone ends up on Spinalonga.'

Katerina had not meant her words to sound so blunt, but in any case Maria did not react. She was keeping her emotions in check. It was someone else who was walking around the island. The real Maria was far away, lost in thought.

The graves were all unmarked, for the simple reason that they were shared. There were too many deaths here to allow anyone the luxury of solitude in the afterlife. Unlike most graveyards, which were situated around the church so that all who worshipped were constantly reminded that they would die, this one was secluded, secret. No one on Spinalonga really needed a memento mori. They all knew too well that their days were numbered.

Just before they came full circle they passed a house that was the grandest Maria had seen on the island. It had a large balcony and a porticoed front door. Katerina paused to point it out.

'Officially that's the home of the island leader, but when

Nikos took over he didn't want to push the previous leader and his wife out of their home, so they stayed where they were and so did Nikos. The husband died many years ago now, but Elpida Kontomaris is still there.'

Maria recognised the name immediately. Elpida Kontomaris had been her mother's best friend. The harsh fact was that her mother seemed to have been outlived by nearly all around her.

'She's a good woman,' added Katerina.

'I know,' said Maria.

'How do you know?'

'My mother used to write about her. She was her best friend.'

'But did you know that she and her late husband adopted Dimitri when your mother died?'

'No, I didn't. When she died I didn't really want to know about the details of life here any more; there was no need.'

There had been a long period after Eleni's death when even Maria had resented the amount of time that her father spent going to the colony; she had no interest in it once her mother had gone. Now, of course, she felt some remorse.

From almost all points on her walk the village of Plaka had remained in sight, and Maria knew that she would have to start disciplining herself not to glance over there. What good would it do to be able to see what activities people were engaged in across the water? From now on nothing over there had anything to do with her, and the quicker she got used to that, the better.

By now they had returned to the small cluster of houses where they had begun. Katerina led Maria towards a rust-coloured front door and took a key from her pocket. It seemed as dark inside as out, but with the flick of a switch the room was cheered up just a little. There was a dampness about it, as though it had been uninhabited for some time. The fact was that the previous incumbent had languished in the hospital for several months and never recovered, but given the sometimes dramatic recovery that could take place after even the most virulent lepra fever, it was island practice to retain people's homes until there was no further possible hope.

The room was sparsely furnished: one dark table, two chairs and a 'sofa' against the wall which was made of concrete and covered with a heavy woven cloth. Little other evidence of the previous inhabitant remained, except a glass vase containing a handful of dusty plastic flowers and an empty plate rack on the wall. A shepherd's hut in the mountains would have been more hospitable.

'I'll stay and help you unpack,' said Katerina bossily.

Maria was determined to hide her feelings about this hovel and could only do so if she was left her on her own. She would need to be firm.

'That's very kind of you, but I don't want to impose any more on your time.'

'Very well,' said Katerina. 'But I'll pop back later this afternoon to see if there is anything I can do. You know where I am if you need me.'

With that she was gone. Maria was glad to be alone with her own thoughts. Katerina had been well-meaning but she detected a hint of fussiness and had begun to find her twittering voice faintly irritating. The last thing Maria wanted was for anyone to tell her how to arrange her house. She would turn this miserable place into a home and she would do so herself.

The first thing she did was to pick up the vase of pathetic plastic roses and empty it into the bin. It was then that despondency overtook her. Here she was in a room that smelt of decay and the damp possessions of a dead man. She had held herself in check until this moment but now she broke down. All those hours of self-control and false good cheer for her father, for the Papadimitrious and for herself had been a strain, and the awfulness of what had happened now engulfed her. It was such a very short journey that had marked the end of her life in Plaka and yet the greatest distance she had ever travelled. She felt so far from home and everything that was familiar. She missed her father and her friends and lamented more than ever that her bright future with Manoli had been snatched away. In this dark room she wished she was dead. For a moment it did occur to her that perhaps she *was* dead, since hell could not be a gloomier or less welcoming place than this.

She went upstairs to the bedroom. A hard bed and a straw mattress covered with stained ticking were all the room contained, except for a small wooden icon of the Virgin clumsily nailed to the rough wall. Maria lay down, her knees pulled in towards her chest, and sobbed. How long she remained so she was not sure, since she eventually fell into fitful, nightmarish sleep.

Somewhere in the profound darkness of her deep underwater dream, she heard the distant sound of booming drums and felt herself being pulled to the surface. Now she could hear that the steady percussive beat was not a drum at all but the insistent sound of someone knocking on her door downstairs. Her eyes opened and for several moments her body seemed unwilling to move. All her limbs had stiffened in the cold and it was with every ounce of her will that she raised herself off the bed and stood upright. This sleep had been so profound that her left cheek bore the clear impression of two mattress buttons and nothing would have woken her except for what she now realised was the sound of someone almost battering down the door.

She descended the narrow staircase and as she drew back the latch and opened the door, still in a state of semi-consciousness, she saw two women standing there in the twilight. One of them was Katerina; the other was an older woman.

'Maria! Are you all right?' cried Katerina. 'We were so worried about you. We have been knocking on the door for nearly an hour. I thought you might have . . . might have . . . done yourself some harm.'

The final words she blurted out were almost involuntary, but there was a strong basis for them. In the past there had been a few newcomers who had tried to kill themselves, some of them successfully.

'Yes, I'm fine. Really I am – but thank you for worrying about me. I must have fallen asleep . . . Come in out of the rain.'

Maria opened the door wide and stepped aside to let the two women in.

'I must introduce you. This is Elpida Kontomaris.'

'Kyria Kontomaris. I know your name so well. You were my mother's great friend.'

The women held on to each other's hands.

'I can see so much of your mother in you,' said Elpida. 'You don't look so very different from the photographs she had of you, though that was all long ago. I loved your mother, she was one of the best friends I ever had.'

Katerina surveyed the room. It looked exactly as it had done many hours ago. Maria's boxes stood unopened and it was obvious that she had not even attempted to unpack them. It was still a dead man's house. All Elpida Kontomaris saw was a bewildered young woman in a bare, cold room at just the time of day when most people were eating a warm meal and anticipating the familiar comfort of their own bed.

'Look, why don't you come and stay with me tonight?' she asked kindly. 'I have a spare room, so it will be no trouble.'

Maria gave an involuntary shudder. Chilled by her situation and the dampness of the room, she had no hesitation in accepting. She remembered passing Elpida's house earlier that day and with her womanly eye for detail recalled the elaborate lace curtains that had covered the windows. Yes, that was where she would like to be tonight.

For the next few nights she slept in Elpida Kontomaris's house and during the day would return to the place which was to become her own home. She worked hard to transform it, whitewashing her walls and recoating the old front door with a bright, fresh green that reminded her of the beginning of spring rather than the tail-end of autumn. She unpacked her books, her photographs, and a selection of small pictures which she hung on the wall, and ironed her embroidered cotton cloths, spreading them on the table and on the comfortable chairs that Elpida had decided she no longer needed. She put up a shelf and arranged her jars of dried herbs on it, and made the previously filthy kitchen a hostile place for germs by scrubbing it until it gleamed.

That first dark day of despondency and despair was left behind, and though she dwelt for many weeks on what she had lost, she began to see a future. She thought much of what life with Manoli would have been like and began to question how he would have reacted in difficult times. Although she missed his levity and his ability to make a joke in any situation, she could not imagine how he would ever have tolerated adversity if it had come their way. Maria had only tasted champagne once, at her sister's wedding. After the first sip, which was full of fizz, the bubbles had disappeared, and she reflected on whether marriage to Manoli would have been rather like that. She would never know now and gradually she gave him less and less thought, almost disappointed in herself that her love seemed to evaporate by the day. He was not part of the world that she now occupied.

She told Elpida about her life from the day her mother had left: how she had looked after her father, about her sister's marriage into a good family, and about her own courtship and engagement to Manoli. She talked to Elpida as though she was her own mother, and the older woman warmed to her, this girl she had already known from her mother's descriptions all those years before.

Having overslept and missed it on the first afternoon, Maria went later that week for her appointment with Lapakis. He noted her symptoms and drew the location of her lesions on a diagrammatic outline of the body, comparing his observations with the information that Dr Kyritsis had sent him and noting that there was now an additional lesion on her back. This alarmed him. Maria was in good general health at present, but if anything happened to change this, his original hopes that she had a good chance of survival might come to nothing.

Three days later Maria went to meet her father. She knew that he would have set off punctually at ten to nine to bring Lapakis across, and by five minutes to she could just about make out his boat. She could see that there were three men aboard. This was unusual. For a fleeting moment she wondered if it was Manoli, breaking all the rules to come and visit her. As soon as she could distinguish the figure in the boat, however, she saw that it was Kyritsis. For a moment her heart leapt, for she associated the slight, silver-haired doctor with the chance of a cure.

As they bumped gently into the buoy, Giorgis threw the rope to Maria, who tied it expertly to a post as she had done a thousand times before. Though he had been anxious about his daughter, he was careful to conceal it.

'Maria . . . I am so pleased to see you . . . Look who is here. It's Dr Kyritsis.'

'So I can see, Father,' Maria said good-naturedly.

'How are you, Maria?' enquired Kyritsis, stepping nimbly from the boat.

'I feel absolutely one hundred per cent well, Dr Kyritsis. I have never felt anything else,' she replied.

He paused to look at her. This young woman seemed so out of place here. So perfect and so incongruous.

Nikos Papadimitriou had come to the quayside to meet the two doctors, and while Maria stayed to talk to her father, the three men disappeared through the tunnel. It was fourteen years since Nikolaos Kyritsis had last visited, and the transformation of the island astonished him. Repairs to the old buildings had been started even then, but the result had exceeded his expectations. When they reached the hospital, he was even more amazed. The original building was just as it had been, but a huge extension, equal in size to the whole of the old building, had been put up. Kyritsis remembered the plans on Lapakis's office wall all those years ago and saw immediately that he had fulfilled his ambition.

'It's astonishing!' he exclaimed. 'It's all here. Just as you wanted it.'

'Only after plenty of blood, sweat and tears, I can assure you – and most of those from this man here,' he said, nodding his head towards Papadimitriou.

The leader left them now and Lapakis showed Kyritsis proudly around his new hospital. The rooms in the new wing were lofty, with windows that reached from floor to ceiling. In the winter, the sturdy shutters and thick walls shielded patients from battering rains and howling gales, and in the summer the windows were thrown open to receive the soothing breeze that spiralled up from the sea below. There were only two or three beds to each room and the wards had been designated for either men or women. Everywhere was spotlessly clean, and Kyritsis noticed that each room had its own shower and washing cubicle. Most of the beds were occupied but the atmosphere in the hospital was generally still and quiet. Only a few patients tossed and turned, and one moaned softly with pain.

'Finally I've got a hospital where patients can be treated as they should be,' said Lapakis as they returned to his office. 'And moreover a place where they can have some self-respect.'

'It's very impressive, Christos,' said Kyritsis. 'You must have worked so hard to achieve all this. It looks exceptionally clean and comfortable – and quite different from how I remember it.'

'Yes, but good conditions aren't all they want. More than anything they want to get better and leave this place. My God, how they want to leave it.' Lapakis spoke wearily.

Most of the islanders knew that drug treatments were being worked on, but little seemed to have come their way. Some were sure that within their lifetime a cure would be found, though for many whose limbs and faces were deformed by the disease it was no more than a dream. A few had volunteered to have minor operations to improve the effects of paralysis on their feet or to have major lesions removed, but more than that they did not really expect.

'Look, we've got to be optimistic,' said Kyritsis. 'There are some drug treatments under trial at the moment. They don't work overnight, but do you think some of the patients here would be prepared to try them?'

'I'm sure they would, Nikolaos. I think there are some who would try anything. Some of the wealthy ones still insist on doses of hypnocarpus oil, in spite of the cost and the agony of having it injected. What do they have to lose if there's something new to try?'

'Actually quite a lot at this stage . . .' replied Kyritsis

thoughtfully. 'It's all sulphur-based, as you probably know, and unless the patient is in generally good health the side-effects can be disastrous.'

'What do you mean?'

'Well, anything from anaemia to hepatitis – and even psychosis. At the Leprosy Congress I've just been to in Madrid, there were even reports of suicide being attributed to this new treatment.'

'Well we'll have to think very carefully about which, if any, of our patients act as guinea pigs. If they have to be strong in the first place, there are plenty who would not be up to it.'

'Nothing has to be done straight away. Perhaps we could start by drawing up a list of suitable candidates and I can then discuss the possibility with them. It's not a short-term project – we probably wouldn't begin to inject for several months. What do you think?'

'I think that's the best way forward. Having a plan at all will seem like progress. Do you remember the last time we compiled a list of names here? It seems so long ago, and most of the people on it are dead now,' said Lapakis gloomily.

'But things are different today. We weren't talking about a real, tangible possibility of a cure in those days; we were simply trying to improve our methods of preventing contagion.'

'Yes, I know. I just feel I've been treading water here, that's all.'

'That's perfectly understandable, but I do believe there's a future to look forward to for some of these people. Anyway, I shall be back in a week, so shall we have a look at some names then?'

Kyritsis took himself back to the quayside. It was now midday and Giorgis would be there to collect him as arranged. A few heads turned to look at him as he made his way back down the street, past the church, the shops and the *kafenion*. The only strangers these people ever saw were newcomers to the island, and no newcomer ever walked with such purpose in his stride as this man. As the doctor emerged from the tunnel and the choppy late October sea came into view, he saw the little boat bobbing up and down a hundred metres or so off the shore, and a woman standing on the quayside. She was looking out to sea but heard his step behind her and turned. As she did so, her long hair blew up in wisps around her face and two large oval eyes gazed at him with hope.

Many years earlier, before the war, Kyritsis had visited Florence and seen Boticelli's captivating image of the Birth of Venus. With the grey-green sea behind her and her long hair caught by the wind, Maria strongly evoked the painting. Kyritsis even had a framed print on his wall at home in Iraklion, and in this young woman he saw the same shy half-smile, the same almost questioning incline of the head, the same just-born innocence. Such beauty in real life, however, he had never seen. He was stopped in his tracks. At this moment he was not regarding her as a patient but as a woman, and he thought her more beautiful than anyone he had ever seen.

'Dr Kyritsis,' she said, rousing him from his reverie with the sound of his own name. 'Dr Kyritsis, my father is here.'

'Yes, yes, thank you,' he blustered, suddenly aware that he must have been staring.

Maria held the boat fast for a moment as the doctor climbed in, and then she released it and tossed him the rope. As Kyritsis caught it he looked up at her. He needed one more glimpse, just to make quite sure he had not been dreaming. He had not. The face of Venus herself could not have been more perfect.

Chapter Eighteen

AUTUMN IMPERCEPTIBLY TURNED to winter and the musky smell of wood smoke pervaded the air on Spinalonga. People went about their daily business wrapped from head to foot in every woollen layer they possessed to defend themselves from the cold, for whichever way the wind blew this small island caught its full force.

In Maria's house the spirits of past inhabitants had been banished. Every picture, cloth and piece of furniture was now hers, and a glass dish of lavender and rose petals in the middle of the table scented the air with its sweet fragrance.

To Maria's surprise, her first few weeks on the island passed quickly. There was one moment alone that left her with a distinct sense of unease. She had just moved out of Elpida's warm and rather grandly furnished home into her own more familiar surroundings. As she turned the corner from the small alleyway into the main street to buy some groceries she physically collided with another woman. She was much smaller than Maria, and as they stepped away from each other Maria saw that she was considerably older too. Her face was furrowed with deep lines and so gaunt that her ear-lobes, which were greatly enlarged by leprosy, were monstrously accentuated. The old woman's walking stick had gone flying halfway across the street.

'I'm so sorry,' said Maria breathlessly, holding the woman's arm and helping her to regain her balance.

Dark beady eyes glared into Maria's.

'Just be more careful,' the woman snapped, grabbing her stick. 'Who are you anyway? I've not seen you before.'

'I'm Maria Petrakis.'

'*Petrakis!*' She spat the name out as though it had all the sourness of an olive eaten straight from the tree. 'I once knew someone called Petrakis. She's dead now.'

There was a note of triumph in her voice, and Maria immediately realised that this bent crone was her mother's old enemy.

The two women went their separate ways. Maria continued up the hill to the bakery, and when she glanced back to see where Kyria Kroustalakis had gone, she saw that she was standing at the bottom of the street by the old communal tap, staring up at her. Maria quickly looked round again. She shuddered.

'Don't worry,' said a voice behind her. 'She's pretty harmless really.'

It was Katerina, who had seen the collision between Maria and her mother's old enemy.

'She's just an old witch marinaded in her own bitter juices, a viper who's lost her venom.'

'I'm sure you're right, but she does a good impression of a snake who could still bite,' said Maria, her heart beating slightly faster than usual.

'Well, believe me, she can't. But what she is good at is

spreading bad feeling – and she's certainly succeeded at that with you.'

The two women continued up the street together, and Maria decided that she would give Kristina Kroustalakis no further thought. She had already seen that many people on Spinalonga accepted their situation, and the last thing any of them needed was someone who undermined this.

A more welcome encounter with part of her mother's past was her first meeting with Dimitri Limonias. Elpida invited them to her home one evening and both approached the meeting with some trepidation.

'Your mother was extremely kind to me,' Dimitri began, once drinks were poured and both were seated. 'She treated me like her own son.'

'She loved you like her own son,' said Maria. 'That's why.'

'I feel I should apologise in some way. I know that everyone thought I was responsible for giving her the disease,' said Dimitri hesitantly. 'But I've talked to Dr Lapakis about this at length and he thinks it is highly improbable that the bacteria were passed from me to your mother. The symptoms are so slow to develop that he thinks we contracted it quite independently from each other.'

'I don't believe any of that matters now,' said Maria. 'I'm not here to blame you. I just thought it would be a good idea to meet. You're almost like a brother after all.'

'That's a very generous thing to say,' he said. 'I don't feel as though I have much of a family any more. My parents have both died and my brothers and sisters were never exactly in the habit of writing letters. No doubt they're all ashamed. God knows, I do understand that.'

Several hours passed as the two talked about the island, the school and Eleni. Dimitri had been lucky. During his time on Spinalonga he had enjoyed the loving care of Eleni and then Elpida. One was an experienced mother and the other had treated him as the precious child she had always yearned for, giving him love and attention that sometimes almost swamped him. Maria was glad to have met this quasi-half-brother and the pair would often meet for coffee or even for supper, which she would cook while Dimitri enthused about his work. He currently had fourteen children in the school and aimed to get them reading by seven years old. Spending time with someone who was driven by his working life made Maria realise that being a leper was not going to dominate her every waking hour. A fortnightly appointment at the hospital, a compact house to keep neat and tidy, a small allotment to tend to. Along with the meetings with her father, these were the cornerstones of her single, childless existence.

To start with, Maria was nervous about telling her father that she had struck up a friendship with Dimitri. It might seem like a betrayal, as the family lore had always been that it was this boy who had infected Eleni. Giorgis had spent enough time with Lapakis to know that this was not necessarily the case, so when Maria made her confession that she was now Dimitri's friend, her father's reaction was unexpected.

'What's he like then?' he asked.

'He's about as dedicated as Mother was,' she answered. 'And he's good company too. He's read every book in the library.'

This was no mean feat. The library now had over five hundred books, most of them sent from Athens, but Giorgis was unimpressed by this. There were other things he wanted to know.

'Does he talk about your mother?'

'Not much. He probably thinks that would be insensitive. He did once tell me that his life was better here than it would have been if he hadn't had to come to Spinalonga.'

'That's an odd thing to say,' exclaimed Giorgis.

'I get the impression life was really hard for his parents and he certainly would never have become a teacher . . . Anyway, how's Anna?'

'I don't know really. I suppose she's all right. She was supposed to come and see me on the feast of Agios Grigorios but she sent a message saying she wasn't well. I really don't know what's wrong with her.'

It was always the same story, Maria thought. Promised meetings and last-minute cancellations. It was a pattern Giorgis expected now, but from afar Maria continued to be annoyed by her sister's callous disregard for the man who had struggled so hard to bring them up.

Within a month Maria knew she needed something to occupy her and picked a battered notebook off her shelf. It contained all her handwritten instructions on the use of herbs. *For healing and cure*, she had written on the title page in her neat, schoolgirl script. In the context of leprosy, those words looked so naïve, so optimistic, so entirely far-fetched. There were, however, plenty of other ailments that people suffered from on Spinalonga, from stomach disorders to coughs, and if she could relieve them of those as she had done so successfully in her old life, then it would be a worthwhile contribution.

Maria was bubbling over with news of her plans when Fotini came to visit her one day, telling her how she planned to scour the uninhabited, rocky part of the island for herbs as soon as spring came.

'Even on those limestone cliffs with the salt spray there's apparently plenty of sage, cistus, oregano, rosemary and thyme. Those will give me the basic means of providing remedies for general ailments and I'll try to cultivate other useful plants on my allotment. I'll need to get approval from Dr Lapakis, but once I've done that I'll advertise in *The Spinalonga Star*,' she told Fotini, who, on this chilly day, was warmed to see her dear friend so full of fire and enthusiasm.

'But tell me what's going on in Plaka,' Maria asked, never one to keep the conversation one-sided.

'Not much really. My mother says that Antonis is as grumpy as ever and it's high time he found himself a wife, but Angelos met a girl last week in Elounda that he seems very keen on. So who knows, perhaps one of my bachelor brothers might be married before long.'

'And what about Manoli?' asked Maria quietly. 'Has he been around?'

'Well, Antonis hasn't seen him on the estate quite so much . . . Are you sad about him, Maria?'

'It probably sounds awful, but I don't miss him as much as I thought I would. I only really think about him when we're sitting here talking about Plaka. I almost feel guilty about not feeling more. Do you think that's strange?'

'No, I don't. I think it's probably a good thing.' Since Fotini had been on the receiving end of Antonis's gossip about Maria's fiancé all those months ago, she had never entirely trusted

Manoli, and she knew it would be better in the long term if Maria could put him to the back of her mind. After all, there was no chance that she would ever marry him now.

It was time for her to go. Maria looked down at her friend's swollen belly.

'Is it kicking?' she asked.

'Yes,' replied Fotini. 'All the time now.'

Fotini was nearing the end of her pregnancy and beginning to worry about the rough waters she had to cross to see her friend.

'Perhaps you shouldn't be coming across now,' said Maria. 'If you're not careful you'll be giving birth in my father's boat.'

'As soon as I've had the baby I'll be straight back,' Fotini reassured her. 'And I'll write. I promise.'

By now Giorgis had established a firm routine for seeing his daughter on Spinalonga. Though Maria was comforted by the idea that her father came and went sometimes several times a day, it made no sense for her to see him each time. She knew it would be wrong for both of them to meet so often; it would be to pretend that life was going on just as it had before, simply in a different location. They decided to limit themselves to three encounters a week, on Mondays, Wednesdays and Fridays. These days were the high points of her week. Monday would be Fotini's day once she had resumed her visits, Wednesday was the day Dr Kyritsis visited, and on Fridays she saw her father alone.

In mid January Giorgis brought the exciting news that Fotini had given birth to a son. Maria wanted all the details.

'What's his name? What does he look like? How much does he weigh?' she asked excitedly.

'Mattheos,' replied Giorgis. 'He looks like a baby and I've no idea what he weighs. About the same as a bag of flour, I suppose.'

By the following week, Maria had embroidered a tiny pillowcase with the baby's name and date of birth and filled it with dried lavender. *Put it in his cradle*, she wrote in a note to Fotini. *It'll help him to sleep.*

By April, Fotini was ready to come and see Maria again. Even with her new responsibilities as a mother, she still knew the minutiae of everything that happened in Plaka and her antennae were well tuned to the comings and goings of its inhabitants. Maria loved to hear the gossip but also listened intently as her friend described the trials and pleasures of her new state of motherhood. For her part she shared all that took place on Spinalonga, and their talks always lasted for well over an hour, with hardly a pause for breath.

The Wednesday encounters with Dr Kyritsis were a very different matter. Maria found the doctor a little disconcerting. It was hard to disassociate him from the moment when the diagnosis had been delivered, and his words still echoed in her mind: '. . . leprosy is present in your body.' He had condemned her to a living death and yet he was also the man who now held out a tenuous promise that one day she might be free of the disease. It was confusing to link him with the worst and possibly the best of all things.

'He's very aloof,' she said to Fotini one day when they were chatting, sitting together on the low stone wall that surrounded one of the shade-giving trees by the quayside. 'And a bit steely, like his hair.'

'You make it sound as though you don't like him,' Fotini responded.

'I'm not sure I do,' answered Maria. 'He always seems to stare at me, and yet it's as though he's looking through me as if I'm not really there. He seems to make my father cheerful, though, so I suppose that's a good thing.'

It was strange, reflected Fotini, how Maria kept bringing this man into the conversation, especially if she didn't really like him.

Within a few weeks of Kyritsis's first visit, the two doctors had short-listed the cases that they would monitor for suitability for drug treatment. Maria's name was among them. She was young, healthy, newly admitted and in all ways an ideal candidate, and yet for reasons that Kyritsis could not explain even to himself, he did not want her to be in the first group that they would begin to inject several months from now. He struggled against this irrationality. After years of delivering unwelcome diagnoses to people who deserved so much better, he had trained himself to limit his emotional involvement. This objectivity made him imperturbable, even expressionless sometimes. Though Dr Kyritsis cared about humankind in a general sense, people tended to find him cold.

Kyritsis decided to cut the list from twenty to fifteen and these cases he would monitor closely over a period of months to decide on dosage and suitability. He omitted Maria's name from the final list. He did not need to justify this decision to anyone but he knew it was the first action he had taken in perhaps his entire career which was not governed by reason.

He told himself it was in her best interest. Not enough was known about the side-effects of some of these drug doses and he did not want her to be in the front line of an experiment. She might not be up to it.

One morning early that summer, during the journey over from the mainland, Kyritsis asked Giorgis whether he had ever been further than the great gateway of Spinalonga.

'Of course not,' replied Giorgis with some surprise. 'I've never even thought of it. It wouldn't be allowed.'

'But you could visit Maria in her own home,' he said. 'Almost entirely without risk.'

Kyritsis, now familiar with Maria's symptoms, knew that the chances of Giorgis Petrakis contracting leprosy from his daughter were a million to one. There were no bacteria on the surface of Maria's flat skin patches, and unless Giorgis came into direct contact with any broken skin there was virtually no chance at all of him being infected.

Giorgis looked thoughtful. It had never occurred to either him or Maria that they could spend any time together in Maria's house. It would be infinitely more civilised than seeing each other on the quayside, windswept in winter and sun-scorched in summer. Nothing would be more wonderful.

'I shall speak to Nikos Papadimitriou about it and seek Dr Lapakis's opinion, but I see no reason why it should not happen.'

'But what would they think back in Plaka if they knew I was going into the colony rather than just delivering goods on to the quayside?'

'If I were you I would keep quiet about it. You know as well as I do what visions people over there have of life here.

They all think leprosy is spread in a handshake, or just by being in the same room as a sufferer. If they thought that you were drinking coffee in the same house as someone with the disease I think you know what the consequences of that might be.'

Giorgis knew better than anyone that Kyritsis was right. He was all too familiar with the prejudices against lepers and for so many years had been obliged to listen to the ignorant views – even of men who called themselves his friends – on the subject. What a dream, however, to sit and share a pot of coffee or a glass of ouzo once again with his lovely daughter. Could it really happen?

That day Kyritsis spoke to the island leader and solicited the views of Lapakis. When he saw Giorgis that night he was able to give him official approval for his visits.

'If you wish to invite yourself through that tunnel,' he said, 'you may.'

Giorgis could hardly believe his ears. He could not remember feeling such excitement for a very long time and was impatient to see Maria so that he could tell her what Kyritsis had suggested. That very Friday morning, as soon as he stepped off the boat, she knew something was up. Her father's face gave it away.

'I can come to your house!' he blurted out. 'You can make coffee for me.'

'What? How? I don't believe it . . . are you sure?' Maria said with incredulity.

It would be such a simple thing, but so precious. Like his wife and daughter before him, Giorgis entered with trepidation the dark tunnel which led through the heavy fortified wall. When he emerged into the bright light of the leper colony it was as much of a revelation to him as it had been to them. The early June day was already warm, and though the clear light would later dissolve into a haze, the sharp colours of the scene that confronted Giorgis almost dazzled him. A profusion of crimson geraniums cascaded out of huge urns, a candy-pink oleander gave shade to a litter of tortoiseshell kittens and a deep green palm waved gently next to the sapphire door of the hardware store. Shiny silver pans hung down in a string and glinted in the sunlight. Huge pots of bright green basil stood outside almost every door ready to give flavour even to dull dishes. No, it was not as he had imagined it.

Maria was as excited as her father, but at the same time slightly nervous about his presence. She did not want him wandering too far into the leper colony, not just because he would invite stares and curiosity but because his presence could cause jealousy and resentment among the other lepers. She wanted to keep her father to herself.

'It's this way, Father,' she urged, leading him off the main street and into the little square where her house was situated. She unlocked her front door and led the way in. Soon there was an aroma of coffee in the small house as it bubbled up through the percolator on the stove, and a plate of baklava stood on the table.

'Welcome,' Maria said.

Giorgis did not really know what he had expected, but it was not this. It was a replica of his house in Plaka. He recognised photographs, icons and pieces of china which matched his own at home. Dimly he recalled that Eleni had asked for some plates and cups from the family set so that she would be eating from the same crockery as her family. After that, those pieces had gone to Elpida, who had kept some of his wife's possessions when she died, and now they were in Maria's hands. He also saw the cloths and throws which Maria had spent so many months embroidering, and a wave of sadness passed over him when he thought of Manoli's house in the olive grove where she should have been living, had things worked out as originally planned.

They sat down at the table and sipped their coffee.

'I never thought I would sit at a table with you again, Maria,' he said.

'Neither did I,' Maria answered.

'We have Dr Kyritsis to thank for this,' said Giorgis. 'He's got some rather modern views, but I like this one.'

'What will your friends in Plaka say when you tell them that you have started coming into the colony?'

'I shan't tell them. You know what they'd say. They're as stuck in their views about Spinalonga as they ever were. Even though there's a strip of water dividing them from here, they're convinced leprosy will be carried across on the air to infect them. If they knew I was coming into your house, they'd probably ban me from the bar!'

The last comment may have been flippant, but Maria still expressed concern.

'It's probably best that you keep it to yourself then. No doubt it worries them enough that you come over here as often as you do.'

'You're right. You know some of them even think that I somehow managed to carry germs across from here to infect you back in Plaka.'

Maria was horrified at the idea that her leprous state might be used to fuel such fears on the mainland and it alarmed her that her father might be faced with prejudice even from his oldest friends, men he had grown up with. If only they could see them now: a father and his daughter sitting at a table, eating the sweetest pastries that money could buy. Nothing could have been further from the conventional image of a leper colony. Even her irritation at the thought of all the ignorant talk on the mainland could not spoil this moment.

When they had finished their coffee, it was time for Giorgis to go.

'Father, do you think Fotini would come one day?'

'I am sure she would, but you can ask her when she comes on Monday.'

'It's just that . . . this is so like normal life. Sharing a drink with someone. I can't tell you what it means to me.'

Maria, usually so steadfast at controlling her emotions, had a catch in her voice. Giorgis stood to go.

'Don't worry, Maria,' he said. 'I am sure she will come – and so will I.'

The two of them walked back to the boat and Maria waved him goodbye.

As soon as he returned to Plaka, Giorgis wasted no time in telling Fotini that he had been into Maria's house, and without even hesitating, his daughter's oldest friend asked whether she would be able to do the same. Some people would have considered this reckless, but Fotini was more enlightened about the way in which leprosy could be spread than others, and on her next visit, as soon as she got off the boat, she seized Maria's arm.

'Come on,' she said. 'I want to see your home.'

A broad smile spread across Maria's face. The two women sauntered through the tunnel and were soon at the door of Maria's house. The coolness of the interior was welcome, and instead of strong coffee they drank *kanelada*, the chilled cinnamon drink they had both loved as children.

'It's so kind of you to come here to see me,' said Maria. 'You know, I never pictured anything but loneliness here. It makes so much difference having visitors.'

'Well it's much nicer than sitting on that wall in the heat,' said Fotini. 'And now I can picture where you really live.'

'So what's new? How's little Mattheos?'

'He's wonderful, what more can I say? He's eating a lot and growing very big.'

'It's just as well he likes his food. He does live in a restaurant after all,' commented Maria with a smile. 'And what's happening in Plaka? Have you seen my sister lately?'

'No. Not for a long time,' Fotini said thoughtfully.

Giorgis had told Maria that Anna came to see him quite regularly, but now she wondered if that were really true. If Anna had turned up in her shiny car, Fotini would have known about it. The Vandoulakis family had been angry in the extreme when they learned of Maria's leprosy and it had not surprised her at all that Anna had not written since she came to Spinalonga. Neither would it really surprise her if her father had lied about her sister's visits.

Both women were silent.

'Antonis sees her from time to time, though, when he's working,' Fotini said at last.

'Does he say how she looks?'

'Fine, I think.'

Fotini knew what Maria was really asking. Was her sister pregnant? After all those years of marriage, it was high time that Anna had a child. If not, there must be a problem. Anna was not expecting a baby, but there was something else happening in her life that Fotini had thought long and hard about telling Maria.

'Look, I probably shouldn't tell you this, but Antonis has seen Manoli coming and going from Anna's house.'

'That's allowed, isn't it? He is family.'

'Yes, he is family, but even members of your family don't need to visit every other day.'

'Perhaps it's to discuss estate business with Andreas,' Maria said matter-of-factly.

'But he doesn't go when Andreas is there,' said Fotini. 'He goes during the day, when Andreas is out.'

Maria found herself being defensive.

'Well it sounds to me as though Antonis is spying.'

'He isn't spying, Maria. I think your sister and Manoli have grown rather close.'

'Well if they have, why doesn't Andreas do something about it?'

'Because he has absolutely no idea that it's going on,' said Fotini. 'It wouldn't even occur to him. And what he doesn't see or think about, he need never know about.'

The two women sat in silence for a moment, until Maria got up. She pretended to busy herself with washing their glasses but nothing took her mind away from what Fotini had just told her. She was thoroughly agitated, suddenly remembering her sister's rather edgy behaviour all those months ago when she and Manoli had visited. It was perfectly feasible that there might be something going on between them. She knew her sister was more than capable of such infidelity.

With sheer vexation she twisted the cloth round and round inside the glasses until they squeaked. As ever her thoughts were with her father. She felt keenly, even in anticipation, his ever-deepening shame. As for Anna, was she not the only one of the three Petrakis women who still had the possibility of a normal, happy life? Now it sounded as though she was doing everything she could to throw it all away. Maria's eyes pricked with tears of anger and frustration. She would hate Fotini to think that she was jealous. She knew Manoli would never be hers but it was hard nevertheless to bear the idea of him being with her sister.

'You know, I don't want you to think I care about Manoli any more, because I don't, but I do care about my sister's behaviour. What's to become of her? Does she really think that Andreas will never find out?'

'She obviously thinks he won't. Or if she does, it doesn't bother her. I'm sure the whole thing will just fade out.'

'That's probably optimistic, Fotini,' Maria said. 'But there's nothing we can do about it, is there?'

The two sat in silence for a moment before Maria changed the subject.

'I've started using my herbs again,' she said, 'with some success. People are beginning to come to me now and the *dictamus* worked almost immediately for an elderly gentleman with a stomach disorder.'

They continued to chat, though Fotini's revelation about Anna weighed heavily on their minds.

* * *

The relationship between Anna and Manoli did not, as Fotini predicted, fade out. On the contrary, the spark between them was rekindled and a fire soon smouldered. Manoli had been entirely faithful to Maria while they were engaged to be married. She was perfect, a virgin, his Agia Maria, and undoubtedly she would have made him a happy man. Now she was a fond memory. The first few weeks after Maria had gone to Spinalonga he had been listless and unhappy, but the period of mourning the loss of his fiancée soon passed. Life had to go on, he had thought to himself.

Like a moth to a flame he was drawn back to Anna. She was still there in that house, so close, so needy and somehow so gift-wrapped in her tightly fitted ribbon-trimmed dresses.

It was around lunch time one day, his old habitual visiting time, when Manoli let himself into the kitchen at the big house on the estate.

'Hello, Manoli.' Anna greeted him without surprise and with enough warmth to melt the snows on Mount Dhikti.

His confidence that she would be pleased to see him was matched by her arrogance. She had known that he would come, sooner or later.

Alexandros Vandoulakis had recently handed the entire estate over to his son. This gave Andreas huge responsibilities and less and less time at home, and soon Manoli was seen leaving his cousin's house more often than just on alternate days. He was now there every day. Antonis was not the only person aware of this. Many of the estate workers knew about it too. There was a double safety net that Anna and Manoli relied on: Andreas was too busy to notice anything himself, and it was worth more than any man's job to approach their boss with tales about his wife. For these reasons they could enjoy each other with impunity.

There was nothing that Maria could do and the only influence Fotini had was to urge her brother to keep it to himself. If Antonis mentioned it to their father, Pavlos, then it was bound to reach Giorgis, since the two men were great companions.

Between Fotini's visits, Maria tried to put her sister to the back of her mind. Her inability to influence the situation was not determined only by the distance between them. She knew that even if she was still on the mainland, Anna would have been doing just what she liked.

Maria began to look forward to the days when Kyritsis came across, and always made sure she was at the quayside to meet her father and the silver-haired doctor. One fine summer day Kyritsis stopped to talk. He had heard from Dr Lapakis of Maria's skills with herbal cures and tinctures. A firm believer in modern medicine, he had long been sceptical about the power of the sweet, gentle flowers that grew on the mountainsides. What strength could they possibly have when compared with twentieth-century drugs? Many of the patients he saw on Spinalonga, however, talked of the relief they had experienced through some of Maria's concoctions. He was prepared to relax his cynicism, and told her so.

'I know conviction when I see it,' he said. 'I've also seen some real evidence on this island that these things can work. I can hardly continue to be a sceptic, can I?'

'No, you can't. I'm glad you admit it,' said Maria, with a note of triumph. It gave her huge satisfaction to realise that she had successfully persuaded this man to change his views. Even greater was her satisfaction when she looked at him and saw his face break into a smile. It transformed him.

Chapter Nineteen

THE DOCTOR'S SMILE changed the climate around him. Kyritsis had not been given to smiling in the past. Other people's misery and anxiety were the cornerstones of his life and rarely gave him cause for levity or pleasure. He lived alone in Iraklion, working long days in the hospital, and the few waking hours he had outside it were spent reading and sleeping. Now, at last, there was something else in his life: the beauty of a woman's face. To the hospital staff in Iraklion and to Lapakis and the lepers who were now regular patients he was just the same as he always had been: a dedicated, single-minded and unnervingly serious – some would say humourless – scientist. For Maria he had become a different person. Whether he would be her salvation in the long term she did not know, but he saved her in a small way every time he crossed the water by making her pulse quicken. She was a woman again, not just a patient waiting on this rock to die.

Though the temperatures began to drop during those first days of autumn, Maria felt an increasing warmth in Nikolaos Kyritsis. When he arrived on the island each Wednesday he would stop to talk to her. First of all it would be just for five minutes, but as time went on it was for longer on each occasion. Eventually, meticulous about punctuality and the need to be on time for his hospital appointments, he began to arrive earlier on the island to allow himself enough time to see Maria. Giorgis, who always rose at six o'clock in the morning, was perfectly happy to bring Kyritsis over at eight-thirty rather than nine and observed that the days when Maria had come to talk to him on Wednesdays were over. She still met the boat, but not to see her father.

Usually a man of few words, Kyritsis talked to Maria about his work back in Iraklion and explained the research with which he was involved. He described how the war had interrupted everything and told her what he had been doing during those years, painting a detailed description for her of a war-blasted city where every last trained medical person was required to be on duty almost round the clock to care for the sick and wounded. He told her about his travels to international conferences in Egypt and Spain where the world's experts on leprosy treatment gathered to share their ideas and to give papers on their latest theories. He told her about the various cures that were currently being tried out and what he really thought of them. Occasionally he had to remind himself that this woman was a patient and might eventually be a recipient of the drug therapy that was being trialled on Spinalonga. How strange, he sometimes found himself thinking, to have found such friendship on this small island. Not only his old friend, Christos Lapakis, but this young woman too.

For her part Maria looked at him and listened, but offered very little of her own life in return. She felt she had little to share. Her existence had become so small, so limited, so narrowly focused.

As Kyritsis saw it, people on Spinalonga were living a life that he might almost have envied. They came and went about their business, sat in the *kafenion*, saw the latest films, went to church and nurtured friendships. They lived in a community where everyone knew each other and had a common bond. In Iraklion he could walk the length of the bustling street every day for a week and not see a familiar face.

As vital to Maria as the conversations with Dr Kyritsis were her weekly meetings with Fotini, but these she anticipated half with dread these days.

'So has he been seen leaving the house this week?' she asked as soon as Giorgis was out of earshot.

'Once or twice,' answered Fotini. 'But only when Andreas was there too. The olive harvest has started so he is around more. Manoli and Andreas are supervising the presses and apparently they both go back to the big house for dinner.'

'Perhaps it was all in your brother's imagination, then. Surely if Manoli and Anna were lovers he wouldn't go for dinner there with Andreas?'

'Why not? It would be *more* likely to arouse suspicion if he stopped going there.'

Fotini was right. Anna was spending many an evening perfectly coiffed, manicured and poured into immaculately well-fitted dresses, playing the twin roles of good wife to her husband and welcoming hostess to his cousin. It was no more than Andreas expected of her. She carried the situation off effortlessly and the chances of her fluffing a line or casting a giveaway glance were almost non-existent. For Anna the under-currents only added to the frisson of being on an imaginary stage, and on the days when her parents-in-law were there it created additional tension, increasing her excitement and the sublime thrill of concealment.

'Did you enjoy our evening?' she would ask Andreas later in the blank darkness of their ample bed.

'Yes, why?'

'I was just asking,' she would say, and as they began to make love she felt the weight of Manoli's body and heard his deep groans. Why should Andreas question such pleasure? Afterwards, he lay silent and breathless in the dark shuttered room, the unsuspecting victim of her passion for another man, a man with whom she had only made love in broad daylight.

For Anna there was no conflict in this situation. Since she had no choice in the matter of her passion for Manoli, her infidelity was almost justified. He had appeared unannounced in her life and her reaction had been spontaneous. Free will played no part in her response to him and it had never occurred to her that it could. Manoli's presence electrified her, aroused every hair on her body and made every square centimetre of her soft, pale skin yearn to be touched. It could never be any other way. I can't help it, she said to herself as she brushed her hair in the morning on the days when Andreas had left for the furthest area of the estate and she expected Manoli to appear in her kitchen at lunchtime. There is nothing I can do. Manoli was her husband's blood relative. With all the will in the world she could not have driven him away. She was a trapped but uncomplaining victim, and even though it was happening under his own roof Andreas had not the slightest inkling that Anna was betraying him in his own bed, with the framed *stephana*, the marriage crowns, witnessing her act of perfidy.

Andreas did not spend much time thinking about Manoli. He was glad that he had returned from his travels but he left any worrying about him to his dear mother, who fretted that her nephew was in his thirties and not yet married. Andreas was sorry that the marriage to his wife's sister had encountered such an insurmountable obstacle, but he supposed that sooner or later his cousin would find another suitable woman to bring into the family. As for Eleftheria, she was sorry that her nephew's sweet bride had been snatched away but was even sorrier to have a nagging suspicion that some affinity existed between Manoli and her daughter-in-law. She could not quite define it and indeed sometimes told herself it was in her imagination. It was as fleeting as a shape in a cloud.

Maria shuddered to think of how Anna might be behaving. Her sister had never bothered with caution and nothing would change that now. Her real concern, however, was not Anna herself but the impact of her behaviour on their father. There was not one secure element in that poor dear man's life, she thought.

'Has she no shame?' she muttered

'I'm not sure she has,' said Fotini.

The women tried to talk of other things, but conversation always began and ended with talk of Anna's infidelity and speculation on how long it would be before Anna cast a careless glance in Manoli's direction that might just make Andreas pause for a moment and wonder. Little by little, any residual feelings Maria might have had for Manoli evaporated. The only certainty she had was that there was nothing she could possibly do.

It was now late October. The winter winds were gaining

strength and would soon penetrate the thickest overcoats and the heaviest of woollen wraps. It seemed to Maria that it was uncivilised to stand here in the perishing cold talking to Dr Kyritsis, but the thought of giving up their conversations was unbearable. She loved talking with this man. They seemed never to run out of things to say, even though she felt she had so little of interest to tell him. She could not help comparing the way he spoke to her with the way Manoli had talked. Her fiancé's every sentence had been full of playful banter, but with Kyritsis there was not a flicker of flirtation.

'I want to know what it's really like to live here,' he said to her one day as the wind gusted around them.

'But you see the island every week. You must be as familiar with how it looks as I am,' she said, rather puzzled by his statement.

'I look at it, but I don't see it,' he said. 'I see it as an outsider passing through. That's very different.'

'Would you like to come to my house and have some coffee?' Maria had quietly practised saying these words for some time, but when they finally came out she hardly recognised her own voice.

'Coffee?' Kyritsis had heard her clearly enough, but repeated the word for want of something to say in response.

'Would you?'

It was as though she had disturbed him from a reverie.

'Yes, I think I would.'

They walked together through the tunnel. Though he was the doctor and she the patient, they walked side by side, like equals. Both of them had passed through the Venetian walls a hundred times, but this was a different kind of journey.

Kyritsis had not walked a street like this in the company of a woman for years, and Maria, walking along with a man who was not her father, felt self-conscious in a way she thought she had left behind with childhood. Someone might see her and jump to the wrong conclusion. 'It's the doctor!' she wanted to shout, desperate to spare herself from gossip.

Quickly she showed the way into the small alleyway close to the end of the tunnel and they entered her house. Maria began making coffee. She knew Kyritsis did not have long and would want to be punctual for his first appointment.

While Maria busied herself finding sugar, cups and saucers, Kyritsis looked about the room. It was much more comfortable and colourful than his own small apartment in Iraklion. He noticed the embroidered cloths, the picture of the young Kyria Petrakis with Maria and another girl on the wall. He saw a neat row of books, a jug containing leafy sprigs from an olive tree and bunches of lavender and herbs hanging to dry from the ceiling. He saw order and domesticity and felt warmed by them both.

Now that they were on Maria's terrain, he felt he could get her to talk about herself. There was one burning question he wanted to ask. He knew so much about the disease, its symptoms, its epidemiology, its pathology, but of course he did not know what it really *felt* like to have leprosy and until now he had never thought of asking one of his patients.

'How does it feel . . .' he ventured, 'to be a leper?'

The question seemed so personal, but Maria did not hesitate to answer.

'In some ways I feel no different now than I did a year ago, but I *am* different because I've been sent here,' she said. 'It's a bit like being in prison, for someone like me who's not affected by the disease day to day. Except there are no locks on the door, no bars.'

As she said this, her mind went back to that cold autumn morning when she had left Plaka to come to Spinalonga. Life on a leper colony had certainly not been what she had wished for, but she paused for a moment and wondered what it would have been like had she married Manoli. Would that have been another kind of prison? What sort of man would betray his own family? What Judas would abuse the kindness and hospitality that had been shown him? She had been taken in by his charm but realised now that circumstances might have spared her. This was a man with whom she had not once had a conversation that touched anything deeper or broader than the olive harvest, the music of Mikis Theodorakis or whether to attend the saint's day celebrations in Elounda. Such *joie de vivre* had attracted her at first but she realised that perhaps there was no more to him than that. Life with Manoli might have been just another kind of life sentence, no better than the one she was condemned to on Spinalonga.

'There are lots of good things, though,' she added. 'Wonderful people like Elpida Kontomaris and the Papadimitrious and Dimitri. They have such spirit and, do you know something, even though they've been here an awful lot longer than I have, they never, ever complain.'

When she had finished speaking, Maria poured coffee into a cup and passed it to Kyritsis. She noticed, too late, that his hand trembled violently, and when he took the coffee, the cup clattered to the ground. A dark puddle spread across the stone floor and there was an awkward silence before Maria rushed to the sink to get a cloth. She sensed his profound embarrassment and was keen to relieve him of it.

'Don't worry, it's fine,' she said, mopping up, collecting the pieces of patterned china in a dustpan as she did so. 'As long as you didn't burn yourself.'

'I'm terribly sorry,' he said. 'I'm terribly sorry to have broken your cup. It was so clumsy of me.'

'Don't worry about it. What's a cup?'

It was, in fact, a special cup, one of the set that her mother had brought from Plaka, but Maria realised that she did not mind at all. It was almost a relief that Kyritsis was not so perfect, not as impeccable in every way as he outwardly appeared.

'Perhaps I shouldn't have come,' Kyritsis mumbled. In his mind, it was a sign that he should not have broken the rules of professional etiquette in which he believed so strongly. By coming into Maria's house for social reasons he had crossed a boundary with a patient.

'Of course you should have come. I invited you and I would have been miserable if you hadn't.'

Maria's outburst was spontaneous, and more enthusiastic than she had really intended. It surprised Dr Kyritsis, but it also surprised her. Now they were even. Both had lost their composure.

'Please stay and have some more coffee.'

Maria's eyes looked into the doctor's so imploringly that he could do nothing but accept. She took another cup from the rack, and this time, once the coffee was poured into it, she left it on the table for him to pick up safely.

They both sipped without speaking. Sometimes there is

awkwardness in silence, but not this time. Eventually Maria broke the spell.

'I hear a few people have started some drug treatment. Is it going to work?' It was a question she had been longing to ask.

'It's quite early days, Maria,' he answered. 'But we have to hold out a little hope. We are aware of some contraindications to the treatment, which is why we have to be cautious at this stage.'

'What kind of drug is it?'

'Its full name is diphenyl sulphone, but it's generally known as dapsone. It's sulphur-based and potentially toxic. The key thing, though, is that any improvement generally takes place over the very long term.'

'So it's no magic potion then,' said Maria, trying not to sound disappointed.

'No, I'm afraid it's not,' said Kyritsis. 'It'll be a while before we really know if anyone will ever be fully cured. I'm afraid no one will be leaving quite yet.'

'So that means you might be able to come for coffee another time?'

'I very much hope so. You make such good coffee.'

Dr Kyritsis knew his answer was somehow gauche and that it implied he was only interested in coming because of the quality of her coffee. That was not at all how it was meant to sound.

'Well, I had better be going now,' he said, trying to cover his embarrassment. 'Thank you.' With that rather stiff farewell, Kyritsis left.

As she cleared the cups and swept the floor to remove the

last shards of the broken cup, Maria heard herself humming. The sensation could only be described as a lightness of heart, an unfamiliar feeling in a grey place, but she would enjoy it and hope against hope that it would remain with her. All day she felt as though her feet did not quite touch the ground. She had much to do but each task felt a pleasure. As soon as she had tidied up, she bundled some of her herb jars into a rough basket and set off to see Elpida Kontomaris.

The elderly woman rarely locked her door, and Maria let herself in. She found Elpida in bed, pale but propped up on her pillows.

'Elpida, how are you feeling today?'

'I am actually feeling much better,' she said. 'Thanks to you.'

'It's thanks to nature, not to me,' Maria corrected her. 'I'm going to make another infusion for you. It's obviously working. You're to have a cupful of this now, one in about three hours, and then I will come back this evening to give you a third.'

For the first time in weeks, Elpida Kontomaris was beginning to feel well again. The griping stomach aches she had been suffering from finally seemed to be on the wane, and there was no doubt in her mind that her improvement was due to the soothing herbal medicines that Maria had been preparing for her. Though the skin on her elderly face sagged and her clothes hung off her like limp rags, her appetite was beginning to return and she could now imagine a time when she might eat properly again.

As soon as she had made sure that Elpida was comfortable, Maria was gone. She would return that evening to ensure that her patient took her next dose, but meanwhile she would spend the day at 'the block', as it was unaffectionately known. The large apartment building situated at the end of the main street was still unpopular. It felt lonely and desolate up there at the top of the hill. People preferred the cosiness of the small Turkish and Italian houses. The proximity of the older houses to each other helped promote a sense of community which mattered more to them than bright strip lighting and modern shutters.

Today Maria went there because four of the apartments were home to lepers who could no longer fend for themselves. These were the cases whose ulcerated feet had led to amputation, whose claw-like hands rendered them incapable of even the simplest domestic tasks and whose faces were deformed beyond recognition. In any other situation, the lives of these disfigured individuals would have been abjectly miserable. Even now several of them lived on the very brink of despair, but the efforts of Maria and a few other women like her never allowed them to go over it.

What these people cherished more than anything was their privacy. For one young woman, whose nose had been destroyed by leprosy and whose eyes were held permanently open through facial paralysis, the stares of her fellow colonists were insupportable. Occasionally she went out at night and crept into the church, alone with the dark icons and the comforting smell of melted candlewax, but otherwise, she would never go out, except for the very short monthly walk to the hospital, where Lapakis would chart any changes to her lesions and prescribe drugs to help lure her mind and body from an almost permanently wakeful state into one of short but blissful sleep. Another, slightly older woman had lost one of her hands. She was paying the highest price for the severe burns she had inflicted on herself while cooking for her family only a few months before coming to the island. Dr Lapakis had done everything he could to try and heal the ulcerated wounds, but the infection had got the better of both of them and his only choice had been to amputate. Her remaining hand was fixed in a claw. She could just about hold a fork, but she could not open a tin or do up a button.

Every one of the dozen or so extreme cases who lived here was hideously scarred. Most of them had arrived on Spinalonga in an acute state of decrepitude, and in spite of the hospital's best efforts to ensure that no long-term damage was done to them by the numbing effects of the disease, it was not always possible to control it. They matched the biblical image of the leper and were as far along the hellish road to disfigurement as anyone could be while still being perceptibly human.

Maria shopped and cooked for these end-stage cases. She hardly even noticed their deformities any more, as she served them lunch and, in some cases, helped to feed them. Always in her mind was the thought that her mother might well have been like this. No one had ever really told her, but as she lifted spoons of rice to their lips, she hoped that Eleni had never suffered as these people did. She regarded herself as one of the lucky ones. Whether or not the new drug treatment worked successfully, these people's broken bodies could never be mended.

Most people on the mainland imagined that all lepers were as ravaged by the disease as these extreme cases and the very thought of their proximity repulsed them. They feared for themselves and for their children and had no doubt that the bacillus that had infected the people on this island could be airborne into their own homes. Even in Plaka there were people with such misconceptions. In the past few years, a secondary reason for resenting the colony had brewed. Greatly exaggerated stories of the Athenians' wealth had whipped people up into a state of increasing rancour, particularly in the poorer hillside communities of Selles and Vrouhas which did not enjoy the reliable income of fishing villages such as Plaka. One minute they feared the idea that they too might end up on Spinalonga; the next they seethed with envy at the idea that the colonists might be living more comfortable lives than they were themselves. Their fears were both ill-founded and deep-rooted.

One day in February a rumour began to circulate. It was sparked by the idle comment of one man, and like a forest fire from a single carelessly dropped match it spread with frightening speed and soon rampaged through every nearby village from Elounda in the south to Vilhadia on the northern coast. It was said that the mayor in Selles had taken his ten-year-old son to hospital in Iraklion. He was to have tests for suspected leprosy. Perhaps the disease was spreading from the island to the mainland. Within a day, the storm clouds of crowd overreaction had gathered. A ringleader in each village and the long-incubated feelings of fear and loathing were all it took for anger to boil over, and people began to descend on Plaka, intent on the island's destruction. Their cause was an irrational one. If Spinalonga was sacked, they reasoned, no further lepers could be sent there and the Greek government would be forced to relocate the colony. They also imagined that once threatened, the influential Athenians would insist on being taken somewhere safer. Either way, it would rid them of this filthy blot on their landscape.

The mob planned to take every fishing boat they could lay their hands on and land under cover of darkness. By five o'clock that Wednesday afternoon there was a gathering of two hundred, mostly men, on the Plaka quayside. Giorgis saw the first trucks arrive and heard the commotion as people spilled out of them and made their way down to the quayside. Like the other villagers of Plaka, he was aghast. It was time for him to go over to collect Kyritsis, but first he had to force his way through the crowd to find his boat. As he did so, he caught snatches of conversation.

'How many can we fit into a boat?'

'Who's got the petrol?'

'Make sure there's plenty!'

One of the ringleaders spotted the old man getting into his boat and addressed him aggressively.

'Where do you think you're going?'

'I'm going across to collect the doctor,' he answered.

'What doctor?'

'One of the doctors who works over there,' answered Giorgis.

'What good can doctors do for lepers?' the ringleader sneered, playing to the crowd.

As the group laughed and jeered, Giorgis pushed his boat away from the quay. His whole body quaked with fear and his hand trembled violently on the tiller. The little boat fought hard against the choppy sea, and never had the journey seemed longer. From some way off he could see the dark silhouette of Kyritsis, and eventually he was bringing the boat close to the stony wall.

The doctor did not bother to tie the boat up, but instead climbed straight in. It had been an arduous day and he was eager to get home. In the half-light, he could hardly see Giorgis's face under his hat, but the old man's voice was unusually audible.

'Dr Kyritsis,' he almost choked, 'there's a crowd over there. I think they're planning to attack Spinalonga!'

'What do you mean?'

'Hundreds of them have arrived. I don't know where from, but they're getting some boats together and they've got cans of petrol. They could be on their way any time now.'

Kyritsis was dumbstruck both by the stupidity of these people and by fear for the islanders. There was little time. He had a very swift choice to make. It would be wasting valuable minutes if he went back inside the great walls to warn the lepers. He had to get to the mainland to talk these lunatics out of their plan.

'We need to get back – *fast*,' he urged Giorgis.

Giorgis swung the boat around. This time the wind was behind him, and the caique covered the distance between island and mainland in no time at all. By now the people on the quayside had lit their torches, and as the small boat reached the shore another truckload of men was arriving. There was a ripple of excitement as Giorgis brought the boat in, and when Kyritsis disembarked the crowd parted to make way for a tall, broad-shouldered man who was clearly their spokesman.

'So who are *you*?' he mocked. 'Coming and going from the leper colony as freely as you like?'

The noisy crowd fell silent to listen to the exchange.

'My name is Dr Kyritsis. I am currently treating a number of patients on the island with new drug therapy. There are signs that this could lead to a cure.'

'Oh!' the man laughed sarcastically. 'Listen, everybody! Do you hear that? The lepers are going to get better.'

'There is a very strong chance of it.'

'Well supposing we don't believe that?'

'It doesn't matter if *you* don't believe it.' Kyritsis was dramatic in his emphasis. He focused on the ringleader. He could see that this bully would be nothing without his mob.

'So why is that then?' the man said with scorn, surveying the crowd who stood expectantly on the quayside, their faces lit by the flickering torches. Now he was trying to whip them up. He had misjudged this slight man who seemed to command more attention than he would have expected for someone of his stature.

'If you lay so much as a finger on a single one of those lepers out there,' said Kyritsis, 'you will find yourself in a prison cell darker and deeper than your worst nightmares. If even *one* of those lepers dies, you will be tried and convicted for murder. I will personally see to it.'

There was a stir amongst the crowd and then it fell silent again. The leader could sense that he had lost them. Kyritsis's firm voice penetrated the silence.

'Now what do you plan to do? Go home quietly or do your worst?'

People turned to each other and small huddles formed. One by one, torches were extinguished, plunging the quayside almost into darkness. One by one the crowd walked quietly to their vehicles. All their resolve to destroy Spinalonga had evaporated.

As the leader made his way alone back to the main street, he cast a backward glance at the doctor.

'We'll be looking out for that cure,' he shouted. 'And if it doesn't come, we'll be back. You mark my words.'

Giorgis Petrakis had remained in his boat during this confrontation, watching first with fear and then with admiration as Dr Kyritsis diffused the mob. It had seemed so unlikely that a lone individual could deter the force of this gang of thugs that had appeared hell-bent on destroying the leper colony.

Kyritsis had seemed to be completely in control, but inwardly he had feared for his own life. Not just that. He had feared for the life of every leper on the island. Once his heart ceased to feel that it would burst from his chest, he realised there was something specific that had given him the courage to stand up to the crowd: it was the possibility that the woman he loved had been in danger. He could not deny it to himself. It was Maria he had been desperate to save.

Chapter Twenty

IT DID NOT take long for word to get around Spinalonga that an uprising against the island had been quelled. Everyone soon knew that Dr Kyritsis had single-handedly dispersed a rowdy mob and for that he was the hero of the hour. He returned the following Wednesday as normal, and his anticipation at seeing Maria was more intense than ever. The realisation that he had such strong feelings for her had taken him by surprise, and he had thought of little else all week. She was on the quayside to meet him, a familiar figure in her green coat, and today a broad smile stretched across her face.

'Thank you, Dr Kyritsis,' she said, before he had even stepped off the boat. 'My father told me how you stood up to those men and everyone here is so grateful for what you did.'

By now Kyritsis was on dry land. Every part of him wanted to take her in his arms and declare his love, but such spontaneous behaviour went against a lifetime of reticence and he knew that he could not do it.

'Anyone would have done the same. It was nothing,' he said quietly. 'I did it for you.'

Such unguarded words. He knew he should be more careful.

'And for everyone on this island,' he added hastily.

Maria said nothing and Kyritsis had no idea whether she had even heard him. As usual they walked together through the tunnel, their feet crunching on the gravelly surface, and neither of them spoke. There was a silent acknowledgement that Kyritsis would come to her home for coffee before going on to the hospital, but as they reached the bend in the tunnel he saw immediately that today something was different. It was dark at the exit, and the usual view of Spinalonga's main street was obscured. The reason for this soon became clear. A huge crowd of perhaps two hundred had gathered there. Nearly every inhabitant of the island who was fit enough had made his or her way from home to greet the doctor. Children, young people and the elderly with their sticks and crutches had all turned out that chilly morning, hats on, collars up, to express their gratitude. As Kyritsis emerged, applause broke out all around him and he stopped in his tracks, taken aback to be the centre of attention. As the clapping died down, Papadimitriou stepped forward.

'Dr Kyritsis. On behalf of every inhabitant of this island, I would like to thank you for what you did last week. We understand that you saved us from invasion and in all likelihood from injury or death. Everyone here will be eternally grateful to you for that.'

Expectant eyes gazed at him. They wanted to hear his voice.

'You people have as much right to life as anyone on the

mainland. As long as I have anything to do with it, no one will destroy this place.'

Once again applause broke out, and then the islanders gradually drifted away and went about their daily business. Kyritsis had been overwhelmed by the ovation and was relieved when he was no longer the centre of so much attention. Papadimitriou was now at his side and walking along with him.

'Let me accompany you to the hospital,' he said, unaware that this deprived the doctor of precious moments with Maria. With the milling crowd Maria already knew that she could not expect Kyritsis to come to her house. It would be entirely inappropriate. She watched his receding figure and returned to her home. Two cups sat in the middle of her small table, and as she filled one and sat down to drink the coffee which had been brewing on her stove she addressed an imaginary figure sitting across the table.

'Well, Dr Kyritsis,' she said. 'You're a hero now.'

Meanwhile, Kyritsis thought of Maria. How could he possibly wait until the following Wednesday to see her? Seven days. One hundred and sixty-eight hours. There was, however, plenty to distract him. The hospital was under pressure. Dozens of the lepers were in need of urgent attention, and with only two people running the entire place, Lapakis and Manakis were more relieved than ever to see him.

'Good morning, Nikolaos!' cried Lapakis teasingly. 'The finest doctor in Crete, and now the Saint of Spinalonga!'

'Oh come on, Christos,' replied Kyritsis, slightly abashed. 'You know you would have done the same.'

'I'm not sure, you know. By all accounts they were pretty rough.'

'Well all that was last week,' said Kyritsis, brushing the episode to one side. 'We need to get on with today's issues. How are our test patients doing?'

'Let's go into my office and I'll put you in the picture.'

On Lapakis's desk was a tower of files. He picked them up one by one and gave his friend and colleague a brief description of the current state of each patient receiving the drug treatment. Most of the fifteen were showing signs of a positive reaction, though not all.

'Two of them are in a severely reactive state,' said Lapakis. 'One of them has had a temperature of around 104 degrees since you last came, and Athina just told me that the other kept the whole island awake last night with her screams. She keeps asking me how she can have no sensation in her arms and legs and yet feel such terrible pain. I haven't got an answer for her.'

'I'll take a look at her in a minute, but I think the best thing now would be to withdraw the treatment. There's a good chance that there might be some spontaneous healing and the sulphone could do some damage if that's the case.'

When they had taken a brief look through the notes, it was time for the two doctors to do the ward rounds. It was a grim business. One of the patients, who was covered with pus-filled swellings, wept in sheer agony as Lapakis applied a solution of trichloracetic acid to dry the lesions. Another listened quietly as Kyritsis suggested that the best way of dealing with the dead bones in his fingers would be amputation, a simple operation which could be done without anaesthetic, such was the absence of physical sensation in that part of the body. For another there was a visible surge of optimism as Lapakis described the tendon transplant he planned to do on his foot to enable him to walk again. At each bedside, the doctors agreed with the patient what the next stage would be. For some it was the prospect of pain-relieving injections, for others it might be the excision of lesions.

The first of the outpatients then began to arrive. Some merely needed new dressings for their ulcerated feet, but for others the treatment was more gruelling, particularly for a woman who required the excision of a lepromatous growth in her nose and the application of a dozen adrenaline swabs in order to stem the bleeding.

All of this took until mid-afternoon, and then it was time to see the patients who were receiving the new treatment. One thing was becoming clear. Several months into the trial, the new doses of drug therapy were producing encouraging results and the side-effects which Dr Kyritsis had been wary of had not materialised among most of these cases. Each week he had been on the lookout for symptoms of anaemia, hepatitis and psychosis, all of which had been reported by other doctors involved in the administration of dapsone, but he was relieved that none of these were present here.

'We've taken all our guinea pigs up from twenty-five to three hundred milligrams of dapsone twice a week now,' said Lapakis. 'That's the most I can give them, isn't it?'

'I certainly wouldn't recommend anything higher, and if that's giving us these results I think we should regard it as the upper limit, especially given the length of time they'll all be having the injections. The most recent directive is that we should continue to prescribe dapsone for several years after the patient's leprosy has ceased to be active,' said Kyritsis, adding after a pause: 'It's a long haul, but if it leads to a cure I don't think any of them will complain.'

'What about starting the treatment with the next group?'

Lapakis was both excited and impatient. No one would be bold enough to claim that these lepers had been cured, and it would be a few months until they actually ran tests to see whether the leprosy bacillus had been eliminated from their systems. He had a gut feeling that after all these years of talk, false starts and no real faith in a cure, a turning point had been reached. Resignation, even despair, could now be replaced with hope.

'Yes, there's no point in waiting. I think we should select the next fifteen as soon as possible. As before, they should be in good general health,' said Kyritsis.

With every bone in his body, he wanted to make sure that Maria was among the list of names, but he knew it would be unprofessional to exert his influence. His mind had drifted from discussion of the new treatment to thoughts of when he would see Maria again. Each day would seem an age.

The following Monday, Fotini arrived on the island as usual. Maria wanted to tell her about the hero's welcome Dr Kyritsis had received the previous week, but she could see that Fotini was bursting with news. She had hardly got inside Maria's door before she came out with it.

'Anna's pregnant!'

'At last,' Maria said, unsure whether this news was good or bad. 'Does my father know?'

'He can't do, otherwise he would have said something to you, surely?'

'I suppose he would,' she said thoughtfully. 'How did you find out?'

'Through Antonis, of course. By all accounts the estate has been buzzing with speculation for weeks!'

'Tell me then. Tell me what they've been saying,' said Maria, impatient for detail.

'Well, for weeks and weeks Anna wasn't seen outside the house and there were rumours of ill-health, and then one day last week she finally reappeared in public – having put on a very noticeable amount of weight!'

'But that doesn't necessarily mean she's pregnant,' exclaimed Maria.

'Oh yes it does, because they've announced it. She's three and a half months gone.'

In her first few months of pregnancy, Anna had been racked by sickness. Every morning and throughout the day she heaved and retched. Nothing she ate stayed inside her, and for several weeks her doctor was doubtful that the baby would survive at all. He had never seen a woman so ill, so reduced by pregnancy, and once the vomiting subsided there was a new problem. She began to bleed. The only way she might save this baby now was to have complete bed-rest. It seemed, however, that the child was determined to cling on, and in her fourteenth week of pregnancy everything stabilised. To Andreas's great relief Anna then rose from her bed.

The gaunt face that had stared back at Anna from the mirror only a month before was now rounded once more, and as she turned sideways she could clearly see a bump. Her trademark slim-fitting coats and dresses had been put in the back of the wardrobe and she now wore more voluminous clothes, under which her belly slowly swelled.

It was an excuse for celebration on the estate. Andreas threw open his cellar, and early one evening under the trees outside the house all his workers came to drink the best of the previous year's wine. Manoli was there too, and his was the loudest voice among them as they toasted the forthcoming child.

Maria listened in disbelief as Fotini described these recent events.

'I can't believe she hasn't made a point of going to see Father,' she said. 'She never thinks of anyone but herself, does she? Do I tell him, or wait until she gets round to it?'

'If I were you, I would tell him. Otherwise he's bound to hear it from someone else.'

They sat in silence for a while. The expectation of a child was normally a cause for great excitement, especially among women and close relations. Not this time, though.

'Presumably it's Andreas's?'

Maria had said the unsayable.

'I don't know. My hunch is that even Anna doesn't know, but Antonis says that gossip is still rife. They were all happy to drink to the new baby's safe arrival, but behind Andreas's back there was plenty of whispering and speculation.'

'That's not really surprising, is it?'

The two women talked for a while longer. This significant family development had swept other events aside and temporarily diverted Maria's thoughts from Kyritsis and his gallant behaviour the week before. For their first meeting in many weeks, Fotini found she was not listening to Maria's continual chatter about the doctor. 'Doctor Kyritsis this,

Doctor Kyritsis that!' she had teased Maria who had turned the colour of a mountain poppy when Fotini pointed out this slowly growing obsession.

'I'll have to tell Father about Anna as soon as I can,' said Maria. 'I'll tell him as though it's the best news ever and say Anna has been too sick to come and see him. It's half true anyway.'

When they got back to the quayside, Giorgis had offloaded all the boxes he was delivering and was sitting on the wall under the tree, quietly smoking a cigarette and surveying the view.

Though he had sat here a thousand times, weather and light combined together to produce a different picture every day. Sometimes the barren mountains that rose up behind Plaka would be blue, sometimes pale yellow, sometimes grey. Today, with the low clouds across the landscape, they were not visible at all. Parts of the sea's surface were whipped up by wind, creating areas of light spray that swirled about across the water like steam. The ocean was masquerading as a seething cauldron of boiling water, but in reality it was as cold as ice.

The sound of the women's voices disturbed him from his reverie, and he stood up to get the boat ready to go. His daughter hastened her step.

'Father, don't rush away. There's some news. Some really good news,' she said, doing her best to sound enthusiastic. Giorgis paused. The only good news he ever hoped for was that Maria might one day say she could come home. It was the only thing in the world he prayed for.

'Anna is having a baby,' she said simply.

'Anna?' he said vaguely, as though he had almost forgotten

who she was. 'Anna,' he repeated, staring at the ground. The truth was that he had not seen his elder daughter for over a year. Since the day that Maria had started her life on Spinalonga, Anna had not visited even once, and as Giorgis was *persona non grata* at the Vandoulakis home, contact had ceased. Initially this had been a source of great sadness, but with the passage of time, though he knew the paternal tie would always remain, he began to forget about his daughter. Occasionally he would wonder how two girls born of the same mother and father and treated the same way from the day they were born could turn out so differently, but that was about all the thought he had given to Anna of late.

'That's good,' he said at last, struggling to find a response. 'When?'

'We think it's due in August,' replied Maria. 'Why don't you write to her?'

'Yes, perhaps I should. It would be a good excuse to get in touch.'

What reaction should he have to hearing about the impending arrival of his first grandchild? He had seen several of his friends in a state of high exuberance when they became grandfathers. Only the previous year his greatest friend Pavlos Angelopoulos had celebrated the birth of Fotini's baby with an impromptu session of drinking and dancing, and it seemed that the entire population of Plaka had descended on the bar to celebrate with him. Giorgis did not picture himself making merry on *tsikoudia* when Anna's baby arrived, but it was, at least, an excuse to write to her. He would ask Maria's help in composing a letter later that week, but there was no hurry.

Two days later it was time for Kyritsis's visit. When he came to Spinalonga he had to rise at five a.m., and after his long journey from Iraklion the last few miles were full of anticipation for the taste of strong coffee on his lips. He could see Maria waiting for him, and today he inwardly rehearsed the words he was going to say to her. In his head he saw a version of himself that was articulate but full of passion, calm but fired with emotion, but as he got off the boat and was confronted by the face of the beautiful woman he loved, he knew that he should not be so hasty. Though she looked at him with the eyes of a friend, she spoke to him with the voice of a patient, and as her doctor he realised that his dreams of confessing his love were but that. Dreams. It was out of the question to cross the barrier created by his position.

They walked through the tunnel as normal, but this time, to his relief, there was no one cheering him at the end of it. As usual the cups were on the table, and Maria had saved time by making the coffee before he arrived.

'People are still talking about the way you saved us,' she said, taking a pot off the stove.

'It's very nice of them to be so appreciative, but I am sure they'll forget about it soon. I just hope those troublemakers keep away in future.'

'Oh, I think they will. Fotini told me it was all sparked by the rumour that a local boy had been taken to Iraklion for leprosy tests. Well, the child and his father returned last weekend. They'd been on a trip to see the boy's grandmother in Hania and decided to stay there for a few days. He wasn't ill at all.'

Kyritsis, listening intently to Maria, resolved to keep his

feelings under control. To do otherwise would be wrong, a transgression of his position.

'We've had some very encouraging results from the drug testing,' he said, changing the subject. 'Some of the patients are really showing an improvement.'

'I know,' she said. 'Dimitri Limonias is one of them, and I was talking to him yesterday. He says he can already feel a change.'

'Much of that could be psychological,' said Kyritsis. 'Being put on any kind of treatment tends to give patients a huge boost. Dr Lapakis is compiling a list of people from whom we will select the next group. Ultimately, we hope almost everyone on Spinalonga will be given the new drugs.'

He wanted to say that he hoped she would be on that list. He wanted to say that all his years of research and testing would be worthwhile if she was saved. He wanted to say that he loved her. None of those words came.

Much as he would have loved to linger in Maria's pretty home, he had to leave. It was hard to face yet another seven days before seeing her again, but he would not tolerate bad time-keeping in himself or others and knew that they would be waiting for him up at the hospital. Wednesdays were like a shaft of sunlight in the darkness of a strenuous, overworked week for Dr Lapakis and Dr Manakis, and this made Kyritsis's assiduous punctuality even more important. The extra workload that had been created for these two doctors in administering the drug therapy was taking them over the edge of endurance. Not only did they have to treat the patients who were in lepra reaction, but they also now had people who were suffering from the side-effects of the drugs. On many nights now, Lapakis was not leaving the island until ten o'clock, sometimes returning again at seven in the morning. Soon Kyritsis would have to consider increasing the frequency of his visits to Spinalonga to twice or even three times a week.

Within a couple of weeks, Dr Lapakis had shortlisted his next group of candidates for treatment. Maria was one of them. One Wednesday in mid-March, when the wild flowers were beginning to spread across the slopes on the north side of Spinalonga and the tight buds on the almond trees were bursting into blossom, Kyritsis went to find Maria in her house. It was six o'clock and she was surprised to hear a knock on the door at that time. She was even more amazed to see the doctor standing there, when she knew he was usually hurrying to meet her father in order to begin his long journey back to Iraklion.

'Dr Kyritsis. Come in . . . What can I get for you?'

The evening light glowed burnt amber through the gauze curtains. It was as though the village outside was going up in flames, and for all Kyritsis cared at this moment, this could have been the case. To Maria's surprise, he took both her hands.

'You're going to start treatment next week,' he said, looking directly into her eyes and, with absolute certainly, he added, 'one day you're going to leave this island.'

There were so many words he had rehearsed, but when the moment came he declared his love with a soundless gesture. For Maria, the cool fingers that grasped hers and lightly pressed them were more intimate, more articulate, than any arrangement of words about love. The life-giving sensation of flesh on flesh almost overwhelmed her.

In all those hours of discussion when she and Kyritsis had sat together talking of abstract things, she had been aware that even in the chinks where silence crept in she felt complete and content. It was just like the feeling she got when she found a lost key or a purse. After the frantic search and then the discovery, there was a sense of peace and wholeness. That was what being with Dr Kyritsis was like.

She could not help comparing him with Manoli, whose flamboyant talk and flirtatious behaviour flowed out of him unchecked, like water from a burst pipe. On their very first meeting at the Vandoulakis home, he had grabbed her by the hands and kissed them as though he was passionately in love. Yes, that was just it: she knew with absolute certainty that Manoli had not been passionately in love with her, but with the *idea* of being passionately in love. And here was Kyritsis, who gave every indication of not recognising his own feelings. He had been much too busy and preoccupied with his work even to acknowledge the signs or the symptoms.

Maria looked up. Their eyes and hands were now locked together. His was a look that overflowed with kindness and compassion. Neither of them knew how long they stood like this, though it was enough time for one era of their lives to end and another to begin.

'I will see you next week,' Kyritsis said finally. 'By then I hope Dr Lapakis will have given you a date for starting treatment. Goodbye, Maria.'

As he left her house, Maria watched Kyritsis's slight frame until it disappeared round the corner and out of sight. She felt she had known him for ever. It was in fact more than half her life ago that she had first set eyes on him, when he came to visit Spinalonga in the days before the German occupation. Though he had made little impression then, she now found it hard to remember what it had felt like *not* to love him. What had lived in that great space that Kyritsis now occupied?

Though no recognisable words of love had been spoken between Maria and the doctor, there was still plenty to tell Fotini. When she arrived the following Monday, it was patently obvious to her that something had happened to her oldest friend. Theirs was a friendship that could pick up a subtle sign of mood change; the merest hint of unhappiness or ill-health was always betrayed in hair that seemed dull, skin that was sallow or eyes that lacked their usual sparkle. Women noticed these things in each other, just as they noticed a gleam in the eye or a lingering smile. Today Maria was radiant.

'You look as though you have been cured,' Fotini joked, putting her bag down on the table. 'Come on, tell me. What's happened?'

'Dr Kyritsis—' Maria began.

'As if I couldn't have guessed,' teased Fotini. 'Go on . . .'

'I don't know what to tell you, really. He didn't even say anything.'

'But did he *do* anything?' urged Fotini, with the fervour of a friend eager for detail.

'He held my hands, that's all, but it meant something. I'm sure of it.'

Maria was conscious that hand-holding might sound insignificant to someone who was still part of the great outside world, but even on mainland Crete a certain formality between men and women was still the norm for unmarried people.

'He said that I would be starting treatment soon and that I might one day leave this island . . . and he said it as though he cared.'

All of this might have seemed feeble evidence of love. Fotini had never even met Kyritsis properly, so who was she to judge? In front of her, though, she had the sight of her greatest friend suffused with happiness. That much was very real.

'What would people here think if they knew there was something between you and the doctor?' Fotini was practical. She knew how small-town people talked, and Spinalonga was no different from Plaka, where a relationship between a doctor and his patient would keep the gossips on their doorsteps well into the small hours.

'No one must be allowed to know. I'm sure that a few people have noticed him coming out of my house on Wednesday mornings, but nobody has said anything. At least not to my face.'

She was right. A handful of people with vicious tongues had tried to spread the word, but Maria was well liked on the island, and malicious talk only tended to stick when someone was already halfway to being unpopular. What concerned Maria more than anything was that people might think she was getting preferential treatment; first place in a queue for injections, for example, or some other kind of perk, however meagre, would be enough to spark jealousy. That would reflect badly on Kyritsis and she was determined to ensure that no criticism attached itself to him. People like Katerina Papadimitriou, who had proved rather interfering, had seen Kyritsis leave her house on many occasions, and for someone who wanted to be in control of everything around her, this was disturbing. The leader's wife had done all she could to find out from Maria why Kyritsis came, but Maria had been deliberately unforthcoming. She had a right to her privacy. The other source of trouble was Kristina Kroustalakis, the unofficial town-crier, whose attempts to discredit Maria in some way had continued relentlessly for the past year. She went into the *kafenion* every evening and, on the basis of no evidence at all, dropped hints to anyone she met that Maria Petrakis was not to be trusted.

'She's carrying on with the specialist, you know,' she would say in a stage whisper. 'You mark my words, she'll be cured and off the island before any of us.'

It kept her going, this mission to stir up anger and discontent. She had tried – and failed – to do the same with Maria's mother; now she would do her best to destabilise the daughter's peace of mind. Maria, however, was strong enough to withstand such behaviour and enough in love with the doctor to make her happiness untouchable.

Maria's course of treatment began that month. Her symptoms had been slow to develop since she arrived on the island, with the anaesthetic patches on her skin spreading only marginally during the past eighteen months. Unlike so many of her fellow islanders, she had not experienced numbness in the soles of her feet and the palms of her hands, which meant she was unlikely to be vulnerable to the sores and ulcers which had cost so many of her fellow lepers the ability to walk and fend for themselves. If a sharp stone found its way into her shoe she soon knew about it, and her lithe hands curled around the handles of the big cooking pots she used at the 'block' as readily as they had ever done. This made her one of the lucky ones, but there was, nevertheless, an extraordinary relief in the sense that, finally, something was being done to combat the disease. Though it had not yet devastated her body, it had already done plenty of damage to her life.

The springtime wind, the Sokoros, blew from the south, finding its way between the mountains to the Gulf of Mirabello, where it whipped the sea into a white frenzy. Meanwhile on land the trees, now full of leaves in bud, began to whisper. How much better a sound than the rattle of dry, barren branches. Now that it was nearly May, the sun came out strongly and reliably each day and drenched the landscape in colour. Monochrome sky and rock had vanished and the world now put on its blue, gold, green, yellow and purple. Throughout early summer, birdsong was noisily exuberant, and then came two months when nature stood still in the breathless air and the scent of roses and hibiscus hung heavily on the air. Leaves and flowers had strained to emerge from dormant winter trees and plants and remained perfect through June and July before curling, scorched and dry, in the heat of the sun.

Dr Kyritsis continued to visit Maria at home once a week. They continued to say nothing of their feelings towards each other and there was an element of magic in their silence. It had the perfect fragility of a soap bubble rising into the sky, so visible, so multicoloured, but best left untouched. Maria one day found herself wondering how much her mother and father had ever spoken about love. She guessed correctly that they rarely had; in their happy marriage, there had seemed no need to mention something so certain, so unequivocal.

Throughout these summer months Maria, and now over half the population of Spinalonga, continued with the dapsone treatment. They knew it did not mean an overnight cure – or, as the more sardonic of them called it, 'reprieve from the gallows' – but at least it gave them hope, and even those still waiting for their treatment bathed in reflected optimism. Not everyone thrived, however. In July, having started her course only two weeks earlier, Elpida Kontomaris went into lepra reaction. Whether or not it was a consequence of the drug treatment, the doctors could not be sure, but they stopped giving her the injections straight away and did what they could to relieve the agony she was in. Her temperature raged out of control and for ten days did not drop below 105 degrees. Her body was now covered in ulcerated sores and every nerve felt tender; there seemed to be no position in which she was comfortable. Maria insisted on visiting her and, against all the rules of the hospital, Dr Lapakis allowed her into the small ward where the old lady lay, sobbing and sweating by turns.

Through her half-closed eyes, she recognised Maria.

'Maria,' she whispered hoarsely, 'they can't do anything for me.'

'Your body is fighting the disease. You mustn't give up hope,' Maria urged. 'Especially now! For the first time ever, they are so confident of a cure.'

'No, listen to me.' Through a burning, uncontrollable wall of pain, Elpida pleaded with Maria. 'I've been ill for so long. I just want to go now. I want to be with Petros . . . Please tell them to let me go.'

Sitting on an old wooden chair by her bed, Maria took

the woman's limp hand. Was this, she wondered, the same death that her own mother had suffered? The same violent battle where a weary body found itself under attack with no means of defence? She had not been there to say farewell to her mother, but she would stay with Elpida until the end.

At some point during that hot night, Athina Manakis came to relieve her.

'Go and get some rest,' she said. 'You won't do yourself any good if you sit here all night without anything to eat or drink. I'll stay with Elpida for a while.'

By now, Elpida's breathing was shallow. For the first time, it seemed that she was out of pain. Maria knew she might not have long and did not want to miss the moment of her going.

'I'll stay,' she said firmly. 'I must.'

Maria's instincts were right. A short while later, in the quietest hour of the night, between the very last moments of human activity and the first stirring of the birds, Elpida gave a final sigh and was gone. At last she was released from her ravaged body. Maria wept until her body was drained of tears and energy. Her grief was not just for the elderly woman who had given her so much friendship since she had arrived on the island, but for her own mother, whose last days might have been as agonising as Elpida's.

The funeral was an event which brought everyone on the island pouring down to the little church of St Pantaleimon. The priest conducted the service in the doorway so that the hundred or so who stood outside in the sun-baked street could share it with those who were crammed into the cool interior. When the chanting and prayers were over, the flower-covered coffin was carried at the head of a long procession which made its way slowly up the hill past the hospital and the 'block' and round to the unpopulated side of the island, where rocks fell away into the dark Stygian waters. Some of the older people sat on their wooden-saddled donkeys to make this long journey; others took each step carefully and slowly, reaching the cemetery long after the body had been lowered into the ground.

It was the last week of July and the saint's day for St Pantaleimon was on the twenty-seventh of the month. It seemed both a good and a bad time for such a celebration. On the one hand, with one of the most beloved members of the community so recently buried, the patron saint of healing seemed not to have been doing his job. On the other, many people on Spinalonga who had been receiving the drug treatment were showing early signs of recovery. For some, their lesions no longer seemed to be spreading; for others, as blood returned to tissue, paralysis appeared to be reversed. At least for a few it seemed as though a miracle might be about to take place. St Pantaleimon's birthday party must go ahead, even if people thought they should be in mourning for a lost friend.

Special breads and pastries were baked the night before, and on the day itself people filed through the church to light their candles and say a prayer. In the evening there was dancing and the singing of *mantinades*, and the half-heartedness which had characterised some recent festivals was absent. When the wind gusted in their direction, the people of Plaka could hear the occasional strains of lyre and bouzouki as they drifted across the water.

'People need a future,' Maria remarked to Kyritsis when he was sitting at her table the following week. 'Even if they're unsure about what it's going to bring.'

'What do you hear them saying?' he asked. She was his earpiece in the real world of the leper colony.

'No one talks about leaving yet,' she said. 'I think we all realise it's still early days. But the mood has changed. The people who haven't started their treatment are getting restless too. They know it matters.'

'It does matter. It might seem slow, but I promise you it really is going to make a difference.'

'How slow will it be?' she asked. The question of how long it was all going to take had never really been broached.

'Even when the disease has ceased to be active, we would need to continue with treatment for one or two years, depending on the severity of the case,' he replied.

In the timescale of this ancient disease, the oldest known to mankind, one or two years was the blink of an eye. But as Kyritsis looked at Maria, he realised that it seemed an eternity to him. It did to her too, though neither of them was likely to say so.

As if to balance death with birth, news came at the end of August that Anna's baby had been born. Giorgis arrived one Friday morning to tell Maria. He had not yet seen the child, a girl, but Antonis had come hotfoot to Plaka the previous day to tell him. It had not been an easy birth. Anna had been ill for some weeks at the end of the pregnancy and the labour had been difficult and protracted. Though she was still weak, the doctor assured her she would make a quick recovery, ready to have another. Nothing was further from her mind. The baby, fortunately, was healthy and now thriving.

The birth of a child in the family had softened Alexandros Vandoulakis towards Giorgis Petrakis and he now felt that it was an appropriate moment for reconciliation. The old man had had sufficient time out in the cold. A few days later an invitation arrived for him to attend the baptism. This would take place the following week and would be followed by feasting and merrymaking, for which Cretans needed little excuse. The arrival of a child in the Vandoulakis family after nearly a decade of waiting was a reason for great thanksgiving and celebration in both the family and the community beyond it. No one welcomed the disruption of the natural order which occurred when the people who owned the land and provided jobs failed to produce children. Now that Anna Vandoulakis had given birth to one child, none doubted that she would produce another and that the next time it would be a boy. That would ensure, once and for all, that the old patterns would continue for the next generation.

The baptism took place in the same church in Elounda where Anna and Andreas had been married nine years earlier. How much had changed since then, reflected Giorgis as he sat on a hard wooden seat at the back of the church waiting, along with dozens of others, for his daughter and her husband to arrive with the baby. He had arrived as late as he could and now sat hunched inside his jacket, keen to avoid conversation with other members of the Vandoulakis family, whom he had not seen for nearly two years now. Alexandros and Eleftheria were already at the front of the church when he arrived, and next to them was Manoli, who was talking animatedly to the people in the row behind him, his hands waving about as he told some anecdote that left his audience helpless with laughter. He was as handsome as ever, his dark hair slightly longer than Giorgis remembered it and his teeth gleaming white against his tanned skin. He must miss Maria, he mused, to have still not found another girl to be his wife. Then the congregation rose. The priest had entered and was processing down the aisle, followed by Andreas and Anna. She carried a tiny bundle of white lace.

Giorgis was immediately struck by the appearance of his daughter. He expected to see the radiance of motherhood, but instead it was an almost gaunt figure who wafted past him. He thought back to how Eleni had looked after the birth of their two children and remembered how she had maintained a healthy fullness that seemed natural to someone who had been carrying a child all those months. Anna, however, was as slim as a young vine and looked as fragile. It was a long time since he had seen her, but her physique was not as he had expected. Andreas looked just the same, thought Giorgis, rather stiff and upright and as aware as ever of his place in the world

The buzz of lively chatter stopped and a hush descended on the congregation, as though no one wanted to wake the baby. Though she was blissfully unaware of anything but the warmth of her mother's arms around her, it was a significant moment for the child. Until baptised, Sofia, as she was to be named, was exposed to the 'evil eye', but once the ritual had taken place her spiritual safety would be guaranteed.

As the rest of the gathering once again took their seats, Manoli stepped forward. Aside from the priest and the baby, he was the key figure at the baptism: the *nonos*, the godfather. In accordance with Cretan tradition, a child was given one godparent, who was the most important person in his life after his mother and father. As the congregation watched and listened to the priest's incantations and saw the waters washing away the baby's nonexistent sins, the spiritual bond between Manoli and Sofia was forged. He was handed the baby and now kissed her forehead. As he did so, the indescribably sweet essence of newborn infant enveloped him. Nothing seemed more natural than to treasure this tiny weightless being.

In the final stage of the ritual, a pure white ribbon was hung round Manoli's shoulders by the priest and knotted to create a symbolic circle embracing both man and child. Manoli looked down at the baby's sweet face and smiled. She was awake now, and her dark, innocent eyes gazed unfocused into his. On his face she would have seen a look of pure adoration, and no one doubted for a second that he would forever love and cherish his godchild, his precious *filiotsa*.

Chapter Twenty-one

AFTER THE BAPTISM, Giorgis hung back as the crowd made their way out of the church's great double doors and into the sunshine outside. He wanted to see his granddaughter up close but also he wanted to speak with her mother. Until now Anna had not even been aware that her father was there, but as she turned to leave the church she spotted him and waved enthusiastically across the sea of people who were now making their way past him, resuming the conversations they had started before the service began. It seemed like an age before she reached him.

'Father,' she said brightly, 'I'm so pleased you could come.'

She spoke to him as though he were some old friend or distant relative with whom she had long since lost touch but with whom she was quite pleased to resume an acquaintance.

'If you really are so pleased I came, why haven't you been to see me for over a year? I've not been anywhere,' he said, adding pointedly: 'Except Spinalonga.'

'I'm sorry, Father, but I wasn't well at the beginning or end of the pregnancy, and these summer months have been so hot and uncomfortable.'

There was no point in being critical of Anna. There never

had been. She had always managed to twist criticism round and make the accuser feel guilty; the disingenuity of her manner was only what he had expected.

'Can I meet my granddaughter?'

Manoli had lingered at the front of the church while a group gathered around him to admire his god-daughter. She was still bound to him within the white ribbon and he appeared to have no intention of letting her go. It was loving, but also proprietorial, the way in which he held her so close. Finally he made his way up the aisle towards the man who had so nearly become his father-in-law. They greeted each other and Giorgis studied what he could see of his little granddaughter, who was buried deep in many layers of lace and once again fast asleep.

'She's beautiful, isn't she?' said Manoli, smiling.

'From what I can see of her she is,' replied Giorgis.

'Just like her mother!' continued Manoli, glancing up at Anna with laughter in his eyes.

He had not really given Maria a second thought for months but felt he ought to enquire after her.

'How is Maria?' he asked, his voice sufficiently full of concern and interest to fool anyone who might overhear into thinking that he still cared for her. It was the question Anna should have asked, and she now stood quietly to hear the answer, wondering after all whether Manoli still carried a flame for her sister. Giorgis was more than happy to talk about his younger daughter.

'She is quite well and her symptoms haven't really got worse since she's been there,' he said. 'She spends most of her time helping the lepers who can't look after themselves. If they need a hand with their shopping and cooking she does it for them, and she still does a lot with her herbal cures as well.'

What he did not mention was that most of the islanders were now undergoing treatment. There was no point in making too much of it, because even he did not know what it really meant. He understood that the injections they were having could alleviate symptoms, but more than that he did not know. He certainly did not believe in a cure for leprosy. It was pure fantasy to imagine that the oldest disease in the world could be eradicated, and he would not let himself indulge in such a dream.

As he finished speaking, Andreas came over.

'Kalispera, Giorgis. How are you?' he asked rather formally. The appropriate niceties were exchanged and then the moment came for them all to leave the church. Alexandros and Eleftheria Vandoulakis hovered in the background. Eleftheria was still embarrassed by the gulf that existed between themselves and Giorgis Petrakis, and privately she felt a great deal of pity for the old man. She did not, however, have the guts to say so. This would have been to defy her husband, who felt as keenly as ever the shame and stigma of having such a close connection with the leper colony.

The family were the last to leave the church. The bearded priest, magnificent in his gilded crimson robes and tall black hat, stood laughing in the sunshine with a group of men. All around him women in bright floral dresses chattered and children ran about, dodging the adults and squealing as they gave chase to each other. There was to be a party tonight and a sense of excitement hung in the air like an electric charge.

The wall of shimmering heat that met Giorgis when he

emerged from the marble coolness of the church of Agios Grigorios made him feel light-headed. He blinked in the glare and beads of perspiration rolled down his cheeks like cool tears. The collar of his woollen jacket prickled uncomfortably at his neck. Was he to stay with this crowd and make merry through the night? Or should he return to his village, where the familiarity of every winding street and worn front door gave him comfort? As he was about to try and slip away unnoticed, Anna appeared at his side.

'Father, you must come and have a drink with us. I insist on it,' she said. 'It'll bring the baby bad luck if you don't.'

Giorgis believed as much in the influence of fate and the importance of trying to ward off evil spirits and their malicious power as he did in God and all his saints, and not wishing to bring any misfortune to this innocent baby he could not refuse his daughter's invitation.

The party was already in full swing when he parked his truck under a lemon tree at the side of the long driveway that led to the Vandoulakis home. On the terrace outside the house, a group of musicians was playing. The sounds of lute, lyre, mandolin and Cretan bagpipe wove in and out of each other, and though the dancing had not yet begun, there was a keen sense of anticipation. A long trestle table was laid out with rows of glasses, and people helped themselves from barrels of wine and took platefuls of *meze*, small cubes of feta cheese, plump olives and freshly made *dolmades*. Giorgis stood for a while before helping himself to some food. He knew one or two people and for a while engaged in polite conversation with them.

When the dancing began, those who wished to do so joined

in, while others stood around to watch. Glass in hand, the old man looked on as Manoli danced. His lithe figure and energetic steps made him the centre of attention, as did his smile and the way in which he shouted instructions and encouragement. In the first dance he whirled his partner round and round until it made onlookers dizzy to watch. The regular thump of the drum and the passionate insistence of the lyre had the power to mesmerise, but what held the audience spellbound was the spectacle of someone entirely transported by the rhythmic beat of the music. They saw in front of them a man with the rare ability to live for the moment, and his sheer abandon showed he did not give a damn what people thought.

Giorgis found his daughter standing by his side. He could feel the heat from her body, even before he saw she was there, but until the music stopped there was no purpose in speaking. There was too much noise. Anna folded her arms and unfolded them and Giorgis could sense her agitation. How desperately she seemed to want to be among the dancers, and when the music stopped and new people filtered into the circle and others bowed out, she quickly slipped in to take her place. Next to Manoli.

A different tune struck up. This one was more sedate, more stately, and the dancers held their heads high and rocked backwards and forwards and to left and right. Giorgis watched for a few moments. As he caught sight of Anna through the forest of arms and spinning bodies he could see that she had relaxed. She was smiling and making comments to her partner.

While his daughter was immersed in the dance, Giorgis took the opportunity to leave. Long after his small truck had bumped its way down the track and out on to the main road, he could still hear the strains of music in the air. Back in Plaka, he stopped at the bar. It was where he would find the easy camaraderie of his old friends and a quiet place to sit and think about the day.

It was not Giorgis who described the baptism to Maria the following day but Fotini, who had been given a detailed description by her brother, Antonis.

'Apparently he hardly put the baby down for a minute!' raved Fotini, outraged at the man's audacity.

'Do you think that annoyed Andreas?'

'Why should it?' asked Fotini. 'He clearly doesn't suspect a thing. Anyway, it left him free to circulate with his neighbours and the other guests. You know how focused he is on everything to do with the estate – he loves nothing more than talk of crop yields and olive tonnage.'

'But don't you think Anna wanted to hold her?'

'I don't honestly think she's that maternal. When Mattheos was born I couldn't bear him to be out of my arms. But everyone is different and it really doesn't seem to bother her.'

'And I suppose Manoli had the perfect excuse to monopolise her. Everyone expects it of the godfather,' said Maria. 'If Sofia *is* his child, it will have been the one day of his life when he could make a fuss of her like that without anyone questioning it.'

Both women were silent for a while. They sipped their coffee and finally Maria spoke.

'So do you *really* think Sofia is Manoli's child?'

'I have absolutely no idea,' answered Fotini. 'But he certainly feels a strong bond with her.'

Andreas had been delighted by the birth of Sofia, but became anxious about his wife during the next few months. She looked ill and tired but seemed to perk up when Manoli came to call. At the time of the baptism Andreas had been unaware of the strong current that flowed between his wife and cousin, but in the months that followed he began to question the amount of time that Manoli spent in their home. His position as a member of the family and now *nonos* to Sofia was one thing, but his frequent presence in the house was another. Andreas began to observe how Anna's mood could change the minute Manoli left, from frivolous to frowning, from gay to grumpy, and noticed how her warmest smiles were reserved for his cousin. He tried to put these thoughts from his mind for much of the time, but there were other things to arouse his suspicion. One evening he returned from the estate to find the bed unmade. This happened several more times, and on two other occasions he noticed that the sheets had only been roughly straightened.

'What's wrong with the maid?' he asked. 'If she's neglecting her duties, she ought to be sacked.'

Anna promised to talk to her, and for a time there was no more cause for complaint.

Life on Spinalonga continued just as before. Dr Lapakis came and went each day and Dr Kyritsis got approval from the hospital in Iraklion to increase his visits from once to three times each week. One particular autumn evening as he made his journey from Spinalonga to Plaka, something struck him forcibly. Dusk had already fallen; the sun had dropped behind the mountains, depriving the whole strip of coastline of its light and plunging it into near darkness. When he looked round, however, he saw that Spinalonga was still bathed in the golden glow of the last of the sun's rays. It seemed to Kyritsis the right way round.

It was Plaka that had many of the qualities you would expect of an island – insular, self-contained and sealed against the outside world – whereas Spinalonga hummed with life and energy. Its newspaper, *The Spinalonga Star*, still edited by Yiannis Solomonidis, carried digests of world news along with comment and opinion. There were also reviews of films which were due to be shown in forthcoming months, and extracts from the writings of Nikos Kazantzakis. Week by week they serialised his visionary book *Freedom and Death* and the inhabitants of the colony devoured every word, waiting each week for the next instalment, which they would then discuss in the *kafenion*. When the Cretan writer was awarded the World Peace Prize in June that year, they even reprinted his acceptance speech. 'If we do not want to allow the world to sink into chaos, we must release the love which is trapped in the heart of all humans,' Kazantzakis had said. The words resonated with readers on Spinalonga, who were all too aware of the mayhem and suffering that they had been protected from both in Greece and further afield by being incarcerated on the island for so long. Many of them relished the chance to stretch their intellects, and they would sit for hours chewing the cud over the latest sayings of this literary and political Goliath, as well as other contemporary authors. Several of the Athenians had books sent out each month to augment the sizeable library already on the island which was free for everyone to use. Perhaps because they dreamed of leaving, they continually looked outwards, beyond the place where they lived.

The *kafenion* and the taverna overflowed with customers in the evening and now even had competition in the form of a second small taverna. The allotments round the back of the island all looked as though they would yield good crops that summer, and there was plenty to buy and sell in the twice-weekly market. The island had never been in such good shape; not even when the Turks first built their homes had conditions been so comfortable.

Occasionally Maria allowed herself a moment of frustrated outburst with Fotini.

'It's almost more agonising now that I know there's a chance we might be cured,' she said, gripping her hands together. 'Can we dream or should we just be happy with the present?'

'It's never a bad thing to be content with the present,' said Fotini.

Maria knew her friend was right. She had nothing to lose if the here and now could be enough. One thing that did prey on her mind, however, was the consequence for her of being cured.

'What would happen then?' she asked.

'You'd be back with us in Plaka, wouldn't you? Just as you were before.'

Fotini appeared to be missing the point. Maria stared down at her hands and then looked up at her friend, who was crocheting the edge of a baby's coat as they talked. She was pregnant again.

'But if I was no longer on Spinalonga, I would never see Dr Kyritsis again,' she said.

'Of course you would. If you weren't living here he'd no longer be your doctor and things might be different.'

'I know you're right, but it fills me with dread,' said Maria. She pointed at the newspaper which lay on her table, open at the serialised extract from Kazantzakis's book. 'See that,' she said. '*Freedom and Death.* It sums up my situation exactly. I might get my freedom, but when I do it'll be no better than death if I can't see Dr Kyritsis any more.'

'Has he still not said anything to you?'

'No, nothing,' Maria confirmed.

'But he comes to see you every week. Doesn't that say enough?'

'Not quite,' Maria said bluntly. 'Though I do understand why he can't say anything. It wouldn't be the right thing to do.'

Maria betrayed none of her anxiety when she saw Kyritsis. Instead she used the time with him to ask for advice in helping the cases she looked after in the 'block'. These were people who needed immediate relief from the aches and pains they endured on a daily basis. Some of their problems were irreversible, but others could be alleviated with the right physiotherapy. Maria wanted to make sure she was advising them correctly on exercising, since some of these cases rarely got to see a doctor. More vigorously than ever she threw herself into her work. She was not going to dwell on what she regarded as the remote possibility of leaving Spinalonga. Repatriation would bring such mixed feelings, not just for her but for so many others. Spinalonga was a safety net for them, and the thought of leaving it was bittersweet. Even when they were no longer infectious, many of them would carry the scars of the disease, the strangely pigmented skin, the twisted hands, the deformed feet. The rehabilitation of such cases would be another lifetime's work.

Unbeknown to her, the doctors were testing and retesting the patients who had been the first to receive the treatment, just over a year before. Five of them appeared to be entirely free of the bacillus. One of these was Dimitri Limonias; another was Theodoros Makridakis. During all those years since Papadimitriou had beaten him to the position of leader, Makridakis had maintained his political opposition to the Athenians, who had effortlessly made themselves the ruling class. Now portly and white-haired, he still stood for election, but each year, as the support for Papadimitriou became stronger, the number voting for Makridakis diminished. He hardly minded at all. Why should he? The living conditions for all of them had improved exponentially since he had arrived on the island all those years ago, and he knew as well as anyone that this had largely been thanks to his Athenian friends. His attitude to them had softened over the years and he only maintained his opposition so that he could sustain a lively debate with them in the *kafenion*.

At the tail end of a long and arduous day, Kyritsis and Lapakis sat down to review some test results. Something had become very obvious.

'You know we'll soon have a good case for letting these patients go, don't you?' said Kyritsis with a rare smile.

'I do,' replied Lapakis. 'But we'll need government approval first and they may be reluctant to give it so soon.'

'I'll request their release from here on condition that they continue to have treatment for a few months afterwards and check-ups for another year after that.'

'Agreed. Once we've got government authority, we'll tell the patients, but not before.'

Weeks passed before a letter came. It stated that the patients would have to test negative for a whole year before they could be let off the island. Kyritsis was disappointed by the delay this would entail, but even so the goal he was aiming for now seemed within reach. Over the next few months the tests remained clear, and it looked as though the first dozen could be gone by Christmas.

'Can we tell them yet?' asked Lapakis one morning. 'Some of them keep asking when and it's hard to keep fobbing them off.'

'Yes, I think it's time. I believe there's no danger now of a relapse in any of these cases.'

The first few patients greeted the announcement of their clean bill of health with tears of joy. Though they promised to keep the news to themselves for a few days, neither Lapakis nor Kyritsis imagined for a moment that they could possibly do so.

At four o'clock Dimitri arrived and sat waiting his turn. The patient before him, the woman who worked in the bakery, emerged tear-stained, dabbing at her scarred cheeks with a large white handkerchief. She must have been given some bad news, thought Dimitri. At two minutes past four, Kyritsis put his head round the door and called him in.

'Sit down, Dimitri,' said the doctor. 'We have some news for you.'

Lapakis leant forward, his face beaming.

'We have been given permission to release you from the colony.'

Dimitri knew what he was supposed to feel, but it was as though the numbness that used to afflict his hands had returned and this time taken his tongue. He remembered little of life before Spinalonga. It was his home and the colonists were his family. His real family had long since stopped communicating with him and he would have no idea how to find them now. His face had become very disfigured on one side, which was not a problem here, but in the outside world it would single him out for attention. What would he do if he left, and who would teach in the school?

A hundred questions and doubts whirled around in his mind and a few minutes went by before he could speak.

'I would rather remain here while I have a function,' he said to Kyritsis, 'than leave all of this behind and go into the unknown.'

He was not alone in his reluctance to leave. Others also feared that the visible legacy of the disease would always remain with them and mark them out, and they needed reassurance that they might be able to reintegrate. It was like being a guinea pig all over again.

In spite of the misgivings of these few, it was a momentous occasion in the island's history. For more than fifty years lepers had come but never gone, and there was thanksgiving in the church and celebration in the *kafenion*. Theodoros Makridakis and Panos Sklavounis, the Athenian who had set up the thriving cinema, were the first to leave. A small party gathered by the entrance to the tunnel to bid them farewell, and both of them fought back tears, with little success. What weight of mixed feelings burdened them as they shook hands with the men and women who had been their friends and companions for so many years. Neither of them knew what life over that strip of water held for them as they boarded Giorgis's waiting boat to pass from the known into the unknown. They would travel together as far as Iraklion, where Makridakis would try to pick up the threads of his former life, and Sklavounis would take the boat to Athens, knowing already that his former career as an actor could not be resumed. Not the way he looked now. Both men would keep a tight hold on the medical papers which declared them 'Clean'; there would be several occasions over the following few weeks when they would be obliged to show them in order to verify that they were officially free of the disease.

Months later, Giorgis brought letters to Spinalonga from the two men. Both described the great hardship of trying to fit back into society and told how they were treated as outcasts by anyone who identified them as men who had once lived in the leper colony. Theirs were not encouraging tales, and Papadimitriou, who was the recipient, shared them with no one. Others from the first treatment group had also now left. They were all Cretan and had been welcomed by their families and found new work.

The pattern of recovery continued during the following year. The doctors kept meticulous records of everyone's date of first treatment and how many months the test had shown up as negative.

'By the end of this year we'll be out of a job,' said the sardonic Lapakis.

'I never thought that unemployment would be my aim in

life,' replied Athina Manakis, 'but it is now.'

By late spring, save for a few dozen cases who had reacted so badly against the treatment that they had been obliged to stop undergoing it, and some who had not responded at all, it was clear that the summer could bring a widespread clean bill of health. By July there were discussions on Spinalonga between the doctors and Nikos Papadimitriou regarding how all this should be managed.

Giorgis, who had ferried that first batch of cured men and women away from Spinalonga, now counted the days until Maria might be on his boat once again. The inconceivable had now become a reality and yet he feared there might be some hitch, some unforeseen problem that had not yet been envisaged.

He kept both his excitement and his anxieties to himself and many times had to bite his tongue when he overheard the usual tactless banter in the bar.

'Well I for one shan't be putting up the bunting to welcome them back,' said one fisherman.

'Oh, come on,' responded another. 'Have a bit of sympathy with them.'

Those who had always been more openly resentful of the leper colony remembered with some shame the night when plans to raid the island had nearly got out of hand.

In Lapakis's office early one evening, the island leader and the three doctors were discussing how the event should be marked.

'I want the world to know that we're leaving because we're cured,' said Papadimitriou. 'If people leave in twos and threes and steal off into the night it gives out the wrong message to everyone on the mainland. Why are they sneaking away? they'll ask. I want everyone to know the truth.'

'But how do you suggest we do that?' asked Kyritsis quietly.

'I think we should all leave together. I want a celebration. I want a feast of thanksgiving on the mainland. I don't think it's too much to ask.'

'We have those who aren't cured to think about too,' said Manakis. 'There's nothing for them to celebrate.'

'The patients who are facing longer-term treatment,' said Kyritsis diplomatically, 'will also be leaving the island, we hope.'

'How's that?' asked Papadimitriou.

'I am currently awaiting authority for them to be transferred to a hospital in Athens,' he answered. 'They will receive better care there, and in any case the government won't fund Spinalonga once there are too few people here.'

'In that case,' said Lapakis, 'can I suggest that we allow the sick to leave the island before the cured. I think it would be easier for them that way.'

They were all in agreement. Papadimitriou would have his public display of this new freedom, and those who were yet to be cured would be tactfully transferred to the Hospital of Santa Barbara in Athens. All that remained now was to make the arrangements. This was to take several weeks, but a date was soon set. It was to be 25 August, the feast of Agios Titos, the patron saint of all Crete. The only one among them who harboured any misgivings about the fact that Spinalonga's days as a leper colony were now numbered was Kyritsis. He might never see Maria again.

Chapter Twenty-two

1957

As they would have done in any normal year, the residents of Plaka made preparations for the saint's day feast. This year would be different, however. They would be sharing the celebrations with the inhabitants of Spinalonga, their close neighbours who had existed only in their imaginations for so many years. For some it would mean welcoming home almost forgotten friends; for others it would mean confronting their own deep prejudices and trying to suppress them. They were to sit down at a table and share food with their hitherto unseen neighbours.

Giorgis was one of very few people who had known the reality of the colony. Many others on the mainland had for years enjoyed the financial benefits of having such an institution across the water, supplying them with much of what they consumed, and for them the prospect of the colony's closure meant a loss of business. Others admitted to themselves that they felt a certain relief at the thought of Spinalonga's demise. The sheer volume of sick men and women over the water had always worried them, and in spite of the knowledge that this disease was less contagious than many others, they still feared it as they would bubonic plague. These people kept their minds closed to the fact that leprosy could now be cured.

There were some who keenly anticipated the arrival of their guests for this historic night. Fotini's mother, Savina Angelopoulos, still cherished the memory of her friend Eleni whose loss she had grieved for many years, and to see Maria free again would be pure joy. It would mean only one tragedy, not two. Apart from Giorgis, Fotini rejoiced more than anyone. She was to be reunited with her best friend. No longer would they need to meet in the semi-darkness of Maria's house on Spinalonga. Now they would be able to sit on the bright restaurant terrace chewing over the events of the day while the sun went down and the moon came up.

In the steamy heat of this August afternoon, in the taverna kitchen, Stephanos was cooking up great metal dishes of goat stew, swordfish and rice pilaff, and the *zakaroplastion*, the patisserie, was baking trays of honeysweet *baklava* and *katefi*. This would be the feast to end all feasts in its lavish offerings of food.

Vangelis Lidaki relished such an event. He enjoyed the emotional temperature created by a day so out of the ordinary, and also knew what it must mean to Giorgis, one of his most regular if least talkative customers. It occurred to him too that some of the inhabitants of Spinalonga might become new citizens of Plaka, swelling the population and increasing his own business. Success for Lidaki was judged by the number of empty beer and raki bottles that rattled around in his old crates at the end of each day, and he hoped that the volume of these might swell.

Feelings among the lepers were as mixed as the feelings of the people about to receive them. Some of the members of the colony dared not admit even to themselves that their departure filled them with as much dread as had their arrival. The island had given them undreamt-of security and many dreaded losing that. Some of the islanders, even though there was not a mark, not a blemish, to indicate that they had been leprous, were full of trepidation that they would never be able to live a normal life. Dimitri was not the only one of the younger islanders to have no memory of anywhere other than Spinalonga. It had been their world, with everything outside it no more real than pictures in a book. Even the village they looked at across the water each day seemed little more than a mirage.

Maria had no problem remembering life on the mainland, although it seemed that the past she looked back on was someone else's, not her own. What would become of a woman who had lived the best part of her twenties as a leper and who would be considered an old maid back on the mainland? All she could really see as she looked across the continually churning, undulating waters was the uncertainty of it all.

Some people on Spinalonga had spent the month before departure carefully packing each and every possession to take with them. There were several who had received a warm response from their families when they had written to tell them the good news of their release and who expected a kind welcome. They knew they would have somewhere to unpack their clothes, their china, their pots, their precious rugs. Others ignored what was about to happen, carrying on the routine of daily life until the very last minute as though it was never going to change. It was a hotter than ever August, with a fierce Meltemi that blew the roses flat and sent shirts flying from washing lines like giant white gulls. In the afternoons, everything but the wind was subdued. It continued to bang doors and rattle windows while people slept in shuttered rooms to escape the heat of the sun.

The day for departure came, and whether people had prepared themselves or not, it was time to leave. This time it was not only Giorgis who went to the island, but half a dozen other village fishermen who finally believed they had nothing to fear and would help ferry people away from Spinalonga with all their worldly possessions. At one o'clock in the afternoon on 25 August, a small flotilla could be seen approaching from Plaka.

A final service had been held in the tiny church of St Pantaleimon on the previous day, but people had filed through the church to light candles and mumble their prayers for many days before that. They came to give thanks, and as they took deep breaths to calm their unsteady nerves, inhaling the heady, treacle-thick scent of the candles that flickered around them, they prayed to God that He would give them the courage to face whatever the world across that narrow strip of water brought them.

The elderly and those still sick were helped on board first. Donkeys worked hard that day, plodding back and forth through the tunnel bearing people's possessions and pulling carts piled high with boxes. A great mountain of goods built up on the quayside, turning a long-held dream into the tangible reality of departure. It was only now that some of them really believed this old life was ended and a new one was to begin. As they made their way through the tunnel they imagined they could hear their own heartbeats drumming against its walls.

Kyritsis was officiating on the quayside in Plaka, ensuring that those who were still sick and being taken back to Athens to continue treatment were carefully dealt with.

Among the last few left on the island were Lapakis and Maria. The doctor had needed to clear up the final pieces of paperwork and had packed all the necessary folders in a box. These medical records gave his patients a clean bill of health and would be in his own safe-keeping until everyone had crossed the water. Only then would he distribute them. They would be the islanders' passports to freedom.

Leaving the little alleyway from her house for the final time, Maria looked up the hill towards the hospital. She could see Lapakis making his way down the street, struggling with his cumbersome boxes, and set off to help him. All around her were signs of hasty departure. Until that final hour, a few had refused to believe that they were really leaving. Someone had failed to fasten a window and it now banged in the breeze; several shutters had come loose from their catches and curtains flapped around them like sails. Cups and saucers sat abandoned on tables in the *kafenion*, and in the school room an open book lay on a desk. Algebraic formulae were still scratched in chalk on the blackboard. In one of the shops a row of tins remained on a shelf as if the shopkeeper had imagined he might open it up again some day. Bright geraniums planted in old olive oil drums were already wilting. They would not be watered that night.

'Don't worry about me, Maria,' said the doctor, red in the face. 'You've got plenty to think about.'

'No, let me help you. There's no reason why you should break your back for us any more,' she said, taking one of the smaller record boxes. 'We're all healthy now, aren't we?'

'You certainly are,' he replied. 'And some of you can go away and put this whole experience behind you.'

Lapakis knew as soon as he had said it how hard this would probably be, and was embarrassed at his own thoughtlessness. He fumbled his way towards the words that he thought would give greatest comfort.

'A new beginning. That's what I mean . . . You'll be able to have a new beginning.'

Lapakis was not to know it, but a new beginning was exactly the opposite of what Maria wanted. It suggested that everything of her old life on the island would be swept away. Why should he know that the most precious thing of all was something she would never have found but for her exile on this island and that, far from wanting to leave everything of her life on Spinalonga behind, Maria wanted to take the best of it with her?

As she took a last look up the main street, acute feelings of nostalgia almost made her swoon. Memories rolled one after the other into her mind, overlapping and colliding. The extraordinary friendships she had formed, the camaraderie of laundry days, the merrymaking on feast days, the pleasure of seeing the latest films, the satisfaction in helping people who really needed her, the unwarranted fear when fierce debates raged in the *kafenion*, mostly between the Athenians and usually on subjects that seemed to have little relevance to their own day-to-day lives. It was as if no time at all had elapsed between the moment she had stood on this spot for the first time and now. Four years ago she had been full of hatred for Spinalonga. At the time, death had seemed infinitely preferable to a life sentence on this island, but now here she was, momentarily reticent about leaving. In a few seconds, another life would begin, and she did not know what it would hold.

Lapakis read all this in her face. For him, as well, life was to bring new uncertainties now that his work on Spinalonga was over. He would travel to Athens to spend a few months with the lepers who were going to the Santa Barbara hospital and still needed treatment, but after that his own life was as unmapped as the moon.

'Come on,' he said. 'I think we should go. Your father will be waiting for us.'

They both turned now and walked through the tunnel. The sound of their steps reverberated around them. Giorgis was waiting at the other end. Drawing deeply on a cigarette, he sat on the wall in the shade of a mimosa tree watching for his daughter to emerge from the tunnel. It seemed as though she would never come. Apart from Maria and Lapakis, the island was now evacuated. Even the donkeys, goats and cats had been ferried across in a scene reminiscent of Noah's Ark. The last boat, except for this, had departed ten minutes earlier and the quayside was now deserted. Close by, a small metal box, a sheaf of letters and a full packet of cigarettes had been dropped, all testimony to the hurried departure of the final group. Perhaps there had been a hitch, Giorgis thought in a panic. Maybe Maria could not leave after all. Perhaps the doctor had not signed her papers.

At the moment when these rogue thoughts had taken on an uncomfortable reality, Maria emerged from the black semicircle of the tunnel and ran towards him, her arms outstretched, all second thoughts and doubts about leaving the island forgotten as she embraced her father. Wordlessly he basked in the sensation of her silky hair against his rough skin.

'Shall we go?' Maria asked, eventually.

Her possessions were already loaded on board. Lapakis got on first and turned to take Maria's hand. She put one foot on the boat. For a fraction of a second the other remained on the stony ground, and then she lifted it. Her life on Spinalonga was over.

Giorgis untethered his old caique and pushed it away from the quayside. Then, nimbly for a man his age, he jumped aboard and swung the boat around so that it was soon heading away from the island and out towards the mainland. His passengers faced towards the front of the boat. They watched the sharp point of the prow which, like an arrow, sped swiftly towards its target. Giorgis was wasting no time. His view of Spinalonga was still all too clear. The dark shapes of the windows looked at him like hollow, sightless eyes and their unbearable emptiness made him think of all those lepers who had ended their days afflicted by blindess. Suddenly he had a vision of Eleni as she was the last time he ever saw her, standing on that quayside, and for a moment the joy of having his daughter close by him was forgotten.

It was only a matter of minutes now before they were to land. The little harbour in Plaka was crowded with people. Many of the colonists had been greeted by family and friends; others simply hugged each other as they touched their native land for the first time in as many as twenty-five years. The noisiest contingent were the Athenians. Some of their friends and even colleagues had travelled all the way from their city to celebrate this epoch-making day. There would be no time for sleep tonight, and tomorrow morning they would all make their way back to Iraklion for the return journey to Athens. For now they would teach Plaka a thing or two about the art of making merry. Some of them were musicians and had already practised that morning with the locals, forming an impressive orchestra of every instrument, from lyre and lute and mandolin to bouzouki, bagpipe and shepherd's flute.

Their new baby, Petros, in arms, Fotini and Stephanos were there to greet Maria, along with Mattheos, their little brown-eyed boy, who danced about with excitement in the heady atmosphere, not at all aware of the significance of the day but delighted by the suggestion of carnival in the air.

'Welcome home, Maria,' said Stephanos. He had stood back as his wife embraced her best friend, waiting his turn to greet her. 'We are so glad that you are back.'

He began to lift Maria's boxes and load them on to his pick-up truck. It was only a short distance to the Petrakis house, but too far to carry everything by hand. The two women crossed the square, leaving Giorgis to tie up the boat. They would go on foot. Trestle tables were already set up and chairs were laid out in groups. Bright little flags traced the four sides of the square and fluttered gaily across its diagonals. It would not be long before the party began.

By the time Maria and Fotini arrived at the house, Stephanos had already unloaded the boxes, which now sat inside the door. As she went in, Maria felt a pricking sensation on the back of her neck. Nothing had changed since the day she left. All was immaculately in place just as it always had been: the same embroidered sampler with its welcoming '*Kali Mera*' – 'Good Morning' – that her mother had completed just in time for her marriage hung on the wall opposite the door to greet visitors, the same collection of pans hung near the fireplace and the familiar set of flower-sprigged china plates was ranged on the rack. Inside one of her boxes Maria would soon find some matching ones and the parts of the service would be united once again.

Even on such a luminous day, it was gloomy in this house. All the old familiar objects might still be in their places, but the walls themselves seemed to have absorbed the profound misery that had been endured within them. They exuded the loneliness of her father's previous few years. Everything appeared to be the same, but nothing was as it had been.

When Giorgis walked in a few moments later, he found Stephanos, Fotini, Petros and Mattheos, who was clutching a small posy of flowers, and Maria all crowded into the little house. At last it seemed that some fragments of his life were fitting back together. His beautiful daughter was standing in front of him, one out of the three women in the framed photograph he looked at each and every day. In his eyes, she was lovelier than ever.

'Well,' said Fotini. 'I shouldn't stay too long – there's food still to be prepared. Shall we see you back in the square?'

'Thanks for everything. I'm so lucky to be coming back to old friends like you – and a new friend as well,' she said, looking towards Mattheos, who now plucked up the courage to step forward and give her the flowers.

Maria smiled. They were the first flowers she had been given since Manoli had presented her with some four years earlier, only a week before she had gone to be tested for leprosy. The little boy's gesture touched her.

It was more than half an hour later, changed into a different dress and with her hair brushed until it gleamed more brightly than the mirror itself, that Maria felt ready to go out and face the curiosity of the inhabitants of Plaka. Despite the welcome that some of her neighbours would give her, she knew that others would be scrutinising her and looking for signs of the disease. They would be disappointed. Maria did not bear the slightest trace. There were several on whom the disease had taken a greater toll. Many would hobble for life on their crippled feet, and the unlucky few who had lost their sight would forever be reliant on their families. For the majority, however, lesions had vanished, ugly skin pigmentations had faded to invisibility, and feeling had returned to the places where anaesthesia had numbed them.

Maria and her father walked together towards the square.

'I won't believe it until I see it,' said Giorgis, 'but your sister has said she might come tonight. I got a note from her yesterday.'

'Anna?' said Maria, astonished. 'With Andreas too?'

'So she said in her letter. I suppose she wants to welcome you back.'

Like any parent, he yearned for reunion and assumed that Anna thought it a good moment to make up for her negligence over the past few years. If he could have two daughters back instead of one that would make him happier than ever. For

Maria, on the other hand, a meeting with Anna tonight was a prospect that she did not relish. Celebration not reconciliation was the purpose of today: every last leper on Spinalonga was finally to be given his liberty.

In her Elounda home, Anna was preparing herself for the party in Plaka, carefully pinning her hair and meticulously applying her lipstick so that it followed precisely the curve of her full lips. Sitting on her grandmother's lap, Sofia watched intently as her mother painted her face until her cheeks were as highly coloured as a doll's.

Ignoring both his mother and his daughter, Andreas marched in.

'Aren't you ready yet?' he asked Anna coldly.

'Almost,' she replied, adjusting her heavy turquoise necklace in the mirror and lifting her chin to admire the effect before spraying herself with a storm cloud of French perfume.

'Can we go then?' he snapped.

Anna seemed oblivious to her husband's icy tones. Eleftheria was not. She was discomfited by the way her son addressed his wife. She had not heard this coolness of tone before, nor seen him give her such glaring looks, and she wondered whether Andreas had, at last, woken up to the familiarity that now existed between his wife and Manoli. She had once mentioned her concerns to Alexandros. It was a mistake. He was angry and swore to boot out 'that good-for-nothing Don Juan' if he crossed any boundaries. After that, Eleftheria had kept her worries to herself.

'Night-night, sweetheart.' Anna turned to her little daughter, whose chubby arms reached out towards her. 'Be good.'

And with that she planted a perfect imprint of her lips on Sofia's forehead and left the room.

Andreas was already waiting in the car, the engine revving. He knew why his wife was taking such meticulous care with her appearance, and it was not for him.

It was something extraordinarily small that had finally made Andreas face the fact that his wife was being unfaithful to him: an earring under his pillow. Anna was always meticulous about removing her jewellery and carefully laying it inside a velvet-lined drawer in her dressing table before she went to bed, and Andreas knew he would have noticed if she had come to bed wearing her gold and diamond earrings the previous night. He said nothing when he saw the glint of gold against the white linen as he climbed between his otherwise immaculate sheets, but his heart turned to ice. In that instant, his *philotemo*, the very sense of honour and pride that made him a man, was mortally wounded.

Two days after that he came home in the early afternoon, parking his car some distance away and walking the last fifty metres to his house. He was not surprised to see Manoli's truck parked outside. He had known it would be there. Opening the front door quietly, he stepped into the hallway. A clock ticked but otherwise the house was deadly quiet. Suddenly the silence was shattered. A woman wailed. Andreas gripped the banister, repulsed, sickened by the sound of his wife's ecstasy. His instinct was to leap the stairs two at a time, burst into his bedroom and tear them both limb from limb, but something stopped him. He was Andreas Vandoulakis. He had to act in a more measured way and he needed time to think.

* * *

As Maria approached the square there was already an immense crowd gathered there. She spotted Dimitri standing at the centre of a small group along with Gerasimo Vilakis, who had run the colony's *kafenion*, and Kristina Kroustalakis, who was smiling. It made her almost unrecognisable. All around was the buzz of excited talk and the faint strain of music as someone strummed a bouzouki at the far end of the street. Greetings were called from left and right as she came into the open space. She met many boisterous families and friends from Athens and was introduced by them as *Agia* Maria or 'the herbal magician'. The latter pleased her, though being sanctified most definitely did not.

The last few hours had been so momentous that she had given little thought to Dr Kyritsis. There had been no goodbye, so she was sure they would meet again. It could not be soon enough. Coming into the thick of the crowd, Maria felt her heart lurch as though it might dislodge itself from her chest. There he was, sitting at one of the long tables with Lapakis. In the mêlée he was the only person she saw, his silver hair almost luminous in the fading light. The doctors were deep in conversation, but eventually Lapakis looked up and noticed her.

'Maria!' he exclaimed, getting to his feet. 'What a great day for you. What is it like being home after all this time?'

Fortunately it was not a question she was really expected to answer and if it had been she would not have known where to begin or where to end. At this moment, Papadimitriou and his wife approached, with two men who bore such a close resemblance to Papadimitriou that it went without saying that they were his brothers. The island leader wanted his family to meet the men who were responsible for giving them a new life. There would be a thousand toasts later, but they wanted to be the first to say thank you.

Kyritsis stood back but Maria could feel the pressure of his gaze, and as Lapakis talked to the Papadimitrious, he drew Maria to one side.

'Can I have a moment of your time?' he asked politely, but loudly enough to be heard above the noise. 'Somewhere quieter than here,' he added.

'We could walk down to the church,' she answered. 'I want to go in and light a candle.'

They left the packed square where the cacophony of excited voices had reached a deafening pitch. As they walked the length of the empty street towards the church, the crowd sound became little more than a background hum. A sense of impatience determined Kyritsis's next action. Enough of this woman's life had been taken away by the disease and every second seemed one too many lost. His restrained bedside manner left him for a moment and boldness took over. By the entrance to the church door, he turned to face her.

'I have something to say. It's very simple indeed,' he said. 'I would like you to marry me.'

It was a statement, not a question. And it was as if no reply was required. For some time now, there had been no real doubt in Maria's mind that Kyritsis loved her but she had forced herself to stop imagining that this might have some kind of resolution. She had found it safer in the past few years to banish daydreams as soon as they had started to take shape and to live in the here and now where disappointment could not lay waste her fantasies.

For a moment she said nothing, but looked up at him as he held her by the shoulders, his own arms outstretched. As though she needed persuasion that he meant it, he filled her silence.

'There has never been anyone who has affected me as you have. If you don't wish to marry me, I shall go away and you need never think of me again.' His hands had tightened their grip on her shoulders. 'But either way, I need to know now.'

So it *was* a question. The moisture had drained from her mouth and a supreme effort was required to regain control of her tongue.

'Yes,' was the single, husky syllable that she was capable of expelling. 'Yes.'

'You will?' Kyritsis seemed astounded. This dark-haired woman, this patient of his whom he felt he knew so well and yet still knew so little about, was agreeing to be his wife. His face broke into a smile and Maria's mirrored it, dazzlingly. Uncertainly at first, and then with increasing passion, he kissed her, and then, suddenly aware of how they must look in the deserted street, they pulled apart.

'We must return to the celebrations,' said Kyritsis, speaking first. His sense of duty and correctness was even more keenly developed than her own. 'People might wonder where we are.'

He was right: they needed to return because it was a night for everyone to share before they went their separate ways. By the time they got back to the square, the dancing had begun. A huge circle had formed and a slow *pentozali* dance was in progress. Even Giorgis had joined in. The man who so often sat in the shadows at any event had come forward and now wholeheartedly joined the merrymaking.

Fotini was the first to spot her friend's return in the company of the doctor, and she knew beyond a shadow of a doubt that Maria, at last, had the opportunity for happiness. The pair had chosen not to say anything tonight – they wanted Giorgis to be the first to know, and the heady atmosphere of this *panegyri* was not where they wanted to tell him their news.

When Giorgis came to find them at the end of the dance, he had only one question on his lips for Maria.

'Have you seen Anna? Is she here?'

In the past few years, he had more or less abandoned hope of his family ever being together, but today there was a chance of it. He was puzzled by Anna's continuing absence, though; she had, after all, promised to be here.

'I am sure she will come, Father, if she said she would,' Maria reassured him, though the words sounded hollow to them both. 'Why don't we have another dance,' she suggested. 'You seem to have the energy.' She led her father back to the fray and they joined in as a new dance began.

Fotini was busy carrying plates of food to the table. She noticed the doctor observing Maria dancing and felt happier than ever that her dearest friend had found such a fine man. By now it was dark, the wind had dropped and there was not a ripple in the sea. The temperature seemed not to have fallen even by one degree since that airless afternoon, and when people came to sit out between dances, they thirstily gulped back tumblers of sharp wine, slopping much of it in the dust. Maria returned from her dance, found her place at

Kyritsis's side and they simultaneously lifted their glasses. It was a silent toast.

Anna and Andreas were nearly in Plaka now. Neither had spoken throughout the journey. Both were lost in their own thoughts. It had occurred to Andreas that Manoli might resume his engagement to Maria now that she was back, and as they approached the village and could see the thronging crowd he broke the silence, taking pleasure in provoking his wife with the suggestion.

'*Manoli?* Marry *Maria*? Over my dead body!' she screamed with a passion he had never seen in her before. The barriers were down now. 'What makes you say that?' Anna could not let it drop.

'Why shouldn't he? They were engaged and about to get married before,' he taunted her.

'Shut up. Just shut up!' She lashed out at him as he parked the car.

The violence of Anna's response had shocked Andreas.

'My God!' he roared, defending himself from the hard blows that rained down on him. 'You love him, don't you!'

'How *dare* you say that!' she screeched.

'Go on, why don't you admit it, Anna! I'm not a complete fool, you know,' he said, trying to regain control over his voice.

Anna was silent, as though her fury had momentarily subsided.

'I know it's true,' said Andreas, almost calm now. 'I came home early one day last week and he was there with you. How long. . . . ?'

Anna was now crying and laughing at the same time, hysterical. 'Years,' she spluttered. 'Years and years . . .'

It seemed to Andreas that Anna's scarlet lips smiled as though even now she was lost in some kind of ecstasy. Her denial would have given him a place to retreat, the possibility that he was wrong after all, but her admission was the greatest mockery of all. He had to wipe that rictus grin from her face.

In one deft movement he reached inside his jacket pocket and drew out his pistol. Anna was not even looking. Her head was tilted back, the round beads of her necklace vibrating with her laughter. She was delirious.

'I've never . . .' she gasped, now completely crazed with the excitement of telling him the truth, 'I've never loved anyone as much as Manoli.' Her words lashed out like a whip, cracking the air around him.

In the main square, Kyritsis watched as the first of the fireworks was let off into the limpid sky. Rockets would be sent into the air every hour until midnight, each one exploding with a violent bang and a shower of sparks that were reflected like gems in the still sea. As the first volley of fireworks came to an end there was a moment's quiet before the band thought it worthwhile striking up again. Before they could do so, however, there were two more loud and unexpected bangs. Kyritsis turned his face upwards, expecting to see a shower of glittering sparks descending from the sky, but it was immediately apparent that there would be none.

A commotion had broken out around a car parked near the square. It had been seen drawing up only a few minutes earlier and now a woman lay sprawled in the passenger seat. Kyritsis started to run towards it. For a moment it seemed as though the rest of the crowd was petrified into inactivity. Disbelief that such an act of violence could intrude on this merrymaking almost paralysed them, but they cleared a path to let him through.

Kyritsis felt the woman's pulse. Although it was weak, there was still a sign of life.

'We need to move her,' he said to Dr Lapakis, who was now at his side. Rugs and pillows had miraculously appeared from a nearby house and the two men carefully lifted the woman down on to the ground. At their request, the crowd of onlookers moved to a respectful distance to let them do their work.

Maria had worked her way to the front to see whether there was anything she could do to help. As they laid the woman down on the blanket, she realised who it was that they held in their blood-stained embrace. Many in the crowd now recognised her too and there was a collective gasp of horror.

There was no mistaking her. Raven haired, full-bosomed and clad in a dress now soaked with blood that no one else at this gathering could have afforded in a month of feast days, it was, without any doubt at all, Anna Vandoulakis. Maria knelt down beside her on the rug.

'It's my sister,' she whispered through her sobs to Kyritsis. 'My sister.'

Someone in the crowd was heard to shout: 'Find Giorgis!' and seconds later Giorgis was kneeling by Maria's side, weeping silently at the sight of his elder daughter, whose life was ebbing away before them all.

In a few minutes it was all over. Anna never regained consciousness, but her dying moments were spent with the two people who loved her most, praying fervently for her salvation.

'Why? Why?' repeated Giorgis through his tears.

Maria knew the answer but she was not going to tell him. It would only add to his grief. Silence and ignorance were what would help him more than anything at this moment. He would learn the truth soon enough. What would haunt him always was that in a single evening, he had celebrated the return of one daughter and lost the other for ever.

Chapter Twenty-three

WITNESSES SOON EMERGED from the crowd. One bystander had heard a couple arguing through the open window of the car when he had passed it a few minutes before the gunshots, and a woman claimed to have seen a man running off down the street immediately afterwards. This information sent a group of men off in the direction of the church, and within ten minutes they had returned with their suspect. He still held the weapon in his hand, and made no attempt to resist arrest. Maria knew his identity before she was told. It was Andreas.

There was a profound sense of shock in Plaka. It had always promised to be a memorable night, but not quite in this way. For a while people stood around in small groups and talked in low voices; it had not taken long for word to pass around that it was Maria's sister who had been shot dead, and that Anna's husband had been arrested for the crime. An extraordinary party had come to an untimely end and there was no choice but to wind up the evening and go their separate ways. The musicians dispersed and the remains of the food were put away; muted goodbyes were said as the Athenians began to leave, taken by their families and friends to start a new life.

Those with shorter distances to go had been offered beds by local people for the night and were to stay until the following day, when they would start their journeys back to their villages and towns in other parts of Crete. Andreas Vandoulakis had been taken away under police escort to spend the night in an Elounda cell and Anna's body was carried to the small chapel by the sea, where it was to remain before burial.

The daytime temperature had not dropped. Even now, when night was almost giving way to breaking day, there was a breathless warmth in the air. For the second time in twenty-four hours, Giorgis's small house was overcrowded. Last time his visitors had been looking forward to a celebration. This time they prepared for a great lamentation. The priest had visited but when he could see that little comfort was to be given in such tragic circumstances, he left.

At four o'clock in the morning Giorgis climbed, exhausted, to his room. He was numb and did not know whether this was grief or perhaps a sign that he was no longer capable of feeling at all. Even Maria's long-awaited return felt like nothing now.

Kyritsis had stayed for an hour or so, but there was no more he could do tonight. Tomorrow, which was already today, he would help them make arrangements for the funeral, but meanwhile he would snatch a few hours' sleep in a spare room above Fotini and Stephanos's taverna.

At the least interesting of times the villagers loved to gossip, but now they scarcely had time to draw breath. It was Antonis who was able to shed some light on the events leading up to Anna's killing. In the early hours of the morning, when a few of the men still sat around a table in the bar, he related what he had observed. A few weeks before, he had noticed that Manoli always seemed to slip away for several hours in the middle of the day. It was circumstantial evidence, but even so it might go some way towards explaining what had driven Andreas to murder his own wife. During this period, Andreas's mood had darkened by the day. He was ill tempered with everyone with whom he came into contact and his workers had begun to live in fear of him. A gathering thunderstorm rarely brought such tension. For so long Andreas had been kept in the dark, blissfully unaware of his wife's behaviour, but once he had emerged blinkingly into the daylight and seen the truth, there had been only one course of action. The drinkers in the bar were not unsympathetic, and many agreed that being cuckolded would drive them to murder. A Greek's manhood would not stand such ignominy.

Lidaki seemed to be the last one to have seen Manoli, who had now disappeared without trace, though his precious lyre still hung on the wall behind the bar.

'He came in here about six o'clock last night,' he said. 'He was his usual cheerful self and he certainly gave the impression he was going to stay for the celebrations.'

'No one seems to have seen him after that,' said Angelos. 'My hunch is that he felt awkward about seeing Maria.'

'Surely he doesn't still feel under obligation to marry her?' chipped in another voice.

'I doubt it, knowing Manoli, but it might have kept him away all the same,' said Lidaki.

'Personally I don't think it has anything to do with Maria,' said Antonis. 'I think he knew that his time was up.'

Later that morning Antonis went up to Manoli's home. He held nothing against this charming but feckless individual; he had been a good companion and drinking partner, and even the passing thought that he could be lying in his house in a pool of blood could not be ignored. If Andreas had killed his wife, it might not have been beyond him to kill his cousin too.

Antonis peered through the windows. Everything looked just as normal: the unruly mess of a bachelor home, with pots and plates piled up in no apparent order, curtains half drawn, a trail of crumbs across the table and an uncorked, two-thirds-empty bottle of wine; all of this was what he would have expected to see.

He tried the door and, finding it open, ventured inside. Upstairs in the bedroom, in a scene which might well have simply been further evidence that the person who lived here had no regard for tidiness, there were signs of a hasty departure. Drawers were pulled open and items of clothing spilled out like a volcanic eruption. Wardrobe doors gaped to reveal an empty rail. The unmade bed with its skewed sheets and flattened pillow was as Antonis might have expected, but what really gave him the clue that the feeling of emptiness in the house was possibly a permanent one were the picture frames that lay face down on the surface of a chest of drawers in the window. It looked as though they had been knocked over in haste, and two of the frames were empty, their contents hurriedly ripped out. All the signs were there. Manoli's truck had gone. He could be anywhere in Greece by now. No one would be looking for him.

* * *

Anna's funeral was not to take place in Plaka's main church, where Andreas had sought shelter, but in the chapel on the outskirts of the village. This small building overlooked the sea and had an uninterrupted view of Spinalonga. Nothing but salt water lay between the chapel's burial plot and the lepers' final resting place where the remains of Anna's mother lay in the ground.

Less than forty-eight hours after the death, a small, darkly clad group gathered in the damp chapel. The Vandoulakis family was not represented. They had remained firmly within the four walls of the Elounda house since the murder. Maria, Giorgis, Kyritsis, Fotini, Savina and Pavlos stood with their heads bowed as the priest prayed over the coffin. Wafts of incense billowed from the censer as lengthy intercessions were said for the forgiveness of sins before the comforting words of the Lord's Prayer were uttered almost inaudibly by them all. When it was time for the interment, they moved outside into the relentless glare of the sun. Tears and perspiration mingled to flow down their cheeks. None of them could quite believe that the wooden box soon to disappear into the darkness contained Anna.

As the coffin was lowered into the ground, the priest took some dust and scattered it crosswise over the remains.

'The earth is the Lord's,' he said, 'and all who dwell on it.' Ash from the censer floated down to mix with the dust, and the priest continued: 'With the spirits of the righteous made perfect in death, give rest to this the soul of thy servant . . .'

The priest's delivery had a singsong lilt. These words had been spoken a thousand times, and they held the small congregation spellbound as they poured from his scarcely parted lips.

'O pure and spotless Virgin, intercede for the salvation of your servant's soul . . .'

Fotini contemplated the notion of a pure and spotless Virgin interceding on Anna's behalf. If only Anna herself had remained a little more spotless, they might not be standing here now, she thought.

By the time the service was drawing to a close, the priest was in competition with an army of a thousand cicadas, whose unrelenting noise reached a climax as he came to the closing words.

'Give her rest in the bosom of Abraham . . . May your memory be everlasting, our sister, and worthy of blessedness.'

'Kyrie Eleison, Kyrie Eleison, Kyrie Eleison.'

A few minutes passed before anyone could bring themselves to move. Maria spoke first, thanking the priest for conducting the ceremony, and then it was time to walk back into the village. Maria went home with her father. He wanted sleep, he said. That was all he wanted. Fotini and her parents would return to the taverna to find Stephanos, who had been minding Petros and playing with the carefree Mattheos on the beach. It was the quiet mid-afternoon hour. Not a soul stirred.

Kyritsis would wait for Maria on a shady bench in the square. Maria needed to get away from Plaka just for a few hours and they planned to drive to Elounda. It would be the first journey she had made in four years, apart from the short one which had brought her from Spinalonga to the mainland. She yearned for an hour or so of privacy.

There was a small *kafenion* she remembered by the water's edge in Elounda. Admittedly it had been somewhere she used to go with Manoli, but that was all in the past now. She would not let thoughts of him follow her. As they were shown to a table where the sea lapped gently on the rocks below them, the events of the past forty-eight hours already seemed distant. It was as though they had happened to someone else, somewhere else. When she looked across the water, however, she could clearly see Spinalonga. From here the empty island looked just the same as it ever had, and it was hard to believe it was now completely devoid of human life. Plaka was out of sight, concealed behind a rocky promontory.

It was the first opportunity Maria and Kyritsis had had to be alone since the moment outside the church on the night of the feast. For perhaps one hour her life had held such promise, such a future, but now she felt that this great step forward had been counteracted by several back. She had never even addressed the man she loved by his Christian name.

When he looked back on this moment some weeks later, Kyritsis blamed himself for rushing in. His overexcitement at the prospect of their future together bubbled over into talk of his apartment in Iraklion and how he hoped it would be adequate for them.

'It isn't very spacious, but there is a study and a separate guest room,' he said. 'We can always move in the future if we need to, but it's very convenient for the hospital.'

He took her hands across the table and held them. She looked troubled. Of course she did. They had just buried her sister, and here he was, impatient as a child, wanting to talk about the practicalities of their life together. Clearly Maria needed more time.

How comforting, the sensation of his hands clasping hers, full of such warmth and generosity, she thought. Why couldn't they just remain here at this table for ever? No one knew where they were. Nothing could disturb them. Except her conscience, which had followed them here, and now nagged at her.

'I can't marry you,' she said suddenly. 'I have to stay and look after my father.'

The words seemed to Kyritsis to have come out of the clear blue sky. He was shocked. Within minutes, though, he saw it made perfect sense. How could he have expected everything to continue on its former path, given the dramatic events of the past two days? He was a fool. How could this woman, whom he had been drawn to as much by her integrity and selflessness as by her beauty, be expected to leave her bereaved and distressed father? For his whole life rationality had ruled him, and the one moment when he had denied it to let his emotions take their turn, he had stumbled.

One part of him wanted to protest, but instead he held on to Maria's hands and gently squeezed them. He then spoke with such understanding and forgiveness that it almost broke her heart.

'You're right to stay,' he said. 'And that's why I love you, Maria. Because you know what's right and then you do it.'

It was the truth, but even more so was what he said next.

'I shall never love anyone else.'

The owner of the *kafenion* kept his distance from their table. He was aware that the woman had broken down in tears and he did not like to intrude on his customers' privacy. There had not been any raised voices, which was unusual for a row, but it was then that he observed the sombre way in which the couple were dressed. Except for old widows, black was unusual for a summer's day, and it dawned on him that perhaps they were in mourning.

Maria eased her hands away from Kyritsis's grasp and sat with her head bowed. Her tears flowed freely now and ran down her arms, her neck and between her breasts. She could not stop them. The restrained grief at the graveside had only temporarily held back the overwhelming sorrow that now burst its dam and would not abate until every last drop of it had poured out and drained away. The fact that Kyritsis was so reasonable made her weep all the more and made her decision all the more lamentable.

Kyritsis sat looking at the top of Maria's bowed head. When the shaking had subsided, he touched her gently on the shoulder.

'Maria,' he whispered. 'Shall we go?'

They walked away from their table, hand in hand, Maria's head resting on Kyritsis's shoulder. As they drove back to Plaka, in silence, the sapphire-blue water still sparkled, but the sky had begun to change. It had started its subtle transition through azure to pink, and the rocks took on the same warm tones. At last this terrible day was beginning to fade.

When they reached the village, the doctor spoke.

'I can't say goodbye,' he said.

He was right. There was too much finality about the word. How could something that had never really begun come to an end?

'Neither can I,' said Maria, now perfectly in control.

'Will you write to me and tell me how you are? Tell me what you're doing? Tell me how life is for you in the free world?' asked Kyritsis with forced enthusiasm.

Maria nodded.

It was pointless prolonging the moment. The sooner Kyritsis went, the better it would be for both of them. He parked outside Maria's house and got out to open the passenger door. Face to face they stood, and then for a few seconds they held each other. They did not so much embrace as cling to each other, like children in a storm. Then, with great strength of will, they simultaneously released each other. Maria immediately turned away and went into her house. Kyritsis climbed back into his car and drove away. He would not stop until he got back to Iraklion.

The unbearable silence inside the house quickly drove Maria back out into the street. She needed the sound of the cicadas, a dog barking, the buzz of a scooter, squeals of children. All of these greeted her as she walked towards the centre of the village where, in spite of herself, she glanced up the street to check whether Kyritsis's car was still in sight. Even the trail of dust his wheels sent into the air had already settled.

Maria needed Fotini. She walked quickly to the taverna, where her friend was spreading the tables with paper cloths, snapping lengths of elastic around them to keep them from blowing away in the wind.

'Maria!' Fotini was pleased to see her friend, but dismayed at the sight of her ashen face. Of course, it was not surprising she looked so pale. In the past forty-eight hours she had returned from exile and seen her sister shot and buried. 'Come and sit down,' she said, pulling out a chair and guiding Maria into it. 'Let me get you something to drink – and I bet you haven't eaten all day.'

Fotini was right. Maria had not eaten for over twenty-four hours, but she had no appetite now.

'No, I'm fine. Really I am.'

Fotini was unconvinced. She put the list of things that needed to be done before the first evening customers arrived to the back of her mind. All of that could wait. Drawing up another chair, she sat down close to Maria and put her arm around her.

'Is there anything I can do?' she asked tenderly. 'Anything at all?'

It was the note of kindness in her voice that sent Maria shuddering into sobs, and through them Fotini could make out a few words that gave away the reason for her friend's ever-deepening misery.

'He's gone . . . I couldn't go . . . couldn't leave my father.'

'Look, tell me what happened.'

Maria gradually calmed down.

'Just before Anna was shot, Dr Kyritsis asked me to marry him. But I can't leave now – and that's what I would have to do. I would have to leave my father. I couldn't do that.'

'So he's gone away, has he?' asked Fotini gently.

'Yes.'

'And when will you see him again?'

Maria took a very deep breath.

'I don't know. I really don't know. Possibly never.'

She was strong enough to mean it. The fates had been vengeful so far, but with each blow Maria became more resistant to the next.

The two friends sat for a while, and eventually Stephanos came out and persuaded Maria to eat. If she was going to make such a sacrifice for her father, then she might as well be strong enough to be useful. It was all completely pointless if she made herself ill.

As night fell, Maria rose to go. When she reached her house, it was still shrouded in silence. Creeping up to the spare bedroom, which would now be hers again, she lay down on the bed. She did not wake until late the following morning.

Anna's death left a trail of other disrupted and destroyed lives. Not just her sister's, her father's and her husband's, but her daughter's too. Sofia was not yet two years old, and it was not long before she noticed the absence of her parents. Her grandparents told her that they had both gone away for a while. She cried at first, and then began the process of forgetting. As for Alexandros and Eleftheria Vandoulakis, in one evening they had lost their son, their hopes for the future and the reputation of the family. Everything that had ever worried them about Andreas marrying beneath his class had been fulfilled to the letter. Eleftheria, who had been so willing to accept Anna Petrakis, had to face the bitterest disappointment. It was only a short time before Manoli's absence was brought to their attention and they worked out for themselves what had led to the horrifying events of the feast of Agios Titos. That woman had brought the deepest shame on them all, and the thought of their son languishing in his prison cell was a daily torture.

Andreas's trial in Agios Nikolaos lasted three days. Maria, Fotini and several other villagers were called as witnesses, and Dr Kyritsis came from Iraklion to testify, remaining afterwards only briefly to speak to Maria. Eleftheria and Alexandros sat impassively in the gallery, both of them gaunt with anxiety and shame at being on such public display. The circumstances of the murder were hung out and aired for the whole of Crete to salivate over, and the daily newspaper ran every last sensational detail. Giorgis attended throughout. Though he wanted justice for Anna, he was never in any doubt that it was his daughter's behaviour that had triggered Andreas's violent reaction, and for the first time in fourteen years he was glad that Eleni was not there.

Chapter Twenty-four

1958

FOR SEVERAL MONTHS there was no communication between the Vandoulakis and Petrakis families. There was Sofia to consider, however, and for her sake this ice age had to pass. Eleftheria would have come round to a point of reconciliation more speedily than her husband, but even Alexandros, given time to reflect, began to see that it was not only his own family who had suffered. He realised that the damage sustained had been heavy on both sides and, with an almost mathematical precision that was strictly in character, he weighed up their respective losses. On the Vandoulakis side: one imprisoned son, one disgraced nephew, one family name brought to ruins. On the Petrakis side: one dead daughter, a family depleted by murder and before that by leprosy. By his powers of reckoning, the equation balanced. The person who stood in the middle was Sofia, and it was the responsibility of all of them to knit some kind of a life together for the little girl.

Alexandros eventually wrote to Giorgis.

We have had our differences, but it is time to end them. Sofia is growing up without her parents and the best thing we can offer her is the love and companionship of the remaining members of her family. Eleftheria and I would be very happy if you and Maria would join us for lunch next Sunday.

Giorgis did not have a telephone in his home, but he hurried straight to the bar and used the one there. He wanted to let Alexandros know immediately that they accepted the invitation and would both be happy to come, and he left a message with the Vandoulakis housekeeper to say so. Maria, however, had mixed feelings when she read the letter.

'"Our *differences*"!' she said mockingly. 'And what does he mean by that? How could he describe the fact that his son killed your daughter as "our differences"?'

Maria was incandescent with rage.

'Does he accept no responsibility? Where is the remorse? Where is the apology?' she screamed, waving the letter in the air.

'Maria, listen. Calm down. He doesn't accept responsibility because he bears none,' said Giorgis. 'A father can't be responsible for all the actions of his child, can he?'

Maria reflected for a moment. She knew her father was right. If parents did carry the burden of their child's mistakes, it would be a different world. It would mean that it was Giorgis's fault that his elder daughter had driven her husband to shoot her through her own reckless and unfaithful behaviour. That was clearly absurd. She had to concede the point, if reluctantly.

'You're right, Father,' she said. 'You're right. The only thing that really matters is Sofia.'

Some kind of rapprochement was forged between the families after this, with unspoken acknowledgement that there was fault on both sides for the catastrophe that had damaged them all. Sofia, from the very beginning, was well cushioned. She lived with her grandparents but every week she would go down to Plaka and spend a day with her other grandfather and Maria, who would dedicate themselves to her entertainment. They would go out on boat trips, catch fish and crabs and sea urchins, paddle in the sea and go for short walks along the cliff path. At six o'clock, when they delivered Sofia back to her grandparents' house near Elounda, they would all be tired out. Sofia had the adoring attention of three grandparents. In some ways, she was lucky.

As spring turned into early summer, Kyritsis counted that two hundred days had passed since Anna's burial and the day he had driven Maria to Elounda and realised that their future was not going to be spent together after all. Every day he struggled to stop himself thinking of what might have been. He lived the same disciplined existence he had always lived: into the hospital on the dot of seven-thirty in the morning and out again at nearly eight at night, with a solitary evening of reading, studying and letter-writing ahead of him. It occupied him thoroughly, and many envied his dedication and his apparent absorption in what he did.

Within weeks of the patients' exodus from Spinalonga, news that the island was no longer in use as a leper colony had spread across Crete. It meant that many who had feared to reveal potential leprosy symptoms emerged from their villages and came to seek help. Now that they knew treatment would not mean incarceration in the leper colony, they were unafraid to reveal themselves and came in waves to see the man who was known to have brought the cure for leprosy to Crete. Though modesty prevented Dr Kyritsis from basking in this glory, his reputation spread. Once diagnosis had been confirmed, sufferers would come to him for regular injections of dapsone, and usually, in the space of a few months, as doses were gradually raised, improvements would begin to show.

For many months Kyritsis continued his work as head of department in the bustling main hospital of Iraklion. There should have been nothing more rewarding than seeing his patients walk away from him cured of the disease and discharged for good. All he felt, however, was a terrible emptiness. He felt this in the hospital and he felt it in his home, and each day became more of an effort than the last as he dragged himself from his bed and back to the hospital. He even began to question whether he really had to administer the drugs himself. Could someone else not take his place? Was he really needed?

It was during this time of feeling dispensable inside the hospital and empty outside it that he received a letter from Dr Lapakis, who, since Spinalonga had closed, was now married and had taken up the post of head of dermatovenereology at the general hospital in Agios Nikolaos.

My dear Nikolaos,

I wonder how you are. Time has gone so quickly since we all left Spinalonga and in all those months I fully intended to get in touch with you. Life is busy back here in Agios Nikolaos and the hospital has greatly expanded since I was here full time. Do come and see us if you would like a break from Iraklion. My wife has heard so much about you and would love to meet you.

Yours,
Christos

It set Kyritsis thinking. If someone he respected as much as Christos Lapakis found fulfilment working in Agios Nikolaos, then perhaps the choice was his. If Maria was not able to come to him, he would have to go to her. Every Tuesday, Crete's daily newspaper carried advertisements for hospital vacancies and each week he would scan them, hoping to find work closer to the woman he loved. The weeks passed and several suitable jobs were advertised in Hania, but these would take him even further from his desired destination. Disenchantment set in, until one day he received another letter from Lapakis.

Dear Nikolaos,

I hope all is well with you. You'll think me henpecked I am sure, but I am planning to give up my job here. My wife wants to live closer to her parents in Rethimnon so we shall be moving in the next few months. It just occurred to me that you might be interested in taking over my department. The hospital is expanding rapidly and there could be a bigger opportunity later on. Meanwhile, I thought I should let you know of my plans.

Yours,
Christos

Although nothing had ever been said, Lapakis knew that his colleague had formed a bond with Maria Petrakis, and he had been dismayed to learn that Kyritsis had returned to Iraklion alone. He surmised that Maria had felt obliged to stay with her father and regarded the whole situation as a terrible waste.

Kyritsis read and reread the letter before putting it into the top pocket of his white coat, where he reached for it several times during the day and ran his eyes over the words again and again. Although a job in Agios Nikolaos would close all kinds of doors in his career, there was one door in his life which would open: the opportunity to live closer to Maria. That night he wrote to his old friend and asked him how he should pursue this opportunity. There were formalities to be attended to, other candidates to be interviewed and so on, Lapakis replied, but if Kyritsis could write a formal letter of application within the week, then it was likely that he would be considered for the post. The truth of it, as both of them well knew, was that Kyritsis was overqualified for the job. Moving from the headship of a department in a city hospital to the same position in a smaller hospital meant that no one doubted he could do the job, and the hospital was delighted, if slightly mystified, that someone of his calibre and reputation should have applied. He was summoned for interview and it was only a matter of days before he then received confirmation that they would like to award him the post.

Kyritsis's plan was to establish himself in his new life before he contacted Maria. He did not want her to raise any objections to the apparent turnaround in his career and planned simply to present the situation as a fait accompli. Less than a month later, now established in a small house not far from the hospital, he set off to Plaka, which was only twenty-five minutes' drive away. It was a Sunday afternoon in May, and when Maria opened her front door to see Kyritsis standing there, she paled with surprise.

'Nikolaos!' she gasped.

A small voice then piped up. It seemed to come from Maria's skirt, and a face appeared from behind her at not much higher than knee level.

'Who is it, Aunt Maria?'

'It's Dr Kyritsis, Sofia,' she replied in a scarcely audible voice.

Maria moved aside and Kyritsis stepped over the threshold. She looked at his back as he passed her, the same neat, straight back that she had watched so many times when he had left her home to walk up the main street of Spinalonga to the hospital. Suddenly it seemed only a moment since she had been on the island, day-dreaming of a future.

Maria trembled as she laid out cups and saucers, and they clattered noisily. Soon she and Kyritsis were as comfortably seated as they could be on the hard wooden chairs, sipping their coffee just as they used to on Spinalonga. Maria struggled in vain to think of something to say. Kyritsis, however, came straight to the point.

'I've moved,' he said.

'Where to?' Maria asked politely.

'Agios Nikolaos.'

'Agios Nikolaos?'

She almost choked on the words. Astonishment and delight

mingled in equal measure as she struggled to imagine the implications of his announcement.

'Sofia,' she said to the little girl, who was sitting at the table, drawing, 'why don't you go upstairs and find that new doll to show Dr Kyritsis . . .'

The little girl disappeared upstairs to fetch her toy, and now Kyritsis leaned forward. For the third time in her life Maria heard the words: 'Marry me.'

She knew that Giorgis was able to look after himself now. They had come to term's with Anna's death and Sofia had brought pleasure and distraction into their lives. The distance to Agios Nikolaos meant that Maria could visit her father several times a week and still see Sofia as well. It took less than a second for all of this to go through her head, and before she took her next breath she had given him her answer.

Giorgis returned soon after. He had not been as happy since the day he learned that Maria was cured. By the next day, news had travelled all around Plaka that Maria Petrakis was to marry the man who had cured her, and preparation for the wedding began immediately. Fotini, who had never lost hope in the prospect of Maria and Kyritsis marrying, threw herself into the plans. She and Stephanos were to host the party before the wedding service and their friends would all crowd into the taverna for a great feast afterwards.

They set a date with the priest for two weeks hence. There was no reason to wait any longer. The couple had a house to move into, they had known each other for some years and Maria already had a trousseau, of sorts. She also had a dress, the one she had bought for her wedding with

Manoli. For five years it had lain in the bottom of a chest, wrapped in layers of tissue. A day or two after Kyritsis's second proposal, she unfolded it, shook out the creases and tried it on.

It still fitted as beautifully as it had done on the day it was purchased. She was physically unchanged.

'It's perfect,' said Fotini.

On the eve of the wedding the two women were together at Fotini's, planning how Maria should wear her hair.

'You don't think it's bad luck marrying in the same dress I was to have worn for a different wedding? A wedding that never took place?'

'Bad luck?' replied Fotini. 'I think you've run out of bad luck now, Maria. I must confess I think Fate did have it in for you, but not any more.'

Maria was holding the dress up to herself in front of the long mirror in Fotini's bedroom. The frothy tiers of its full, lacy skirt cascaded around her like a fountain and the fabric swished about her ankles. With her head thrown back, she began to twirl around like a child.

'You're right . . . you're right . . . you're right . . .' she chanted rhythmically, breathlessly. 'You're right . . . you're right . . . you're right . . .'

Only when she was dizzy did Maria stop spinning and throw herself backwards on to the bed.

'I feel,' she said, 'like the luckiest woman alive. No one in the whole world could be as happy as I am.'

'You deserve it, Maria, you really do,' replied her oldest friend.

There was a knock on the bedroom door and Stephanos put his head into the room.

'Sorry to disturb you,' he said jokingly. 'We've got a wedding happening here tomorrow and I'm trying to prepare the feast. I could really do with a hand.'

The two women laughed, and Maria jumped off the bed, throwing the dress across a chair. Both of them raced downstairs after Stephanos, giggling like the children they had once been, their excitement at the prospect of Maria's big day filling the air.

They woke up to a clear May day. Every last inhabitant of the village emerged to follow the bridal procession the short distance from Maria's home to the church at the other end of the village. They all wanted to be sure that the beautiful dark woman in white was safely conducted to the ceremony and that nothing, this time, would get in the way of her and a happy marriage. The doors of the church were left open during the ceremony and the crowd craned their necks to catch a glimpse of the proceedings at the far end of the aisle. Dr Lapakis was the best man, the *koumbaros*. He was a familiar figure in Plaka – people remembered his daily comings and goings to Spinalonga – but fewer villagers remembered Kyritsis. His presence had been a fleeting one, though they were all well aware of his significance in the evacuation of the leper colony.

As the pair stood at the altar, the priest crowned them with the woven halos of flowers and grasses. There was absolute silence in the church and the crowd standing in the sunshine outside were hushed as they strained to hear the words.

'The servant of God, Maria, is crowned to the servant of

God, Nikolaos . . . In the name of the father and of the son and of the Holy Spirit, now and ever unto the ages. O Lord our God, crown them with your glory.'

They all then listened as the priest read from the familiar marriage texts, St Paul's letters to the Ephesians and to St John. There was nothing hurried or perfunctory about the service. This was the most solemn and binding of ceremonies and its duration reinforced its significance to the two who stood at the altar. Over an hour later, the priest drew the proceedings to a close.

'Let us pray for the groom and the bride. That they may have mercy, life, peace, health and salvation. May Christ, our true God, who by his presence in Cana of Galilee approved the dignity of marriage, have mercy upon us, O Lord Jesus Christ, have mercy upon us.'

A resounding 'Amen' reverberated through the church and finally the deed was done. Sugared almonds were distributed to everyone in the congregation and all of those who had stood outside. They were a symbol of the abundance and joy that everyone hoped Maria and Kyritsis would now enjoy. There was not a soul who wished them anything else.

Giorgis had sat in the front pew of the church with Eleftheria and Alexandros Vandoulakis. It was a public symbol of their reconciliation, and between them sat little Sofia, charmed and excited by the pageantry and colour of the wedding. For Giorgis there was a strong sense of a new beginning and a certainty that all the woes of the past were firmly behind him. It was the first time in years that he had felt at peace.

When Maria emerged, crowned, with her silver-haired

groom, the crowd cheered and then trailed after them in the sunshine to the taverna, where the merrymaking would begin. The feast that Stephanos laid on for all the guests that night was munificent. Wine flowed and corks popped from bottles of *tsikoudia* long into the night. Under the stars, the musicians plucked and bowed until the dancers' feet were numb. There were no fireworks.

They spent the first two nights of their marriage in a grand hotel overlooking the harbour in Agios Nikolaos but were both eager to begin the next stage of their lives. Maria had been to the house which was to be their marital home on several occasions in the two weeks leading up to the wedding. It would be the first time she had lived in a big bustling town and she relished the prospect of this change. The house was on a steep hill close to the hospital and had a wrought-iron balcony and floor-to-ceiling windows, as did all the others in the street. It was a tall, narrow house with two flights of stairs, and the paintwork was the palest aquamarine.

Dr Kyritsis himself was new to the town, so it did not attract gossip when he brought home his bride, and the place was sufficiently far from Maria's old home for her to be able to start afresh. No one knew of her medical history here, except her husband.

Fotini was the first to visit, with Mattheos and baby Petros, and Maria proudly showed her round.

'Look at these huge windows!' exclaimed Fotini. 'And you can see the sea over there. And look, boys, there's even a little garden!'

The house was grander and more spacious than any in Plaka and the furniture less rough and ready than the village style which most people still had at that time. The kitchen too was a good deal more sophisticated than the one Maria had been brought up with: for the first time in her life she had a fridge, a modern cooker and an electricity supply that did not suddenly shut down with no notice.

For a few months, life could not have been more perfect. Maria loved her new home on the hill near the hospital, and soon it was decorated to her taste and hung with the samplers she had embroidered as well as framed photos of her family. One morning in early September, however, she heard the bell of their newly installed telephone. It was Giorgis, who rarely rang her, so she knew immediately that something was amiss.

'It's Eleftheria,' he said in his usual blunt manner. 'She passed away this morning.'

In the past few months Giorgis had grown close to the Vandoulakis couple, and Maria could detect the sorrow in his voice. There had been no warning of illness and no signs of the stroke which had taken the elderly woman so suddenly and unexpectedly. The funeral was held a few days later, and it was only at the end of the ceremony, when Maria saw her little niece hand in hand with her two grandfathers, that the reality of the situation dawned on her. Sofia needed a mother.

She could not shake the thought off. It followed her, stuck to her like the spines of a thistle clinging to wool. The little girl was only just three years old – what was to happen to her? Suppose Alexandros died too? He was at least ten years older than Eleftheria had been so it was perfectly possible that this could happen, and she knew Giorgis would never manage to look after her on his own. As for her father, in spite of

Andreas's plea for leniency at the trial, the judge had passed a harsh sentence that ensured he would not be out of prison until Sofia was at least sixteen.

As they sipped their glasses of wine in the semi-darkness of the Vandoulakis drawing room in Elounda, a room that seemed purpose-made for mourning, with its forbidding family portraits and heavy furniture, the solution seemed more and more perfect. This was not the time to discuss it with anyone, although she now ached to share it. It felt as though the walls themselves murmured as people adopted the low, restrained tones of those who felt that even the clink of a glass might ruin the strict sobriety of the atmosphere. All the while Maria wanted to stand on a chair and make an announcement about what she wanted to do, but she had to wait an hour or so until it was time to leave before confiding in Kyritsis. Before they were even in their car she seized his arm.

'I've had an idea,' she blurted out. 'It's about Sofia.'

There was no need for her to say any more. Kyritsis had been mulling over the very same possibility.

'I know,' he replied. 'The little girl has lost two mothers now, and who knows how long Alexandros will live after this?'

'He was devoted to Eleftheria and he's heartbroken. I can't imagine how life will be for him without her.'

'We need to think about this carefully. It might be the wrong time to suggest that Sofia comes to live with us, but being with her grandfather won't be a long-term solution, will it?'

'Why don't we go and talk to him about it in a few days' time?'

Only two days later, having telephoned ahead to let him

know they would like to come, Maria and Nikolaos Kyritsis found themselves once again in Alexandros Vandoulakis's drawing room. The once statuesque man seemed to have shrunk since the funeral, when he had held his head high and proud throughout the service.

'Sofia has already gone to bed,' he began, pouring them both a drink from a bottle which stood on the sideboard. 'Otherwise she would be here to say hello to you.'

'It's about Sofia that we've come,' began Maria.

'I thought it might be,' said Vandoulakis. 'The matter scarcely warrants discussion.'

Maria paled. Perhaps they had made a terrible faux pas in coming.

'Eleftheria and I had a discussion a few months ago on this very subject,' Vandoulakis began. 'We talked about what would happen to Sofia if one of us died – though of course we were assuming it would be me who would go first. What we agreed was that if one of us were left on our own, the very best thing for our granddaughter would be for her to be taken care of by someone younger.'

Alexandros Vandoulakis had spent decades being in command, but even so it astonished them that he had so completely taken charge of the situation. They did not have to say another word.

'The finest solution for Sofia would be if she went to live with you,' he said, addressing them both. 'Would you consider it? I know you are very fond of her, Maria, and as her aunt you are the closest of all her blood relations.'

For a few moments Maria struggled to speak, but Kyritsis managed to say everything that was necessary.

The next day, when Kyritsis had finished work at the hospital, he and Maria returned to the Vandoulakis home and between them began to prepare Sofia for the next stage of her life. By the end of the following week she had moved to the house in Agios Nikolaos.

At first Maria was nervous. Within a year of leaving Spinalonga she had become a wife and now, almost overnight, the mother of a three-year-old. She need not have feared, however. Sofia led the way and adapted happily to being with a couple who were so much younger and more energetic than her grandparents. In spite of her traumatic start in life, she was an apparently carefree child and loved the company of other children, which she soon found in abundance in their very own street.

Kyritsis had also been anxious about becoming a parent. Although he had always numbered a few children among his patients, his contact with anyone as young as Sofia had been limited. The little girl was wary of him too, at first, but then realised that with the slightest provocation she could make his serious face crease into a smile. Kyritsis began to dote on her and was soon frequently castigated by his wife.

'You do spoil her,' wailed Maria, when she saw how Sofia ran rings around Nikolaos.

As soon as Sofia went to school, Maria began to train to work in the hospital dispensary. It seemed a perfect complement to her work with natural herbs, which she also continued to practise. Once a week Maria, who had learned to drive since her marriage, took Sofia to her paternal grandfather's house, where she would spend the night in the bedroom that was kept for her there. The next day, when Maria collected her, they would usually continue to Plaka, where they saw Giorgis. Almost every visit they would see Fotini too and Sofia would play on the beach below the taverna with Mattheos and Petros while the two women caught up on the minutiae of each other's lives.

Life continued in this happy and settled way for a while. Sofia enjoyed the routine of seeing both her grandfathers once a week and the excitement that growing up in a busy harbour town offered a child. Eventually the knowledge that Maria and Nikolaos were not her real parents slipped out of memory's reach. The house where they lived in Agios Nikolaos was all she would ever be able to recollect of early childhood. The only gap in any of their lives was a sibling for Sofia. It was a subject they rarely spoke about, but it weighed heavily on Maria that she had not produced a child of her own.

When Sofia was nine, Alexandros Vandoulakis died. He passed away peacefully in his sleep having tied up every last detail of his will, leaving the estate to be split between his two daughters and their families and a generous lump sum of money in trust for Sofia. Three years later, Giorgis became bed-ridden after a chest infection and moved to the house in Agios Nikolaos to be cared for by Maria. Over the next two years, his teenage granddaughter spent hours each day sitting on his counterpane playing backgammon with him. One autumn day, just before Sofia's return from school, he died. Both the women in his life were inconsolable. Their only real comfort was to see the throng that gathered for his funeral. It was held in Plaka, the village where he had spent almost his entire life, and the church was filled with well over a hundred villagers, who remembered with great affection the taciturn fisherman who had borne so much misfortune so uncomplainingly.

One chilly morning, early the next year, a typed envelope bearing an Iraklion postmark arrived. It was addressed to 'The Guardians of Sofia Vandoulakis'. Maria's stomach lurched when she saw the name. It was not one that Sofia had ever known she possessed and she snatched the letter up from the doormat and immediately stashed it at the back of a drawer. There was only one source for a letter addressed in such a way and Maria was full of trepidation; she planned to wait until her husband returned before finding out whether her fears were justified.

At about ten that night, Nikolaos arrived home from a long day at the hospital. Sofia had gone to bed an hour earlier. With some formality, Nikolaos slit the envelope with his silver opener and drew out a stiff sheet of paper.

To Whom It May Concern

They were together on the settee, their legs touching, and Nikolaos's hand quivered slightly as he held the letter out for both of them to read.

We regret to inform you that Andreas Vandoulakis passed away on 7th January. The cause of death was pneumonia. Burial will take place on 14th January. Please confirm receipt of this letter.

Yours faithfully,
Governor, Prison of Iraklion

For a few moments, neither of them spoke. But they read, and re-read, the perfunctory note. Andreas Vandoulakis. His was a name which had carried such connotations of wealth and promise. It was hard to believe, even after the dreadful events over a decade earlier, that the life of such a privileged individual had finally ended in a damp prison cell. Without speaking, Nikolaos got up, returned the letter to its envelope and crossed the room to lock it in his bureau. There was no chance that Sofia would ever find it there.

Two days later, Maria was the only mourner as Andreas's coffin was lowered in to a pauper's grave. Neither of his sisters attended. They would not even have considered it. As far as they were concerned, their brother had been as good as dead for a very long time.

By now it was the late 1960s and the first wave of tourists began to arrive in Crete, many of them visiting Agios Nikolaos, which became a magnet for northern Europeans beguiled by the sunshine, the warm sea and the cheap wine. Sofia was fourteen and becoming wilful. With parents who were so conventional and such pillars of the community, she soon found that an effective way to rebel was to hang around in the town with boys from France and Germany who were only too pleased to keep the company of a beautiful Greek girl with a gloriously buxom figure and waist-length hair. Although Nikolaos hated to be in any conflict with Sofia, in the summer months battles became an almost daily occurrence.

'She's inherited her mother's looks,' despaired Maria late one night when Sofia had failed to return home. 'But it now looks as though she might have her character too.'

'Well, I think I finally know which side of the nurture versus nature debate I'm on,' said Kyritsis ruefully.

Though she was rebellious in other ways, Sofia worked hard at school, and when she reached the age of eighteen it was time to consider university. It was an opportunity that had never been open to Maria and was one that both she and Nikolaos wanted for her. Maria assumed that Sofia would go to Iraklion for her studies, but she was disappointed. From childhood Sofia had watched large boats coming and going from mainland Greece. She knew that Athens was where Nikolaos had studied, and this was where she wanted to go. Never having left Crete herself, Maria was filled with trepidation at Sofia's ambition to go further afield.

'But the university in Iraklion is as good as any on the mainland,' she said, appealing to Sofia.

'I'm sure it is,' Sofia replied. 'But what's wrong with going somewhere further away?'

'Nothing's wrong with it at all,' Maria replied defensively. 'But Crete seems a big enough place to me. It has its own history and its own customs.'

'That's precisely the point,' snapped Sofia, showing a steely determination that nothing could bend. 'It's too wrapped up in its own culture. It seems almost sealed off from the outside world sometimes. I want to go to Athens or Thessalonika – at least they connect with the rest of the world. There's so much happening out there and we're never even touched by most of it here.'

She was displaying a desire to travel that was only natural for a girl at her stage of life. Nowadays everyone of her age seemed keen to go off and see more of the world. Maria dreaded it, though. As well as her own fears at losing Sofia, it raised in her mind the question of Sofia's paternity. Manoli would have talked like that, about Crete being a small island on a very large planet and how exciting the possibilities were beyond it. There was something strangely familiar about this wanderlust.

By the time June came, Sofia had made her decision. She was going to Athens and her parents would not stand in her way. At the end of August she would be sailing away.

The night before their daughter was to take the boat to Piraeus, Maria and Nikolaos were sitting in their garden under an ancient vine which dripped with ripening bunches of purple-hued grapes. Sofia was out. Nikolaos nursed the last few drops of a large balloon of Metaxa.

'We have to tell her, Maria,' he said.

There was no reply. During the past few months the two of them had gone over and over the arguments for telling Sofia that they were not her true parents. It was when Maria had eventually admitted the possibility that Manoli might have been Sofia's father that Kyritsis had finally made up his mind. The girl had to know. Now there was a chance that her father could be living and working in Athens, or anywhere else for that matter, she had to be told the truth. Maria knew that Nikolaos was right and that Sofia must be told before she left for Athens, but every day she deferred the moment.

'Look, I don't mind doing the talking,' said Nikolaos. 'I just think the time for procrastination is over.'

'Yes, yes. I know you're right,' Maria said, taking a deep breath. 'Let's tell her tonight.'

They sat in the warmth of the summer night, watching moths twirl like ballerinas in the candlelight. Occasionally the silence would be disturbed by the rustle of a lizard, its tail catching a dry leaf before it made its vertical dash up the wall of the house. What did those bright stars have in store for her family? wondered Maria. They seemed always to be watching, knowing the next chapter before she did. It grew late and still Sofia did not return, but they were not going to give up and retire to bed. They could not postpone what they had to do for yet another day. By a quarter to eleven the temperature had dropped and Maria was shivering.

'Shall we go inside?' she said.

Time dragged its heels for the next fifteen minutes, but eventually they heard the front door slam. Sofia was back.

Part 4

Chapter Twenty-five

As Fotini reached this point in the story, she was suddenly overwhelmed by the responsibility of describing the emotions of someone who was more than capable of telling her own tale. Although Fotini knew as well as anyone else alive how Sofia must have felt, who could tell the story better than she who had taken the blows of truth first hand? It was Sofia who, on that August night, had tried and repeatedly failed to catch her breath when her parents revealed that they were not really her parents at all; she who had had to face the fact that her real mother was no longer alive, and that there was no certainty about the identity of her natural father. She could never be sure of anything ever again. If the earth had undulated beneath her feet and the island of Crete been shaken by a great seismic movement she could not have felt more insecure.

Fotini realised there was only one thing to do, and all it would take was a phone call to Sofia in London. She slipped away, leaving Alexis to contemplate the now familiar view of Spinalonga.

As soon as she picked up the telephone, Sofia knew who it was who was calling.

'Fotini! Is that you?'

'It is me. How are you, Sofia?'

'Very well, thank you. Has my daughter Alexis been to visit you? I gave her a letter for you.'

'She most certainly has been to see me and she's still here now. We've had a very rewarding time together and I've done almost everything you asked.'

There was a moment's hesitation at the other end of the line. Fotini felt a sense of urgency.

'Sofia, how long would it take for you to get here? I've told Alexis all I can, but there are some things that I don't feel right about telling her. She has to leave soon to meet up with her boyfriend, but if you could get here before she goes, we could all have a couple of days together. What do you think?'

Again, silence at the other end.

'Sofia? Are you still there?'

'Yes, I'm still here . . .'

It was such a spontaneous invitation. There were a thousand reasons why Sofia could not drop everything and fly out to Greece, but there were enough very good reasons why she should, and almost instantly she decided to put the objections to one side. She would get herself to Crete by the following day, come what may.

'Look, I'll see if I can get a flight. It would be lovely to come to Plaka after all this time.'

'Good. I shan't tell Alexis, but I'll keep my fingers crossed you'll be able to get here.'

Sofia had no problem getting a seat on a flight to Athens. At this stage of the season there was little demand and there was a plane leaving Heathrow that afternoon. She hurriedly packed a small bag and left a message on Marcus's answer phone to explain where she was going. Take-off was on time, and by eight o'clock that night she was speeding in a taxi towards Piraeus, where she caught the night boat to Iraklion. As the ferry tilted this way and that on its southward course, Sofia had plenty of time to become anxious about what she was going to face when she arrived. She could not quite believe she had made this decision. Going to Plaka would be a journey so laden with memories that she was surprised at herself, but Fotini had sounded so insistent. Perhaps it really was about time she faced her past.

The following morning, less than twenty-four hours since the telephone conversation between the two women, Fotini saw a car drawing up in the side road near the taverna. A well-rounded blonde woman stepped out. Though it was twenty years since she had seen her and her fair hair could have thrown her off the scent, Fotini realised immediately who it was. She hurried out to meet her.

'Sofia, you're here. I can't believe it!' she exclaimed. 'I wasn't sure you'd come!'

'Of course I've come. I've wanted to come back for years but there just never seemed the right moment. And anyway, you never invited me,' she added teasingly.

'You know you don't have to wait for invitations to come here. You could have come any time you liked.'

'I know.' Sofia paused and looked around her. 'It all looks just the same.'

'Nothing much has changed,' Fotini said. 'You know what these villages are like. The local shop paints its shutters a different colour and there's an outcry!'

As she had promised, Fotini had not breathed a word to Alexis about her mother's impending arrival, and when the younger woman appeared on the terrace, bleary-eyed with sleep, she was astounded to see her mother, and wondered at first whether the previous evening's brandy was responsible for giving her hallucinations.

'Mum?' was all she could say.

'Yes, it is me,' replied Sofia. 'Fotini invited me and it seemed a good opportunity to come over.'

'It's such a surprise!' her daughter replied.

The three women sat around a table and sipped cold drinks in the shade of an awning.

'How has your trip been?' asked Sofia.

'Oh, so-so,' said Alexis with a noncommittal shrug of her shoulders. 'Until I got here. And then it became much more interesting. I've had a fantastic time in Plaka.'

'Is Ed here with you?' Sofia asked.

'No. I left him in Hania,' Alexis said, looking down at her coffee. She had scarcely given him a thought in the past few days and suddenly felt a pang of guilt that she had abandoned him for so long. 'But I plan to go back tomorrow,' she added.

'So soon?' exclaimed Sofia. 'But I've only just got here.'

'Well,' said Fotini carrying more drinks to the table, 'we haven't got much time then.'

All three of them knew that there was an agenda. Why else would Sofia have come? Alexis's head was still spinning from everything that Fotini had told her over the past few days, but she knew there was a final chapter. This was what her mother was here to provide.

Chapter Twenty-six

IT WAS THE night before Sofia was to leave for Athens to begin her life as a student at the university. Her trunk only had to be transported a few hundred metres down the road to the port and loaded on to the ferry, and its next stop, like hers, would be the capital of Greece, three hundred kilometres away to the north. Sofia's resolve to spread her wings was balanced by an equal amount of anxiety and fear. Earlier that day she had fought the temptation to unpack each and every item and put them back where they had always belonged: clothes, books, pens, alarm clock, radio, pictures. Leaving the known for the unknown was hard, and she perceived Athens as a gateway to either adventure or disaster. The eighteen-year-old Sofia could not imagine a middle ground. Every bone in her body ached with the anticipation of homesickness, but there was no going back now. At six o'clock she went out to meet her friends, to say goodbye to the people she was leaving behind. It would be a good distraction.

When she returned, on the stroke of eleven, she found her father pacing up and down the room. Her mother sat on the edge of a chair, her hands clasped tightly together, her knuckles white with tension. Every muscle in her face was taut.

'You're still up! I'm sorry I'm so late,' Sofia said. 'But you didn't have to wait up.'

'Sofia, we wanted to talk to you,' said her father gently.

'Why don't you sit down,' suggested her mother.

Sofia immediately felt uncomfortable.

'This all seems a bit formal,' she said, throwing herself into a chair.

'There are one or two things we feel you ought to know before you go off to Athens tomorrow,' said her father.

Now her mother took over. After all, most of it was her story.

'It's hard to know where to begin,' she said. 'But there are a few things we want to tell you about our family . . .'

That night they told her everything, just as Fotini had related it to Alexis. Not the slightest suspicion or unguarded word had given Sofia any forewarning, and she was totally ill equipped to deal with such revelations. She saw herself standing on a high mountain where layers of secrecy had been laid down over the millennia, each stratum of rock and stone hardening across the previous one. They had kept every last detail from her. It seemed like a conspiracy. When she reflected on it, there must have been dozens of people who knew about her mother's murder, and each and every one of them had maintained their silence for all those years. And what about the speculation and gossip that must have ensued? Perhaps people who knew her still whispered behind her back as she passed: 'Poor girl. I wonder if she ever found out who her father was?' And she could imagine the malicious susurration, the mutterings about leprosy: 'Fancy that,' they must have said. 'Not just one, but two cases in her family!' All those stigma that she had blithely carried about with her for years and years but not been in the least bit aware of. A disfiguring disease, an immoral mother, a murderer for a father. She was utterly repulsed. Her ignorance had been nothing less than bliss.

She had never questioned that she was the product of these two people who sat in front of her. Why should she? She had always imagined that her looks were a mixture of Maria's and Kyritsis's. People had even said so. But she was no more a blood relation of the man she had always called father than of any man she might meet in the street. She had loved her parents unquestioningly, but now that they were not her parents, were her feelings for them different? In the space of an hour, her entire life history had changed. It had dissolved behind her and when she looked back, there was a void. A blank. A nothingness.

She received the news silently and felt sick. Not for a moment did she think of how Maria and Kyritsis might be feeling or what it had cost them to tell her the truth after all this time. No. This was *her* story, *her* life that they had falsified, and she was angry.

'Why didn't you tell me all this before?' she screamed.

'We wanted to protect you,' said Kyritsis firmly. 'There seemed no need to tell you before.'

'We have loved you as your own parents would have loved you,' interjected Maria pleadingly.

She was desperate enough to be losing her only child to university, but even more distressed that the girl who stood in front of her and looked at her as though she was a stranger would no longer regard her as her mother. Months and years had gone by when the fact that Sofia was not their own flesh and blood had had no relevance, and they had loved her all the more perhaps because they had been unable to produce children of their own.

At this moment, however, Sofia just saw them as people who had lied to her. She was eighteen, irrational, and resolved now in her desire to invent a future for herself where she would be in command of the facts. Her anger gave way to a *froideur* that brought her emotions under control but chilled the hearts of the people who loved her most in the world.

'I'll see you in the morning,' she said, getting up. 'The boat leaves at nine.'

With that, she turned on her heel.

The following morning Sofia was up at dawn doing her final packing, and at eight o'clock she and Kyritsis loaded her luggage into the car. Neither of them spoke. All three of them drove down to the port, and when the moment came, Sofia's farewells were perfunctory.

She kissed each of them on both cheeks.

'Goodbye,' she said. 'I'll write.'

There was a finality about her adieu that gave no promise of short-term reunion. They trusted her to write, but they knew already that there was no purpose in watching for letters. As the ferry pulled away from its moorings, Maria was certain this was the worst that life could bring. People standing beside them were waving a loved one a fond farewell, but of Sofia there was no sign. She was not even on deck.

Maria and Kyritsis stood watching until the boat was a speck on the horizon. Only then did they turn away. The emptiness was unbearable.

For Sofia, the journey to Athens became a flight from her past, from the stigma of leprosy and the uncertainty of her parentage. A few months into her first term, she was ready to write.

Dear Mother and Father (or should I call you Uncle and Aunt? Neither seems quite right any more),

I am sorry things were so difficult when I left. I was terribly shocked. I can't even begin to put it into words and I still feel sick when I think about it all. Anyway, I am just writing to let you know that I am settling in well here. I am enjoying my lectures, and though Athens is much bigger and dustier than Agios Nikolaos, I am getting used to it all.

I will write again. I promise.

Love,
Sofia

The letter said everything and nothing. They continued to receive notes that were descriptive and often enthusiastic but gave away little of how Sofia was feeling. At the end of the first year, they were bitterly disappointed, if not entirely surprised, when she did not return for the vacation.

She became obsessed with her past and decided to spend the summer trying to trace Manoli. At first the trail seemed warm and she followed a few leads around Athens and then other parts of Greece. Then her sources became imprecise, phone books and tax offices for example, and she simply knocked on the door of any stranger who happened to be called Vandoulakis; the two of them would then stand there awkwardly before Sofia briefly explained herself and apologised for troubling them. The trail, such as it was, went stone cold, and one morning she woke up in a hotel in Thessalonika wondering what on earth she was doing. Even if she found this man, she would not know for sure if he were her father. Would she, in any case, prefer her father to have been a murderer who had killed her mother, or an adulterer who had abandoned her? It was not much of a choice. Should she not turn away from the uncertainty of her past and build a future?

At the beginning of her second year, she met someone who turned out to be a much more significant figure in her life than her father, whoever he might have been. He was an Englishman by the name of Marcus Fielding and he was on sabbatical at the university for a year. Sofia had never met anyone quite like him. He was big and bearish with a pale complexion that tended to blotchiness when he was embarrassed or hot, and he had very blue eyes, which were a rare thing to see in Greece. He also looked permanently crumpled in a way that only an Englishman could.

Marcus had never had a real girlfriend. He had generally been too wrapped up in his studies or too shy to pursue women, and he had found the sexually liberated London of the early 1970s intimidating. Athens during the same period was well behind in this revolution. In his first month at the university he met Sofia in a whole group of other students and thought her the most beautiful woman he had ever seen. Though she seemed quite wordly, she was not unapproachable, and he was astonished when she accepted an invitation from him.

Within weeks they were inseparable, and when it was time for Marcus to return to England she made the decision that she would forgo the rest of her course in order to go with him.

'I have no ties,' she said one night. 'I'm an orphan.'

When he protested, she assured him it was true.

'No, really, I am,' she said. 'I have an uncle and aunt who brought me up but they're in Crete. They won't mind me going to London.'

She said no more about her upbringing and Marcus did not pursue it, but what he did insist was that they should marry. Sofia needed no persuasion. She was completely and passionately in love with this man and knew beyond a shadow of a doubt that he would never let her down.

One chilly February day, the kind when frost lingers until midday, they married in a south London registry office. The invitation, an informal one, had stood on the high shelf above Maria and Nikolaos's fireplace for a few weeks. It would be the first time they had seen Sofia since the day she had sailed out of their lives. The searing pain of abandonment that they had felt so keenly at first gradually eased and gave way to the dull ache of acceptance. They both approached the wedding with a mixture of excitement and trepidation.

They liked Marcus instantly. Sofia could not have found herself a kinder, more dependable man, and to see her so content and secure was as much as they could have wished for, even if it was tainted by the fact that there was little likelihood now that she would ever return to settle in Crete. They enjoyed the English wedding, though it seemed to lack all the ritual and tradition that they were used to. It was just like an ordinary party except there were a few speeches, and what was strangest of all was that the bride did not really stand out from the other guests, dressed as she was in a red trouser suit. Maria, who spoke no English at all, was introduced to everyone as Sofia's aunt, and Nikolaos, who spoke excellent English, as her uncle. They remained at each other's side throughout, Kyritsis acting as translator for his wife.

Afterwards they stayed in London for two nights. Maria, particularly, was baffled by this city where Sofia had now chosen to live. It was another planet to her, a place that throbbed incessantly with the sound of car engines, monstrous red buses and heaving crowds filing past windows of slim mannequins. It was a city where, even if you were a resident, the chances of bumping into anyone you knew were non-existent. It was the first and last time Maria ever left her native island.

Even with her husband Sofia had explored the no-man's-land between secrets and lies. She convinced herself that concealment, the act of *not* telling something, was very different from telling something that was untrue. Even when her own children were born – Alexis, the first of them, only a year after the wedding – she vowed never to speak to them of her Cretan family. They would be guarded from their roots and forever protected from the deep shame of the past.

In 1990, at the age of eighty, Dr Kyritsis died. Several short obituaries, no more than a dozen or so lines long, appeared in British newspapers, praising him for his contribution to leprosy research, and Sofia carefully cut them out and filed them away. In spite of an age gap of nearly twenty years, Maria survived him by only five years. Sofia flew out to Crete for a perfunctory two days for her aunt's funeral and was overwhelmed by guilt and loss. She realised that her eighteen-year-old self had shown nothing but self-centred ingratitude in the way she had left Crete all those years before, but it was too late now to make amends. Far, far too late.

It was at this point that Sofia decided she would finally erase her background. She disposed of the few keepsakes of her mother's and her aunt's that lived in a box at the back of her wardrobe, and one afternoon, before the children returned home from school, a stack of yellowing envelopes with Greek stamps was burned on the fire. She then removed the backing from the framed photograph of her uncle and aunt and discreetly tucked the newspaper cuttings précising Kyritsis's life to a few sentences behind the picture. This record of their happiest day now lived by Sofia's bedside and was all that remained of her past.

By destroying the physical evidence of her history, Sofia had tried to shrug off her background but the fear of its discovery ate into her like a disease and, as the years passed, the guilt over how she had treated her aunt and uncle intensified. It sat in the pit of her stomach like a stone, a regret that sometimes made her feel physically sick when she realised there was nothing she could do to make amends. Now that her own children had left home, she felt more keenly than ever the agony of remorse and knew for certain that she had caused unforgivable pain.

Marcus had known better than to ask too many questions and went along with Sofia's desire to avoid any reference to her past, but as the children grew up, the Cretan characteristics were unmistakable: in Alexis the beautiful dark hair and in Nick the black lashes that framed his eyes. All the while Sofia feared that her children might one day discover what sort of people their ancestors had been, and her stomach churned. Looking at Alexis now, Sofia wished she had been more open. She saw her daughter scrutinising her as though she had never seen her before. It was her own fault. She had made herself a stranger both to her children and to her husband.

'I am so sorry,' she said to Alexis, 'that I've never told you any of this before.'

'But why are you so ashamed of it all?' Alexis asked, leaning forward. 'It's your life story, sort of, but at the same time you played no part in it.'

'These people were my flesh and blood, Alexis. Lepers, adulterers, murderers—'

'For goodness' sake, Mum, some of these people were heroic. Take your uncle and aunt – their love survived everything, and your uncle's work saved hundreds, if not thousands, of people. And your grandfather! What an example he'd be to people nowadays, never complaining, never disowning anyone, suffering it all in silence.'

'But what about my mother?'

'Well, I'm glad she wasn't *my* mother, but I wouldn't blame her entirely. She was weak, but she'd always had that rebellious streak, hadn't she? It sounds as though she always found it harder than Maria to do what she was meant to. It was just the way she was made.'

'You're very forgiving, Alexis. She was certainly flawed, but shouldn't she have fought harder against her natural instincts?'

'We all should, I suppose, but not everyone has the strength. And it sounds as though Manoli exploited her weakness as much as he possibly could – just as people like that always do.'

There was a pause in their exchange. Sofia fiddled anxiously with her earring as though there was something she wanted to say but she could not quite spit it out.

'But you know who behaved worse than anyone?' she eventually blurted out. 'It was me. I turned my back on those two kind, wonderful people. They'd given me everything and I rejected them!'

Alexis was stunned by her mother's outburst.

'I just turned my back on them,' Sofia repeated. 'And now it's too late to say sorry.'

Tears welled up in Sofia's eyes. Alexis had never seen her mother cry.

'You mustn't be too hard on yourself,' she whispered, drawing her chair up close and putting an arm around her mother. 'If you and Dad had dropped a bombshell like that on me when I was eighteen, I would probably have done just the same. It's totally understandable that you were so angry and upset.'

'But I still feel so guilty about it, and I have done for so many years,' she said quietly.

'Well, I don't think you need to now. It's the past, Mum,' said Alexis, holding her closer. 'From everything I've heard about Maria, I think she probably forgave you. And you wrote letters to each other, didn't you? And they came to your wedding? I'm sure Maria wasn't bitter – I don't think she had it in her.'

'I hope you're right,' said Sofia, her voice muffled as she struggled to suppress her tears. She looked away towards the island and slowly regained her composure.

Fotini had listened quietly to this exchange between mother and daughter. She could see that Alexis was making Sofia look at the past from a new perspective, and decided to leave them alone together for a while.

The Vandoulakis tragedy, as it was known, was still chewed over in Plaka, and the little girl who had been left without a father or mother had not been forgotten by those who had witnessed the events of that memorable summer night. Some of those people still lived in the village. Fotini strolled into the bar and had a quiet word with Gerasimo, who then gesticulated frantically to his wife. They would drop everything and come; their son could serve behind the bar for a while. All three of them hastened to the taverna.

At first Sofia did not recognise the small group who had appeared at a table close to where she and Alexis were sitting but as soon as she was aware that the elderly man was mute, she realised who it was.

'Gerasimo!' she cried. 'I remember you now. Weren't you working in the bar here when I used to come and visit?'

He nodded and smiled. The fact that Gerasimo was dumb had intrigued the little Sofia. She remembered being slightly afraid of him, but also recollected how much she enjoyed the iced lemonade he made specially for her whenever she and Maria called in at the bar, which was where they usually went to meet her grandfather. She had more difficulty remembering Andriana. Though she was now plump and terribly afflicted with varicose veins, which were ill concealed by her thick stockings, Andriana reminded Sofia that she had been a teenager when Sofia used to come to Plaka. Sofia dimly remembered a beautiful but rather languid girl who would usually be sitting outside the bar chatting to her friends while groups of teenage boys hung around, leaning nonchalantly on their mopeds. Fotini had found the brown envelope of photographs again, and once more they were spread out on the table and the family likenesses between Sofia, Alexis and their ancestors marvelled over.

The taverna was closed that night, but Mattheos, who was soon to take over his parents' business, now arrived. He had grown into a mountain of a man, and Sofia and he embraced enthusiastically.

'It's so good to see you, Sofia,' he said warmly. 'It's been such a long time.'

Mattheos began to lay a long table. One more guest was still to arrive. Fotini had telephoned her brother Antonis earlier that day, and at nine o'clock he arrived from Sitia. He was now very grey and quite stooped, but he still had those dark, romantic eyes that had drawn Anna to him all those years ago. He sat between Alexis and Sofia and after a few drinks he lost his shyness about talking English after so many years without practice.

'Your mother was the most beautiful woman I ever saw,' he said to Sofia, adding as an afterthought, 'apart from my own wife, of course.'

He sat quietly for a moment before he spoke again.

'Her beauty was a gift as well as a curse, and a woman like her will always drive some men to extreme behaviour. It wasn't all her fault, you know.'

Alexis watched her mother's face and could see that she understood.

'*Efharisto*,' Sofia said quietly. 'Thank you.'

It was well past midnight, and the candles had long since guttered to extinction, before everyone round the table got up to leave. Only a few hours later both Alexis and Sofia needed to be on the road, Alexis to retrace her steps to Hania to meet up with Ed, and her mother to catch the ferry back to Piraeus. For Alexis it was as though a month had passed since she had arrived, even though it was actually only a few days. For Sofia, in spite of the fact that her visit had been fleeting, its significance was immeasurable. Embraces as warm as the day itself were exchanged, and fond promises made to return the following year for a longer and more peaceful stay.

Alexis drove her mother to Iraklion, where Sofia was to catch the night ferry back to Athens. There was not a moment of silence on the journey as their conversation flowed. Once she had dropped her mother, who would happily spend the day in the city's museums before catching the ferry that night, Alexis carried on towards Hania. She had resolved the mystery of the past; today the future would be her concern.

Nearly three hours later she arrived back at the hotel. It had been a long, sweaty journey and she was desperate for a drink, so she crossed the road to the closest bar, which overlooked the beach. Ed was there, sitting alone and gazing out to sea. Alexis moved towards him quietly and took a seat at his table. The scrape of her chair alerted him to her presence and he looked round, startled by the noise.

'Where the *hell* have you been?' he shouted.

Apart from the message she had left for him four days earlier to say that she would be staying in Plaka for a couple of nights, she had not contacted him. Her mobile phone had been switched off.

'Look,' she said, knowing she had been wrong to be so out of touch, 'I'm really sorry. It all got very involved and somehow I lost track of time. Then my mum came over and—'

'What do you mean, your mum came over? So you were having some kind of family reunion or something and just forgot to tell me about it! Thanks a lot!'

'Listen . . .' Alexis began. 'It was really important.'

'For God's sake, Alexis!' he groaned with sarcasm. '*What* is more important? Buggering off to see your mother, who you can visit any day of the week when you're at home, or having this holiday with me?'

Ed did not expect an answer to this. He had already sauntered across to the bar to get himself another drink, his back turned to Alexis. She could see the anger and resentment in the line of his shoulders, and while they were still turned she slipped quickly and silently away. It took her a matter of minutes at the hotel to stuff all her clothes into a bag, grab a couple of books from the bedside table and scribble him a note.

Sorry it's ended like this. You never did listen.

There was no 'Love Alexis', no row of kisses. It was the end. She could admit it to herself now. There was no love left.

Chapter Twenty-seven

ALEXIS WAS SOON back on the road to Iraklion. It was already four in the afternoon and she would have to put her foot down to reach it by seven o'clock, in time to return the hire car and catch the ferry which left at eight.

As she drove along the smooth road, which hugged the coastline and gave her a continuous and spectacular view of the sea, a feeling of euphoria swept over her. To her left there was nothing but blue: azure sea and sapphire sky. Why were feelings of misery called 'the blues'? she wondered. This bright sky and sparkling water seemed integral to her ecstatic sense of wellbeing.

With the windows wound down and warm air blowing through, her hair flickered behind her like a dark stream and she sang along loudly and passionately to 'Brown-Eyed Girl' as the cassette whirred round in the car's cheap tape deck. Ed hated Van Morrison.

This exhilarating journey lasted a little more than two hours, and as she rattled along, fear of missing the boat kept her foot firmly pressed on the accelerator. There was nothing quite like the sense of abandon she got at the wheel of a car.

With only moments to spare, she dealt with the irritations

of dispensing with the hired car, purchased her ticket for the ferry and climbed the ramp which brought her into the bowels of the ship. She was all too familiar with the stench of fumes that greeted passengers boarding a Greek ferry but knew that in an hour or two she would acclimatise. Cars were still being driven on, and freight was being loaded on to the deck, along with plenty of commotion and shouting from a crowd of dark-haired men yelling at each other in a language that she was still ashamed she knew so little of. In this particular situation, it was probably just as well. She saw a door marked 'Foot passinjers' and disappeared gratefully through it.

Somewhere on this boat, she knew she would find her mother. There were two lounges, one for smokers, another much emptier one for non-smokers. A group of American students occupied the latter, while in the former there were several dozen big family groups returning to mainland Greece after their holidays to relatives in Crete. They were vociferous and all appeared to be haranguing each other, though in truth they were probably simply discussing whether to have toasted sandwiches now or later on in the journey. Alexis could not find her mother on this level so she went up on deck.

In the fading light she saw Sofia at the far end, towards the prow. She was sitting alone, her small travel bag at her feet, looking across at the twinkling lights of Iraklion and the vaulted arches of the great arsenal built by the Venetians. The pristine walls of the solid sixteenth-century fortress which stood guard over the harbour could have been built yesterday.

A day earlier it was Alexis who had been amazed to see her mother. This time it was Sofia's turn to be surprised by the sight of her daughter.

'Alexis! What are you doing here?' she exclaimed. 'I thought you were going back to Hania.'

'I did.'

'But why are you here then? Where's Ed?'

'Still in Hania. I left him there.'

There was little need to explain, but Alexis wanted to talk.

'It's all over. I realised how pointless it was, how half-hearted,' she began. 'When I sat listening to Fotini describe your family and what they went through, what really struck me was how powerfully they loved each other. It was through sickness and health, thick and thin, until death parted them . . . I knew I didn't feel like that about Ed – and I certainly wouldn't feel like that about him in twenty, or even ten years' time.'

In the decades since Sofia had turned her back on the people and the place that had nurtured her into adulthood, she had never perceived it all so clearly. Her daughter had made her look at these ancestors of hers as though they were characters in a drama. At last she saw not humiliation but heroism, not perfidy but passion, not leprosy but love.

Everything was in the open now, the wounds were exposed to the air and at last there was the possibility of healing. There was no shame in any of it. She no longer had anything to hide and for the first time in twenty-five years her tears flowed unchecked.

As the cumbersome ferry moved slowly out of the harbour and blasted its horn into the still night air, Alexis and Sofia stood against the railings, catching the breeze on their faces. Arms entwined, they looked back across the pitch-black water until, gradually, the lights of Crete faded into the distance.

Leprosy:
A Continuing Problem in the Twenty-First Century

Although leprosy has been eradicated in the United States, it is still a major health problem in developing countries. In 2004 more than 400,000 new cases were diagnosed, around 70 percent of these in India. Leprosy (also known as Hansen's disease) is caused by a germ similar to that which causes tuberculosis. It attacks the nerves of the hands, feet, and face and, if left untreated, can take away the ability to move fingers, toes, and eyelids. It can also destroy the ability to feel pain so that those affected are prone to injury and burns that can result in serious infections and ultimately the lost of fingers, toes, and sight. The longer the disease is left undetected, the more often it is that the deformities so often associated with leprosy will occur. When these deformities are coupled with the social stigma born out of fear and misunderstanding, those affected are often rejected by family and community. This means that many are afraid to come forward to seek treatment in the early stages of the disease.

To do your part to help those afflicted with the disease, contact American Leprosy Missions (ALM):

American Leprosy Missions
1 ALM Way
Greenville, SC 29601
Phone: (864) 271-7040 or (800) 537-7679
Fax: (864) 271-7062
www.leprosy.org